MONTANA

LOOK FOR THESE EXCITING WESTERN SERIES FROM BESTSELLING AUTHORS WILLIAM W. JOHNSTONE AND J.A. JOHNSTONE

The Mountain Man
Luke Jensen: Bounty Hunter
Brannigan's Land
The Jensen Brand
Smoke Jensen: The Early Years
Preacher and MacCallister
Fort Misery
The Fighting O'Neils
Perley Gates
MacCoole and Boone
Guns of the Vigilantes
Shotgun Johnny
The Chuckwagon Trail
The Jackals
The Slash and Pecos Westerns
The Texas Moonshiners
Stoneface Finnegan Westerns
Ben Savage: Saloon Ranger
The Buck Trammel Westerns
The Death and Texas Westerns
The Hunter Buchanon Westerns
Will Tanner, Deputy US Marshal
Old Cowboys Never Die
Go West, Young Man

Published by Kensington Publishing Corp.

MONTANA

A Novel of Frontier America

WILLIAM W. JOHNSTONE
and J.A. JOHNSTONE

PINNACLE BOOKS
Kensington Publishing Corp.
www.kensingtonbooks.com

PINNACLE BOOKS are published by

Kensington Publishing Corp.
119 West 40th Street
New York, NY 10018

PUBLISHER'S NOTE: Following the death of William W. Johnstone, the Johnstone family is working with a carefully selected writer to organize and complete Mr. Johnstone's outlines and many unfinished manuscripts to create additional novels in all of his series like The Last Gunfighter, Mountain Man, and Eagles, among others. This novel was inspired by Mr. Johnstone's superb storytelling.

First Printing: February 2024
ISBN-13: 978-0-7860-5079-6
ISBN-13: 978-0-7860-5080-2 (eBook)

10 9 8 7 6 5 4 3 2 1

Printed in the United States of America

PROLOGUE

From the May issue of Big Sky Monthly Magazine
by Paula Schraeder

The bestselling T-shirt for tourists at Wantlands Mercantile in Basin Creek has an image of a colorful trout in the center circle and these words on the front.

WELCOME TO CUTTHROAT COUNTY

We're Named After Montana's
State Fish

But on the back is the image of a tough-looking, bearded cowboy wearing an eyepatch and biting down on a large knife blade, with these words below.

But WATCH Your Back

Yes, this is Cutthroat County, all 1,197 square miles, according to the US Geological Survey's National Geospatial Program, with 31.2 of those square miles water. According to the 2020 US Census Bureau, the county's population is a healthy 397, though the sunbaked, silver-headed lady working the counter at Wantlands Mercantile when I dropped in on a windy but wonderfully sunny June afternoon told me differently. "Oh, 'em guvment volunteers mighta missed a coupla dozen or so. Folks live here 'cause they've lived here all their lives. Or they come because—"

I waited. Finally, I had to ask, "Why do folks come here?"

"To hide," she said.

Having been in Cutthroat County for three days, I know there must be roughly 1,130 square miles (not including the 31.2 miles of water) for anyone to hide.

It seemed like a good place to hide.

And getting to Basin Creek wasn't easy.

I left Billings early in the morning in my Toyota Camry, winding through plenty of Big Sky country, and after hitting the turnoff north at Augusta, I drove and drove and drove, with nothing to see but pastures and open country.

Aside: A truck driver at a Great Falls coffee shop on my way back home laughed when he heard my story.

"Was it at night?" he asked.

"No, sir," I told him.

"You should drive through there at night. It's like you're in a [expletive] bowl." He sipped his latte. "Liked to've sent me to the looney bin a time or two."

Back to my trip: Finally, reaching a crossroads store, I stopped for coffee and confirmation. "Is this the right way to Basin Creek?" I asked the young Native man who rang me up.

"Yes." He took my money.

He must have read the skepticism on my face. Then he smiled, tilted his head north, and confirmed it. "Just keep going that way, and drive till you reach the end of the earth."

Cutthroat County is bordered by the Blackfeet Indian Reservation on the north, the Ponoká (Elk) Mountains to the east, the Always Winter mountain range on the west, and US Highway 103 on the south. If you are driving to Glacier

National Park or the Canadian entry point at Milk River City, it's a good idea to take your potty break at Basin Creek. Maybe top off the gas tank, as well. (That crossroads station I stopped at on the drive north has no gasoline for sale; I did not have courage enough to use the outhouse.) There are only two gas stations in Cutthroat County, and both are in Basin Creek.

"That's not exactly true," I was later told.

"Roscoe Moss has a pump at Crimson Feather [a community of four trailers and a ranch far to the east of where owner Garland Foster has brought in wind turbines]. At least when the Conoco truck driver—there's a refinery in Billings, you know—remembers to stop on the first of the month. 'Course, old Roscoe's prices are higher than a loan shark's interest rates, and his pump is slower than spring getting here."

The speaker, a handsome man of slightly above average height, dark hair flecked with gray, and the darkest eyes I've ever seen, paused to sip coffee—black (his third cup since I'd been interviewing him)—and appeared to be counting the other gas pumps.

"And most ranchers and mining companies have their own pumps," he continued. "Though some stopped after they had to dig up their old pumps and haul them away. EPA thing, if I remember right." His smile was disarming. "But you're too young to remember leaded gasoline."

He did not appear to be flirting. But he sure was charming.

"If you run out of gas, there's a pretty good chance someone will top you off with enough to get you to East Glacier. Maybe as far as Cut Bank." The disarming man was John T. Drew, Cutthroat County sheriff, one of those fellows "*who's lived here all their lives.*"

"Well," he politely corrected, "if you don't count four-and-a-half years in Bozeman." He points to the Montana State University diploma—criminal justice—on the wall to the right of the window overlooking the county courthouse grounds.

Those four and a half years might be the only period of time when any Drew male had not dined, slept, and worked in Cutthroat County since long before Cutthroat County was carved out of Choteau County in 1891. I pointed out the first Maddox to set foot in Cutthroat County was a mountain man—perhaps *seven, eight, nine generations ago*.

Drew smiled and shrugged—"I've never figured the math"—then nodded at the diploma. "Math's why it took me an extra semester to get that sheepskin on the wall."

"Do people hide here?" I asked.

"People escape here," he said, the smile still warm. "Tourists come here to fly-fish for cutthroat trout or to pick up one of those T-shirts Maudie sells by the scores during peak season. The three-hundred and ninety-seven folks who call this patch of heaven home live here because they love it. Because this country's in their blood. The air's clean. The water's pure. And if you don't mind a whole lot of winter most years, it's a good place to call home."

Sixty years ago, Cutthroat County made national headlines for being the last of the Old West towns. The sprawling Maddox Ranch, now headed by Ashton Maddox, was likened to the Ponderosa of TV's *Bonanza*. The county sheriff then—John Drew's grandfather—was called a real Matt Dillon, the character played by James Arness in the long-running western series *Gunsmoke*.

Tourists from across the world flocked to Cutthroat County not just to go trout fishing in America but to see the wildest Wild West. A Montana state tourism guide raved about four guest ranches—three of which boasted to be real, working ranches—and a restored historic hotel. Two stables offered guided horseback rides along the county's myriad peaks, valleys, and creeks. A plan was to turn part of the long abandoned railroad tracks, originally laid in the 1890s, into an Old West tourism train complete with a coal-powered locomotive and mock gunfights and train robberies.

That boom lasted slightly less than a decade.

A few years later, Cutthroat County, and especially Basin Creek, got statewide attention and a joke on *The Tonight Show* [though I have been unable to confirm it since there's no video on YouTube] as a speed trap.

Drew laughed at that memory. "Well, the town speed limit was thirty-five, and my daddy did not like speeders. Maybe because his daddy preferred riding a horse than driving that Ford Galaxy. We have Ford Police Interceptor SUVs now, by the way. But we're getting some pressure from the state to move to hybrids. If we get another electric charging unit, we might go for that. But that's up to the county. And the annual budget."

Today, no 1890s train runs through Basin Creek. There aren't even any iron rails anymore. The only electric-charging station in the county is at my motel, though the Wantlands Mercantile is investigating the costs and reliability of adding one in the next two years. The restored historic hotel burned down twenty-five years ago. The site is home to the cinder block Wild Bunch Casino, where cowboys, sheepherders, townspeople, and a few passing tourists drink beer and play video poker, video keno, video blackjack, video slots, while Chuckie Corvallis serves up food. The day's special was $7.99 for Tater-Tot Casserole.

I opted for coffee and the soup of the day, cream of mushroom, probably straight from a can.

There's a NO SMOKING sign on the outside door, but Chuckie Corvallis was lighting a new filterless Pall Mall with the one he'd just burned down to almost nothing.

"It's my place," he said when he noticed my questioning, healthy-lung face. "I own this place. I can smoke if I wanna. Nobody else can. Ain't my law. It's the [expletive] feds."

Aside: By the time our interview was over, I had to race back to my motel room, shower twice, and find a laundromat to rid my clothes of tobacco stink.

"What happened to Basin Creek?" I asked Corvallis.

"The [expletive] government. [Expletive] feds. [Expletive expletives]. Folks stopped carin' 'bout their country. Hippies. Freaks. Now it's the [expletive expletives] and their [expletive] ignoramus politics. [Expletive] 'em." He pulled hard on his cigarette and blew smoke. "Pardon my [expletive] French."

Both town stables have been paved over. On one site sits my quaint motel.

Things, however, are changing in Basin Creek.

A month before my arrival, newcomer Elison Dempsey announced his candidacy for Cutthroat County sheriff—a position that has been held almost exclusively by Drews since the county's founding. Dempsey heads the Citizens Action Network, a quasi-military vigilante group, which MSNBC said nothing is "quasi" about it. Dempsey has been getting plenty of press, statewide, regionally, and nationally.

Tan, clean-shaven, his dark hair buzzed in crew-cut fashion, and white teeth, he looks like he might have been an Olympic track star or boxer. Smiling after I told him that, he corrected me.

"I might have done well in the biathlon. I'm a great skier, downhill or cross-country. Out here, it's good to be able to ski. Winters can be long, and skiing sure beats snowshoeing when it's forty below zero. But I am an excellent marksman. Rifle. Shotgun. 45. automatic."

A Colt .45 was holstered on his hip. The rack behind him in his massive four-wheel-drive Ford carries a lever-action Winchester, a twelve-gauge pump shotgun, and a lethal-looking assault rifle, perhaps an AK-47. I don't know. And I don't want to ask.

"I do have a concealed carry permit," he assures me when he notices my focus on the automatic pistol. "You can ask our soon-to-be ousted sheriff." He chuckles. "All the members of C.A.N. have concealed carry permits, too. But as you can see, we *conceal* nothing."

Dempsey volunteered to take me on a tour of Cutthroat County. His truck gets eight miles a gallon, he said, but told me not to worry.

The gas container in the bed of the Ford looks like it could refill an aircraft carrier.

"The problem here," he said as he slowed down and pulled off the road, "is that two men run this county." He nods at a gate on the left. The arched sign above the dirt road reads MADDOX CATTLE COMPANY. An encircled *M*—a brand well recognized across Montana—hangs just below the company's name.

"There's one of them. Ashton thinks he's God," Dempsey said. "Maddoxes have been gods here for too long. Maddoxes and Drews. It's time for someone to put both of those gods in their place."

Dempsey wore a camouflage T-shirt that appeared painted to his chest and upper arms. It was not a tourist T-shirt from Wantlands Mercantile, but a red, white, and blue Citizens Action Network T-shirt.

CUTTHROAT COUNTY

C.A.N.!

WE WILL!

Citizens Action Network

He flexed his muscles and grinned, showing those white teeth. "And I happen to be Zeus, Hercules, and Apollo rolled into one."

For the record, Ashton Maddox declined my multiple interview requests.

"Who's the other god?" I asked.

He snorted. "You just spent a couple hours with him in the sheriff's office. You know that. For more than a century—two centuries really—this county has been all Drew and all Maddox. I'm here to change that. And I will. For the better."

Several miles up the road, we turned onto another two-track. An hour later, I was thinking *No one's going to find my body. Ever!*

Dempsey finally stopped, rolled down his window, and nodded at a ramshackle building. "Here's another problem nobody seems to want to fix."

Figuring it was abandoned, I stared at the *house*, if that's the right word. One wall was made of straw bales. The rest that I could see appeared to be made of anything and everything someone could throw together. Wooden crates. Driftwood. Broken two-by-fours. Cans. Cinderblocks. Dirt. The window—singular—was apparently made of Coke bottles and Mason jars.

"Someone lives there?" I finally asked.

"If you call that living," Dempsey answered.

I was about to ask what someone who lived there does. Maybe it was a line camp for Ashton Maddox. Then I remembered the lady at Wantlands Mercantile.

They hide.

"You've heard of folks wanting to live off the grid?" Dempsey asked.

"Sure, but—"

"You can't get farther off the grid than Cutthroat County and fifteen miles off the highway." Dempsey shifted the gear into first and we pulled away.

"He's not so bad. I mean, he likely paid money for four or five acres. Land's cheap here. This ain't Livingston or Missoula. If he's registered to vote, I like him. He can vote for me come November. I don't care what party he belongs to. See, I'm running as an independent. I like all folks, those who don't break the law, I mean. Maybe he grows a little grass. Does some illegal trapping. There's a good crick four miles northeast. Poaches a pronghorn or takes an elk out of season.

I don't know. Maybe he's like you. Wants to be a real writer. A real Louis L'Amour."

I let him know. "I am a *real* writer."

A half hour later, he stopped again. "Here's another problem," he said, pointing at another rundown trailer home. "The dude that lives here is a poacher. See, that good-looking deputy that Drew got himself, she was pulling off the road a deer that got hit by a tourist on the way back from Glacier. This dude comes by in that Jap rig and asked if he could take the deer carcass. Deputy Mary Broadbent let him. That's illegal.

"This isn't deer season. She broke the law. Broadbent, I mean. When I heard of it, I told Drew. He didn't do a thing. So I called Trent, the local game warden here. He didn't do a thing. Because if Ashton Maddox isn't ruling Cutthroat County, John T. Drew is."

We drove back to the main highway, and headed back to Basin Creek. When we saw two hitchhikers, Dempsey swore, blew the horn, and floored the rig, sending the lean man and tall woman jumping over the ditch and almost falling against the barbed-wire fence.

"That's another problem," Dempsey said after he stopped laughing. "Blackfeet Indians keep coming down here, taking jobs away from folks who live here and want to work."

I didn't bring up the fact that Cutthroat County covers what once was Blackfeet country and that anyone has the right to work anyplace in America.

He had to slow down when we found ourselves behind a semi hauling cattle.

"And there's the final biggest problem in Cutthroat County. I aim to fix it once I send John T. Drew to pasture," Dempsey said.

I smelled cattle manure over diesel.

"You won't believe this, lady, but this spring, we had a

report of rustling here. Cattle rustling. Just like you'd see in an old movie on Channel 16."

"Rustling?"

He nodded, then named his suspects, but I left them out of this article. My editor and publisher have a policy that they don't want to be sued for libel.

Elison Dempsey said he had reached out to George Grimes, a noted Texas Ranger recently retired, and the subject of last year's action movie titled *Beretta Law*. He asked him to join C.A.N. as a stock detective, but fears the fee George Grimes demands is far more than C.A.N. can afford.

Grimes could not be reached for comment.

"Is rustling why Garland Foster put up wind turbines on his ranch?" I asked.

"Foster is a fool" was all Dempsey would say. "He won't vote for me. But he'll be the only one."

When I reach Garland Foster by telephone, he laughed when I asked for a response to being called a fool. "Been called worse, little lady." He still reaps millions from his Florida condos and myriad business interests in Texas, many Great Plains states, and in Mexico, Central and South America. He moved from southern Texas after the death of his wife four years ago.

Dempsey isn't the only person who has criticized Foster.

"Ashton Maddox hates my guts," Foster said with another chuckle. "But it's not my fault his granddaddy had to sell off part of that big ol' Circle M spread during the Great Depression. I just happened to have a few million bucks to spend and thought Montana would sure beat the heat in Florida, Texas, and Mexico. I didn't know a blasted thing about Sacagawea Pasture when I paid cash for eleven sections [7,040 acres] of real estate."

Sacagawea Pasture, according to legend once property of Maddoxes and Drews, has a name that dates to the 1840s, but the Maddox and Drew names go back even further in Montana lore and legend and actual history.

So why, I asked, is a longtime cattle rancher turning to wind turbines?

"More sheep than cattle," he corrected. "Least for the past coupla years. Wind turbines don't smell like cattle or sheep, and while beef and wool prices fluctuate, the wind always blows in this country."

"What about rustling?" I ask.

Foster laughed. "Nobody's rustled one of my turbines yet."

Back in town, John T. Drew confirmed there had been one report of rustling on a small ranch. He and both deputies were investigating. "Not to sound like a fellow running for public office, but I cannot comment further because this is an active investigation." He smiled that disarming smile again.

"Elison Dempsey says he has offered his Citizens Action Network volunteers to help with your investigation," I told him.

The sheriff nodded. "Elison Dempsey says lots of things. Offers a lot of things. Most of them I ignore. No, I reckon I ignore anything Dempsey says. But I did tell him and some of his C.A.N. folks they are welcome to volunteer for the county's search and rescue team.

"There's a lot of country for hikers, hunters, and anglers to get lost in," he explained, "and a lot of my time as county sheriff is spent searching and rescuing, not citing speeders who think all Montana highways are autobahns."

I asked about the controversy with Mary Broadbent, game warden Ferguson C. Trent, and the deer given to a so-called squatter.

"Deputy Broadbent told that man he could have the deer as long as he told the game warden about it the next morning, which he did." Drew smiled. "No sense in letting good deer meat rot when it could feed a family for a week. I'm partial to backstrap myself."

That was confirmed by Trent of the state Department of

Fish, Wildlife and Parks. Not the backstrap part. But that the taker of the deer did call Warden Trent about taking the roadkill for many suppers.

Drew stared at me. "This place can still be the frontier."

I asked about Mary Broadbent, who, like Ashton Maddox, declined to talk to me for this article.

The sheriff's smile was gone, and the eyes again hardened. "She's a good deputy."

I looked around the office and kept looking.

"You look confused, Miss Schraeder," he said politely.

I was. "Do you have a dispatcher? I mean, where do calls come in? If you're patrolling how do you—"

"Nine-one-one calls go to Cut Bank in Glacier County. Those are relayed here." The smile returned. "We're small. But we are efficient."

"Do you think you'll win reelection?"

"That's up to the voters."

"Are things changing in Cutthroat County?" I asked.

"Nothing ever stays the same." The look on his face tells me he's okay with change . . . unlike some Westerners I've interviewed over the years. "We've never been on CNN or *Face the Nation* or NPR till recently. That takes some getting used to. But if that brings us some tourist dollars that won't hurt us. We thank *Big Sky Monthly Magazine* for sending you here.

"Just remind your readers we indeed have speed limits. If you speed here, you'll get pulled over. And fined. And if you commit a major crime, there's one thing you need to know."

"What's that?"

There was that smile again. "The judge might not be in town for some time. Our jail holds ten comfortably. But it's like any jail anywhere. It loses its uniqueness after a few hours."

The jail is in the basement of the combination county courthouse and town hall, a rectangular two-story building of limestone that is dwarfed by Basin Creek's biggest structure, a leaning wooden granary next to the old depot in what is called Killone Memorial Park.

Abe Killone was a rancher who paid out of his own pocket for the construction of the county courthouse. He was murdered on the streets of Basin Creek in 1917.

Except for the bathrooms, the entire eastern wing of the first floor holds the county library. Several rooms labeled STORAGE, and town-related government offices (or desks) are also on the first floor: Mayor Sabrina Richey, Tax Assessor Henry Richey, and the constable Derrick Taylor, though he likes to call himself the town marshal. His hours are the same as the county's justice of the peace, 9:00 A.M.–noon Mondays, and 1:00–4:00 P.M. Thursdays.

Other kiosks are scattered across the western side of the dark building for the school superintendent, clerk, and recorder, while the county's road department, treasurer, and assessor have their own offices.

"They keep the important stuff downstairs," librarian Phyllis Lynne told me. "So people don't have to walk up those stairs."

Don't worry. The building is ADA compliant. An elevator at the far corner was completed in 1992. County Manager Dan O'Riley told me, "It runs like it was put in in 1492."

His offices are upstairs, along with Sheriff Drew's and the three elected county commissioners, chairwoman Grace Gallagher, Sid Pritchard, and Mack "Yes, it's my real name. Wanna see my birth certificate?" McDonald. They are responsible for the hiring of all nonelected county officers, including the county coroner and county attorney. Cutthroat County went to a county commissioner management style in 1948.

Most of the second floor covers what's officially called the Cutthroat County Courthouse/Basin Creek Municipal Building, even if the court is hardly used . . . for trials, anyway. Town hall meetings are sometimes held there, and the public school put on a presentation of *Inherit the Wind* three years ago.

The clerk, James Alder, says the last criminal case tried was six months ago. "Connie Good Stabbing stole a truck to get back to the rez. Well, she said she borrowed it. Dom Purcell pressed charges. But they reached a plea deal while the jury was deliberating. So everybody was happy. The jurors got paid for their time, Connie had to paint the Catholic church here in town and pay Malone a 'rental fee' and reimburse him for gas."

I stared at him, and expected to wake up in front of an *Andy Griffith* rerun on MeTV.

"It's not always this tame," John T. Drew said when I found my way back to his office. "And it's a long way from Mayberry."

There have been four deaths over the past eighteen months, two in traffic accidents (neither involving alcohol), one hiker who met up with a bear in the Ponoká range, and this past December, a cowboy on Garland Foster's ranch was killed while working alone. Apparently he was killed in what the coroner called "a horse wreck."

The coroner, George J. White, by the way, does not live in Cutthroat County. He resides in Havre, Hill County seat and "a bit of a haul" from Basin Creek. The county attorney lives in Choteau, Teton County seat and "not as far away as Havre," attorney Murdoch Robeson tells me over the phone, "but it sure ain't close."

"Does that work?" I asked Dan O'Riley, who was standing in the doorway to the sheriff's office.

"It has to. Lawyers can't make a living in Cutthroat County. Coroners don't have much to do here, either."

I asked O'Riley why Elison Dempsey was talking about the need for his Citizens Action Network in a town and county like this. "He told me Cutthroat County needs a change and a lot of illegal activity goes unreported."

O'Riley laughed. "Most illegal activity goes unreported everywhere, miss. But how much illegal activity do you think you can find in a county of fewer than four hundred people?"

Dempsey also said he would reopen the investigation into the death of one of those traffic accidents. A single-car accident that claimed the life of forty-nine-year-old Cathy Drew, wife of Sheriff John T. Drew.

Disgusted as this makes me, I have to bring that up to the charming sheriff because those charges have been flying around the state—and on some cable news networks—since Mrs. Drew was found in her overturned Nissan Rogue on US Highway 103 between 12:30 and 4:15 A.M. on Friday, December 3, 2021. She was rushed to a Missoula hospital and pronounced dead on arrival.

Drew sighed. "US Highway, so Montana State Police troopers were the primary on that. They handled the investigation. Best guess is that she swerved, overcorrected. I'm a cop. I don't like best guesses. I'd like to know for sure what happened. But I have gotten mighty sick of Elison Dempsey and one of these days, he's going to wish he kept his mouth shut."

Dan O'Riley quickly changed the subject. "You read enough history books on Montana and you'll come across lots of names you'll still find on the list of registered voters."

"Like Drew and Maddox?" I asked.

"More than that," O'Riley said. "My ancestors came here in 1881. But I'm a newcomer. You don't read anything about Dempseys."

"There you have it," Elison Dempsey yelled when I met him at the Busted Stirrup Bar in Basin Creek. "If your roots don't go back to fur trappers and cattle rustlers and Indian killers, you got no right to live in Cutthroat County. That's what I'm fighting. That's why I'm running for sheriff. And that's why the truth will come out and I will be elected."

Yet, when I left my motel, and drove down Main Street, I saw Sheriff John T. Drew getting out his Interceptor in front of the county-town courthouse. I stopped, rolled down the window, and thanked him for all his help.

His eyes were mellow again, and he leaned against the passenger door. "You're welcome back anytime, Miss Schraeder."

"You haven't read my story yet."

His grin widened and his eyes twinkled. "Most likely, I won't. No offense. I just don't like reading about me or Drews or Maddoxes. Got enough of those yarns growing up."

Well, we heard the stories, too, read the novels, some so-called histories, and heard the schoolground rhymes even when I was a child.

Pew Pew
Marshal Drew
Killed a Maddox
Times Thirty-two
Pew Pew
Marshal Drew

"Drive safe," the sheriff said, tipped his hat, and stepped back. "And watch your speed. Remember what I told you. A person can wait a long time before the judge comes to town."

As I headed out of Basin Creek to return to Billings I made sure I didn't go a hair over thirty-five miles per hour and just to be safe, kept my Camry at sixty-five as I headed out of Cutthroat County, the last frontier in Montana.

But a frontier that is rapidly changing.

DAY ONE

WEDNESDAY

CHAPTER 1

After opening the back door, Ashton Maddox stepped inside his ranch home in the foothills of the Always Winter Mountains. His boots echoed hollowly on the hardwood floors as he walked from the garage through the utility room, then the kitchen, and into the living room.

Someone had left the downstairs lights on for him, thank God, because he was exhausted after spending four days in Helena, mingling with a congressman and two lobbyists—even though the Legislature wouldn't meet till the first Monday in January—plus lobbyists and business associates, then leaving at the end of business this afternoon and driving to Great Falls for another worthless but costly meeting with a private investigator. After crawling back into his Ford SUV, he'd spent two more hours driving only twelve miles on the interstate, then a little more than a hundred winding, rough, wind-buffeted miles with hardly any headlights or taillights to break up the darkness, which meant having to pay constant attention to avoid colliding with elk, deer, bear, Blackfoot Indian, buffalo, and even an occasional moose.

Somehow, the drive from Basin Creek to the ranch road always seemed the worst stretch of the haul. Because he knew what he would find when he got home.

An empty house.

He was nothing short of complete exhaustion.

But, since he was a Maddox, he found enough stamina to switch on more lights and climb the staircase, *clomp, clomp, clomp* to the second floor, where his right hand found another switch, pushed it up, and let the wagon wheel chandelier and wall sconces bathe the upper story in unnatural radiance.

Still running, the grandfather clock said it was a quarter past midnight.

His father would have scolded him for leaving all those lights on downstairs, wasting electricity—not cheap in this part of Montana. His grandfather would have reminded both of them about how life was before electricity and television and gas-guzzling pickup trucks.

Reaching his office, Ashton flicked on another switch, hung his gray Stetson on the elk horn on the wall, and pulled a heavy Waterford crystal tumbler off the bookshelf before making a beeline toward the closet. He opened the door and stared at the mini–ice maker.

His father and grandfather had also rebuked him for years about building a house on the top of the hill. "This is Montana, boy," Grandpa had scolded time and again. "The wind up that high'll blow you clear down to Coloradie."

Per his nature, Ashton's father had put it bluntly. "Putting on airs, boy. Just putting on airs."

What, Ashton wondered, *would Grandpa and Daddy say about having an ice maker in his closet?* "Waste of water *and* electricity!"

Not that he cared a fig about what either of those hard rocks might have thought. They were six feet under. Had been for years. But no matter how long he lived, no matter how many millions of dollars he earned, he would always hear their voices.

Grandpa: *The Maddoxes might as well just start birthin' girls.*

Daddy: *If you'd gone through Vietnam like I did, you might know a thing or two.*

Ashton opened the ice maker's lid, scooped up the right number of cubes, and left the closet door open as he walked back to the desk, his boot heels pounding on the hardwood floor. Once he set the tumbler on last week's Sunday *Denver Post*, which he still had never gotten around to reading, he found the bottle of Blanton's Single Barrel, and poured until bourbon and ice reached the rim.

Grandpa would have suffered an apoplexy had he known that a Maddox paid close to two hundred bucks, including tax, for seven hundred and fifty milliliters of Kentucky bourbon. Both his grandpa and father would have given him grief about drinking bourbon anyway. As far back as anyone could recollect, Maddox men had been rye drinkers.

The cheaper the better.

"If it burns," his father had often said, "I yearns."

Ashton sipped. *Good whiskey is worth every penny,* he thought.

Glass still in his hand, he crossed the room till he reached the large window. The heavy drapes had already been pulled open—not that he could remember, but he probably had left them that way before driving down to the state capital.

They used to have a cleaning lady who would have closed them. One of the hired men's wife, sweetheart, concubine, whatever. But that man had gotten a job in Wyoming, and she had followed him. And with Patricia gone, Ashton didn't see any need to have floors swept and furniture dusted.

He debated closing the drapes, but what was the point? He could step outside on the balcony. Get some fresh air. Close his eyes and just feel the coolness, the sereneness of a summer night in Montana. Years ago, he had loved that—even when the wind come a-sweepin' 'cross the high plains. Grandpa had not been fooling about that wind, but Ashton Maddox knew what he was doing and what the weather was like when he told the man at M.R. Russell Construction Company exactly what he wanted and exactly where he wanted his house.

Well, rather, where Patricia had wanted it.

Wherever she was now.

He stood there, sipping good bourbon and feeling rotten, making himself look into the night that never was night. Not like it used to be.

"You can see forever," Patricia had told him on their first night, before Russell's subcontractor had even gotten the electricity installed.

He could still see forever. *Forever.* Hades stretching on from here north to the Pole and east toward the Dakotas, forever and ever and ever, amen.

The door opened. Boots sounded heavy on the floor, coming close, then a grunt, the hitching of jeans, and the sound of a hat dropping on Ashton's desk. "How was Helena?" foreman Colter Norris asked in his gruff monotone.

"Waste of time." Ashton did not turn around. He lifted his tumbler and sipped more bourbon.

"You read that gal's hatchet job in that rag folks call the *Big Sky Monthly*?"

"Skimmed it. Heard some coffee rats talking about it at the Stirrup."

"Well, that gal sure made a hero out of our sheriff."

Ashton saw Colter's reflection in the plate glass window.

"And made Garland Foster sound like some homespun hick hero, cacklin' out flapdoodle about cattle and sheep prices and how wind's gonna save us all." Holding a longneck beer in his left hand, Colter lifted his dark beer bottle and took a long pull.

Ashton started to raise his tumbler, but lowered it, shook his head, and whispered, "'while beef and wool prices fluctuate, the wind always blows in this country.'"

The bottle Colter held lowered rapidly. "What's that?"

"Nothing." Ashton took a good pull of bourbon, let some ice fall into his mouth, and crunched it, grinding it down, down, down.

The foreman frowned. "Thought you said you just skimmed that gal's exposé." Colter never missed a thing—a sign, a clear shot with a .30-.30, a trout's strike, or a half-baked sentence someone mumbled.

Raising the tumbler again, Ashton held the Waterford toward the window. "He didn't put up those wind turbines," he said caustically, "because of any market concerns." He shook his head, and cursed his neighboring rancher softly. "He put those up to torment me. All day. All night."

A man couldn't see the spinning blades at that time of night. But no one could escape the flashing red warning lights. Blinking on. Blinking off. On and off. Red light. No light. Red light. No light. Red light. Red . . . red . . . red . . . red . . . all night long. All night long till dawn finally broke. There had to be more wind turbines on Foster's land than that skinflint had ever run cattle or sheep.

Ashton turned away and stared across the room. Colter held the longneck, his face showing a few days growth of white and black stubble and that bushy mustache with the ends twisted into a thin curl. The face, like his neck and wrists and the forearms as far as he could roll up the sleeves of his work shirts, were bronzed from wind and sun and scarred from horse wrecks and bar fights. The nose had been busted so many times, Ashton often wondered how his foreman even managed to breathe.

"You didn't come up here to get some gossip about a college girl's story in some slick magazine," Ashton told him. "Certainly not after I've spent three hours driving in a night as dark as pitch from Helena to here by way of Great Falls."

"No, sir." The man set his beer next to the bottle of fine bourbon.

"Couldn't wait till breakfast, I take it." Ashton started to bring the crystal tumbler up again, but saw it contained nothing but melting ice and his own saliva. "I figured not."

Few people could read Colter's face. Ashton had given up

years ago. But he didn't have to read the cowboy's face. The voice told him everything he needed to know.

Colter wasn't here because some hired hand had wrecked a truck or ruined a good horse and had been paid off, then kicked off the ranch. Colter wasn't here because someone got his innards gored by a steer's horn or kicked to pieces by a bull or widow-making horse.

Frowning, Ashton set the glass on a side table, walked to the window, found the pull, and closed the drapes. At least he couldn't see those flashing red lights on wind turbines any longer.

Walking back, his cold blue eyes met Colter's hard greens. "Let's have it," Ashton said.

The foreman obeyed. "We're short."

Ashton's head cocked just a fraction. No punch line came. But he had not expected one. Most cowboys Ashton knew had wickedly acerbic senses of humor—or thought they did—but Colter had never cracked a joke. Hardly even let a smile crack the grizzled façade of his face. Still, the rancher could not believe what he had heard.

"We're . . . *short*?"

Colter's rugged head barely moved up and down once.

Ashton reached down, pulled the fancy cork out of the bottle, and splashed two fingers of amber beauty into the tumbler. He didn't care about ice. He drank half of it down and looked again at his foreman.

No question was needed.

"Sixteen head. Section fifty-four at Dead Indian Pony Crick." His pronunciation of *creek* was same as many Westerners.

Ashton took his glass and rising anger to the modern map hanging on the north-facing wall, underneath the bearskin. Colter left his empty longneck on the desk and followed, but the foreman knew better than to point.

Ashton knew his ranch, leased and owned, better than

anyone living. He found section fifty-four quickly, pointed a finger wet from the tumbler, and then began circling around, slowly, reading the topography and the roads. "You see any truck tracks?"

"No, sir. Even hard-pressed, a body'd never get a truck into that country 'cept on our roads. What passes for roads, I mean. Our boys don't even take ATVs into that section. Shucks, we're even careful about what horses we ride when working up there."

Ashton nodded in agreement. "Steers? Bull or . . . ?"

"Heifers."

"Who discovered they were missing?"

"Dante Crump."

Ashton's head bobbed again. Crump had been working for the Circle M for seven years. He was the only cowboy Ashton had ever known who went to church regularly on Sundays. Most of the others were sleeping off hangovers till Mondays. A rancher might question the honesty of many cowboys, but no one ever accused Dante Crump of anything except having a conscience and a soul.

Ashton kept studying the map. He even forgot he was holding a glass of expensive bourbon.

Colter cleared his throat. "No bear tracks. No carcasses. The cattle just vanished."

"Horse tracks?" Ashton turned away from the big wall map.

The cowboy's head shook. "Some. But Dante had rode 'cross that country—me and Homer Cooper, too—before we even considered them cattle got stoled. So we couldn't tell if the tracks were ours or their'uns."

"Do we have any more cattle up that way?" Ashton asked.

"Not now. We'd left fifty in the section in September. Dante went there to take them to the higher summer pasture. Found bones and carcasses of three. About normal, but he took only thirty-one up. So best I can figure is that sixteen got rustled."

"*Rustled.*" Ashton chuckled without mirth. The word sounded like something straight out of an old Western movie or TV show.

"Yeah," the foreman said. "I don't never recollect your daddy sayin' nothin' 'bout rustlers."

"Because it never happened." Ashton let out another mirthless chuckle. "I don't even think my grandpa had to cope with rustlers, unless some starving Blackfoot cut out a calf or half-starved steer for his family. Grandpa had his faults, but he wasn't one to begrudge any man with a hungry wife and kids." He sighed, shook his head, and stared at Colter. "You're sure those heifers aren't just hiding in that rough country?"

The man's eyes glared. "I said so" was all he said.

That was good enough for Ashton, just as it had been good enough for his father.

"Could they have just wandered to another pasture?"

"Homer Cooper rode the lines," the foreman said. "He said no fence was down. Sure ain't goin' 'cross no cattle guards, and the gates was all shut and locked."

They studied each other, thinking the same thought. An inside job. A Circle M cowboy taking a few Black Angus for himself. But even that made no sense. No one could sneak sixteen head all the way from that pasture to the main road without being seen or leaving sign.

"How?" Ashton shook his head again. "How in heaven's name . . . ?"

Colter shrugged. "Those hippies livin' 'cross the highway on Bonner Flats will say it was extraterrestrials." Said without a smile, it probably wasn't a joke.

In fact, Ashton had to agree with the weathered cowboy.

The *Basin River Weekly Item* had reported cattle turning up missing at smaller ranches in the county, but Ashton had figured those animals had probably just wandered off. The ranchers weren't really ranchers. Just folks wealthy enough to buy land and lease a pasture from the feds for grazing and have themselves a quiet place to come to and get a good tax break on top of it. Like that TV director or producer or company executive who ran buffalo on his place and had his own private helicopter. There were only two real ranchers left in Cutthroat County, though Ashton would never publicly admit that Garland Foster was a real rancher. He'd been mostly a sheepman since arriving in Cutthroat County, and he was hardly even that anymore.

Ashton looked at the curtains that kept him from seeing those flashing red lights all across Foster's spread. "How did someone manage to get sixteen Black Angus of our herd out of there? Without a truck or trucks. Without being seen? That's what perplexes me." He moved back to the map, reached his left hand up to the crooked line marked in blue type—*Dead Indian Pony Creek*—and traced it down to the nearest two-track, then followed that to the ranch road, then down the eleven miles to the main highway.

Colter moved closer to the map. Those hard eyes narrowed as he memorized the topography, the roads, paths, streams, canyons, everything. Then he seemed to dismiss the map and remember the country from personal experience, riding a half-broke cowpony in that rough, hard, impenetrable country in the spring, the summer, the fall. Probably not the winter, though. Not in northern Montana. Not unless a man was desperate or suicidal.

His head shook after thirty seconds. "I can take some boys up, see if we can find a trail."

Ashton shook his head. He had forgotten about a wife who had left him, had dismissed a fruitless trip to the state capital, and then an even more unproductive meeting in a Great Falls coffee shop with a high-priced private dick. "No point in that," he said. "They stole sixteen head of prime

Black Angus because we were sleeping. Anyone who has lived in Montana for a month knows you might catch Ashton Maddox asleep once, and only once. I'll never make that mistake again. They won't be back there. Any missing head elsewhere?"

"Nothin' yet," Colter replied. "But I ain't got all the tallies yet."

Ashton remembered the bourbon and raised the tumbler as he gave his foreman that look that needed no interpretation. "I want those tallies done right quick. There's one thing in my book that sure hasn't changed since the eighteen hundreds. *Nobody* steals Circle M beef and gets away with it."

CHAPTER 2

One of these days, Mary Broadbent thought, *I'll learn how to cook.*

Then she wouldn't have to eat breakfast at the Wild Bunch Casino.

At 7:19 A.M. the counter was packed. She had learned fast after arriving in Basin Creek two years back that she was not the only person in Cutthroat County who couldn't cook.

A highway construction worker in his orange safety vest and hard hat was shouting for another Coors when he turned to see Mary walk inside. His mouth hung open for what seemed like minutes, and then he spun around on the dingy black stool and called out to the waitress, "Make it a coffee, sweetheart. Don't leave room for any milk or nothin'."

His friends chuckled and went about mopping up runny eggs with biscuits straight from a package and slurping down their coffees. A pockmarked teen turned around from a video keno game and smiled at her, then winked. She shook her head, thought about asking him if his mama and daddy knew he was cutting class this morning, but then realized the boy had probably dropped out of school in eighth grade.

She dismissed eating at the counter and found a table near the big window. A truck driver sat alone at one table, waiting on his breakfast, and tourists—a balding man, plump wife, two grade-school-age kids, likely home-schooled since it was early May—sat with their specials of the day. They'd be the ones in the SUV rental out front. Probably on their way back from Glacier National Park to the airport. Billings . . . Great Falls . . . maybe Missoula . . . possibly as far away as Salt Lake City or Denver. She'd seen the silver Chrysler Pacifica parked in front of a unit at the Cowboy Up Motel yesterday evening.

The boy stared wild-eyed at the automatic pistol holstered on her hip.

"Don't stare," his father whispered over his coffee.

"She's got a gun," the boy whispered back. "She's a cop."

"A policeman." The mother gasped, looked up at Mary, and smiled. "Sorry. A policewoman."

"Like Angie Dickinson." The truck driver laughed at his joke. The parents, it appeared, were too young to remember television from the 1970s.

Fact was, Mary Broadbent was too young to have seen the original run of that series, but she had heard so many references to *Police Woman*, she had grown used to it. She had googled the show just to see what the fuss was about, and quickly decided there were worse actresses to be compared to than Angie Dickinson.

Mary had blond hair, blue eyes, too, but any resemblance probably ended there. She was short. At five foot, two inches, barely tall enough to get into Montana Law Enforcement Academy, and four inches above the minimum height to be a United States Marine. But she was solid, strong, and smart. Of course, she could never wear tights the way Angie did in *Rio Bravo*—the only movie Mary could recall ever seeing Angie Dickinson in.

Pulling out the chair, Mary removed her hat, laid it on the other side of the table, and sat down. The little girl, maybe five years old, stared over her cereal bowl.

Mary smiled. The girl smiled back.

"Are you having a nice vacation?" Mary asked.

The girl shook her head. "We haven't seen a bear or eagles."

Mary nodded, leaned forward, and whispered in a conspiratorial tone, "Want to know something?"

The parents looked on in silence. The boy's mouth hung open, unable to believe a sheriff's deputy was talking to his kid sister.

"I've lived here just over two years, and I've never seen a bear once." *Well,* she thought, *not a live one.*

"Really?"

"Cross my heart," Mary said, and looked up at Polly Poe, the redheaded waitress who had been working there forever.

"Coffee and the Number Four."

"What I figured," Polly said, and went back to the counter.

"How about an eagle?"

Mary blinked, found the girl again, and smiled.

"Yes. I have seen eagles. Which way are you going from here?"

"East Glacier," the father answered.

She had guessed wrong. They had not come from but were going to. Vacation had just started. No wonder the girl hadn't seen an eagle yet. "Well, when you get into the Always Winter Mountains, just look high in the trees along the river. And if you're going into the park, I'm pretty sure you'll spot many an eagle. Some osprey, too."

The boy found his voice. "What's an osprey?"

"A raptor," Mary said. "Like an eagle. Looks like a bald eagle a bit. They both have white heads, but the eagle's is solid white. And the eagle is bigger. The osprey's body is white, the eagle's dark. Both are absolutely beautiful to see." She smiled.

Polly came with her coffee and a glass of water.

Mary let the tourists get back to their breakfast, and she stared out the window as Basin Creek came to life. Across the street, a Chevy truck stopped, and two men climbed out, walked to the bed, and pulled out a sign. She let out a sigh as the two men began pounding a sign into the grass.

ELISON DEMPSEY C.A.N. & WILL!
VOTE DEMPSEY FOR SHERIFF

Too bad, she thought. If she were outside, she could cite them for illegal parking, but they'd be gone by the time she got across the street. And John would chastise her for writing a ticket for a village offense when her jurisdiction was Cutthroat County . . . and for giving Carl Lorimer more copy to fill his *Basin River Weekly Item.*

A black sedan caught her eye next as it turned left, which meant coming in from the north, and parked next to her navy blue Interceptor. A white-haired man stepped out, glanced at Mary's SUV, and reached back inside his car, over the driver's seat and into the passenger side. He pulled out a cowboy hat, and settled it on his head. As though that made him a cowboy. It was a cheap hat, probably off the shelf at the Wantlands Mercantile. New, black, it had the standard curled brim and ubiquitous cattleman crease. He wore jeans and a blue shirt. The boots were scuffed, worn, with those awful-looking ultra-wide, flat toes.

He walked away from the car, which chirped as he hit the lock button on the keychain, and walked inside. Having paid his bill, the truck driver stopped and sucked in his stomach as he let the man in the new cowboy hat slide past him.

The car . . . the man . . . seemed familiar.

"See ya, doll," the trucker called to Polly, nodding at the cash and change by his empty plate, and left the restaurant for his Mack truck and empty trailer.

The newcomer looked at the table and sat down. He didn't

even look at the counter or the other tables. He sat and looked out the window.

He was neither handsome nor ugly. Average height and weight. The type of man most people would hardly give a second glance. But there was something about him, the way he looked, held himself. His eyes studied everything outside the window.

Now, if she were a suspicious detective, Mary would try to figure out what he was up to. But what would anyone be up to in Basin Creek? Planning a bank heist? There was a First Bank branch in the courthouse, which was little more than an ATM. Most people did their banking in Choteau or Cut Bank. Construction workers, and sometimes even Mary, often cashed their checks at the Wantlands Mercantile, where Dottie took out only a couple of dollars for the trouble—during peak season, anyway. She'd charge more in winter when money got tight throughout the county.

But Mary was pretty sure the man looked familiar because she had seen him on a poster. Maybe if she had gotten more sleep last night . . .

Polly hurried over with a rag. Maybe she thought the guy would steal her tip. She said, "Lemme clean this up for you, mister."

The man reached over, grabbed the bills and change, and held them out for her, smiling.

"Why, thank you, hon," Polly said, and took the money and stuffed it inside the apron pocket. She busied herself wiping down the table. That trucker ate like a pig. Then Polly stepped back, shoved the rag inside the back pocket of her jeans, wiped her hands on the front pant legs and smiled. "Coffee?" she asked.

"Hot tea?" he asked.

"We can do that for you, yes sir." Polly bit her lower lip. "Let's see. I think we got black tea, and lemon tea, or I can pour you some iced tea—unsweetened—and put it in the microwave."

"Your choice." He smiled again.

Mary didn't recognize the voice.

Smitten, Polly said, "I'll fetch you a menu. Our special today's corned beef hash." Leaning forward, she whispered, "But it's straight out of a can, and not from one of them factories that make good canned food, but the cheap stuff. I'd go with the bacon and sausage or eggs, if I was you."

"Just tea for now," the man said.

Something about him remained familiar, but Mary still couldn't place him.

Polly said to Mary, "I'll have yours right out."

"Are you a real cop?"

Forgetting about the man, Mary sighed and looked over at the boy.

"Bryant, don't be rude, " the dad scolded.

The mother sang out, "We don't call them cops, son. They are police officers."

"Actually," Mary said, making herself smile, "I'm a sheriff's deputy."

"You mean you can arrest people?" the boy asked.

"If I have to," Mary said, putting on her charm.

"You ever shot a criminal?"

She leaned forward and narrowed her eyes. "Not yet."

The boy found his glass of milk and guzzled it.

The mother mouthed a silent, "I am so sorry."

Mary shrugged that off and gave that pleasant smile.

The dad paid the bill, stood up, and the family left in a hurry, the little girl staring at Mary through the large window, till they reached the minivan. By the time the Chrysler van pulled out of the parking lot, Polly was putting a bowl in front of Mary, then grabbing the money on the vacant table. She didn't wipe it down but hurried to a table by one of the video poker games where someone was asking for another Pepsi.

How anyone could drink a Pepsi at eight in the morning was beyond Mary. She found the spoon, and looked up. John T. Drew stood in front of her, wearing his Stetson, which was well-worn, battered, and custom-made, and smiled.

"Good morning, Sheriff," Mary said.

Drew nodded. "Deputy Broadbent." He looked at the vacated table.

"Join me?" Mary asked, and nodded at the empty chair.

"Don't mind if I do." He dragged the chair out, sat into it smoothly, and pulled off his hat, which he laid crown down on the empty chair.

Mary's oatmeal was skimpy on the raisins this morning as she thought, *No, that man did not have the look of a tourist.* But she turned her attention to her boss.

"I'll fetch you some coffee, Johnny," Polly told Drew. "You want the special?"

Drew nodded at Mary's bowl. "That'll do."

"Oatmeal." Polly snorted. "You turning yuppie on us, Johnny?"

"Just watching my figure."

She laughed and moved off toward a construction worker waving his empty cup of coffee.

"How'd last night go?" Drew asked.

Mary shrugged. "Well, I had to run Connie Good Stabbing to the rez."

"All the way?" After Polly poured his coffee, Drew opened a packet of what passed for cream, dumped it into the cup, and stirred it absently with a spoon.

"Just to the turnoff." Mary smiled, watching Polly serve tea to the stranger. "Hassun was waiting in his pickup."

Smiling, Drew put the spoon on a napkin, picked up the cup, and said, "He's a good dad. Good man. Patient." He took a sip, made a face.

Mary grinned. "It's not Starbucks."

"No, it's not." He drank more though. "That's a long, lonely drive in the middle of the night."

"I would have enjoyed company." She stretched out her right leg and tapped his toe with her boot.

He did not try to hide the grin, but he did pull his feet in to avoid any more such distractions. "No deer carcasses this time?" he asked.

She frowned. He might have been joking, but sometimes it was hard to tell with the sheriff.

"No deer. No speeders. No wrecks. No—" She looked at the stranger sipping tea.

"I put you on the roster for the highway. Traffic. But school zone till nine. Then just make sure nobody still thinks our highways are the autobahn."

Mary turned back to her boss.

"You up for that?" the sheriff asked. "I mean a day shift after a night shift is never much fun."

Mary slid her bowl away. She had finished most of it, and it wasn't like they served real oatmeal there, anyway.

Polly was back, asking the man from the sedan if he wanted more tea or to order some breakfast, but was told he was fine with tea. He handed her a five-dollar bill and told her to keep the change. Polly then started telling John T. Drew about the aches she was having in her back at nights, as if Drew had more than basic medical training.

Mary wished the waitress would finish complaining and remember the big tip she was getting. Mary didn't get to spend much time with John on workdays. She looked at her watch. She'd have to leave now before the schoolkids—all seventy-eight of them—started to go to the campus that held the combined grade, middle, and high schools.

When Polly finally left, Mary sighed with relief and smiled at the sheriff. "I can sleep in tomorrow, right?"

He found his billfold and dropped some bills by the oatmeal bowl. John T. Drew gave her that look that almost made her blush. “I wouldn’t count on it,” he whispered.

She did blush then. Rising, she found her hat, glanced again at the man with the tea, and headed for the door, daydreaming about the night to come. A night with Sheriff John T. Drew alone to herself, after she finished her shift.

CHAPTER 3

There were no reserved parking spots for law enforcement or other emergency vehicles in front of the Cutthroat County Courthouse/Basin Creek Municipal Building. Not that John T. Drew, Mary Broadbent, or Denton Creel ever had trouble finding a place near the front door. Drew eased his Interceptor next to the fire hydrant and smiled, knowing how Fire Chief Bobby Ward would give him grief about that. It was their running joke.

For that early on a Wednesday morning, the number of cars in front of what Drew fondly called "the old Bailey Building and Loan," in homage to one of his favorite movies, came as a surprise. He recognized Dan O'Riley's Dodge Ram. He also knew who owned the top-of-the-line Ford Expedition that had likely set him back eighty or ninety grand. And Ashton Maddox would have paid cash.

After setting the emergency brake, Drew stepped onto the rough pavement, closed the door, hit the lock on his keychain, and stepped onto the sidewalk. He took note of the other cars and figured the county commissioners were meeting. They were part-time politicians who had real jobs and, unlike most politicos, they didn't like sitting in meetings. Since they had just finished their monthly meeting last week, something was up. It had to be Ashton Maddox.

Drew's Justin boots sounded heavily when he entered the old building. He didn't expect to find Constable Taylor in today, as this was Wednesday, but he expected to have his morning chat with school superintendent Nancy Poteet. The library wouldn't open until lunchtime, when some kids from the schoolgrounds would come over to check out books, especially those in Miss King's sixth-grade class. Miss King could have been Methuselah's mother. She had taught Drew way back in the day.

On the way to the staircase, he passed Poteet's desk and saw the note.

Sorry. Taking ambulance-driving class
in Cut Bank today.
Back tomorrow.
NP

Drew found a pen in his shirt pocket, and smiled as he scribbled beneath Poteet's initials.

Who in Cut Bank knows how to drive *anything*?

There was no need to sign the note. She'd know his writing and his humor.

Up the dark stairs, boots echoing even louder, he came to the second floor and headed toward his office, habitually checking the doors of the county attorney and coroner since both rarely came to Basin Creek. School kids had broken in two years ago, sprayed graffiti over Murdoch Robeson's walls and laid a mannequin with an arrow stuck in the dummy's chest across George White's desk. They were caught. Kids didn't realize Basin Creek had modernized enough to have surveillance cameras in the old building, though the place got so dark at night it was a miracle Taylor, Robeson, O'Riley, and Drew had been able to identify the pranksters. Their parents wound up replacing the broken glass and the kids repainted the attorney's walls and spent their next ten Saturdays on litter duty in the town. Knowing the parents of those four boys, Drew figured they didn't sit comfortably for a week of Sundays.

Yes, he thought, stopping at his office. *Sometimes it does seem like Mayberry.* He glanced down the hall at O'Riley's office and heard muffled voices from the meeting room next to it. Well, four of the voices were muffled. Ashton Maddox was bellowing, though Drew couldn't understand the words.

The sheriff fished the key out of his jeans pocket and unlocked the door. Thinking as he always thought, *How many sheriff's departments have locked doors?* he went inside and hung his Stetson on the rack and put his satchel case on the empty seat. He hit START on the coffeemaker and got ready for his morning routine.

Paperwork. The bane of every county sheriff's existence.

He sat at his desk and went over Mary Broadbent's duty log. At least Creel had yesterday and today off, so he had just her report to read, then opened yesterday's mail, which always arrived after lunch when Drew was patrolling. He had returned that afternoon, but never bothered with the mail. He needed something to do in the mornings.

His plan was to file some papers and post two APBs on the bulletin board. He found his MSU Bobcats coffee mug and filled it with better coffee than he'd ever get at the Wild Bunch Casino.

The meeting in the county commissioners boardroom broke up.

"Just see it gets done, Dan," Ashton Maddox thundered, his words bouncing off the walls, then his boots plodding on the tile and down the stairs.

I should have keyed his SUV. Drew grinned at his daydream, found milk not even expired in the minifridge, and was stirring his cup when Dan O'Riley knocked twice and opened the door.

"Got a sec, John?" That was one of the county manager's legendary questions.

Drew nodded, then seeing O'Riley's eyes on the coffee cup, he nodded at the row of fairly clean spares atop the minifridge. "Help yourself," he said, and returned to his desk.

"I'm sure you heard Ashton Maddox's fare-thee-well just now," O'Riley said as he poured coffee into a mug, then settled into one of the two chairs in front of Drew's desk. He was carrying a notepad and a rolled-up newspaper tucked underneath his left armpit.

"I was prepared for it." Drew tasted his coffee, which wasn't bad by his standards. "Saw his rig in front of the old Bailey Building and Loan when I parked."

Settling the notepad and newspaper on his lap, O'Riley sipped coffee, nodded as though he actually liked it, and crossed his left leg over his right. "He called very late last night. I called Grace and Sid. Texted Mack, knowing he'd be on the river guiding some tourists this morning, but just to give him a heads-up in case he ran into Ashton."

Drew took another sip of coffee. He said nothing.

"Ashton said he's missing sixteen head of cattle."

The sheriff's laughter shocked the county manager.

After placing his cup on a highway department report, Drew crossed his arms. "What's he running these days? Five thousand head?"

"I don't think it's that many." Drew frowned.

"It's not far under that, though. Forty-five hundred maybe—for a low in a bad year. And winter wasn't that bad, you know." He shook his head and drank more coffee, but the taste had turned bitter. "The man has a ranch of one hundred and forty-nine thousand acres, more than two-thirds of that deeded and he's complaining that he lost sixteen head."

"At one pasture," O'Riley said.

"Which one?"

"Section fifty-four. Dead Indian Pony Creek."

Drew leaned forward at that detail. "Grizzly?"

O'Riley shook his head. "No sign of that."

"They could have gotten lost. That's rough—" He stopped, pushed back the chair, and shook his head. A rancher could lose a fair amount of cattle around Dead Indian Pony Creek in the summer and fall when the beeves grazed at the higher elevations. But not in winter when the cattle were down on the grasslands. Not unless a big blow came in of a sudden. As he had pointed out, the past winter was mild by Montana standards.

Sure, Ashton Maddox had too many faults to count, but he did know how to manage a ranch, and he wasn't cheap when it came to fences, gates, and cattle guards.

"The way Ashton explained it, Dante Crump—you know how straight he is—rode over to do a count and push cattle up into the high country. They were sixteen head short, not including less than a handful lost during the winter. Sixteen Black Angus heifers, just up and gone."

Black Angus did not just up and go anywhere.

Drew shook his head. "Maybe that story in the *Big Sky Monthly* gave some folks an idea."

Rustling had been mentioned briefly in that piece. At the time, only one ranch had reported the loss of a few head. But now?

O'Riley picked up the newspaper—newcomer Carl Lorimer's *Basin River Weekly Item*—that was published every Thursday morning. Drew rarely read it. Having watched the Missoula newspaper go from a decent-size publication to practically nothing, he never could understand why anyone would start a newspaper these days, especially in a town with one hundred and sixty-nine people and a county with fewer than two hundred and thirty more.

"You see this?" O'Riley asked.

Drew finished his coffee and set the mug on a coaster. "Are you kidding me?"

O'Riley made no expression, but handed the paper over the desk. "Lorimer says five other ranches have reported missing cattle."

The headline read:

GET A ROPE?

CATTLE RUSTLING INCREASES
IN CUTTHROAT COUNTY.

Well, Drew couldn't fault the man's reporting. The Cutthroat County Cattlemen's Association had confirmed that five ranchers had reported loss of cattle to the Montana Department of Livestock's Brand Enforcement Division, District 3. Montana Livestock had put up a $500 reward for information leading to the arrest and conviction of any felony rustler. According to county records, seventy cattle had been reported missing before the sixteen Ashton Maddox had allegedly lost. Mostly heifers, they had a value of over $2,000 per animal, meaning a rough value of $140,000.

But the article took a turn to the absurd.

> Elison Dempsey, running for election as Cutthroat County sheriff against incumbent John T. Drew and leader of the Citizens Action Network volunteer anticrime unit, says it is now official. George Grimes, a noted Texas Ranger recently retired, and the subject of last year's action movie *Beretta Law* will join C.A.N. as a stock detective.

Drew didn't recognize the name of the Montana livestock official who said the department, and the brand inspector for District 3, welcomed any help. But it was the final line of the article that raised the sheriff's blood pressure.

> Drew could not be reached for comment.

"I don't recall being asked for a comment." He handed the paper back to O'Riley.

The county manager shrugged. "He probably would say he called two or three times."

"Got voice mail. And my cell phone works better than most in this—"

"It's really not the point, John." O'Riley was right.

Drew nodded, even though he didn't like the fact that he had let a newspaper article irritate him, especially since it was pretty much spot-on. "Clark Blaine's the brand inspector for District 3. He's a good man. Denton's been working this case—or these cases, I should say with Clark. We've sent alerts on the breeds, ear tags, and brands. But this isn't like the old days. We can't track a truck on a paved road."

O'Riley smiled. "Or hang them." Reading Drew's face, he quickly abandoned his attempt at joking. "Well, you and Clark have another case of rustling on your hands."

"Maddox hasn't filed a complaint to my office," Drew said.

"You didn't expect him to, did you?" O'Riley stood up, found his notepad, but left this week's newspaper. "I'm sure Ashton will let Clark know."

Drew telephoned Denton Creel with the news of the missing cattle at the Circle M Ranch, and told him to check with Clark Blaine and coordinate the investigation. Creel had been around long enough to know the far-from-friendly relationship between Maddoxes and Drews was pushing two centuries.

The rest of the morning went normal. At noon, Drew checked in with Mary Broadbent—nothing much to report, there—and then locked up the office and headed downstairs and into the brisk but pleasant afternoon. Fifty-nine degrees was warm that far north at that time of year. Once in the Interceptor, he drove to the Busted Stirrup Bar, grabbed a chicken sandwich, no mayo, and iced tea to go, then began his patrol.

Two state highways plus US 103 crossed Cutthroat County, but nobody had ever tried to figure out how many county roads there were, since every one of them was dirt. A tourist would have been surprised to learn how many meth labs had been raided in the county by the sheriff's department. Sometimes the deputies were assisted by agents from the Montana Department of Justice's Narcotics Bureau, if, by chance and luck, one of those officers felt like driving to the end of the world.

Drew decided to take Elk Lane and make sure no one had decided to reoccupy the trashed trailer home on the hillside. A meth-head had caused a grass fire two years ago that scorched acres and acres of cattle graze, but left the trailer alone. They had thrown the book at him. 45-9-102: Criminal possession of dangerous drugs. 45-9-103: Criminal possession with intent to distribute. 45-6-102: Negligent arson. And 45-8-313: Unlawful possession of firearm by convicted person.

He wound up taking a plea deal and was doing a five-year stretch in Deer Lodge, but he might already be out on parole, or someone else could have taken up residence in that trailer, though Drew had no plans to search it unless he found something suspicious.

He didn't. But after topping the hill and rolling down to the flats, he spotted a cowboy herding cattle. Harry Sweet was a smart cowhand, using the barbed-wire fence to keep the ten fat beeves in a line.

Drew drove ahead, then stopped, climbed out of the Interceptor, stepped over the ditch, and waited by the fence. He looked at those wood turbines far down the pasture, wondering why some turned and others didn't, and smiled as the cattle trod past. One black heifer stopped briefly and stared at him, but then Harry Sweet cawed like a raven and the animal turned back and hurried along.

A steer had a blue US Department of Agriculture RFID tag on its left ear. The radio-frequency tags were new, but only required for cattle or bison being transported across state lines. In the old days, cattlemen branded young cattle, but in Montana, many still used hot iron. Maddox used ear tags.

Drew remembered hearing the photographer who had come earlier in the year say, "Those ugly ear tags sure ruin photographs."

One of Garland Foster's cowpunchers had said, "Ever been branded, buster?"

The photographer had laughed and then brushed back his long hair to reveal an earring. "No, sir, but I've had my ear pierced. It didn't hurt. And it's pretty. But those things . . . they're just ugly as sin."

Harry Sweet reined his dun gelding over and stopped near the fence. Pushing back his hat, he hooked his knee over the horn, spit out tobacco juice, then nodded. "Sheriff. What brings you to this neck of the woods?"

Drew gestured up the hill. "Just making sure you weren't making meth."

The cowhand smiled a broken-toothed grin. "My teeth look rotted to you?"

"The few you have left? No. Guess I made a long drive for nothing."

Sweet chuckled. "I ain't seen nobody in that old trailer." He waved at the pasture. "You'd never know this was burnt over last year, would you?"

"Two years, I think."

"Maybe so." He looked ahead to make sure none of the animals had started to stray.

"Ashton Maddox says he lost sixteen heifers to rustlers. Section fifty-four over by Dead Indian Pony Creek."

The cowboy shifted the wad of tobacco to his other cheek. "When?"

Drew's head shook. "Dante Crump found them missing a day or two ago when he was pushing them up to the summer graze."

The grin returned. "Ol' Maddox must have blowed a gasket. Someone stole Circle M beef. That'll make the Old Man happy."

"Have you lost any?"

"Not to rustlers. But the Old Man don't run much beef no more. Sheep mostly, and not many of them now that he's got them confounded Don Quixotes."

Drew had never heard of a wind turbine called a Don Quixote, and was surprised Harry Sweet even knew about Quixote.

"The Circle M's the sixth ranch to report a hit by rustlers," Drew said.

Sweet's head bobbed. "I know. The Old Man reads the emails he gets from the Cattlemen's Association. He told me. He also said if I see someone taking one of his critters, to thank the fool and open the gate for him."

That sounded like something Garland Foster would say.

Drew looked at the cattle as they moved along. "Where you driving those? Nothing down that way but Big Coulee."

The cowhand spit, frowned, wiped his mouth, eyed the bovines, shook his head, and finally chuckled. "Tell you the truth, Sheriff . . . since Foster turned to windmillin', there ain't a whole lot for a workin' cowhand like me to do. So I'm . . . well . . . just keepin' in shape."

Drew laughed. "Well"—he nodded a farewell—"if you see or hear anything, let me know."

A cell phone rang. When Drew found it in his shirt pocket, Sweet nodded a goodbye and kicked the gelding into a lope to catch up with his heifers.

The call was dropped. Drew swore softly, leaped the ditch,

and returned to the SUV, which he backed up the hill to the crest where he'd have a stronger signal. He'd recognized the number of the Glacier County Sheriff's Office in Cut Bank. That usually meant one thing. Someone in Cutthroat County had called 9-1-1.

CHAPTER 4

That scribe for the *Basin River Weekly Item* was waiting to ambush Ashton Maddox when he exited the old courthouse building. He had read the publishers bio but couldn't remember all the details.

Carl Lorimer had worked for the *Rocky Mountain Bulletin* in Denver as a cops reporter before that newspaper folded, then got hired by one of those supermarket tabloids. According to the first issue of Montana's newest newspaper, he was a native of Montana, born in Roundup, but his folks moved to California when he was thirteen, and he had moved around since then, while always longing to return to the Big Sky Country. He liked the West, the way people relied on themselves with that rugged independence that made America and the West great. He liked how Montanans were true Americans. Stubbornly independent but willing to give the shirts off their backs to help those in need. Tough. Sometimes violent if necessary. But they tipped their hats to the ladies, and the ladies were strong and feisty, and every man, woman, and child knew good manners.

He seemed to have forgotten the latter.

"You mind not leaning against my SUV?" Ashton said from the sidewalk.

The editor quickly straightened and stepped away from the driver's door of the Platinum Expedition. "Sorry, Mr. Maddox."

He looked to be in his late forties, maybe early fifties, but Ashton Maddox didn't go about guessing ages of men, women, or children, and didn't care a whit for Carl Lorimer.

"Big meeting with the commissioners, I see."

Ashton pushed the button on the keychain and unlocked the door. Grace Gallagher walked down the sidewalk without saying a word and got into her car. Sid Pritchard had parked around the corner. Ashton wondered which one of those had tipped off the newspaperman, but it didn't matter. It wasn't likely Dan O'Riley—the manager wasn't fond of Carl Lorimer, either, but then most politicians didn't like newspaper journalists. Mack McDonald might have called up the editor last night and let him know. McDonald had been advertising his guided fish trips in that weekly paper.

Pulling a skinny reporter's notebook out of the back pocket of his Wranglers, Lorimer got to the point. "Is it true that you lost sixteen head of cattle to rustlers?"

Ashton thought about giving that standard "No comment," but decided everyone already knew the facts by now, so having it out in next week's *Item* wouldn't exactly be the scoop of the century. "It's true," he said, moving toward his SUV.

"Lou Hyman lost fifteen head. That hurts him, I'd think, a lot more than you losing sixteen heifers. But here's what Hyman said." Lorimer read from his notes. "'We used to hang cattle thieves in Montana way back in the territorial days, and even into statehood. But now we've gone from hanging those dirtbags to fining them a pittance.'" The reporter looked up from the notebook, turned the page, and pulled a pen from his denim shirt pocket. "Would you agree with that, Mr. Maddox?"

"The fine is from five thousand dollars to fifty thousand

dollars," Ashton said. "Or a prison sentence of up to ten years. Or both. That isn't want I'd call a pittance."

Lorimer scribbled and smiled. "That's a great quote, sir."

"Glad I could help." Ashton's tone was meant to be sarcastic. He moved to the driver's-side door.

"Anything else for the record?" the editor asked.

"Not at this time."

"What about the hiring of George Grimes as a stock detective for the Citizens Action Network?"

Ashton's hand was about to open the Expedition's door, but it froze there as he looked back at Lorimer.

"You haven't heard?" Before Ashton could reply, the editor grinned, nodded his head, and said, "Oh, that's right. Of course. You were down in Helena so you probably didn't see last week's edition. I don't have a copy on me, but I'll mail you one. Maybe then you'll subscribe." He laughed at his joke, even if he was undoubtedly hoping Ashton Maddox would help pay his bills.

Finally, Lorimer explained. "Elison Dempsey offered that Texas Ranger—ex-Ranger, I mean—a job as a stock detective." He closed his eyes and seemed to recite from an article he had written. "To assist the investigations being conducted by the Department of Livestock's District Three inspector and bring an end to this outrageous criminal activity."

"I don't know George Grimes. And I hardly know Dempsey."

That, Lorimer did not write in his notebook. "Did you see *Beretta Law*?"

"I don't watch movies. I run a ranch." Ashton opened the car door.

"Before you go, sir, I was hoping I might talk to you about a history article I want to write."

Ashton found the handhold, but did not climb into the big SUV.

"I want to compare what's happening today, the cattle rustling in Cutthroat County, to what happened back in 1891."

1891. Ashton wet his lips.

"Those were wild times," Lorimer said. "At least based on what I've found out in the library and some old newspaper accounts online. I have an appointment next week at the Montana State Historical Society in Helena to do more research. This story would be about how some things have changed. I mean, Basin Creek—the actual creek, I mean—is now Basin River." He laughed. "Why didn't the town ever change its name?"

He probably wasn't actually asking Ashton. The question was more rhetorical.

"And we have cell service . . . more or less on cloudy or stormy days. And you can drink expensive bourbon . . . if you drive to Great Falls."

That wasn't exactly true. Monty Bell managed to get a bottle of Blanton's every month, but he sure charged Ashton a hefty convenience fee.

"But we still have cattle rustling. Would you like to tell me any stories you heard about those days . . . from the Maddox point of view."

Ashton got into the truck, but looked at Lorimer before closing the door. He didn't answer the question directly but said, "You should be able to get all you want from the library. Phyllis Lynne will be happy to assist you, I'm sure." He didn't wish him luck with the article.

The door closed, the SUV roared to life, and Ashton Maddox backed up and drove down the street, but he didn't go home. Not yet. He went to the Victorian house Elison Dempsey had been renting. The front yard was filled with I WANT YOU signs for his vigilante group and VOTE DEMPSEY FOR SHERIFF signs for his own massive ego.

He walked past the camo Jeep, two motorcycles, a beat-up

Chevy truck, and the ELISON DEMPSEY FOR CUTTHROAT COUNTY SHERIFF van, and climbed the steps. The boards on the old porch squeaked as he walked to the door and punched the button. He heard the chimes ringing inside, and stepped back.

A punk in fatigues and flak jacket and holding a Draco AK-47 pistol opened the door. "Yeah?"

"Where's Dempsey?" Ashton said.

"Who wants to know?"

"The man who's gonna take that machine gun from you and shove it up your—"

"Let him in, Comanche." Elison Dempsey chuckled from somewhere in the living room.

Comanche? The kid didn't have an ounce of Indian blood in him. And even with that lethal weapon in his hand, he looked about as tough as a sunflower after a weeklong, below-zero cold snap.

The punk's pockmarked face flushed, but he unlatched the screen door, and let Ashton pull it open. The boy stepped away, lowering the short-barreled semiautomatic and glaring at Ashton.

Stepping into a room that smelled of cigarette smoke and marijuana, he found C.A.N.'s leader eating bacon and eggs and drinking coffee spiked with cheap vodka. The bottle, half empty, stood on a coffee table covered with Montana newspapers, national news magazines, and several old *Playboys*. Dempsey wasn't smoking, but some of his men were.

"You hungry?" Dempsey looked up and wiped his mouth with his shirtsleeve. "I think there's some eggs left. And coffee. Plenty of coffee." He nodded at the bottle. "Or whatever suits you."

"You hired George Grimes?" Ashton did not sit down.

"Yeah." Dempsey found the coffee and slurped. "You know him, eh?"

"I know of him. Why on earth would you bring that jackass up here?"

"Because he is news. He makes news."

"He's a train wreck."

Dempsey grinned. "Train wrecks make news all the time. Like airplane crashes. We'll get more attention now with him coming up here. And remember that story that made all the newspapers when he tracked down those kidnappers in the Big Bend?"

Ashton said nothing.

"That made headlines all over. Got him into a movie." Dempsey's eyes squinted as he thought. "Who was the actor that played him in *Beretta Law*?"

Ashton did not answer.

"Hey, I'm bringing in a famous lawman—more famous than that county hick I'm running against. That'll be good for you. And it'll help me get elected."

"I've given you money because I don't like John Drew. Or any Drew. But remember who has been your big campaign donor. My money isn't for some half-crazy Texan." Ashton looked around the room. He could see where his money was going, and it wasn't much better than a wildcat of a Texas Ranger. "You want any more cash from me, you run your ideas, *big or small*, past me first."

Dempsey sighed, but nodded.

"And keep that loose cannon off my ranch, Dempsey."

The man pouted. "You want me to tell Ranger George Grimes to go back to Texas once he gets here?" His face moved from pouting to abject fear.

"It's too late for that. You'd look like the fool you are if Grimes left. I figure my donations to your campaign are what enticed Grimes to head north."

"No, no, sir. We—" Dempsey swore underneath his breath, shook his head, and finally sighed.

Which Ashton Maddox took as a confession.

"I expect my money's worth," he told Dempsey. "Just keep him away from me. And keep him on a tight rein. Or I'll send you to the slaughterhouse. Understood?"

Dempsey's head bobbed. "Sure, Ash, Sure. We'll let him work them other spreads. It'll work out just fine. I know what I'm doing. Trust me."

You know what you're doing. Ashton shook his head, turned around and left the living room. The punk with the machine pistol stared at him, but then pushed the screen door open.

He returned to the ranch and drove straight to Dead Indian Pony Creek, a tiring drive made longer because of all the gates and wire traps.

"Always leave a gate the way you found it," his daddy had always said. "And on my land, you better find it shut."

It was well after noon by the time he reached the pasture where he had lost sixteen heifers. Before climbing out of the Expedition, he opened the glove box and pulled out the snub-nosed Smith & Wesson .38. Once he was out of the SUV, he shoved the revolver into his waistband, closed the door, and walked across the trampled grass. He didn't expect to find anything except cow pies. Dante Crump and Colter Norris had likely covered the ground for hours, and they hadn't found any sign.

Ashton found what he'd expected—a rusted Folger's coffee can, firepits, beer bottles, cigarette butts. He hiked up a deer trail, gave up on discovering anything there, and cut down the slope till he heard the gurgling of the creek.

Where Dead Indian Pony Creek bent southward, he knelt and studied the tracks of shod horses and cloven hooves of cattle that led to the water. He dipped his hand into the cool, clear water, and splashed the back of his neck, and thought. *What was it that newspaperman had said back in town?*

About Basin Creek now known as Basin River, and why the town never changed its name to match the creek that had been promoted to river? Something like that.

Another memory brought a brief smile. *His grandfather saying he never understood why anyone would call a town a crick. "Tadpoles and fish don't live in towns, cowboys and petticoats don't live in cricks and rivers."*

Ashton sighed. The old man had a point.

Rising, he waded through the water, which didn't even reach his calves, and kept following the horse and cattle tracks, not that he thought they belonged to the stolen heifers. Likely they were made by Dante Crump when he had pushed the cattle that remained up to the high country.

Ashton found a quarter and an arrowhead, and pocketed both.

For two hours, he worked up a sweat moving through the pasture east and west. He became thirsty. Should have brought a water bottle with him, but kept going for fifteen more minutes, before coming to his senses.

The elevation here wasn't that bad—forty-five hundred feet—but dehydration could turn serious. No one knew he was there, and it wasn't like he'd have much of a cell phone signal, if any. He caught his breath, turned back, and headed back for the creek.

"If you drink fast-flowing water, you're safe," his grandfather had told him. "Just don't drink water that's not running fast. That's where the germs get you."

He had bottled water in the Ford, and he walked through the shallow creek, stepped onto the other bank, and was halfway to the SUV when he stopped, turned, and returned to the creek. Kneeling again, he fingered the cloven hoofprint nearest the gurgling water and looked across the small creek to the other bank, the other tracks of cattle and horses that disappeared in the grass. He looked at his fingers on the track right before him, and again at those across the water. Then he turned and stared at the gurgling creek, the blooming bushes, trees, wildflowers, and rocks on both sides of the banks.

No one had found any suspicious tracks. No one had seen any trucks on the roads he had taken to get here. No one had found anything. Heifers did not just disappear. And Ashton Maddox didn't believe in alien spaceships and insane religious zealots sacrificing bovines or ripping out their innards for scientific studies.

Something else came to him. Something his father had told him his grandfather had said.

"You can't track a man through water."

CHAPTER 5

She'd be glad when this day was over.

Not that it had been bad. Like most Wednesdays Mary Broadbent worked, she had the morning shift at the school, making sure tourists and locals saw her Interceptor and paid attention to the SCHOOL-ZONE sign. The last ticket she wrote back in June of last year, the driver complained he didn't see any flashing lights to warn him he was in a school zone.

Flashing lights? In Basin Creek. That was a laugh.

She had told him, "Six-year-olds with book bags holding hands with their eleven-year-old siblings didn't give you any idea?"

The man had called her something nasty, so she had cited him for a seatbelt violation, too.

No speeders today. She had helped walk a few girls across the street. The Yarborough kid always said she wanted to be a police girl just like Deputy Mary.

"You still want to be a sheriff's deputy, Annabelle?" Mary had asked this morning.

"Uh-huh. Just like you. Except I don't want yeller hair."

"You can have any color hair you want, according to the Montana Law Enforcement Academy."

"Or no hair. Like Deputy Denton."

Mary couldn't hold back the laugh. "He has some hair," she'd said.

"That's why he don't never take off his hat."

Mary had managed to stifle a chuckle by the time they reached the gate that led to the school compound.

"You'll make a fine deputy, Annabelle. See you tomorrow."

A classmate asked the girl why she wanted to be a cop.

Mary heard the answer as she waited for the rest of the kids to get across the street.

"So I can shoot my pesty brother."

Basin Creek Constable Derrick Taylor would handle the afternoon crossing duties, so Mary spent the rest of the day on patrol, driving south on the state Highway 60, commonly called Neely Road. Not much traffic, but there rarely was on Wednesdays, especially before school let out for the summer. That would be in another week and a half.

She turned off the highway onto Basin River Road, noting the high water, typical for spring runoff, and stopped when she saw Mack McDonald's Chevy van. He had two customers this morning, probably Montana Department of Transportation cronies who were supposed to be working.

She rolled down the window and asked, "Catch anything?"

"Not in the river," one of the customers said, "but in Mack's beaver pond. We let them go."

"See anybody?"

"Here?" Mack snorted. "Just you, girlie. Johnny taking good care of you?"

Oh, she thought, *if only you knew.*

But she sniggered and said, "Well, he sent me to check on you. Make sure you weren't over the limit."

He laughed. "Tell him that Fergie already cited us for all sorts of wildlife conservation felonies."

She laughed, rolled up the window, and headed along the riverside till the dirt road turned back north. Back to Highway 60, south to US 103, and even that highway was practically abandoned. Back to 60 and up to Montana 76—people called it the Custer Highway though George Custer never made it that far into Montana. The only good part about the drive was the county paid for the gas.

That was pretty much how her workday went. Dull, but a pretty day. She'd brought her own lunch, PB&J sandwiches, parmesan cheese crisps, and an apple and ate at Mack McDonald's beaver pond. Actually, it was the beaver's pond, of course, but it happened to be on Mack's property. She didn't see any beaver, but entertained herself by flipping some cheese crisps into the water, and smiled as cutthroat and brownies enjoyed a free lunch, which got her thinking maybe a parmesan crust over trout fried in olive oil with a bit of minced garlic would be nice. Maybe she'd cook that . . . *no, maybe John would cook that* the next time he came over.

He kept saying he would teach her how to cook one of these days.

Wednesday. As boring as a day could be. The highlight was when she gave directions to Kalispell. "Oh, sir, you took the wrong turn at Scapegoat." How anyone could take a wrong turn at that ghost town was beyond her. A sign—about the only thing there was to see in Scapegoat—gave directions and miles. The man actually said he and his wife were going to a funeral. They'd never make it on time, not even close, but Mary didn't tell them that. She did tell them not to speed. Then she drove north, past Basin Creek. The only car she saw was a dark sedan pulled off on one of the road's few turnouts. Thinking it was her best chance to bring in some money to the county, she slowed down, then saw the driver talking on his cell phone. He had stopped to take or make his call, so no hands-free violation there. She kept going, passed the Murdoch spread, and on to the windmill ranch of Garland Foster. She remembered the rig she had seen last night after she had dropped off Connie Good Stabbing and was heading home.

That had been last night's highlight. Asking a couple of strangers if they needed any help.

"Honest, Officer," the younger of the two had said, "we were just . . . ummmm . . . potty break?"

"I understand."

You didn't find rest stops anywhere in Cutthroat County.

This afternoon, she saw a cattle rig heading south, carrying sad-looking cows.

She didn't think there was any point in driving all the way to the Blackfoot rez, so she turned around, and drove back toward Basin Creek. Even chatter on the police radio had been nonexistent.

At least she could sleep in tomorrow, one of her days off. John Drew was good about that. Work a day shift, then night shift, or vice versa, and you'd have the next day off. Even if John had to cover for you. And the sheriff in this county was on call 24/7.

Mary let off the accelerator and focused on the car heading north. She hit the radar, and the black Mercedes flew past. The radar read 113.

She had already hit the lights and was turning sharply.

Wyoming plates. 2021 Mercedes-AMG C-63 S. 113 in a 65. She radioed that in, floored the Ford, and thought *today is going to be all right. Forty-eight miles over the limit. The judge will like this, all right.*

The driver—the same one who had been on his cell phone at the turnout—pulled over quickly and turned off the ignition. Mary ran the plates. No warrants. Clean. She opened the door, got her ticket book, wet her lips, and slowly approached the man who thought he was Mario Andretti. She needed to find a new racecar driver. She had used Andretti too many times.

The window had been rolled down. The driver's hands remained atop the steering wheel. He was used to this.

Mary relaxed just a bit, though she kept her right hand on the handle of the Glock Model 17.

The wind picked up.

When she reached the side of the car, she recognized him. The tea drinker from the Wild Bunch Casino. Now she recalled the black sedan. “License and registration,” she said.

“Sorry, officer.” The man had both docs out of his wallet and handed them over. That was it. No plea. No anger.

“You were doing one hundred and thirteen, sir.”

The man shrugged. “I’m sorry. I—” He shrugged. No excuses.

Well, that was different. She liked that. “Stay here,” she said, and returned to the car.

Closer to Cut Bank, she radioed the sheriff’s department there to run his plate. It was quicker than waiting for the computer to do the work in that signal-less wasteland. That turned out to be clean, too. But going that fast you didn’t get out of a ticket with “I’m sorry.”

She started to write the ticket when the sedan’s driver-side door opened and the man stepped out and walked toward her.

Mary came out quickly, turned sideways to make herself a smaller target, and partially pulled the nine-millimeter automatic out. “Sir,” she commanded, “I need you to get back in your car, sir. Now.”

The man kept coming, but swaying now. He reached for his collar, jerked it open, popping off a button.

“I”—he gasped—“I don’t feel . . . good . . . of-fi . . . *cer.*” His knees buckled.

Mary shoved the pistol back and ran toward him. She punched her two-way, got ready to call for an EMT, when the man straightened. She knew her mistake. Saw the gun coming up in his right hand. She tried to pull the Glock, but knew she was going to be too late.

“Johnny,” she whispered.

* * *

Ashton Maddox was ticked off. At everyone. First he would ask Colter Norris why a ranch foreman with his experience had not thought about someone using the creek bed to drive stolen cattle. Take them all the way to the bridge at Hoary Marmot, outside Circle M land. Put them in a truck, wait till dark, and drive them to wherever. When he reached the highway, he decided that scolding Dante Crump and his foreman could wait. He had better head north to what everyone called Rodent Road, and see if he could find conclusive proof at the Hoary Marmot bridge that it was what the rustlers had done.

He laughed without mirth.

His grandfather and father had always said he would never make a manhunter. Couldn't track a black bull through two feet of snow.

He saw the flashing lights ahead, and backed off the accelerator. He was doing ninety-two. A state trooper wouldn't have stopped him but one of John Drew's deputies would have likely thrown him in jail.

Something was in the road. A deer. A car was pulled off ahead of the Ford SUV with the red and blue flashing lights. And someone was walking toward the roadkill.

Ashton breathed in deeply. No, that wasn't roadkill. And the man walking held something dark in his right hand. A pistol. And that wasn't a deer in the road. It was . . .

"God in heaven."

He slammed on the brakes, and laid down on the horn. His SUV slid to a stop. Ashton smelled burning rubber. He found the .38 again and jumped outside. Fired once. But the man with the gun did not return fire. He ran. Back to his car. Black.

Maddox charged in pursuit. Tried to make out the plates. The black car sped north. He fired three more times, but didn't think he hit anything. He thought about shooting till he was empty, but stopped. If he kept pulling the trigger, the man could just turn around and drive back to run him over or shoot him dead.

Besides, the black car was almost out of sight.

He reached the woman. "God." He saw the blood. She was dead.

Then groaning, she rolled over.

No. Not dead. But blood covered her face, poured out of both nostrils, and he saw the dark hole on the left side of her forehead. He knelt beside her. She groaned again.

"Hang in there, honey," he said, and looked at the Interceptor. Remembered his cell phone.

Nobody had signals there. But he had heard that you could dial 9-1-1 anywhere and be connected. He sure hoped that was true, because he didn't know what he could do with a police-car radio. His mouth was dry as he punched in the numbers despite two shaking hands. To his relief he heard a human voice.

John Drew stared out the rear window. He hated using that backup camera. It just wasn't the way he'd learned how to drive. The radio buzzed, and he slammed the brake pedal.

"Cutthroat County One, this is Glacier County Two, come in please."

He jerked the emergency brake and grabbed the mic. "Cutthroat County One, I hear you."

"John, Danny." Danny Adams was the chief deputy there.

"Danny. What's up?" John frowned. Usually, a dispatcher relayed the emergency.

"We just got a 9-1-1 call from Ashton Maddox. He was driving north on Highway 60, two miles north of the turnout. He was with one of your deputies, said she was down with a bullet in her head."

She was down. John felt like he had been poleaxed. *With a bullet in her head.*

"He exchanged shots with a man, who fled in a black car—he couldn't tell much else—and sped away north."

Drew punched the gas, swore, let off, and released the brake. "Do you still have Maddox on the line?"

"That's a negative, John. But we're radioing Teton County EMS now. We've also requested a life-flight helicopter out of Missoula International."

John blinked in order to see, then hit the lights, the sirens, and felt the Interceptor leap off the hilltop and land on the road. The tagged heifers being herded by Harry Sweet scattered as he flew past. John T. Drew did not care.

"John." Danny Adams cleared his throat. "You need to slow down, John. And calm down."

He pressed his right foot tighter on the accelerator. "Can you get Maddox back on the line?" he asked.

"We can't do that, John. Get ahold of yourself. Help's on the way."

Now he roared. "Why can't you get that jerk on the line? I want to know what condition my . . . my deputy is in."

The radio crackled.

Then Danny Adams spoke like he always did. Clearly. Concisely. Calmly. "John, I'm not doing that. Maddox had his hands full. He said he had lost her pulse. And was starting CPR."

1891

JUNE

CHAPTER 6

She was dead. Worn out at thirty-two years old.

Napoleon Drew sat at her bedside, stroking her cold, pale right hand. Montana Territory aged a body fast, especially a woman. Especially a woman who had given birth to six babies, four of them still living.

Montana *Territory*. Napoleon sighed. No, Montana was a *state* now. He ought to know that. A state since November 8, 1889, and Cutthroat County had become a new county. Napoleon had been appointed its first sheriff. Officially. Today.

Rebecca almost lived to see it.

The regulator clock began to chime. It was noon. Cutthroat County just became official. And Napoleon Drew soon would be, too.

The baby squalled.

He made himself look across the one-room cabin at the midwife who rocked the newborn, trying with all her might, trying to will the Lord to let that tiny baby girl nurse on a cotton bandanna that had been dipped into a pail of goat's milk.

Four of them still living. Two boys. Two girls. Still living. The look on the woman's face told him that the newborn would shortly follow her mother.

Finally, Napoleon King Drew brought the cold hand to his lips, kissed it, and it laid over Rebecca's breast, atop the other hand. He pushed himself out of the hand-hewn chair, leaned over and kissed her forehead, then brushed her damp yellow hair back and tried to smile.

Fireworks and gunshots blasted outside. He heard old Abe trying to blow that trumpet, someone pounding a drum. Screams, a horse's whinny, all indistinguishable noises. Staring at his wife, he started to bring the blanket up past her stomach, chest, to her neck, and paused just for a moment.

"You almost lived to see history, sweetheart," he whispered. "This piece of country becoming its own county, and your husband being sworn in as its first sheriff." A legal lawman. Not just some vigilante.

He bent down, kissed her lips, and made himself cover her face with the blanket. Turning, Drew found his hat, his coat, considered straightening his tie and collar, but got no further than that thought. Rebecca always told him he looked more comfortable with a loose tie and crooked collar.

"Rakish," she would say, and then give him a wink.

Napoleon pulled the coat on as he crossed the floor, and stopped at his new daughter and the midwife, whose name he had already forgotten. "You need anything?" he asked.

Her head shook. She did not look up from the small, red-faced girl.

"If you do, Miles Seabrook's next door."

Seabrook wouldn't be at the celebration on the Basin Creek square. He dealt poker or faro at the town's best saloon, and rarely rose till well after noon. Then he would sit on his porch reading—reading books—till it was time to tuck a pair of revolvers into his sash, pull up his sleeve garters, and walk to the Hangman's Saloon and Gambling Emporium to take money from suckers.

"I'll have Brockden come over as soon as he can."

Brockden was Basin Creek's undertaker.

After pulling the door open, Drew stepped into the sunshine. Two cowboys spurred their geldings down the street, screaming out curses and whipping their mounts with their hats. At least they weren't shooting pistols in the air. Town Marshal Brent Garfield would frown upon that. Problem with Garfield was that frowning was all that he would do.

After closing the door, Drew stepped onto the weedy path and started for the street. Stopped, drew in a lungful of breath and held it while debating, then exhaled, turned around, and walked back inside.

The midwife did not even look up at him as he strode to the gun case, glanced at the gun belt with the holstered Remington .44 hanging on a hook on the wall, but ignored that and opened a drawer. He grabbed the nickel-plated .38-caliber Colt Lightning, reached back inside, and found the boxes of cartridges. He filled five of the six chambers, leaving the one under the hammer empty—a safety precaution—and slid the revolver into the pocket of his frock coat.

"Dressed for Sunday." That's what his father would have said.

Napoleon did not look at his dead wife's covered body. She would have frowned, displeased with his choice, but not say a peep about it.

When he left the house he did not hesitate. He did not look back. Eugene, at nine Napoleon's oldest child, had saddled the buckskin for his pa. Napoleon straightened the saddle, tightened the cinch, loosened the reins from the post, and stepped into the saddle. Clucking his tongue, he turned the buckskin toward town, and kicked its sides loosely. The gelding snorted, shook its head, but started forward.

Napoleon Drew tried not to think that when he returned home, his wife would not be there.

The fireworks were dying down, but the band still played. Tried to play, anyway. Napoleon painted a smile on his face as he nodded to people he knew, some he liked, most he tolerated, many he knew despised him down to his soul. Folks had come in from all across the new county to celebrate. Governor Toole had sent his regrets, but Napoleon didn't take that personally. The nearest railroad was over in Concord, and the stagecoach ride there from Helena was far from comfortable and farther from reliable. Napoleon knew that firsthand.

He reined up, swung down, and handed the reins to the fellow who worked for the Hun at the livery. A mob of citizens, townsfolk, many of them from the county's two other settlements that weren't big—not that anyone would ever mistake Basin Creek for Virginia City back in the day or Helena or Butte today. But the folks who lived in Crimson Feather and Medicine Pass got a vote for who would lead the county, and most of them backed Napoleon Drew.

He shook hands, bowed, and tipped his hat to women, politely smiling. Shaking more hands. Saying thanks. Nodding politely even when the crowd got too loud that he couldn't hear what the gent in front of him was saying. He made his way to the platform the woodcutters had made for the ceremony, but stopped when he saw the undertaker.

He swallowed, excused himself from a beer jerker and the hotel's cook, and eased past a kid tossing a baseball up in the air and trying, but failing, to catch it.

Brockden must have seen Napoleon out of the corner of his eye, because he shook the hand of the new newspaperman in Basin Creek, and walked straight for Napoleon. He swept off the bowler and gave his grimmest face. "Is she . . . ?"

Napoleon nodded.

"I'm sorry. But it was likely a blessing."

Napoleon made himself nod as if he agreed.

"Let me find my two hired men, Sheriff."

Napoleon tried to smile at the new title.

"I'll send those two boys over and I'll take care of everything. Have you told the Reverend Brooks?"

"I haven't told anyone, Brock, but you."

"All right. What time would you like the funeral?" He sighed.

"It might be two funerals."

Brockden had been in the burying business long enough to perfect that sigh and shake of the head. "I'll take care of everything, Sheriff. How about two o'clock tomorrow? Graveside service at the cemetery. Give people time to have their noon meal and get back home before the afternoon winds start up."

Napoleon must have nodded, because Brockden held out his right hand. They shook, and Napoleon went back to the line of people wanting to congratulate him, wish him luck. He despised that part of the job, but Brockden and others, even Judge Van Gaskin and Theodore Tawny had warned him it was part of the job. A county sheriff wasn't just a lawman. He was also a politician. Well, he would have to become one. The governor had appointed him, but next year Napoleon would have to run for election. Which meant laughing at bad jokes, eating teeth-breaking biscuits, swallowing oversalted stew with a smile, and kissing babies.

Kissing babies.

Rebecca never got to kiss her baby girl.

He wondered if the newborn had already joined her mother.

Then he stepped onto the platform where the fat Baptist preacher and the Frenchy Catholic priest waited beside Judge Van Gaskin, Mayor Carlton Tate, and Marshal Brent Garfield.

The band picked up again. Folks began singing.

For he's a jolly good fellow,
For he's a jolly good fellow,
For he's a jolly good fellow . . .
And so say all of us,
And so say all of us.

Napoleon was relieved when that was over.

Since the judge was Catholic, he asked the priest to hold the Bible. Napoleon put his left hand on the black book, raised his right, and repeated the words the judge told him to say. Mayor Tate, who also served as the representative to the state legislature and the county attorney, pinned the silver five-point star on the lapel of Napoleon's vest.

The band started that racket again. People cheered, sang. Roman candles began popping off. More smiles. More handshakes. Pats on the shoulder.

Finally, Napoleon was free. Buggies started moving down the street, carrying families back to their homes. CLOSED FOR CELEBRATION signs came down from business doors and windows.

He entered Swede's Saloon, which had filled up in a hurry. The Hangman's Saloon and Gambling Emporium didn't open most days till three or four in the afternoon. Men made a space for Drew at the bar, and the Swede poured him a bourbon without even asking. That went down quickly, and the Swede started to refill the shot glass, but Napoleon shook his head, and reached in his vest pocket for two-bits.

But someone pitched a coin on the bar first. "On me, Sheriff."

Napoleon thanked the man, but didn't even look to see who had bought the whiskey, and he made his way out of the small cabin before it became too crowded to even breathe.

By thunder, he thought, *there can't be that many people living in this county.*

He stepped down, looked along the street. He had to get back home. Before the Widow Ashton brought the kids back to the cabin. He had to figure out how to tell those three precious little children that their mother was dead.

Frankie Maddox stepped in front of him, his right hand gripping the butt of his Colt, and Napoleon realized the town was far from deserted. Not everyone had gone to quench thirsts at the Swede's Saloon. He sa[illegible] a newcomer to Basin Creek, standing way o[illegible] And other scribes from the state's presses, in Helena, Bu[illegible] Great Falls. Even Anaconda had sent a reporter up to the new county seat.

"You stole that badge from me, Drew." Frankie Maddox slurred his words.

"Take that up with Governor Toole, Frankie." The new sheriff tilted his head just slightly toward the reporters who stood watching, mouths open, only two of them scribbling words on their notebooks.

Maddox shook his head. "I'm taking it up with you, you back-shootin', kid-killin' vigilante."

"You're drunk." Napoleon wished Garfield would show up. This was a job for the town law. The sheriff was a county man.

Frankie Maddox smiled.

Napoleon faked a sigh and shoved his hands into the pockets of his coat. "I got no fight with you. Go home. Sleep it off. You'll probably beat me in next year's election."

Which wasn't that farfetched of a notion.

"I got a fight with you, Drew." Maddox laughed then, and looked off at the reporters, eager to give them something extra to write about in next week's papers. "They'll be buryin' at least two Drews come tomorrow."

The revolver cocked. It sounded so unnaturally loud.

Cackling, Frankie Maddox staggered just a bit, but kept himself upright, and turned back toward Drew, starting to bring up the long-barreled .45. His eyes widened when he saw the Lightning Drew already held, his arm extended, his body turned sideways, his eyes deadly and unblinking.

"You son of a—" Maddox rushed his arm up too high.

The Lightning coughed. Someone screamed. Frankie Maddox fell flat on his back, the right hand still holding the .45, which was pointed at the sky. He'd pulled the trigger, for the gun belched flame and smoke, and landed next to the dead man's ear.

The echo died down. A few horses screamed or bucked. Men filed out of the Swede's place quickly.

Napoleon lowered the Lightning and walked toward Frankie Maddox, gun still out, but not cocked. You didn't have to cock a double-action Colt before pulling the trigger, but he liked to cock first anyway. It lessened the chances of a bullet firing off to the right. He didn't return the revolver to the pocket of his coat until he stood over the dead man's body, saw those unfocused eyes looking into that big Montana sky.

People started talking, mostly whispering. A woman sobbed somewhere, but not likely over Frankie Maddox.

Napoleon couldn't make out much of the conversation until one man, who had to be standing in front of the Swede's Saloon, said, "By Jacks, makin' us a county ain't changed one blessed thing about this patch of purgatory."

CHAPTER 7

The zebra dun wanted to run. He could smell water now, and everybody in Choteau County—no, it was either Cutthroat County now or about to be soon—knew that the spring at the Widow Jeannie Ashton's place was the deepest, clearest, purest water a body could find in Montana. Stagecoach companies kept pestering her to let them set up a relay or home station, for which they offered her a handsome profit, but she always turned them down.

Which might have been why the Great Northern Railway decided not to lay its tracks through Basin Creek. Well, that's what some people thought. But Murdo Maddox knew better. The railroad company's land grant was the main reason. Geography didn't help, either. Not that it mattered. The way the town and new county kept going, a spur would be built to connect Basin Creek with the rest of this worthless world.

Still, Murdo couldn't wait to see Jeannie Ashton, too. He gave the dun its head, and it moved from that spine-crunching trot to a smooth lope. Once the horse splashed across the little creek, he gave the zebra dun even more rein. He loved the feel of spring air on his face and the movement of a horse underneath him.

At the main trail he made himself pull the reins, and the gelding trotted to the open gate.

He saw the cabin, the barn, the well, laundry on the line, smoke rising from the summer kitchen, horses frolicking in the corral, and chickens running around like they ruled the world. He didn't see Jeannie, but he knew she was home. He saw the phaeton, unharnessed. Then he saw her, where he should have looked first. At the top of the knoll, where her husband was buried.

He would make the dun walk the rest of the way. So as not to disturb the widow. It would also give him a chance to read the sign on the two-hundred-yard path from the main trail to her cabin.

Yeah, Murdo thought, *you are one low-down, untrusting son of a . . .* He sighed. But he couldn't help himself.

Jeannie Ashton had a mind of her own. She was as independent as those wild Blackfoot Indians used to be before white man's bullets, and mostly white man's liquor and smallpox, weakened them to practically nothing. Murdo had proposed to her three times, the first just four months after Artie Ashton had been struck by lightning. Lucky. Likely never knew what killed him. And a dern fool. Carrying an ax over his shoulder with that big sky covered with dark clouds and the wind picking up.

If Murdo proposed today, he'd get put off once more.

But he felt better as he rode. She hadn't had any visitors as far as he could tell. And Murdo Maddox read sign better than most white men in these parts.

He had picked that skill up from Great-grandpa Ebenezer Maddox, who'd come up the Missouri with Lewis and Clark. Legend told the story, he'd helped track down Shoshone horses stolen by Blackfoot Indians. In the late 1830s or early 1840s, Eb Maddox had set up a trading post at Basin Creek, and Maddoxes had been kings of that country ever since.

Of course, if Murdo brought that subject up to Jeannie, she'd point out there happened to be a Drew with Maddox back then. In fact, there had been a debate in Helena over what to name this new county. A fish had beaten out *Maddox* and *Drew*.

There was no sign of a Drew at the moment.

By the way Murdo read the sign, she hadn't had a visitor since he rode over last week. That made him feel light in the saddle, happy as a coyote with a full belly. Satisfied, he let the dun lope up to the corral where he swung down and busied himself leading his horse into the corral to make friends with Jeannie's two geldings and a mare. As she made her way from the grave, Murdo shut the gate, looped the leather over the post, and walked to the well.

Most Maddox men had never been patient, but Jeannie Ashton had helped cure Murdo of that. He lowered the bucket down, heard the splash, then cranked the handle until the bucket came above the granite rocks. Leaning over, he grabbed hold of the bucket and pulled it to the rocky top. He dipped the nearby gourd spoon into the water, came up, and drank.

It tasted so good, so refreshing—*better than brandy,* he thought—and made himself drink again.

She reached the bottom of the hill, and the chickens squawked as she went toward the barn. A rooster stepped out to see what was causing such a commotion.

"You've eaten enough already," she told the fowls as she kept moving toward Murdo and the well.

Her dress was yellow gingham. She wore a wide-brimmed straw hat, and a blue scarf. Her hair was black—dark as any Blackfoot, folks said, and some folks had even dared suggest she was mixed blood.

Those who had said that in front of Murdo Maddox had regretted their choice of words, and never made such a mistake again. Her hair was black, but it was ridiculously curly, draping her narrow shoulders. Few women had enough gumption to keep their hair hanging loosely. Most would have wrapped it in a bun, but Jeannie was about as independent as they came. She smiled.

The smile made Murdo feel years younger, and he found himself smiling back underneath his handlebar mustache. "Good day," he said. "Would you like some water?" He held the gourd spoon toward her.

"Are not you the bold one! Putting your horse into my corral. Helping yourself to my water. Without even asking. Isn't a gentleman supposed to wait until he is asked to step down and visit?"

Murdo's grin stretched. "Not many people have ever even hinted that I might be a gentleman."

"For good reason." Then she laughed. It sounded like she was singing when she laughed.

Murdo grinned, and pushed back the brim of his black hat. "You're looking fine, Jeannie."

"As do you."

He offered the gourd. She shook her head, then changed her mind. Well, it was a warm day, and she had hiked all the way up that hill and down. He filled the gourd and handed it to her, watching her take it, her green eyes holding his as she drank.

"Are you coming back from the big shindig in Basin Creek?" She returned the gourd spoon.

"No. Things didn't work out for me. Or Frankie. I took the trail around Basin Creek."

"Don't be bitter," she said, nodding when he motioned with the spoon to see if she'd care for another drink.

"I'm not bitter." He let the gourd fill with well water and again handed it to the lovely widow. He wanted to end that part of the conversation.

Her head shook in disapproval, but her eyes shown with delight at his stubborn streak. "You are one mule-headed man."

"Yes," he said. "I am."

And she laughed. "Then what brings you all the way down from your ranch?"

"Well, I haven't seen you in more than a week."

"No?" She sipped water.

Murdo had never seen a woman who could look so inviting by just drinking water from an oversized spoon.

"I've seen you."

He wanted to knock that confounded spoon out of her hands and take her into his arms. He imagined her in that four-poster bed, hugging a pillow, dreaming of him, and—

"The Kodak," she said. "Remember?"

"Oh. Yes."

Photographers were everywhere, it seemed, at least the people coming from the east, down south to Yellowstone, or riding the rails from those cold plains in Minnesota and North Dakota to capture all there was to see. Small enough to fit into a valise, a Kodak could capture a likeness in the moment it takes to press a button. The Kodak Number One. One box, one hundred possible pictures, all of which could wind up in a scrapbook. Daguerreotypes and melainotypes were obsolete.

Well, now that he thought about it, he had not seen a daguerreotype in years. If Basin Creek had a photographer, he would soon be out of business.

Knowing how she loved painting sketches and how she had let the traveling photographer stay in the barn for a week last year, Murdo had bought her the Kodak when he had gone to Denver on business. He almost regretted the purchase, except for how much it still delighted her.

"Well, are you hungry?"

His head shook.

"What would you like to talk about?"

"I'd like you to marry me."

"Why don't we talk about . . . Stevenson? Did you finish *The Silverado Squatters*?"

He frowned. "I . . . started it."

"I bet."

She turned. "How about we sit on the porch? I'm a little peaked after my visit with Artie and the girls."

The girls—the two babies who had died so young. Murdo bowed his head and blamed that on Artie. If Jeannie had married a strong man, a man like himself, she would have had boys. Strong boys. Who would have lived a lot longer than four months.

She was already walking toward the cabin. "I have coffee on the stove."

He had no choice but to follow her like a little dog.

To show proper decorum, he stood on the porch when Jeannie went inside to heat up the coffee. Finally, he made himself sit on the bench and stare at the road. He expected the folks who lived down the road would be heading home from town. The circus of swearing in the new county officials in the new county had to be over, but maybe the Swede had gotten a few extra kegs of whiskey. Or brewed some of his own.

Murdo didn't care. It was a pretty day.

He heard Jeannie humming, heard her boots on the wooden floor, then she stepped through the doorway, smiled again at him, and walked over. He rose, again removing his hat, and accepted the china cup, and waited for her to sit in her chair. Her special chair. Once she got settled, he sat back down on the bench.

"Now why would you want to marry me, Murdo Maddox?" she asked, not looking at him, but smiling ever so slightly as she looked at a gelding rolling in the dirt of the corral.

He stared at his cup.

"I don't think you need my one hundred and sixty acres."

"You . . . I . . . I can take care of you."

"Yes. I'm sure you could."

He slurped coffee, felt the back of his neck warm. She always did this. Confounded him. Confused him. Sometimes he thought she was just playing with him. He reined in that temper, and said, "Jeannie, sometimes I wish you would not treat me like a child. I am—" He stopped as a horse thundered down the road. He stood, watched as the rider reined in the bay so hard, it slid past the turnoff to Jeannie's place.

"Mister Maddox!"

He recognized neither horse nor rider. Still holding the coffee cup, he stepped off the porch.

The horse gathered its legs, turned around, then the rider kicked the bay into a trot and came down the path. The horses in the corral approached the edge of the pen, snorting, curious, alert. Murdo Maddox studied the rider.

"That's Brent Garfield," Jeannie said.

Murdo looked back at her. She'd stood, too, but remained on the porch, leaning against the top railing.

Murdo looked back toward the rider. Yes, that's who it was, all right. Brent Garfield, who somehow had managed to get himself hired as the town law in Basin Creek. Murdo felt a touch jealous that a woman had better eyesight than he did, but let it go. The marshal slowed the horse to a walk.

Murdo wondered how Garfield knew where to find him. His seeing her—he couldn't call it courting, not yet anyway—was no secret, but . . . oh, yes. Before turning off on the old trail that skirted west and south around Basin Creek, Murdo had passed a handful of families on the road as they drove wagons or rode horses or mules or walked to see the big show in Basin Creek.

"Mister Maddox!" the town marshal called out again. "It's Frankie."

Murdo drew in a sharp breath. What had that stupid first cousin of his—?

"It's Frankie, Mister Maddox. He's been killed."

Jeannie gasped. "Oh, my God."

Murdo expected her to reach over to steady him, comfort him, though he stood erect. He had not even made a sound. And he was disappointed, maybe even hurt, that Jeannie said nothing, did not grab his arm, or give him a hug.

The worthless lawman stopped the horse.

"Your cousin is dead, sir. Shot dead in town."

That did not surprise him. Frankie was too wild, too mean-spirited, too quick-tempered, and too overconfident to have a long, industrious life. Losing the election as sheriff had left him hitting the jug a lot harder, and he never had been a temperate man.

Murdo heard himself ask, "When?"

Garfield shook his head and tried to catch his breath. Remembering his manners, he removed his hat. "Missus Ashton, I am sorry to have come riding up like this. But it is just—"

"It's quite all right, Mister Garfield," Jeannie said.

"When?" Murdo regretted losing his patience. Not at Marshal Garfield. But in front of Jeannie.

"I guess twenty, thirty, forty minutes ago. I had to find the livery boy to saddle my horse. The Murchisons said they seen you taking the cutoff. That's how I knew to come here." He laughed out of nervousness. "Almost ran right by it, though, didn't I?"

"Who did it?" Murdo asked, but Garfield must not have heard.

"I did run by it. If I hadn't found my wits, probably would have rode all the way to Basin Creek before I—"

"Who killed Frankie?" Surely, the marshal had arrested the killer and put him in jail. Or maybe Frankie had managed to gun down his killer. Frankie was stupid, but he was a Maddox. He was tough.

"I'd already sent Luke Jasper off to your ranch to tell you, sir."

"Would you like some brandy, Mister . . . Marshal?" Jeannie was going crazy. No, no. She was just trying to settle down that incompetent, easily excitable buffoon. And, Murdo realized, calm himself down, too.

"Reckon Luke'll be making a long hard ride for nothing."

"*Brent.*" Somehow Murdo controlled his voice.

The lawman put his hat back on his head, and breathed in deeply. "It was Drew, sir. It was Napoleon Drew."

And Jeannie Ashton whispered, "Oh, my Lord, no. Is Napoleon hurt?"

Chapter 8

Jeannie watched Murdo Maddox lead the zebra dun he had saddled out of the corral to where Marshal Brent Garfield sat on his horse, still blowing hard after the ride from Basin Creek. She wondered if she should say anything. Her lips parted, but she just sighed and watched Murdo put his boot in the stirrup and swing into the saddle. He did not look at Jeannie, he didn't even look at the lawman, just clucked his tongue, and kicked his gelding into a walk. The lawman turned toward Jeannie, and she thought he wanted to say something, but just didn't know what to say, and finally he followed the tough rancher toward the road.

They loped off toward town.

As soon as they disappeared around the bend, Jeannie moved quickly. She kicked out the fire in the outside kitchen and went inside, where she quickly changed into clothes fit for riding. After closing the door to the cabin, she considered the phaeton, but only for a moment. Instead of moving toward the buggy, she headed into the barn.

The chickens eyed her with expectations of a meal, but she hardly even gave them a passing glance. Her focus was the sidesaddle, but she shook her head after short consideration before she picked up Artie's old slick fork. Her husband had never been a top hand, but he knew how important a good saddle was. In this country, a saddle was often worth more than any horse—certainly any horse Artie Ashton could have afforded. He had also been a small man, not much taller than Jeannie, and about as thin as the corral posts.

The saddle fit her well. She had hardly had to adjust the lengths of the stirrups after Artie's fatal run of bad luck. She tossed a blanket and bridle across the seat, and lugged those to the corral.

She could saddle a horse quicker than she could hitch a horse to the phaeton, and she opened the gate and entered the corral with the bridle. *The black,* she thought. *Yes, the black.*

"Come here, Midnight." She whistled.

All of the horses saw the bridle and each one knew what it meant. The black backed up, but Jeannie moved toward him, smiling, cooing, and the gelding succumbed to her charms. The bridle went over, she secured it, and led him out of the corral.

She saddled him quickly, adjusted the position, tightened the cinch, and walked him up the road a few feet, then retightened the cinch before climbing into the saddle. Her woolen hat hung on her back from a braided horsehair stampede string, but she pulled the hat up, secured the string so that the hat would not blow off, and let Midnight trot to the road.

Once she turned the horse down the road, she kicked the gelding's side, and felt the wind in her face, pushing the brim of the cheap hat up, and feeling the glory of being on a horse while at the same time fretting at what must be happening in Basin Creek.

She prayed for Napoleon Drew.

And she prayed for Murdo Maddox.

Murdo's cousin, now deceased, was not worth praying over.

* * *

Lazy and *unproductive* were not words used to describe the people who lived in northwestern Montana. Sure, cowboys would blow their month's wages on liquor or at Sarah Doolittle's house of ill repute, but the next day, or after they got out of jail, they were back at work. Those men of the cloth had a dickens of a time getting their flock to remember that Sunday was a day of rest. Folks bowed their heads in prayer, knelt, crossed themselves, and confessed to the priest, or said "Amen" to the preacher and sang their hymns as best they could. And then went back to work.

Work . . . hard work . . . kept families alive in this country. You worked hard. Or you might die. You might die anyway. Like poor Artie had.

Jeannie felt surprised not to meet anyone traveling down the road from Basin Creek as she loped north. When she reached town, she slowed the black to a walk. Wagons, teams still hitched, crowded the streets. Horses, still saddled, grazed on the lawn that someday might be the site of a real courthouse. As for now, the courthouse was the meeting house some folks said Benjamin Franklin Drew and Eb Maddox put up when they first ventured into the basin in the 1820s—back when Drews and Maddoxes still spoke civilly to one another, just years after those two had come to Montana Territory with Lewis and Clark.

Of course, the cabin had been expanded, but it was easy to tell the newer logs and roof from the original small square building. On most days, anyway.

Jeannie couldn't see much of the building or the grassy lawn surrounding it because of so many people. Folks were talking so much, she could hardly hear her own thoughts as she walked the black slowly, then finally stopped. Every hitch rail and post was crowded. The corral at the livery was full, matching the throng of people surrounding the meeting house.

She sighed, then saw a friendly face on the street, and walked to the surrey. Abe Killone sat on the seat, eating peanuts and pitching the shells into the grass. The rancher smiled at Jeannie and removed his hat. "Mrs. Ashton," he said, and extended the bag of roasted peanuts.

"No, thank you, sir."

Killone ran a good cattle ranch, nowhere near as large as Murdo Maddox's, or even close to Mike McIlhaney's. But no one had ever questioned where Abe Killone got his beef. They might have wondered about the Maddox herd sometimes, Jeannie knew, but those questions were never spoken above a whisper.

Killone was in his forties, had moved up from Colorado, buying cattle and land after the Big Die-up during that awful winter of 1886–87. His eyes were blue, his brown mustache showing more gray now, and he dressed like a hardworking rancher who came to town. His idea of dressing up was wearing a black string tie and a black vest over his blue work shirt. Chaps covered tan trousers, and his boots were stained with horse manure.

He nodded at Midnight. "From the lather on your horse," he said to Jeannie, "I don't need to ask if you've heard what happened."

"I heard," she said, and looked at the crowd.

"I didn't see it." He cracked a nut and popped a peanut into his mouth, then set the sack on the leather seat. "In a day or two, I'll probably be the only man in Cutthroat County who did not see the shooting." He climbed down off the rig. "I might have heard the gunshot, but thought it was just another part of the celebration."

She looked back at him.

He gave his most charming smile. "Would you like me to take your horse, ma'am?"

How did he know? But she did not even consider not handing him the reins. "He's hot. He shouldn't drink—"

"I know horses, Mrs. Ashton." His eyes dazzled her as he took the reins. "He won't drink till he's cooled off." He pointed toward the edge of the crowd. "They're holding an inquest in the old relic of a cabin."

He stepped closer and moved his finger toward the crowd. "You'd never get through the front door. And deputies—who deputized them, I don't know—are keeping folks out of the back. But if you circle around that crowd, I think you can weave your way to the duly sworn in deputies. With your charm and way with words, you might get through. The man at the back door will let you in, too."

She stared at him in bewilderment. "You overestimate my oratory skills, Mr. Killone."

"I think not, ma'am." He pulled the horse toward his buggy. "But if anyone tries to stop you, you just tell them that Abe Killone said to let you pass."

Jeannie thanked him and moved toward the edge of the crowd. Sometimes she wondered why everyone thought only Maddoxes and Drews controlled this section of Montana.

To her surprise, the first line of what she heard one man call *the Winchester quarantine* proved to be an easy line to cross. She simply smiled at a gray-bearded man in buckskins, and he tipped his hat and turned his head, motioning her on through. An even bigger shock was no one in the crowd and none of the other guards questioned why she got through.

The next group of men standing at the back of the rectangular structure appeared much more formidable. These men brandished shotguns and watched her move through the grass, weeds, and rocks till she found herself looking into the dark eyes of a man she did not know, and whose thumbs had already eared back both hammers on the double-barreled monster in his hands.

He said nothing. Just glared.

Jeannie found herself at a loss for words. But she heard a voice.

"Where's your manners, Abilene? Let the lady through."

The short, balding, bespectacled man in a sack suit

removed his bowler and bowed. The guard slowly lowered the hammers on the shotgun, and returned it to his side.

"Thank you, kindly," she told the man with the gun, and walked up to Ira Batts. "And thank you, sir."

"It's my pleasure. We haven't been introduced but I am—"

"Mr. Ira Batts."

He seemed pleased.

"Editor and publisher of our new *Cutthroat County Messenger.*"

"*The,*" he said. "Do not forget the *The*. *The Cutthroat County Messenger*. That gives us more prestige. Not one, but *the* newspaper of record for more than three quarter of a million acres."

"It is too bad acres do not buy newspapers, Mr. Batts."

He laughed, and extended a bent left arm, which she accepted, and he walked her to the rear door.

"They have taken a recess for Judge Van Gaskin's, ahem, constitutional." They stopped at the back door. "I'd recommend our staying here till the judge"—he turned his head to clear his throat—"till the judge returns. The inside of the Union Hall is quite stifling. Van Gaskin ordered the windows shuttered to keep gawkers from interrupting the proceedings. It took an eternity to seat the jury. It took even longer to find Brockden, the county coroner. Seems he got a call during the festivities today."

"I see." She really wanted to go inside just to see Napoleon Drew, see if he was all right. She didn't see Murdo Maddox out there, either, which troubled her. Jeannie wanted to see him, too, just to make sure he didn't do anything rash—anything that might have him appearing before a coroner's inquest.

The newspaper editor-publisher laughed. "Brockden even said he forgot he'd been appointed county coroner, too, when they finally tracked him down."

Jeannie wished she had taken a drink of water. But she wasn't about to ask Ira Batts for one.

"I'll have plenty of news for the second issue of *The Cutthroat County Messenger*," Batts said. "For it has been a busy day for Sheriff Napoleon Drew."

Her head jerked up. Her eyes stared hard.

Batts glanced down, saw her face, and straightened. "Dear me. I fear I have broken news to you. You have not heard?" He did not wait for her to confirm his question. "Old Drew became a widower today. His wife finally gave out. It had been a hard labor. And we just heard the newborn, a little girl, died this day, too."

He shook his head and grinned.

Jeannie tightly shut her eyes. She leaned back against the rough logs, but the newspaperman scarcely even noticed. He was too busy talking, enjoying himself and his words.

"Three deaths in one day. I'll have to hit up H.H. Brockden for an advertisement. Three dearly departed to get ready for burial, and a bonus payment for official county coroner duties."

Biting her lower lip, Jeannie tried to focus. She should go to Napoleon Drew's cabin. Those two sons and the independent daughter that reminded Jeannie of herself would need help. Comforting. More than what the midwife and caretaker could give them. Yet she could not leave until she was certain Napoleon would not be indicted.

Indicted. The word troubled her. *For murder.*

Murdo Maddox would be hoping for that. No, Murdo Maddox did not hope for anything. He demanded things. Well, Murdo demanded *most* things. He had never once tried to strong-arm her into accepting his proposal.

Batts said something. Jeannie opened her eyes and looked up at him, then pushed herself from the log wall.

"Mrs. Ashton? I say, are you all right?"

His mouth opened, then closed as she swallowed. She pasted on her best fake smile. "I am fine, Mr. Batts," she said. "Thank you for your concern."

The bow was gracious. "Not to offend your sensibilities, my dear lady, but I have a flask of most excellent rye. For medicinal purposes, I assure you. If you would like a drink, I am sure I can slip the flask to you with discreetness."

"No, but I kindly thank you." She read the disappointment on his face, but she knew how to correct that. Her head tilted toward the line of trees along the stream that fed Basin Creek. "I believe Judge Van Gaskin is returning," Jeannie said softly.

Batts spun around like he had been called out. "By thunder, yes!" he roared.

Other newspapermen—or so she guessed—rushed toward the approaching man in the black robe who waved them away with his hands and shouted profanities that did not deter them from pounding him with question after question.

At least not until he said, "Boys, if you keep that up, I'll close this courtroom to all you scribes."

Some guards took that as a recommendation that they block the reporters from bothering the judge. The judge stopped in front of Jeannie and Batts and bowed slightly. "Mrs. Ashton"—he extended his hand—"it is always a pleasure to see you . . . even on a day as wretched as this one."

"I was hoping I might be allowed inside the courtroom," she said, remembering to add "Your Honor."

"The honor would be mine," he said, and escorted her into the stifling dark room. "You'll have to sit with the newspaper lice. We're all full up, like Sarah Dolittle's—" He cleared his throat, and Jeannie saw the blush on his cheeks not covered with that thick gray beard. "I mean . . . the churches on Easter Sunday."

"I do not mind," Jeannie said. She found her seat, and as Judge Van Gaskin walked to the rocking chair, she looked at the first row and focused on the back of Cutthroat County Sheriff Napoleon King Drew's head.

CHAPTER 9

"You sure you don't want a lawyer, Napoleon?" Horace Van Gaskin cleared his throat. "I mean, Sheriff Drew."

Drew nodded.

The good citizens of Basin Creek had not gotten to see a good show since a theatrical troupe out of Dublin, Ireland, performed there in 1889 and performed *Romeo and Juliet, H.M.S. Pinafore,* and something called *Mosada* that the Irish really enjoyed.

"Let's get her done, Judge," Drew said.

"All right." Gaskin raised his gavel, clutching the hammer like it was the butt of a revolver and aiming the handle slowly at the jurors and everyone else in the courtroom as he issued a stern warning. "This is a coroner's inquest. This is not a trial. This is what folks do in civilized countries and now that we are Cutthroat County, we are civilized. This inquest will determine whether or not there will be a trial." He swerved to the jurors—mostly townsmen, a farmer, old Alfred Weens who was trying to raise horses a mile or two south of town, and one of Murdo Maddox's hired hands.

Napoleon wasn't sure if anyone was impartial. Impartiality had gotten men killed in some places. But he had to concede the jury was about as even a mix of jurors as anyone could seat. He saw faces of men he might consider friends; he saw faces of men he knew would cheer when he was dead; and he saw faces of men he couldn't say he had ever really met. Not even when he had been campaigning, or what he called campaigning, for county sheriff.

"You jurors will hear the facts. Those facts and nothing but the facts will lead to your verdict. You aren't finding if Sheriff Napoleon Drew is guilty."

A man in the back leaped off a bench and yelled, "You mean *King* Napoleon Drew, don't you, Judge?"

The gavel slammed.

"That's his name, ain't it? King Napoleon. At least he thinks he's—"

Van Gaskin shouted curses above the pounding of his gavel.

Napoleon did not turn around as he heard the sounds, then a crunch behind him, a gasp, and the sound of a man falling onto the wooden floor laid clumsily over hard-packed earth and stone.

Van Gaskin stood. His eyes burned. He pointed down the aisle and bellowed, "Clete. Take that man outside. Strap him to the fence and give him ten stripes. Tell him if I see his ugly face again this month, he'll get the other thirty . . . and I won't be lessening away one."

A deputized guard dragged the unconscious man out of the courthouse. Napoleon couldn't see the man's face, and he had not recognized the voice, but that didn't matter. *King Napoleon*. It wasn't the first time he had heard that one. His name was Napoleon King Drew, King being his mother's maiden name. When kids used to call him King Napoleon, he had always smiled and said, "That fellow in France was just an emperor. Me? I'm a King. But first, I'm Napoleon."

He had thought it funny the first few times. His pals had, too.

But these days, he wished he had been named something duller. Jim or Bob or John or Dick or Sam.

When Clete and the disrupter were gone, and the door closed again, Judge Van Gaskin slammed the gavel and sat down. He picked up his instructions. "I repeat, you aren't finding if Sheriff Napoleon Drew is not guilty. You are finding if there is enough reasonable—look that word up in your Websters, boys, *reasonable*—evidence as put forth and allowed in this proceeding, to take this to trial. If, and only if, you find it is beyond all your doubts—*reasonable doubts*—the sheriff was acting in his full capacity as sheriff, and he was defending his life and person or the lives and persons of innocent bystanders, you will rule that Frank Maddox, God rest his soul, was killed in an act of self-defense. And then we can all go home."

He switched the grip on the gavel and banged it on a wooden square. "Let's get started."

The newspapermen scribbled in their notebooks.

"Mayor Tate," the judge said with a nod. "You're the county attorney now. Call your first witness."

Carlton Tate had been sitting far down the bench from Drew. Trying to disassociate himself, most likely. Or to show he was impartial. Drew could not fault the man for that. As mayor of a town and attorney for a county and a state representative, he did not want to lose any of those jobs. "We call Sheriff Napoleon Drew."

Drew waited for someone to object to his being called *Sheriff*, but hearing nothing but a few soft whispers, he rose and walked to the bench where Judge Van Gaskin swore him in.

Carlton Tate, who had just hours earlier pinned the badge on his vest and shaken his hand, cleared his throat and walked to the table Drew sat behind. "Sheriff, please, in your own words, tell the court what happened."

It sounded, thought Murdo Maddox, *like a pack of lies,* some blood-and-thunder plot straight out of one of those wretched dime novels. To hear *King* Napoleon Drew tell the story he had stepped outside of the Swede's Saloon and found Frank Conner Maddox waiting, his right hand on a holstered Colt revolver. Frank, commonly known as Frankie had accused the new sheriff of stealing the election.

To which the king had said, "You'll have to talk to the governor or"—he nodded at the attorney—"or you, meaning you as our state representative."

Tate nodded. The reporters wrote furiously.

Murdo Maddox frowned, not at the reporters, but at Jeannie Ashton sitting alongside those blood-sucking newspapermen. Looking at that proud, murdering lawman on the witness stand. He hated her for showing compassion for a Drew. And yet he still loved her just the same.

"And what did Frank Maddox do then?" Tate asked.

Murdo Maddox made himself look away from the back of Jeannie's head.

"He said, 'I'm taking it up with you, you back-shooting, kid-killing vigilante,'" the sheriff said. "And I'm fairly sure that is an accurate quote."

Tate tilted his head. "You can recall that quote verbatim but not the other?"

"Yes, sir. The first comment I could pass off to John Barleycorn. The second I took as a threat."

"I see. How long have you been sheriff?"

"Just a few hours."

"But you have been a peace officer before, isn't that correct?"

Napoleon nodded. "I served on committees of law enforcement a few times."

"Committees of law enforcement?" Tate must have been trying to show everyone he was a defense attorney and a prosecutor.

Maddox felt like kicking over the spittoon near him.

This is justice? This is civilization? This is what becoming a county means?

"That's one way of putting it. Some called us a vigilance committee. Others called us vigilantes."

"And some called you killers, isn't that the truth?"

Drew nodded. "Yes, sir. We were called good and bad. But in those days, we were the only law around."

The representative-mayor-attorney nodded and straightened his tie. "Then what happened?"

"I told Frankie he was drunk, and should go home, get some sleep. And I told him I did not want to fight him."

"You did not want to fight him?" The lawyer tried to sound incredulous.

"Yes sir. I did not want to fight him. I told him that. You see, sir"—he turned to face the jury—"my jurisdiction is over the county. This altercation was in the town limits of Basin Creek. I was hoping Marshal Garfield would come and help calm Frankie down."

"But Marshal Garfield did not come to your assistance."

Drew nodded in agreement. "No, sir. Not then. But on a day like this, I am certain he had his hands full."

"Your hands were certainly full."

Drew nodded. "I reckon so. When I told Frankie I didn't want to fight him, he said, 'I've got a fight with you.' To me, that was certainly a threat."

"A threat." Tate nodded again.

"Yes, sir. And then he said that they, meaning the citizens of Basin Creek and/or Cutthroat County, would be burying at least two more Drews tomorrow."

The mayor . . . the county attorney . . . the new county's representative at the legislature cocked his head. "Two *more* Drews?"

"My wife died this morning." Drew's reply sounded toneless. "The infant girl"—his eyes closed, and his voice dropped to a whisper—"a few hours ago."

Murdo Maddox began grinding his teeth at the heavy sighs and gasps that came from all around him.

The judge tapped the gavel. He did not bang it. He did not scream or rail at the people. The gavel tapped a few more times before he laid it aside, and cleared his throat. "The court," he said, "extends its sympathy for your loss." His head raised and he leaned forward and looked into the nearest and farthest men. "I will ask you to refrain yourselves from emotions." He turned to the box of jurors. "And this fact should in no way make this witness more sympathetic to you. A young wife and mother, and a newborn are gone to Glory. They deserve our prayers.

"But we are here for one purpose only. And that is to determine why another man, a man from a prominent family in this county, will also be buried tomorrow." He tapped that wooden block with only his knuckles and nodded at Tate. "Proceed, counselor."

"And then?" Tate asked the lawman.

"I heard and saw Frankie cock his .45."

"And how did you react?"

"Frankie turned to look at some men in the crowd. Just for a moment. He wanted an audience."

The judge cleared his throat and looked sternly at Drew. "That is your opinion, Sheriff, but it is not a fact, which is all this court is interested in hearing." He turned to the jurors. "The comment about the deceased desiring an audience is not to be considered. The comment that he looked away from the marshal can be considered if it has a bearing on what happened afterward."

"Go on," Tate encouraged.

"I had a .38 Colt in my coat pocket," Drew said.

"Do you always go about your business with a revolver in your pocket?" Tate asked.

"No. But I thought it would be less conspicuous than a holstered .44 on my hip. Today was a day of celebration. I did not expect to run into any armed men seeking to do me harm. But I have always been a careful man."

Tate seemed pleased. "Continue."

Drew breathed in and out. "I raised my weapon, and when Frankie turned around and saw that, he tried to kill me."

"Kill you? How so? How could you tell?" Tate stepped back.

"Frankie turned and was bringing up his revolver. Bringing it up toward me. The weapon was cocked. I had no time to ask him to drop the Colt and be placed under arrest. I had no choice but to defend myself. I fired. The bullet took Frankie in the chest. He fell, shot a round straight into the air. And lay still. He was dead by the time I reached him."

Tate entered Frankie's .45 into evidence. He told the judge and the jurors the weapon was found in the deceased man's grip, with one of the five cartridges in the chamber having been discharged recently.

"Did Frankie say anything to you once he saw you had your weapon aimed at his person?" Tate asked.

"He said, 'You son of a—' but did not finish the insult. I pulled the trigger, Frankie fell, shot, and died."

"You have been, if not a county sheriff, a man around violence for a number of years, Sheriff." Tate walked to the jurors. "And I mean that with no disrespect. How many gun battles have you faced in your lifetime, sir? Before today's incident."

"I'm not sure."

"Your best guess?"

"Six. Eight. In which shots were fired."

"Against outlaws and Indians?"

"Mostly outlaws. Or rough men. Rough white men."

"I see. With your experience, after those six or eight gun battles prior to today's encounter, had you not fired your revolver, what do you think would have happened?"

Napoleon Drew frowned while Murdo Maddox clenched his fists so tightly he felt pain all the way to his elbows.

"I believe Frankie Maddox would have been right," Drew answered. "That they would be burying three Drews tomorrow."

"What a mockery!" Murdo Maddox leaped off the bench and swore savagely. He glared not at Napoleon Drew but at Judge Van Gaskin, who found his gavel and beat it furiously.

Two men jerked Murdo back down. He almost punched one of them, and likely would have had a third man not caught his arm. Murdo might still have swung punches at armed deputies and farmers, cowhands and townsmen who tried to stop the brawl. He would have.

Jeannie Ashton knew that.

He would have.

Except he saw her. And he froze. His face did not redden in embarrassment, but turned pale. She thought he might faint.

Instead, he let himself be pushed back down.

The banging stopped, and Judge Van Gaskin put his hands on his hips. "Murdo Maddox, the court will show some leniency here because I know this is a difficult time for you, having lost a cousin. And you have long been an important part of this part of Montana. A founding father, if you will, of Cutthroat County."

When she thought about the judge's statement later that night, Jeannie Ashton would softly chuckle. Murdo Maddox one of Cutthroat County's founding fathers? If he had his way, it would still be uncharted territory, with no one to answer to except himself. He had not liked being in Choteau County, but had accepted it somewhat since the seat, Fort Benton, was a hard—an extremely hard—four-day ride from Basin Creek.

When noises died, except muffled voices from outside and the wind moaning through the cracks in the wood, the judge nodded at Mayor Tate to continue.

"Sheriff, are you absolutely certain you had no other option but to defend yourself this afternoon?"

"I am, sir."

Tate nodded, and suddenly grinned. "Sheriff, this confrontation happened outside of the Swede's Saloon. Is that correct?"

"Yes, sir."

Jeannie briefly closed her eyes. She knew where Tate would take this line of questioning. *That's our mayor, our county attorney, our representative in Helena . . . playing to every person in Cutthroat County to get every vote. Offending no one while offending everyone.*

"Were you leaving the saloon where you ran into the deceased?"

Napoleon Drew did not hesitate. He was too smart for that. "I was."

"Had you been drinking in that saloon?"

"I did."

"Was Frankie Maddox in that place, too?"

"Not that I saw. It was crowded. But I did not see Maddox until I stepped outside."

"How much did you drink?"

"I had one shot of bourbon. Just one. Then I walked outside."

"Had you consumed any liquor before? During today, I mean."

"No, sir. I promised"—he looked at his boots—"I promised . . . Rebecca . . . I'd drink no more than one whiskey a day. Just a shot. Sometimes a beer. But no matter what, just one drink a day."

And sometimes, Jeannie knew, Napoleon Drew didn't even drink anything a day except coffee and water.

"Rebecca being . . . ?"

"My . . . dead wife."

"So you were in no means inebriated or otherwise not in control of your faculties?"

"No, sir."

"You paid for one drink?"

"Yes. No." His head shook. "No. I started to pay the Swede, but someone else paid for the drink. I walked outside. And there was Frankie."

The lawyer looked into the audience. "Well, the chances of this are not good, but is there anyone in this courthouse . . . ?"

Jeannie almost laughed. *This is a courthouse?*

". . . I mean . . . well . . . can anyone here testify to buying the sheriff . . . ?"

A juror slowly raised his hand.

Reporters on both sides of Jeannie laughed and wrote rapidly, their pencils scratching, a few whispering at one another, flipping the pages as the juror rose.

Jeannie did not recognize him.

The judge simply slumped in his chair and shook his head. "Percy Willingham, why didn't you tell me that when we were seating you on the jury?"

"Horace, I didn't think nothin' 'bout it. Plumb forgot it. This ain't been an ordinariest of days."

The reporters cackled and scribbled until the judge pounded the gavel again.

"You're sworn in, Percy," the judge said. "Just stand up and tell the truth."

The tall, redheaded man in overalls and suspenders rose, his Adam's apple bobbing again and again.

The judge asked these questions.

"Did you see Sheriff Drew in the Swede's Saloon today?"

"Yeah."

"What time?"

"Well, after the ruckus stopped in town I hurried over

before the last firecracker popped so I could get close to the bar. But it was already crowded."

Sighing, Van Gaskin closed his eyes. "Did you see Sheriff Drew?"

"Yes, sir. He come in. We was all trying to shake his hand or pat his back."

"Did you see him order a drink?"

"I don't know if I saw that, but the Swede give him one."

"And then?"

"That was it. We was all wantin' . . . well, I guess I can't say all of us was . . . but some of us wanted to buy him another. But he wouldn't take one. I had my quarter in my hand so I give it to the Swede, and Napoleon he walked outside. And, I dunno, a couple of minutes maybe, no more than that, we heard the gunshot. Then we all ran outside. And there was Frankie Maddox, deader than dirt."

Four newspapermen were called to testify as witnesses. Ira Batts was not one of them. Their testimony never departed from what Napoleon Drew had said under oath.

H.H. Brockden was then sworn in and said that from his examination of Frankie Maddox's corpse, he was killed from a single .38-caliber bullet that just missed the heart. From the blood and depth of the bullet, death was not instantaneous but he did not live more than half a minute before giving up the ghost.

The reporter two seats to Jeannie's right whispered, "Giving up the ghost. That's a medical term if I've ever heard one."

"At least it's easy to spell," said the reporter closest to Jeannie.

"Says you."

The judge tapped the gavel and told Percy Willingham to sit down and consider the rest of the evidence introduced and testimony heard.

But that was all there was.

Jeannie listened to the judge as he instructed the jurors, and she looked at the back of Napoleon Drew's head. She had to stop herself from turning around to find Murdo Maddox. The reporters whispered among one another as the jurors were marched by armed guards to another room in the long cabin—actually it had once been an entirely different cabin, maybe a dog trot. Folks couldn't recollect anymore.

Someone whispered, "I wish Percy Willingham would buy me a drink right about now."

It was a loud whispered comment that launched an armada of giggles. Even the judge chuckled as he drank a cup of coffee a guard had brought him.

Fifteen minutes later, the twelve jurors and four guards walked back to the front of the makeshift courtroom. Judge Van Gaskin hit the gavel and said, "Have the gentlemen of the jury reached a verdict."

When Percy Willingham rose, the newspaper journalists laughed until Van Gaskin's gavel silenced them.

"Percy?" The judge sounded weary.

"We have, Hor—Your Honor."

"What say you?"

"We find that Sheriff Napoleon King Drew acted in self-defense and that the homicide—did I pronounce that right?"

More laughter. More pounding of the gavel.

Willingham did not finish, because Judge Van Gaskin was standing, his face red again, pointing that gavel like a handgun. "The ruling of the jury is that the sheriff acted in self-defense. This case is closed. God bless Montana and God save Cutthroat County."

Most of the newspapermen were out of the building before Jeannie could stand.

She started for Napoleon Drew, but knew she'd never reach him. The journalists who did not want to stand in line at the telegraph office to file their accounts already surrounded Judge Gaskin, Mayor Tate, and the new sheriff.

She stepped aside of other well-wishers and tried to find Murdo Maddox, but he was gone. She didn't see him outside. She hurried to Abe Killone.

The Swede's Saloon and Hangman's Saloon and Gambling Emporium were already crowded, and a few people stood outside the hotel restaurant, and more at Doris Caffey's café. Yet the town was slowly clearing out. Men who had been lucky enough to get a seat for the inquest were loading their families onto buckboards or farm wagons or walking back home.

Abe Killone had finished his peanuts, but sat patiently in the carriage when Jeannie reached him. She looked around, but saw no sign of Murdo Maddox's zebra dun.

Killone doffed his hat. "Not guilty I take it?"

"Not guilty."

"I'm glad. You want to sell that horse?"

She made herself grin. "I don't think so. But thank you for your kindness. I made you wait long enough."

"You, Mrs. Ashton, are worth waiting for."

"You, Mr. Killone, are a flirt."

"Yes, ma'am." He hopped down from the buggy, unloosened the reins, and handed them to her. "I led him to the trough over yonder, and let him drink. I'll be heading back to the ranch. It was a pleasure seeing you today, and I'm glad everything worked out all right."

Not everything, she thought.

Murdo Maddox was madder than a hornet. One man was dead. And Napoleon Drew had lost his wife and baby girl. She took the reins, but walked the horse. Walked the horse toward Drew's cabin. Those kids—Eugene, Parker, and that precocious three-year-old, Mary Ellen—would need comforting.

Chapter 10

From *The Cutthroat County Messenger*, Thursday, June 4, 1891

Blood on the streets of Basin creek!

A Celebration is Turned into a Funeral.

Franklin Maddox Hurled to eternity
By Our New County Sheriff's
Deadly Aim!

Coroner's Jury Rules That Maddox
Got What He *Deserved*.

Full Details of Gunfight
& Ruling of the Court

What Will Helena Think?

The birth of Cutthroat County began with the death of one of the county's leading citizens, a thirty-three year-old cowhand, rancher, and explorer—descendant of the first white man to help rid this country of savage redskinned and blackhearted fiends of Indians.

Frank Maddox is dead . . . while jurors and citizens seem to cheer *Long live his murderer!*

Just hours after clocks and watches chimed the new hour and welcomed Cutthroat County into Montana history, and within minutes after Napoleon K. Drew was sworn in as our county sheriff, Frank Maddox was killed with a well-aimed .38-caliber bullet that pierced his heart and sent him to the *streets of gold.*

Our newly elected sheriff celebrated his coronation by entering a shameless den of iniquity. Owned and managed by not a true American, but a foreigner who settled here after men like Murdo Maddox and Michael McIlhaney were civilizing this country with hard work and sweat and decency, it's where Napoleon Drew whet his appetite with spirits most foul.

Yet we cannot fault Sheriff Drew for letting his steel nerves, steady hand, true aim, and a revolver that is almost part of his body bring death to our county seat on our county's first day of existence. For many of us know the hurt, the unbearable pain, that comes with the loss of a loved one.

> *"Ye are of your father the devil, and the lusts of your father ye will do. He was a murderer from the beginning, and abode not in him the truth; because there is no truth in him." John 8:44.*

This day . . . this day of days . . . God saw fit to bring two beloved members of Napoleon Drew's family into His fold. This morning, just before our sheriff took the oath and swore to God to uphold his duties, that same God took away Napoleon Drew's beloved wife.

Yes, Rebecca Langston Drew died—though death might have been a blessing to her kind heart and tired body—just after giving birth to a precious daughter. A girl too weak to name because she was too weak to survive. When the mother, that blessed mother, was called from Montana to the Kingdom of Heaven, the child, the unnamed child, could not hold on. She died.

Who knows how men can stand such anguish? Who knows what death like this—Rebecca was not older than thirty years—can do to a husband and father?

"The Lord is nigh unto them that are of a broken heart; and saveth such as be of a contrite spirit." Psalms 34:18.

Your editor has seen enough heartbreak and reported on many tragic deaths in Boston, Atlanta, Philadelphia, Chicago, Dallas, Trinidad, and Denver. Some men bear the pain and go forward. Some men let the pain tear them apart. And some men kill other men to relieve themselves of the pain. Maybe they hope to be killed.

Perhaps someday their hopes will be granted.

With the devil's brew working in his gut, heart, and soul—though we are skeptical to the latter being in Napoleon Drew's body—Drew stepped outside and gunned down the brother of famed rancher Murdo Maddox. Yes, by blood, Franklin Maddox was just Murdo Maddox's cousin—first cousin, in fact—but the way those two men bonded, you cannot fault this editor for printing the truth.

And the TRUTH is that no matter what the family Bible says, Frankie and Murdo were brothers. They fought together. They roped together. And together they helped make the Circle M Ranch what it is today.

Ask the savage Blackfeet Indians that came to take their scalps. Ask the vicious Shoshones that stole their ponies. Ask the long-dead rustlers who dared to steal their stock. They will all gladly come from the hottest depths of HELL to tell you who sent them to eternal damnation.

But justice is not always just.

The law has spoken, and we must live up to it and uphold it. As the time of vigilantes should be in Montana's history, let us close the book on that lawless time. Let us ask our new sheriff to follow the law. Let us not seek revenge, but fight for justice. Because a *NEW CENTURY* is just around the corner. The *Twentieth Century* beckons us.

But the way of the gun is not the way of justice.

"*Justice, most gracious Duke; O, grant me justice!*" Shakespeare's *The Comedy of Errors*, Act 5, Scene 1.

Citizens of Cutthroat County must decide what legacy shall be passed on. Not only on the first day of Cutthroat County was a man shot dead on our streets, but your dedicated editor, only a resident of Basin Creek for three weeks and five days, learned another crime has occurred within our 1,200 square miles.

Cattle thieves have struck.

Michael J. McIlhaney, whose Rafter 7 outfit helps keep the village of Crimson Feather flush with cash and fine steaks, sent word to this editor that rustlers stole more than 125 head of steers and bred heifers. Always alert, Mr. McIlhaney sent a dozen riders after the low-down thieves but his good men lost the trail at Dead Indian Pony Creek, which is north of the Maddox Circle M grazing land and five miles southeast of Crimson Feather near where the Blackfoot Indians are still allowed to live.

McIlhaney sent word to our sheriff, but, alas, he has been either waylaid by the grief of losing his sickly wife and her last child, or he was too busy reveling in taking the life of yet another innocent man.

DAY TWO

THURSDAY

CHAPTER 11

He switched off the flashing lights a few miles before he exited Interstate 90 and drove through downtown Missoula, past the University of Montana campus and southwest down US 12 until he reached the Clark Fork Medical Center, where he parked the SUV in one of the spaces reserved for non-critical emergency vehicles. After turning off the ignition, he stared at the nondescript building's front doors that kept opening and shutting, letting people in, people out.

Just stared.

It was dark. Had been since he'd reached Great Falls. John T. Drew thought about the phone call he had made before heading into the signal-less country south of Basin Creek. Unable to reach Mr. Broadbent, he'd had to deliver the news to Mary's mother at home. Law enforcement officers were never trained in how to handle those kinds of calls. The big cities had spokespeople to do that, or someone to write a paragraph or two to read over the phone. The only good thing Drew could report was "She's alive, ma'am."

Well, Mary was alive when they'd put her on the helicopter. He'd begged Mrs. Broadbent to wait till morning before making the five-hour drive from Billings to Missoula. Cutthroat County roads were horrible, but I-90 was never a smooth ride, especially during summers. Summers were the time when road crews could finally fix all the damage done during winter. Delays were inevitable. And Montana drivers, Drew included, were all on the crazy side. Margaret Broadbent hadn't answered. She was too busy bawling.

Drew lost track of how long he sat in the parking lot. He lifted his arm and looked at the wristwatch, then focused again on the hospital. He had already forgotten what time it was, but he drew in a deep breath and held it a moment, then unfastened the seatbelt and grabbed the keys and his hat. Once he opened the door, he stood on the pavement and stared at the parking lot lights. They seemed so unnatural. Not what he was used to back home, a long, two hundred and twenty miles—three and a half hours—from there.

He wiped his eyes, steeled his nerves, and only knew he was moving from the sounds his boots made on the asphalt. The last time he had been to that hospital had been to identify Cathy, his wife, a DOA.

A security guard gave him only a passing glance as the doors opened, then closed behind him. He stopped to avoid being trampled by a running kid, and waited for the mother, who didn't look that much older than the boy, to pass in front of him, too, and run down the brat.

Reaching the sprawling, buzzing circular desk, Drew cleared his throat.

A redhead glanced up, then whispered into the phone, "Can you please hold, sir?" She did not wait for an okay, but punched the hold button, and pushed the microphone away from her face. "Sheriff."

"Deputy Sheriff Mary Elizabeth Broadbent was med-evac'd here." He scarcely recognized his voice.

"Yes, sir. She's in surgery. Fourth floor." She pointed. "Elevators are on the right side around the corner. Turn left. You'll find the bullpen, and you can wait there till the doctor . . ." She glanced at a notebook, flipped a page, and looked up. "Doctor Haddad will speak to you as soon as he can."

"Thank you." He turned and followed her directions when she called out to him. He looked over his shoulder.

"I am so sorry, Sheriff. I'm praying she'll be okay."

"Thank you."

The coffee the nurse brought him at the bullpen was worse than what he could find at the Wild Bunch Casino. He drank it anyway, trashed the Styrofoam cup, stood, paced, found the bathroom, paced some more. Sat down. Closed his eyes. Remembered.

"You're from Billings?" he asked.

"All my life." She smiled.

He stared, blinked, glanced at her resumé, and looked at her again. "What makes you want to move all the way from a big city to this remote part of the world?"

"Yellowstone County Sheriff's Department isn't hiring, the police department has no openings, and I don't want to move to Amidon, North Dakota."

He tried not to smile, but failed as her laugh hooked him. Sliding the paper to the pile of papers he had no desire to read, he leaned back. "They teach you anything about Cutthroat County in Billings?"

"A little bit in geography and history. And my parents brought my brother and me here when I was in eighth grade. Well, not here. But we stopped on the way to Glacier one summer."

He nodded. "Lots of people stop here on the way to Glacier. Most of them, though, don't stop."

She smiled again.

He could stare at that smile all day, but he looked away, then dragged the resumé back toward him. He'd just turned fifty years old. She hadn't listed her age, and he couldn't ask, though it would come out in the application. But, criminy, boy, she had to be twenty-five years younger than he was. And Cathy had been gone only a year.

Turning back to the interview, he asked, "What made you join the Marine Corps?"

"It got me out of Billings, and helped pay my way to Missoula. I worked part-time at a security firm."

She went to graduate school, too. Her resumé made him nervous. She was smarter than John T. Drew. But, shucks, who wasn't?

He imagined tuition and dorm rooms and books cost a lot more than it had back in ancient times. When he went to college in Bozeman most of his money had gone to beer. Back in those dark ages he could find beer for two-fifty a six-pack.

"Twentynine Palms?"

She shrugged. "We called it Twenty-nine Stumps. And I never once saw Gomer Pyle."

"You're—" He stopped. If he said she was too young to remember that TV series, he'd get hit with an age discrimination suit. "Well, this isn't California. I imagine Camp Twenty-nine Stumps has more people than you'll see in a month of Sundays up here. But you need to know something about living up here. It's not Billings. It's remote. It's tough, not just in winter, but year round. You've heard tales of pioneers going crazy from the wind, the loneliness. That still happens. And people freeze to death. Lately, we've gotten our share of meth, and once in a while, a local cowboy has way too much to drink and thinks this is still the Old West."

She nodded. "But it's not Billings. Or Slope County, North Dakota."

He took a pen, circled the name of a gunnery sergeant in California and a special investigator for Vibrant Security in Billings, two of her four references. But he figured she already had the job if she was fool enough to accept it.

"Hungry?" he asked as he laid the pen atop the resumé.

"Famished. I could eat anything."

"You haven't had lunch at the Busted Stirrup," he told her.

A year later, on a Friday night, she invited him into her apartment, and he didn't leave till Sunday morning.

Sheriff Drew did not sleep. Couldn't sleep.

"The only people who sleep in hospitals," Denton Creel once told him, "are those on ketamine."

Around two in the morning, a screaming team of doctors, EMTs, and nurses rushed a stretcher down the hallway as nurses held a surgery room door open, and quickly closed it when everyone had gotten inside. He stared at that door just a moment, then looked at the one he had guessed where Mary lay, fighting for her life.

If she weren't already dead.

Denton Creel had buzzed Drew before he left Basin Creek, volunteered to make the drive to Missoula. Or even ride down with him. Shucks, the county could take care of itself for a day or two.

Creel was calling again as another patient was being rushed in. Drew answered the phone, putting a finger in his other ear, remembering what his father had once told him. "Nothing good ever happens after midnight, boy."

The earlier patient looked to have been in a car wreck. Maybe a bar fight. This one, though, was an older woman, probably in cardiac arrest.

"Yeah." Drew waited for Creel.

"Any word?"

"She's still in surgery."

"What was that commotion?"

"Someone else they were bringing into the ER."

"Oh."

"What's going on up there?" Drew shifted the phone to the other ear now that things had quieted down. The signal wasn't the best on Creel's end, but Drew managed to make out what his deputy was telling him.

"State boys are still here at the scene. They just let Maddox go home, but told him to—"

"Why are you still up there?" He barked that so loud, the nurse glared at him.

Creel sighed. "I dunno." The signal dropped for a second. ". . . like I ought to be here. Doing something."

"I'm sorry for snapping," Drew whispered.

"Don't be. I feel like screaming myself."

Denton Creel was a good man. Drew thought he ought to say that, but instead, he sighed, shifted his weight, and said, "You need to get some sleep, Denton."

"We got the plate number," Denton said.

Drew sat up straight. He prayed this part of the conversation would be dropped, and, for once, his prayer was answered. All he heard was "Mary . . ."

When the signal kicked in again, he heard Denton say, "Mary wrote it on the ticket she was going to give him. And the dashcam in her unit confirmed. We got the name, too. From his driver's license. She had that and the insurance card."

"Maddox saw the car. Did he confirm the ID from the driver's license?"

"I didn't catch . . ." Again the signal kicked out. ". . . John."

Drew repeated the question.

"No. Couldn't. Maddox was too far away. He couldn't see . . ."

Drew heard nothing, then ". . . good enough to make out the letters and numbers. But was pretty sure the plate had Steamboat on it. You know. The bucking horse."

"I know."

"The state boys called Wyoming Highway Patrol, Cheyenne Police, and the Laramie County Sheriff's Office. They got a search warrant and were on the way." Denton read the address.

John Drew didn't care a fig about where the guy lived. "What's his name?"

"Terrence. Terrence Abernathy Collins."

Drew started for an ink pen, but stopped. He didn't need to write that name. He'd never forget it.

"Age forty-six. He's some hifalutin . . ." The words became garbled. ". . . can afford a Mercedes. But he sure don't fill . . . who'd shoot a cop over a traffic citation. Far as we . . . he's clean."

Drew glanced at the clock. "It'd take him ten to twelve hours to get to Cheyenne. An APB—"

"Already put out. And the Canada border folks—well, you alerted . . . So did . . ."

Drew wondered if they could put cell phone towers on some of Garland Foster's wind turbines. But he didn't think he had missed much during the call and was thankful for that. The border probably wasn't a feasible escape route. His mind had been clear enough to radio that when he was speeding toward Highway 60, and Danny Adams had been smart enough to have someone do that while he was calling Drew.

"Go home," Drew told Creel. "Get some sleep."

"Well—"

"I need you to get some sleep." Drew knew he had raised his voice when the nurse glared at him again. "Listen," he said, softer now. "First thing in the morning, I want you to drive up to the rez. Get Hassun. Tell him what happened, and ask him to come to the investigation site."

"The state boys will—"

"This happened in Cutthroat County. We're taking lead on this one. It's our case. And Mary's our—"

Soft footsteps sounded, and Drew looked up, sucking in a deep breath and feeling his stomach ache like he had just been punched in the gut. Creel was saying something else, but Drew cut him off.

"Denton. I have to go. Get a couple hours of sleep, then find Hassun. I'll call you later." He ended the call, and pushed himself out of the uncomfortable chair.

Still wearing scrubs and gown, the surgeon walked toward Drew, just now removing the mask and cap covering his crew cut. Doctor Haddad didn't look that much older than Mary Broadbent. "You are Sheriff . . . ?"

"Drew." He held out his hand. "John Drew." He waited.

"Noam Haddad. Chief neurosurgeon here."

Haddad. Reminded Drew of *Hassun*. But just the name.

The handshake was brief. The surgeon's eyes were brown, hard, and he looked exhausted.

The helicopter had taken off from the highway around six o'clock. It was now . . . Drew glanced at the clock on the wall . . . 3:02 A.M.

"She's alive," the doctor said. "But this is a cranial gunshot wound. I need to be honest with you, Sheriff. The mortality rate typically ranges from fifty-one to eighty-four percent."

Drew tried to focus on the first words. *She's alive.*

"She's young, she's strong—quite strong—has a healthy heart. For the moment, we have induced a coma, and I am consulting with Doctor Gottlieb here and via videophone with Doctor Aito Takahash at John Hopkins in Baltimore. We want to see how she's doing before we try to remove the bullet."

Drew swallowed, checked the clock again, and ground his molars. She had been there how long? And they hadn't even operated.

Haddad must have properly diagnosed exactly what was going through Drew's mind.

"Sheriff, brain surgery is always a risk. Tonight was all about stabilization and vital signs. And looking into her brain.

Bullet migration is what we're most concerned about at the moment. Neurologic sequelae can be more than traumatic, it can be fatal. We don't want that. Movement by our surgical tools or the projectile on a whim can lead to an abscess or massive hemorrhage. It's a complicated procedure. We've done a cranial computerized tomography that reveals bone fragments and fragments from the projectile."

"It's called a *bullet*, Doctor." The words fired out of Drew's mouth before he could stop himself.

But the doctor never lost his composure. "It's a bullet. Our guess is nine millimeter."

Drew sighed. "What are her chances?"

"We also have her on antibiotics, antiepileptics, and anti-edema medications. Her heart was beating when she got here."

Doctor Haddad had not, Drew was about to point out, answered the question.

"I'm told someone gave her CPR at the scene," the surgeon said. "Was that you?"

Ashton Maddox. Drew wondered how that hard rock ever took time to take a CPR class. "No." He felt sick. "By the time I reached the scene the helicopter was only ten miles away."

"Well, whoever performed CPR saved your deputy's life." The doctor swallowed. "For now. The rest is up to—" He shook his head. "But she's alive. She's in no apparent distress at this time." He continued to lay out the rest of the situation.

A nine-millimeter bullet had entered the brain at a high velocity. Something called a *nidus*. Something called *brain necrosis*. "We do not want to operate until her vitals are a bit better and we feel that we can remove the projectile without further harming the neurological status."

Suddenly, Drew remembered the Boy Scout five or so years back who had fallen off a rockface at fifty feet. That kid from Denver, sixteen years old, had not survived. Drew headed the county's search and rescue unit, and had helped bring the kid out of the canyon. An ambulance had not rushed the boy to Missoula, but to another hospital in the city. The boy's dad, an assistant scoutmaster, had ridden with Drew to the hospital, where the doctor told the distraught father the grim news.

"What's her GCS?" Drew asked the neurosurgeon.

Noam Haddad gave him more consideration. He probably didn't think anyone not employed at this hospital had ever heard of the Glasgow Coma Scale. He drew in a deep breath, held it for a long while, and exhaled. "Eight."

Drew closed his eyes and expected the surgeon to say that meant nothing at this stage. Maybe he did say it, but all Drew heard was that doc from four years back.

"Your son, I am afraid to report, has a GCS of three, sir. An eight or lower requires intubation, if only to protect airways. A seven or less means the patient is comatose. A three is . . ."

The boy had died twenty-five minutes later.

Numbly, Drew reached into his shirt pocket, found a business card, and held it out for the doctor. "Call me with any updates. Any time."

"Where will you be staying in Missoula?" The doctor took the card, looked at it, and lowered his hand.

Drew shook his head. "I'm heading back to Basin Creek."

"I'd advise against that, Sheriff. It's almost three-thirty. You need sleep. Cutthroat County's better than three hours from here. You're exhausted, and that's not an easy drive for anyone in the daytime."

But Drew found his hat, put it on, and walked toward the elevators. "Call me. With any updates."

Chapter 12

George Grimes did not see why so much of a fuss had been made over Montana. It wasn't near as big as Texas, the roads were crap, nobody knew how to drive, gasoline cost a pretty penny more, and you sure couldn't find even halfway decent enchiladas or chili anywhere. He didn't think the sky was that big, either. West Texas . . . why, a man standing in Plainview could see all the way to Bronte—not that there was much to see. And those mountains up ahead, the Always Winter to the northwest and the Elks—*P* something or other on the road map he had picked up—to the east might be a fair size taller, but he doubted they produced as tough a man and as hard a terrain as the Big Bend country.

But Grimes would say this for Montana: It sure was green at that time of year.

He had driven fifteen hours straight from Houston to Denver, caught a quick nap at a rest stop on I-25, ate what Coloradans called huevos rancheros at some seedy truck stop, and pushed on another eleven hours to Great Falls, where he found a cheap hotel, a bottle of Jack Daniel's, and a prostitute. He could have stayed in a better hotel for the per diem and travel expenses he had arranged with this Elison Dempsey gent, but Grimes was, well, cheap. Just like his daddy. Besides, the Dodge Ram would need an oil change for all the miles he had put on just to get that far.

After kicking the hooker out of his room so he could get some sleep, Grimes had found some moderately decent coffee. Freshly shaved, mustache trimmed, best shirt and best hat on, he started the final leg of the trip. He was halfway sure once he got to Basin Creek—if he could even find that dot on a map—he would give some newspaper interviews, maybe a TV interview or two, look around for a day, then go back home.

Those were his thoughts until he was in a dingy little breakfast joint and FOX News was talking about a shooting of a sheriff's deputy in . . . of all places . . . Basin Creek, Montana.

"Most people have never heard of Basin Creek," the fat news man said.

Grimes had to chuckle when the truck driver sitting a few seats down from him said, "And those who have wish they hadn't."

Grimes wiped his mouth with a paper napkin and leaned back to get a better view of the television screen. A sheriff's deputy—not just that, but a young, female sheriff's deputy—had taken a bullet into the head in what was most certainly supposed to have been a routine traffic stop. Well, now. Providing Elison Dempsey wasn't the sorry son of a dog who had shot that deputy, this job might not be too bad for a rock star Ranger like George Grimes.

He paid for the meal and left the sorry waitress a bigger tip than she deserved. Suddenly he was in a good mood. At the truck, he changed his regular blue law-enforcement tie for a bolo. TV crews and TV viewers seemed to think bolos meant real Texans. Even though most bolo wearers were in New Mexico or Arizona.

At the traffic intersection of a US highway, he eased to the checkpoint at the roadblock, rolled down the window, and crushed out the cigar he had been smoking. He showed the officer his driver's license and the badge he had kept after retiring. The press release . . . and plenty of headlines . . . had used the words *retired from the Texas Rangers after twenty-nine years of service.* Some of those years were good. Some, especially the last two or three years, not so good.

"You're *the* George Grimes?" The cop might have been twenty-five years old, but he looked twelve.

"That's right, Officer. How's that lady cop who got shot doin'?"

"I don't know, sir. She was alive the last I heard. But I haven't heard much the past four hours."

"I take it y'all ain't caught the shooter."

"No, sir. Not yet. But we will."

"I know you will, boy." He took his IDs back and tossed them on the torn passenger seat, about to put the Dodge back into DRIVE.

"Sir?"

He looked at the Montana highway patrol kid, and saw him handing him . . . a ticket book?

"Would you mind, Ranger Grimes, giving me an autograph?"

Grimes chuckled and took the pad and the officer's Bic. "Be right proud to, sonny. Right proud."

Montana, he thought, as he crossed US 103 and saw the sign that read CUTTHROAT COUNTY, *was starting to look a sight better*.

He found Basin Creek easy enough. Saw news vans and a crowd outside something called the Wantlands Mercantile, came to the flashing yellow light, and turned onto Front Street. Downtown wasn't much. The tallest building was a run-down grain silo. The Cutthroat County Courthouse/Basin Creek Municipal Building was a joke. Not a single car was parked out front. He passed a park honoring someone named Killone.

Reaching the stop sign, he found his notebook and flipped to the page with the directions the C.A.N. man had given him. He looked at it once. Three turns later, he knew the house. It had all those stupid campaign signs covering the lawn. If George Grimes had a Victorian home like that and grass like that in the front lawn, no way he'd be covering that lush grass with political lies. Grimes had lived in apartments all his life, except when he'd been stationed in West Texas. Then he'd lived in a dreary adobe bunkhouse where his only visitors were tarantulas, black widows, and rattlesnakes.

After setting the emergency brake, he popped open the glove box and pulled out the single-action Colt. It was the thing he hated most about that pathetic movie they had made about him. *Beretta Law.* He had used Colt revolvers all his life. Cock and fire. And he knew one thing. When a .45 slug from a long-barreled Colt hit someone where it hurt, that person wasn't getting up or squeezing a trigger.

Well, yeah, he had a little stainless-steel .380 automatic strapped over his right ankle, but that was just for added security. At least the Mustang was a Colt. And gave him seven more rounds if needed. Which he never had.

He took a final swig of the coffee he had picked up in Choteau, grabbed the keys— because even in a hayseed little town like this, cops were careful. Walking up the sidewalk, the steps, and across to the covered porch, he hit the doorbell.

Stupid chimes. Just once he wanted to hear that old *ding-dong*.

Footsteps and coughs sounded, and Grimes stepped back, turned sideways, and hooked a thumb over his belt near his back pocket. The jean jacket covered the Peacemaker .45, but he could reach it easy enough.

The door opened, and a skinny human being—if that actually applied to the loser—glared at him. He wore camo fatigues, sandals, no socks. His eyes were red, pupils dilated, and it appeared the kid had not showered or shaved in a month of Sundays. He also held a machine-gun pistol in his left hand, though the muzzle was aimed at the fool's right foot.

"Dempsey here?" Grimes asked.

The boy sniffled, wiped his nose, and tried to look tough. "Who wants to know?"

The retired Ranger thought about punching through the screen, grabbing the throat, pulling the punk onto the porch, and wiping his Tony Lamas over the messy beard. But he smiled and said, "George Grimes."

The head tilted. "You don't look like the George Grimes I saw in that movie."

How many times had he heard that one? He smiled and gave his oft-quoted answer. "That's because I was a sixty-grand-a-year officer of the Department of Public Service. And not a movie star making twenty-five million and a percentage of the box office." He might as well have been speaking Spanish.

Out of the corner of his eye, he saw a white-haired lady walking her beagle. Which meant Grimes couldn't throttle the boy to get an answer.

"Want to see my badge?"

"I thought you got fired."

He wished that old lady had taken her dog to pee somewhere else.

"I *retired*." He leaned forward, though still keeping that smile underneath his mustache, and whispered, "Sonny, my patience has limits."

The kid straightened, sniffled, and nodded down the street. "Dempsey's where everyone else is, I reckon. Where that cop got her head blowed off. Heard him on the radio twice already."

Grimes nodded. "Where's the crime scene?"

It took a while for the kid to understand the meaning of

crime scene, then his nod seemed to signal the same direction. "Just go back to the main highway. Drive north a ways past the Maddox ranch entrance. If you get to the cutoff to Crimson Feather—" He stopped, and laughed. "No, you won't get that far. You'll see the cops. And practically ever'body in Cutthroat County who ain't got a job."

Grimes fought down the desire to ask the boy what his job was and thanked the kid instead, then backed away to the steps. The door was closing when Grimes turned and headed back to the Ram, where the beagle was urinating on the driver's-side rear wheel.

The old lady gasped and scolded the dog. "Rockefeller, no. No. Bad dog." Her white face started to flush.

"Don't worry about that, ma'am," Grimes said, tipping his 6X Silverbelly Resistol and grinning at the dog. "I do that myself after I've had too many beers."

How he loved watching old ladies almost having a stroke.

The Peacemaker went under the seat in case some fool Montana trooper wanted to see his registration and proof of insurance, which he kept in the glove box along with a tire gage, flashlight, and, underneath the gloves and washrag, boxes of ammo for the revolver and the .380 automatic. He left his ID on the passenger seat.

He passed the Circle M sign on the left and saw a puttering old 1970s pickup with Montana plates turn onto a side road on the right. Locals, he figured, knowing to avoid that zoo up the road . . . the crime scene.

Ten minutes later, he was right. It *was* a zoo . . . like every high-profile crime scene he had ever been part of. Not as big a news story as some he had worked in Texas, but he passed a few locals and some cranky tourists mad about being stuck in traffic.

A few gave Grimes the finger as he passed them, his

hazard lights flashing, and he saw the TV news vans, and wondered where they came from. He couldn't even name the capital of Montana. Billings maybe? It sure wasn't Basin Creek.

A uniform stepped onto the southbound lane and held out his left hand, his right hand resting on the holstered sidearm. He looked madder than a hornet, but Grimes smiled, nodded, and kept both hands on the top of the steering wheel. The window was already rolled down. He could hear journalists gossiping, and in his rearview mirror he spotted a couple of other uniforms coming up on both sides of the pickup. One held his automatic out, but his finger was not in the trigger guard.

Montana cops, Grimes decided, weren't all that stupid after all.

The big man, a corporal, from the chevrons on his sleeve, stormed over, stepped back, and demanded. "Mister, what do you think you're doing?" He didn't wait for an answer, but demanded, "License and registration." Didn't even say *please* or *sir*.

Grimes didn't show him either. He flipped open the leather case and the cop saw the DPS badge of a Texas Ranger.

"I'm George Grimes, Corporal," he said in his most gravelly voice. The Texas twang, though, came naturally.

The patrolman looked at the photo ID, then at Grimes, but he didn't mention *Beretta Law*. He cleared his throat, returned the ID, and stepped back. "Yes, sir, Ranger Grimes. If you want to park on the left, that'll be fine. Detective William Ambrose is in charge at the moment, Ranger, sir. He's over by the fence talking on his cell phone." He motioned to a young man in khaki pants, white shirt, blue tie, blue blazer, straw cowboy hat. "The county sheriff is on his way here."

Grimes tossed the ID case back to the passenger seat.

"The sheriff isn't here?" He sounded incredulous because he was. It might be a small town but—

"He was in Missoula with Deputy Broadbent, sir."

Grimes swallowed. "Well"—he nodded—"that's all right, I reckon." He said the words but thought the sheriff was missing a lot of good free advertising on TV. Running for public office, he ought to think about those things and not just the welfare of a cop who worked for him.

"Is . . . ummm . . . Elison Dempsey here?"

The trooper frowned. "Yes . . . sir." He pointed to a van. "DCI has refused to recognize his authority here. He's probably complaining about that to the TV crews."

"DCI?"

"It's our Department of Criminal Investigation, sir."

"I see." Grimes saw some regular traffic in the mirror and nodded again at the corporal. He should park. Let the tourists get on with their vacation. Then find this Will Ambrose. And maybe even Elison Dempsey.

"Thank you, Corporal. I've lost too many Rangers and fellow members of the blue fraternity in my years, son. I do hope that deputy lives. Keep up the good work. And stay safe." He put the Ram into gear.

But the corporal asked one more question. "Sir, what interest do the Texas Rangers have in this investigation?"

"That, Corporal, is what I'm here to find out." He pulled away, found a place to park on the left, and before he could find either Elison Dempsey or the DCI investigator, he was swarmed by camera crews, bright lights, microphones, and newscasters. One was a rather attractive blonde in a low-cut dress.

Montana, Grimes thought, *keeps looking better all the time.*

CHAPTER 13

In the empty house, Ashton Maddox drank his coffee as dawn broke. According to his grandfather clock, he had gotten home at 3:08 this morning. He'd showered, poured himself a double bourbon, and—

No. Ashton rubbed his eyes. He had downed that double bourbon—the first one—before he had showered. Then he had made himself another one, though smaller, on the rocks. After that he had spent fifteen minutes trying to find the right maps, and pored over those for maybe an hour longer, taking notes, plotting various paths. The phone rang every ten minutes or so, but that non-human voice kept telling him *Name Unavailable* or *Call from Helena Montana*, mispronouncing the city and state. Or identifying Dan *Oh-Ri-ley* or *Carl Lo-rim-er*. That's how Ashton knew the shooting was already on cable news television.

He never answered one call, and finally lay down on the sofa at 4:31. The telephone stopped ringing after a time, but when his eyes opened just before dawn, the computerized voice again spoke.

Call from Telephone Number Nine-Eight-Three . . .

He sprang off the couch and rushed to the phone. Montana had only one area code, 406, but he knew only one person who had 983, a newly created area code for the Denver area. He answered it on the third ring. "Baby."

"Daddy," he heard.

He untangled the cord and switched the phone to his other ear.

"What the blazes happened? Why didn't you call me? Are you—" She stopped to catch her breath.

"Aly," he said, "I'm sorry. I'm fine."

"You're all over CNN, Daddy."

He leaned against the desk, trying to think of something he should tell her, but he had said he was fine.

"They say you were shot at. They said you shot back. Some bozo, whoever they hired from Great Falls to get up to Cutthroat County, compared it to the Gunfight at the O.K. Corral."

He swore, and saw the Blanton's Single Barrel he had forgotten to put away. It was too early for bourbon. Besides, the telephone cord wouldn't reach that far. "It wasn't anything like that."

"Did that guy who shot that cop shoot at you?"

He drew in a breath and did not answer.

"That's what I thought, Daddy. Did you actually shoot back at him?"

He wet his lips, debating his answer. Alyson was a smart kid . . . his only child . . . two years out of college and already working as an air traffic controller at Denver International Airport. Ashton could hardly figure out how to get in and out of DIA when he had to fly in there, and his baby girl was helping planes land and take off.

"It's not the first time a Maddox has been shot at, Aly, or the—"

"First time a Maddox has shot back." She'd cut him off and then went silent for ten or fifteen seconds. "I feel like taking a shot at you. You should have called me."

He smiled at that. "The cops didn't let me go until two-something this morning. I didn't want to wake you up."

She sighed.

Ashton wet his lips. "What else did that report on CNN say?"

"You haven't been watching TV?"

"What channel is it on? I don't think I watch anything but the Weather Channel."

The remote was also too far away. He would have to remember how to turn on that Sony that looked larger than one of those old Cinerama screens when his dad had taken the family to see a rerelease of *How the West Was Won* in Kalispell.

"Daddy, I don't know. Channels are different depending on your . . ." She might as well have been speaking Greek.

"That deputy?" he asked. "Did they say anything about her condition?"

"Critical condition with a gunshot wound to her head."

Well, at least she's still alive.

"I think they said a hospital in Missoula. But I was in shock by then."

He wearily exhaled, unable to think of something else to say.

"You were *shot* at!" Alyson flew off the handle again, telling him he could have been killed. That was something he could have laughed off, but then she said words that chilled him.

"Were you trying to get yourself wounded, Daddy? So Mom might come home?"

The bourbon sure would have helped right about then.

The phone line went silent. All he heard were the ticking of the clock and his own breathing.

"Daddy?"

He did not speak.

"I'm sorry, Daddy. That was . . . I . . . I'm upset. I didn't mean that."

"It's all right, Baby," he whispered. He had wondered if his wife would return. Now that he had started seeing—"Look," he told his daughter. "That man was walking toward that officer. You know the county sheriff's department and I don't see eye to eye on anything, but any man I know would have done exactly what I did. That fellow shot that deputy. Put her down. And he was walking toward her to finish the job. I did what I thought was the right thing to do." He almost laughed. "Truth is, I would have done the exact same thing had it been her boss that had a bullet in his brain." He laughed harder. "I can't believe I said that. And don't you tell anyone I said that. Ever. But . . . anyway, that was something I had to do. It was the right thing to do. And it all worked out. I wasn't hurt. The guy didn't even shoot my Expedition. And maybe that deputy will pull through." He heard her sniffle. "It's all right, Aly."

"No." Her sob was audible. "It's not."

"It is. And I'm all right. You're all right. Montana's all right. The world will be okay." Like he used to tell her when she was a baby.

"Do you need me to come up there?"

He laughed. "No. You have a job."

"It's a government job, Daddy. A federal job. I get vacation, you know. And sick leave. And personal leave."

Vacation. Sick leave. Personal leave. Things he still could not comprehend. He had never taken a vacation in his life, unless he counted his honeymoon with Patricia. And that was just a weekend at Many Glacier Lodge up in the national park.

"I'm fine. That guy's probably in Alberta by now. And there were cops all along the highway when I left. And remember . . . what's my last name?"

She sighed.

"Answer me, Alyson."

"It's Maddox."

He laughed. "That's right. And what do Maddoxes do?"

"They take care of themselves."

"Bingo. You working today?"

"Tonight."

"Then you need to get your rest." He heard the door open, and for just a moment, he wondered if he had been wrong. That the man who had shot the deputy was coming in to kill the one witness to the crime. But spurs jingled, and he whispered to his daughter, "Thanks for calling, honey bun."

She sighed again.

"I'll call you later. Gotta go. Sun's up and I have a ranch to run."

"'Bye, Daddy."

"Talk to you later, Aly."

"Love you."

But he didn't hear her. He was already hanging up the phone and turning toward his foreman. "I suppose you've been watching CNN, too," Ashton told him.

When Colter Norris scratched his head and said, "Huh?" Ashton laughed and pointed at the coffeemaker. "Hit that son of a gun and pour yourself a cup. I'm gonna take a quick shower and put on some working clothes." He started for the stairs then stopped and turned back. "Is Dante Crump still around?"

"Havin' his breakfast," Colter said.

"All right. Once you've had your coffee, go back to the bunkhouse. You might as well turn on that stupid TV and see what all went down before the news vans start lining up on the highway outside our gate."

He was moving, glad to be rid of talking to cops and suddenly eager to do things his way, the Maddox way.

"Tell Dante to hitch a horse trailer to the truck and saddle horses for you, him, and me. Good horses. Have Yukon Hearst fix us some sandwiches and some cold drinks and thermoses filled with coffee. We're going hunting."

"Huntin'?"

"For rustlers." Ashton started up the stairs. "Might want

to bring some rubber boots for all three of us. We're gonna get wet."

In the bunkhouse, the cowhands and Hearst, the cook, were staring at the massive TV—bigger even than the one Ashton rarely watched in his big house. They shared the satellite dish, and the Great Falls station came in clearer than any TV image he remembered growing up.

The reporter held a microphone to a ginger-mustached man with a big felt hat, the gaudiest bolo he had ever seen, and an outrageous drawl.

"I just got into town," the big oaf said. "Elison Dempsey brung me up here to help stop rustlin' and clean up the meth operations that are destroying Montana and this good nation's youth." He shook his head and did some *tsk, tsk, tsking*. "I've been deputized by the Citizens Action Committee."

Network, Ashton corrected to himself.

"But I sure wish ol' Dempsey had called for me sooner. I might could've prevented that poor lady deputy from gettin' kilt."

The newsman brought the mic, and the camera, back to his Coppertoned face. "The last report we have, Ranger Grimes, was that the young deputy sheriff was in critical condition but alive at a Missoula hospital."

The Texan shrugged. "Well, with a bullet in the brain, death might be the better alternative than bein' a vegetable the rest of her poor life."

"Why don't someone punch that jackass in the mouth?" Hearst said, dumping scrambled eggs on Dante Crump's plate.

The newscaster began again. "As a Texas Ranger and American crime-fighting legend—" Hearst swore again, but was shushed by young Homer Cooper.

"What advice do you have for our local law enforcement?"

"Best advice I ever give." The former Texas Ranger stared into the camera. "Stay out of my way."

Hearst found the remote and switched to the Weather Channel, which he promptly muted. "Eat yer breakfast and get out of my sight so I can do these dishes," he said, and headed to the coffeepot.

With the boob tube off, Ashton let his workers ask three or four questions about what had happened on the highway yesterday afternoon. He answered tersely and made it clear his employees, full-time or part-time, were not to speak to cops or reporters about the shooting.

Ashton drove the Ford F-450 pickup. The 2015 model with 113,000-plus miles sucked diesel the way Colter drained beer bottles, but it showed no signs of slowing down and could tow a trailer through rougher country than the roads to Dead Indian Pony Creek.

Colter sat in the front passenger seat with the window cracked to keep his cigarette smoke out of his boss's lungs. Dante Crump sat in the back. As low man on the totem pole, it was his job to open and close the gates as the three men moved from pasture to pasture.

Colter turned on the radio, found mostly country music but at last got some actual news from an all-news station in Calgary, though the reception was weak. He soon switched off the radio. Apparently, O.K. Corral-labeled gunfights in the United States weren't that newsworthy in Alberta. He twisted out the smoke and put the butt in the ashtray, which was filled with a week or two's worth of butts and ashes.

"I gotta think they'll have that crime scene roped off for a while yet," Ashton explained. "And every yahoo from the county will be clogging up Highway 60. We'll make better times following the creek on horseback. And we might find something along the way."

"Maybe so." Colter did not look or sound convinced.

"I have not been to the bridge at Hoary Marmot in more than a year," Crump said.

"Longer than that for me," Ashton lied. "That's why I think the rustlers might have chosen that spot." He laughed and shook his head, then slowed as they neared the final gate. "I still have a hard time believing that I'm saying that. Rustlers. In this day and age."

The heavy-duty pickup and trailer behind it slid to an easy stop. Crump stepped out. The idea of rustlers made it seem like Ashton Maddox was living back in the 1800s.

The US Department of Agriculture had come up with ear tags, RFID tags, all sorts of things to help keep track of diseased and stolen cattle. But Maddox cattle would also, always, have brands. And yet someone had stolen some of his beef.

Technology. Progress. But still low-down rustlers.

Criminals always figured out a new way to live off some honest citizen's hard work. That would never end.

The big truck and trailer moved through the last of the latched gates, stopped, and after Crump climbed back inside the truck, Ashton punched the gas. Twenty minutes later, they were bringing the horses out of the trailer.

"We should have driven a truck up to the bridge at Hoary Marmot," Crump said as they rode into the creek. "Then we could drive—"

"Past cops investigating that shooting there and back?" Ashton barked. "Stuck in traffic for who knows how long?"

Colter fired up another cigarette. "Wonder how they're routin' the curious folks around that circus."

"I don't care." Ashton pointed. "You take that side," he told his foreman." Turning in the saddle, he looked at Crump.

"You take the other side." He touched the bay with his spurs and rode ahead. "I'll be up ahead a bit in the middle."

"What are we looking for?" Crump asked. "Exactly?"

"Anything that doesn't belong in this creek."

An hour later Crump had found a fly line over a low branch, the fly long gone. A real nice brown trout had broken the surface and disappeared, startling Colter's sorrel.

"Wish I had that fishing line you saw back aways," the foreman told Crump.

Ashton Maddox found nothing amusing. But he thought he was on the right track. The woods along both sides of the creek bed were thick, and the water had cut through the hard rocks over hundreds of years. The canyon wall moved over their heads, a foot, two feet, then five. Water would have drowned out most of the noise of hooves splashing. If they moved at night, the stars and the moon, always brilliant when it wasn't cloudy, would reflect off the water and guide them.

There were no real rapids. Dead Indian Pony Creek didn't carry much water, even in the wettest of years. Just enough to keep trees and brush, and Circle M livestock, alive. Riding in the creek never became difficult. The water never came up past any of their horses' hocks.

It was a nice day for a ride, but the horses quickly tired of wet feet. Ashton couldn't blame them. The bottoms of his chaps were dripping. When the Dead Indian Pony turned, he saw the rattling old bridge, and he spotted the trail experienced anglers used to come down from the bridge to fish. Turning the gelding toward the bank, he wondered what exactly had he to show for the morning ride.

One broken fly line.

He frowned, ego bruised, disappointed, knowing Colter and Crump probably figured him to be an idiot. Which, since he had found nothing, was a pretty good description of how Ashton felt.

The bridge, at least, would be a nice spot for lunch.

He remembered coming up on Friday nights. *Hoary Marmot Bridge*. Better known back in those days as *Horny Maddox Bridge*. He had even brought Patricia up here a time or two. Just for some necking and petting and sharing a bottle of Mad Dog 20/20—the only booze he could afford for the allowance and later wages his father had given him.

He blocked those memories of nights long ago and a wife who had walked out on him. Focused on better times. Like when he had brought Taisie Neal to the bridge—and they hadn't gone trout fishing.

At least he had better liquor back at the ranch these days. And a healthier allowance.

So far, the trip didn't prove a thing. Maybe at the top of the canyon, he'd find the proof he needed. And if he didn't, he still thought he was right. The creek had to be how those rustlers got his cattle off the property.

His bay was eager to get out of the water and begin the climb up. The horse had made it up maybe fifteen feet, when Ashton reined up quickly and swung to the ground. "Tracks!" He turned back to see Colter handing his reins to Crump, but the foreman wasn't walking up the gravelly slope toward his boss but to the brambles climbing up the canyon side.

Ashton dropped to his knees and slid forward. "Shod horse. And cattle tracks." Straightening, he looked up the canyon. "I knew it. I *knew* it!"

A cow pie rested a few feet ahead, and he slid up, the bay restless and not eager to be pulled by a man walking on his knees. He dropped the reins, knowing the horse wouldn't go far, and reached down and picked up the disc of manure. Pulling off his gloves, he broke it open and let his fingers search for moisture.

Spurs jingled and he turned to see Crump leading two horses and reaching for the reins of his boss's bay.

"Pretty darn fresh." Ashton tossed the manure to the side. "Day. Maybe two." He rose, looked over the saddled horses but could not see his foreman.

"Colter?" he called out. He laughed. "You answering the call of nature?" He felt giddy with excitement.

"Naw."

Turning and looking up, the rancher did not wait. He started up toward the bridge, finding more manure, more tracks. He slipped twice and soon fought for his breath. Why a man would hike up and down this path to catch—and then release—a fish when there were stocked ponds and easier places to reach, he could not guess. His lungs heaved, and he was sweating by the time he reached the top.

There, he had to wait till Crump brought up the horses, then find his canteen to drink rapidly. That done, the cowhand led the horses to the iron railing and tethered them there.

Still holding the canteen, Ashton walked around the dirt road. Tire tracks. Hoof prints. Two trucks, most likely, though one might have been a van. A trailer. His steers had been loaded there, then driven to Highway 60. He drank more water. Finally it struck him. He had solved how the thieves got sixteen heifers out of the pasture without being seen. But he still had no idea who did it.

Spurs sang again as Colter emerged from the trail. His forehead glistened, but that tough cowhand didn't appear to be breathing hard at all.

"I was right." Ashton beamed.

"Yep." The wiry foreman closed the distance and held up his gloved right hand. In it he held a wadded-up empty pack of chewing tobacco, and his calloused fingers began straightening it out, smoothing it. White background. Blue and green letters. Green and brown bars stretching from the triangle center markings like sunbeams.

Ashton knew the label without reading it. Georgia Brand Wintergreen.

"Ain't but one man I know in these parts that chews this brand," Colter said.

CHAPTER 14

Drew had spent more than an hour in the Clark Fork Medical Center parking lot, talking on the radio to the state boys at the scene, and, when county manager Dan O'Riley learned he was on the line, telling him what he could about Mary Broadbent's condition. That doctor, Drew realized, had been absolutely right. He had no business driving all the way back to Basin Creek, but he wasn't going to be anywhere but in Cutthroat County on that day.

Having gassed up in Helena, coffee'd up in Great Falls, and been greeted by daylight and no traffic, he punched the lights on the roof and the pedal to the floor. The radio came alive after he had made himself stop at a Choteau gas station to top off his gas tank, empty his bladder, wash his face, and buy another large cup of strong filling-station black coffee.

Sitting the cup in a holder, he turned off the flashing lights, and slowed down to the speed limit. "I'm on the way, Denton. Left Choteau." He glanced at his watch. "I'm just a few miles south of the state highway."

"Hassun and I are at the scene, Sheriff," Denton Creel told him.

Drew shook his head. "Did you get any sleep?"

The deputy must have driven straight to the reservation to

be back this early with that old Blackfoot tracker. The pause was long.

Creel might have been yawning. "You didn't."

Drew sighed. "What's happening there?"

"They're still going over the turnout inch by inch, it seems. DCI has folks all over the place."

That was good. It was also what Drew expected.

"You wouldn't believe the traffic here, though. I'm about to lend them a hand in that department."

"Ten-four."

"I told the lead investigator you were on the way." Another pause.

Drew stifled another yawn.

"I also told him that we would be primary on this case."

"Who's the lead investigator?"

"Will Ambrose."

That wasn't bad at all. Ambrose was a solid cop, a keen detective. He and Drew had known each other for better than ten years, back when Ambrose was a rookie patrolman and Drew was a part-time deputy for his dad. Ambrose had worked his way up from the highway patrol. He was a nephew to the state attorney general, but that's not how Will Ambrose had gotten to be a top dog in the DCI.

"Bet he didn't like that at all," Drew said.

"Oh, he just grunted."

"What's Hassun doing?"

"Sleeping in my unit."

That was good, too. They might not be getting much sleep for a while.

"Sheriff?"

"Yes, Denton?"

"What about Mary's cat?"

He swore. Drew had forgotten all about Roundabout, that obnoxious tabby feline. He wasn't sure even Mary liked the cat, a stray she had adopted eight months ago. Whenever

Drew went to the apartment, he had to load up on allergy pills, and he still came away with puffy eyes and a runny nose.

"Roundabout will have to take care of herself for a while," he told Creel. "But when you go back to town, stop at the apartment, get Mary's mail, tell the landlady what's going on, and make sure that demon has food and water."

"The landlady's got food and water?"

Drew's eyes closed.

"Oh." Creel laughed. "My brain is dead, Sheriff. All right."

"Ask her to look after the place and the fool cat."

"Copy that."

Drew saw a white van heading west up the road, and knew he was about to cross into Cutthroat County. "US 103 is right ahead, Denton. I'll—

The cell phone on the passenger seat began buzzing. He had a signal again. Then the phone began to ring, the Ian Tyson ringtone, and Drew hit the brakes, turned the emergency lights back on, and pulled onto the shoulder.

"Denton, I have to go. I'll be there directly." He disconnected, and hit the button on the phone. The call went to the speaker. "Billy," he said, and waited.

"Dad. I've been trying to reach you all freakin' night, Dad. How's Mary? It's all over the news. National and lo—"

"Sorry, kid. No signal. Been driving all night from Missoula."

Billy was between his sophomore and junior year at the University of Wyoming in Laramie. Bullpen catcher for the Cowboys varsity baseball team, and spending the summer down there playing on one of those college wooden-bat leagues. Had some host family keeping him and a couple of teammates, both upperclassmen from northern Colorado schools. He was majoring in Outdoor Recreation & Tourism Management at the university's Haub School of Environment and Natural Resources. Drew wasn't sure how canoeing, whitewater rafting, and hiking got a kid a college degree these years, but he had been getting good grades—even in math.

"What happened?" Billy repeated. "How's Mary?"

Drew breathed in, let it out slowly, and said, "She was stable, but critical, at that new hospital off Highway 12 past the college." For the life of him, he couldn't remember the name of the medical center. Man, was he tired.

"The news said Ashton Maddox got into a gunfight with the guy who shot her."

Drew felt a need for something stronger than filling-station coffee. "Yeah. That's what seems to have happened."

"Ashton Maddox?"

Drew did not respond.

"Dad, I'm coming home."

He tensed. "Billy," he said, becoming the patient but stern father. "You've got ball games and—"

"The Laramie Rustlers don't need me. We have four catchers and they're all older and better than I am. Do you know how hard it is to hit with a wooden bat? Don't expect any professional ballplayer, Dad, to get you free tickets to a Rockies game." He was talking fast, and whenever Drew opened his mouth, he couldn't say a thing. "I've got one class. That's over in two weeks, and I can talk to my professor."

"Son . . ."

"I'm coming up, Dad. Don't argue. And don't worry. I'll stop for the night in Billings."

The call ended.

Drew cursed, then he checked his rearview and side mirrors, kept the lights flashing, pulled onto the road, and floored the SUV.

Denton Creel hadn't been kidding about the traffic on the northbound road. Most of what he saw were out-of-state plates, tourists heading to Glacier or maybe Waterton-Glacier

International Peace Park in Alberta. Two eighteen-wheelers were stuck in the traffic.

Drew pulled into the southbound lane and drove at a reasonable, safe speed. The few cars that had been let through at the roadblock up north pulled onto the shoulder and let him pass. When he reached the roadblock, the trooper simply waved Drew through, and he parked the Interceptor between a couple of unmarked units, grabbed his hat, and walked to the turnout still cordoned off by yellow tape and tough-looking state troopers.

A chisel-jawed, crew-cut mountain of a uniformed trooper lifted the yellow tape and allowed Drew to duck underneath. “Sheriff,” the big kid said. Drew just nodded, but then the big man asked, “How’s Mary?”

Drew turned, studied that big chunk of pale granite, and said, “Not good. But alive.”

The rock just nodded, then pointed. “Lieutenant Ambrose is over there.”

“Thank you.”

Drew walked toward Ambrose, who was talking to a tall brunette woman. A uniformed trooper walked over, cleared his throat, and handed Ambrose a paper before nodding in the sheriff’s direction. Seeing Drew, Ambrose told the trooper something, and the uniform walked away. The brunette started to go, but Ambrose must have told her to stay.

Drew covered the distance, and Will Ambrose extended his hand. “Deputy Broadbent?”

Drew shrugged.

Ambrose introduced the brunette, Constance Simar, a lead DNA analyst who had just transferred from the division’s Narcotics Bureau.

They exchanged nods, and analyst Simar started back toward Mary Broadbent’s Interceptor, which was covered with a tent.

Drew didn't know Simar's rank, so he simply called her Agent Simar. She stopped, but Ambrose was already asking the question Drew knew he would be asked.

"You sure you want lead on this, John?" The detective stared at Drew for no more than two seconds before nodding. "I had to ask. We're here to assist you."

Drew nodded, and turned back to Simar. "We have the suspect's driver's license, correct?"

"Yes, Sheriff," and then corrected him. "Alleged driver's license."

"Did you dust it for prints?"

She smiled. "Yes, Sheriff. We did. They are being run as we speak."

"Thank you," he said, and she walked away.

Ambrose gave a smart-aleck grin. "Yeah, I guess you are lead on this one."

Drew saw it but made no reaction.

Ambrose sighed and pointed at the tent-covered SUV. "We've got the whole thing on the unit's camera. You want to watch it, John?"

He didn't. No one wants to see his lover get shot in the head. But it was his job.

The suspect had stepped out of his vehicle and was walking toward Mary's unit. She had gotten out of the car, hand on her weapon, and the audio picked up her instructions to tell him to get back inside his Mercedes. Then he was weaving, gasping, clutching his chest. Mary ran to assist him, and he stopped, pulling out a concealed weapon. Mary stopped, turned, and tried to draw her Glock but the man fired. Mary fell. Then man started for her, then stopped.

That would have been when Ashton Maddox arrived.

The shooter fired, fled to his Mercedes, and took off like a rocket. A moment later, Maddox hurried past the unit, called 9-1-1, then quickly opened Mary's bulletproof vest, tilted her head back as he filled her lungs with his breath, and started CPR.

Watching that did nothing but confirm what Drew already had been told.

"Roadblocks at Glacier, Toole, Pondera, Teton, and Flathead counties," Ambrose said as they walked out from the tent and away from Mary's unit. "APBs all across the Northwest, and Wyoming officials are on the lookout for that Mercedes. Tribal police on the rez notified. The Glacier County sheriff got the alert out fast, and no Mercedes—any Mercedes—have been spotted. Nothing from park rangers in the national park.

"We're focusing on Heart Butte and the rez. This county's not big, but you got a whole lot of ranch roads and BLM roads. I don't think a Mercedes coupe could make it far down many of those but—" He shook his head and cursed. "You passed the units south at the US highway intersection, and we've got the state highways covered, though I don't think the shooter is still in Cutthroat County. If the shooter gets out of Montana, the feds are gonna take over. I don't want that."

"I just want that SOB caught," Drew said.

Ambrose's cell phone rang, but that was good timing. Soft footsteps sounded behind him, and Drew turned to find a coppery-faced man who would make that trooper by the yellow tape look like a fifth-grader.

"Oki, napi," Hassun said, and almost crushed Drew in a bear hug.

Seeing the old man brought back another memory.

The food wasn't great at the casino at Iiníí, but Drew had already warned Mary Broadbent of that fact, while allowing the chow was better than anything she'd get at Basin Creek.

"Unless I cook it," Mary said.

They sat at a table, and a waitress moved from behind the

brightly lit and fairly loud bar, took their orders of coffee and the day's special, and eventually came back with the coffee.

By then Hassun had dragged his chair over and his black eyes were staring hard at Mary Broadbent. "You hire her?" the giant of a Blackfoot asked Drew without taking his eyes off Mary.

"I offered her a job," Drew said. "She took it. Or has taken it. She might change her mind now."

Hassun turned his head just briefly. "You smarter than I thought." Then he looked back at Mary. "You from here?"

"Billings," she said.

He nodded. "I live here," he said. "All my life. Except for two tours in Afghanistan. Marine."

"Semper fi," she said. "I was at Camp Pendleton!"

He laughed. "No fooling?"

"No fooling. But I never got out of the States."

"Wish I never got out of Montana." He shook his head. "Spent six months in Seattle. Ever been to Seattle?"

Mary shook her head.

"Wet." His buddy at the table brought him his cup of coffee, and Hassun thanked the old man, and then took a sip. "They say Seattle has good coffee. But I didn't like it." He clinked his mug against Mary's. "This is coffee I like."

"It is"—she swallowed—"strong."

Hassun nodded. "Good job in Seattle. Good pay. But I come home. Headaches. Headaches all the time. Go to doctor. Doctor does all kinds of tests. Gives me all kinds of pills. I take pills. Nothing cure headaches. Doctor says it's all in my mind. I say, 'I know that, Doc. My head aches. All the time.' Doc sends me to see a—" He bit his lip as he struggled for the word.

"Psychiatrist?" Mary asked hesitantly.

Hassun smiled. "Yes. See if I crazy. I know I am crazy." He drank more coffee. "Head doctor says I don't need no pills. Head doctor says I ain't as crazy as most men she sees. Head doctor says she got the cure for my headaches." The big Blackfoot's eyes were laughing as Mary leaned forward.

Although he'd heard it several times, John Drew had always loved this story. He waited for the punch line.

"Doctor tell me, 'Go home.' So I come back here. Home. And you know what?"

Since his right hand was raising the coffee cup again, Mary reached over and put her hand atop his left one. "You haven't had a headache since."

Hassun's smile beamed brighter than the video lights around the bar.

"She smart, JohnTeeDrew." He always made that name sound like one word. "Too smart to work for you."

Once Hassun lowered Drew back to the ground and the memory of Mary's first meeting with the big Blackfoot faded, Drew looked up into those dark eyes.

"Last night I pray," Hassun told him. "First to the Creator—always first to the Creator—thanking Him for all beautiful things . . . Mother Earth, Father Sky, all living creatures. For *naahks* . . . and for Mary Broadbent." He nodded. "She will live."

Drew wasn't sure, but he thanked Hassun.

"We find this man?" Hassun asked.

"We will find him." Drew nodded at the place where the Mercedes had pulled over. "That's where he parked his car. Will you start there?"

"Yes." Hassun turned and walked toward the spot.

Ambrose cleared his throat, letting Drew know he was off the phone, then called out to the towering uniform built like granite. "Corporal Hazen, take Mr. Hassun to Inspector Evans and tell him to give him a free rein."

The patrolman nodded, and seemed thankful. It wasn't like anyone wanted to try to stop a six-foot-seven, two-hundred-seventy-pound man of iron.

Drew waited, and Ambrose glanced at the cell phone he still held, and slipped it into his jacket pocket.

"That was the Wyoming Highway Patrol," Ambrose said. "Backed up by Cheyenne police, they arrived at the home of Terrence Abernathy Collins. They found the 2021 Mercedes-AMG C-63 S in the garage. Same tags as what showed up on Mary's unit camera and on the ticket she had written out."

Drew checked his watch. It wasn't quite impossible, but it would be nothing short of a miracle that even a speedy Mercedes could make it all the way from there to Cheyenne. Not with APBs out for that car.

"Car's engine wasn't hot. It was downright cold. And Missus Collins says her husband is in London. London, England. He's a researcher. The energy company he works for sent him out on some type of study program. Flew out in early May. Not due back till August tenth. That was confirmed by"—Ambrose glanced at the notes—"Cassadone Energy LTD. And Mr. Collins did not like being interrupted at tea time."

Drew cleared his throat, started to ask, but Ambrose was a smart cop.

"Oh, and Collins, the one in England at least, has dyed his hair. Purple. His wife also said he's going through some . . . things."

CHAPTER 15

Grabbing the bay's reins, Ashton Maddox nodded down the trail that led back to Dead Indian Pony Creek. "You two head back to the truck," he ordered his foreman and best cowboy. "Go back to the ranch—"

"Maybe I ought to ride with you." Colter Norris knew he had committed a faux pas, even if he likely didn't know the meaning of the phrase. He shut up, drew in a breath, and waited for Maddox to finish.

"I'll find our rustler." Maddox took the chewing tobacco package and stuffed it inside the back pocket of his jeans.

"He mightn't 've done no rustling." Colter Norris sure was pushing his luck this afternoon. "Be hard to prove he didn't lose that tobacco pouch whilst he was fishing for trout."

"Let's just see what Harry Sweet tells me." Maddox flipped up the stirrup, and went to work tightening the saddle's cinch. "Then I'll see what Garland Foster has to say about it."

Dante Crump spoke up. "Should we call the sheriff when we get a signal or when we get back to headquarters?"

Is everyone I pay conspiring against me? Maddox thought. "You call Clark Blaine when you get back . . . after you've unhooked the trailer and gotten those horses taken care of. Then get back in that old rig and drive straight to Windmill

Hades. If our good sheriff is at that crime scene, keep your traps shut about this. We'll let the sheriff know when I'm satisfied."

He tugged the horn. The saddle felt set. After a couple of swallows of water, he swung onto his horse, pulled down the brim of his hat, and glared at the two cowboys. "What're you looking at? Get going. Maybe my stolen beef is still on Foster's spread."

"You want a gun?" Colter Norris's eyes were cold.

Maddox patted the pocket of his jacket.

"I have one."

The state cops and even John T. Drew had not confiscated his revolver at the crime scene, though they had bagged the spent casings while wearing surgical gloves. They'd also taken about a dozen photographs of it, and then written down every number and description and measurement of the Smith & Wesson, dusted it for fingerprints, and even taken Maddox's prints. All after telling him he was not a suspect at this time, but they would understand if he wanted to call his attorney. Which he didn't. He kept all of his attorneys in prime beef and ninety-point wines these days. And he wasn't guilty of anything.

"I'll see you across the highway," he said, and kicked the gelding into a lope.

Drew had walked away from Will Ambrose and the other investigators. He put his hands on his hips and tried to clear his head. Hassun had moved from where the Mercedes had been parked onto the paved road. A minority of the uniforms, most of the TV reporters, their camera operators, and even a couple of detectives kept chuckling, though as discretely as possible.

One reporter called out to a uniformed trooper, "Tonto can track a fly on a paved road. Right?"

He began to giggle at his bad joke, but Hassun raised his head, and stared briefly but hard at the TV man, who cleared his throat, and excused himself as he went to hide behind a red, white, and blue news van. The Blackfoot grinned, and went back to kneeling, inching north on the beat-up pavement.

Footsteps sounded behind Drew. He cleared his mind, looked at the purple outlines of the rugged Always Winter range, and caught Will Ambrose in the perimeter of his vision.

"A copied license plate?" Ambrose suggested.

Drew shrugged. "I don't think Wyoming DMV could even screw up that badly."

"From what I could learn about that energy company he works for, it's full of scientists—independent, not government contractors—who are out to save the world." Ambrose lighted a cigarette. "Which explains the purple hair, I guess. Or as his spouse said he's—"

"So someone knows the make and model of Terrence Abernathy Collins's wheels, knows he's leaving the country, knows his wife won't be taking the car out, at least not all the way to Montana, and buys the same model, same color car." Drew shook his head. He tried to think. He took in a deep breath of air, but smelled the cigarette smoke Ambrose tried to keep away.

"Sounds like a Keanu Reeves thriller," Ambrose said.

Drew tried to think of who Keanu Reeves was. Then remembered the last movie he had seen.

"When's the last time you went to a movie?" Mary asked. She had stepped out of her Jeep Renegade, her personal car, and was waiting in the parking lot at the Roaring Falls Theatre in Great Falls—one of those restored old theaters from the golden era of movies, with a balcony and roomy seats and popcorn that tasted like popcorn.

"I took—" He frowned. "It was the one about fly-fishing

in Montana. We drove down to Choteau." He stared at the pavement.

"I'm sorry." She was near him.

He smelled her perfume. Which was nothing like what Cathy ever put on.

Mary's hand found his. Their fingers interlocked. "I wasn't thinking," she whispered.

Drew shook his head. "It's all right." But it wasn't. Not really.

"We had TV," he said, trying to salvage their long drives to Great Falls. "When I was a kid we could get two, sometimes, three channels. No cable. No dish. Basin Creek never had a theater. But when I was in high school, we'd double date. Head to Choteau. If our parents would trust us with a truck."

"Two couples in a truck?"

He had to stop himself from falling into Mary's fascinating eyes. "It had its advantages. Except for the gallon of Brut 33 that Arby Doolittle put on."

Old Arby. *Drew hadn't thought of him since the last high school reunion. Drove semis straight out of high school for some company in Oklahoma City. The first one of Drew's class to get out of Cutthroat County. Blew a front tire on westbound Interstate 40, jumped the median, and ran head-on into an eastbound Kenworth that just couldn't get out of the way. Arby Doolittle. Dead at twenty-seven. There wouldn't be any stories from him at that high school reunion.*

Mary kissed his cheek and stepped back. "And here we are, taking two trucks. With the price of gas like it is."

Well, he deserved that. He didn't feel the need to explain again. Younger deputy seeing the older sheriff. In a small town like Basin Creek where there were no movies to see, gossip was considered first-rate entertainment.

"You wanna see the movie?"

"Come on." She took his hand again and smiled.

In spite of her smile, he thought it was not sincere, that she really wished he would let their relationship be out in the open. He was pretty sure Billy knows, but Drew's son wasn't one to talk too much. "I'll buy the popcorn and Diet Sprites." She pulled him to the old theater, which was showing an old Western with Gary Cooper. Not High Noon. *Another one, but set in Montana.*

Drew frowned. He still couldn't remember the title or what the film was about, and quickly lapsed back into the memory.

"You sure?" he asked, following her.

"I'm sure. You buy supper. We'll split the motel room."

"JohnTeeDrew!"

Drew turned toward Hassun's voice. The big Blackfoot was standing, waving him over. Reporters and cops quit gossiping. Will Ambrose tossed his cigarette butt to the earth, forgetting it was a crime scene, and started forward. Drew passed him quickly, leaped over the yellow tape, and pounded down the pavement as troopers warned the members of the press that they could not come any closer.

Hassun grinned when Drew and Ambrose stopped. The big Indian brought the fingers of his right hand to his nose, sniffed, then extended his hand toward the lawmen. "Man who shot at one who hurt Sweet Mary didn't miss everything," Hassun said, lowering his hand.

Gasoline. Drew sucked in a deep breath. "He hit the gas tank."

Hassun's big head went down, then up.

"Big hole?"

The head shook. "Small gun. But plenty gas come out."

Drew was already trying to do the math. A Mercedes like that would get twenty-five, no more than thirty miles per gallon on the highway. Flooring it to escape the police . . . not that much.

Ambrose was screaming at one of his computer nerds. "How big of a tank does that type of Mercedes hold?" He swore, then bellowed. "And why didn't anyone think to look where Maddox's bullets had hit?" He unleashed a fury of profanity, kicked a stone in his way, and shouted, "Didn't any one of you so-called investigators smell gasoline?"

The shooter hadn't gassed up in Basin Creek. No one had seen him, at least. Few people passing through gassed up in Basin Creek. Most would get gas in Choteau or someplace with cheaper prices—unless they weren't paying attention to the gas gauge.

"Did you have units on all the roads?" Drew turned toward Ambrose as he asked the question.

A tech screamed. "Seventeen-point-four gallons, sir. EPA eighteen city, twenty—"

Ambrose's curses drowned out the highway mileage. "We were so certain the shooter would not have stopped this close to the crime scene." He swore again and slammed his right fist into his left palm. "And those dirt roads are just too tough for that kind of car."

The highway was, as usual, lacking any traffic. Ashton Maddox turned onto the shoulder and headed north for a few miles, then saw the dirt two-track and crossed the pavement. The bay's hooves clopped hard, found the dirt road, and he rode toward the forest of wind turbines that ruined his view every night.

Most people reached Garland Foster's ranch headquarters from the east side by way of Crimson Feather off Montana 76, but it was faster by horseback. It would take Maddox through the pastures cattle and sheep shared with those god-awful monsters of technology. It would also be where he'd find the wintergreen-tobacco-chewing Harry Sweet.

Ashton should feel exhausted. A long day yesterday, then firing shots at a cop-killing fiend in a German car. Well, the deputy wasn't dead yet, maybe thanks to him, but he didn't think a girl like that would survive a bullet to the brain. He'd been questioned over and over by cops about the shooter, the car, what he was doing, where he was going, where he was coming from. Interrogated by everyone except that hard-rock Drew of a county sheriff, who listened and stared, stared and listened, listened and stared.

Incompetent. The men and women of this county were all morons if they thought that was how a peace officer should investigate the shooting of a deputy.

He reined up when he saw the cattle on the northern side of the dirt road. Black cattle. Black Angus. Heifers. USDA ear tags. If there was a Circle M brand on their right hips . . .

He didn't finish the thought and pushed the horse into a lope until he reached the wire trap. After dismounting, he worked the pole and barbed wire until the gate opened, dragged that part of the fence away, and led the bay onto Foster's land. After closing the fence, he led the bay by the reins to the nearest animal chewing her cud and sitting comfortably in a dip, out of the wind and most of the sun.

He swore, called himself stupid. Even Garland Foster wasn't that big of an idiot. This wasn't a Circle M heifer. And that it wasn't branded or tagged shouldn't have surprised Maddox. Foster wasn't a cattleman. He was a millionaire with a bunch of stupid hobbies. Like ranching. And windmilling.

Cursing again for the waste of time, Maddox found the stirrup, and was back in the saddle, spurring the bay up the ridge, heading back to the wire trap when the gelding shied, snorted, and turned northwest. He pulled hard on the reins. And heard the whinny.

The horse snorted, bucked once, but Maddox stopped that

tomfoolery and cursed the bay. The horse pawed the earth with its forefeet and nodded up and down, fighting rein and bit.

Maddox chanced a look and saw the horse a few hundred yards away. "You don't want to play with a Foster horse," he told the bay, and looked again.

It was a saddled horse. But he saw no rider.

He chewed his lower lip, kicked the horse into a trot, and headed for the dark horse, then reined up.

Foster didn't have many hired hands—he didn't need them. He had power companies working on the turbines. He probably drew more from a month's interest from all of his bank accounts than Maddox earned in three good years. But . . . if that was Harry Sweet's horse maybe Sweet had him in the sights of his Winchester. And just because those black heifers weren't branded Circle M did not mean they belonged to Foster.

Ashton reached inside his coat pocket and felt the cold hammer of the snub-nosed .38, which wouldn't do him a lick of good if a Winchester was already aimed at him.

"Don't be stupid," he told himself. "This isn't *Death Valley Days*." He spurred the bay into a lope. But he did not release his grip on the revolver.

The dun snorted, stamped its hooves, reared once. Nervous. Maybe irritated.

Maddox slowed the bay and began singing some Marty Robbins tune as he eased toward the horse. Somehow, the dun settled down just enough for Maddox to get his horse close. The reins dragged the grass. The rotors of the windmill sounded like something from an old sci-fi black-and-white movie. He saw the Boxed S brand. Harry Sweet's horse.

Garland Foster would let a hired hand use his own horses and his own brands. Circle M riders rode Circle M horses. It had been that way as long as there had been a Circle M ranch—because cowboys rode for the brand. Ashton Maddox wasn't about to change that.

He stood in the stirrups and looked across the rolling hills and all those stumps of wind turbines. Nothing.

Cupping one hand over his mouth, he yelled, "Sweet! Harry Sweet!" And got an echo in reply.

You rode here to beat a confession out of Harry Sweet. Now you're acting like you want to save the fool's hide . . . like he got thrown off. Bucked off and started walking back to the ranch. Maddox sat back in the saddle. *Walk twelve, fifteen miles? When Highway 60 is three miles west? Where he could get a ride, eventually . . . to Basin Creek or the rez? And hitchhike to Foster's headquarters? Or call for someone to come pick you up?*

He put his right hand on his thigh, and felt the wadded-up tobacco pouch in his jeans pocket. "Sweet?" he yelled again.

The dun snorted, and moved away ten yards or so.

Whoomph! Whoomph! Whoomph! . . . answered the rotors of the line of wind turbines.

Then he saw something at the base of one of those god-awful monstrosities and loped the distance, stopping the bay when he realized what lay underneath one of those ugly monsters. He swung down, didn't bother to ground-rein or hobble the bay, and jogged the last twenty yards to Harry Sweet.

Stretched out like he was taking a nap. With the top of his head bashed in.

Maddox saw the post that must have been used. He picked it up. Then realizing what he held, he tossed it aside and took several steps back. The bay whinnied.

Harry Sweet was dead. Murdered.

And then, from out of nowhere, a voice drawled, "Well, well, well. Look what I see here."

The accent was Texan.

George Grimes had gotten more than his fifteen seconds of fame, or however long that saying went, with the TV crews, a radio kid, and some snot-nosed reporter from a newspaper in Great Falls. He had hoped someone from the Associated Press would be there, but, well, a part-timer for the cable news shows would be just as good.

He met Elison Dempsey, whose handshake was as feeble as a corpse's. Dempsey suggested they return to town, where they could talk in private, and there wasn't much to do anymore now that the Citizens Action Network and Dempsey had gotten plenty of press.

"I know where your headquarters is," Grimes said. "You go back home. I'll call on you directly. But, well, where am I staying?"

Dempsey grinned. "We have rented you an apartment. Basin Creek Apartments."

What else would a joint be named in that two-bit town?

Grimes made his head nod. Well, he was used to apartments, and the motel he had passed looked about as run-down as most of the buildings he had seen on Front Street. And it did appear to be within walking distance to the Busted Stirrup Bar and that casino, the name of which he had already forgotten.

"Sounds fine." It didn't, but it would have to do. This wasn't El Paso or Austin. It wasn't even Hen Egg or Webb City along the Tex-Mex border.

"The landlady's name is Cindy Kristiansen," Dempsey said. "She's expecting you. What's your brand of liquor? I'll have some sent over. And I'll have something at C.A.N. headquarters, better known as my house." He laughed like he might have thought it was funny.

"I drink what I'm given," Grimes said. "As long as it's Jack."

The idiot politician—*no, that's redundant*—wanted to say more, but George Grimes wanted to get away. He had worked many times with county sheriffs and cattlemen's associations in Texas. Finding rustlers was one thing. But a cop-killer—the girl had to be dead by now—was something different.

A Montana murder solved by a one-time big-time Texas Ranger? That would get him back inside *Time*. Would've been on the cover had those terrorists blown up whatever it was that time.

Dempsey kept spouting out words, but Grimes had quit listening. The cops were now all in a rage about a gas tank being punctured. It would take them awhile to get a plan in action. That's why George Grimes had liked being a Texas Ranger. Like the saying went, *One riot, one Ranger*. He climbed into the pickup, cranked it up, backed onto the pavement, and took off north.

The first dirt road on the left had a gate. Locked or unlocked, a man who had just shot a cop wouldn't have wanted to monkey with a gate. And from the looks of those mountains off to the left, that wasn't a road you took a Mercedes coupe down. The cops back at the crime scene had been talking about some cutoff to Crimson Feather, which sounded like the title of a bad 1950s B Western. That would be obvious.

The cutoff, according to the Montana map Grimes had, was a couple of miles up the road on the right. But the next road that headed east, well, that's where Grimes turned. He put the truck into four-wheel drive, and bounded along, saw a good-sized elk bounding across the lane in front of him and wondered when he had last tasted elk stew.

This road wasn't on the map. It might be a dead-end. But when it curved northeast, Grimes felt better. Then he saw the pathetic excuse of a trailer home. And parked in front of it—or in back of it, since an overgrown driveway led down from another dirt road that had to be the Crimson Feather Cutoff—was a dust covered Mercedes coupe.

"Bingo." He grabbed the Colt, fetched the bolt-action, telescoped .300 Winchester Magnum from behind the seat, and walked cautiously to the coupe. It didn't fit in front of the rancid shell of a trailer home. Perhaps a meth lab. Or crack. Something like that. But no one had been living there for years.

No one who had just shot a cop would have tried hiding in that trailer, either.

Grimes didn't bother wasting time checking the Mercedes. He knew he was on the right trail, and those dimwit Montana cops would eventually stumble their way to it soon enough. He had to hurry if he was going to get to hog some headlines.

Grimes walked to the road. He saw footsteps. Since they led to the pasture across the dirt road, he moved cautiously. Knelt by a post and looked at all those blessed wind turbines. He saw a horse. Saddled. No rider. And then he saw a man on a horse. Riding.

Now what are the chances of me sneaking up on that owlhoot? Pretty good, he thought.

That fool wasn't paying attention to anything but that turbine. Grimes cursed. He should have thought to bring binoculars. But the man had his horse running fast. Right to the closest turbine.

It didn't make complete sense. Actually it didn't make sense at all. That cop-shooter should be miles away. Grimes had put his hand on the hood of the Mercedes, and it was colder than cans of Lone Star beer at the Homestead Bar back home.

Dropping to his belly, Grimes took off his hat and eased it carefully underneath the barbed wire. He hated getting the Resistol dirty. It had set him back three hundred bucks. Then rifle in both hands, he belly-crawled beneath the lowest strand of wire, then came up to his knees slowly. He put the cowboy hat back on his head, and rose into a crouch.

Watching, he decided the man wasn't much of a hunter.

Grimes shoved the Colt into the back of his jeans as the Winchester was all he needed. Keeping the man and horse in sight, mostly the horse, he started half jogging his way behind and around the man on the horse. The horse might signal

Grimes's presence. But that would be all right. From that distance, a scoped Winchester would beat a fool ninety-nine times out of a hundred.

Seven minutes later, he saw the unmoving figure of a man stretched out underneath the turbine. The man who had ridden over pitched something to the ground. That man looked excited. The fellow on the ground looked like a corpse. The living man's horse didn't like being around a dead man.

Grimes slipped off the safety of the .300 and brought it to his shoulder. *Here come the headlines again,* he thought.

And yelled, "Well, well, well. Look what I see here."

When the man turned around, Grimes got a clear view of his head and upper chest in the scope of his rifle. "Hands up," he called out. "I'm arrestin' you for suspicion of murder as a duly appointed officer of the Citizens Action Committee . . . I mean . . . *Network.*"

1891

July

CHAPTER 16

Napoleon Drew pushed himself away from the desk and rubbed his eyes. No one had warned him that being a county sheriff, even in a small county like Cutthroat, required so much bookkeeping and papers to sign. Thirty-four years old and he was about to become the first Drew to have to find an eye doctor to fit him with a pair of spectacles, though his grandfather sure could have used some, as well as his father, the last few years of their lives.

And Napoleon had only had that chunk of tin on his lapel for a month or thereabouts.

After rubbing his eyes, he looked across the room, trying to focus on the WANTED posters tacked on the wall. The cabin door opened, and he swung around as the Widow Claudia Jenks stuck her head inside.

Napoleon glanced at the clock. By thunder, it was pushing three-thirty. He had been doing bookkeeping and stuff since before eleven. Slowly, he rose and looked at the prim, proper, and pompous old biddy. He expected she had some complaint about the Hangman's Saloon and Gambling Emporium. Or maybe she had some complaints about the rowdy behavior of some of the locals during the celebration last week of the country's founding. Then he could direct her to the town marshal and remind her, once more, that his jurisdiction was for the county, not Basin Creek's town limits.

"Missus Jenks," he said. "What can I do for you?"

"Sheriff." She struggled with the summer wind to control the door she held open.

"Yes, ma'am." Napoleon waited.

"You should head over to your place."

He waited for more.

"It's a disgrace. Just a disgrace."

His place probably was. He had buried a wife a month ago. His three kids had no mother to keep them under control. He was going blind with paperwork. And there was no school during the summer, but usually Miss Lois DeForrest watched over Eugene, Parker, and Mary Ellen.

Then he tensed. The grippe had been making its rounds across Cutthroat County. Leviticus Stern had been suffering so much, he had put a bullet through his brain two weeks back.

"What is it?" Napoleon managed to ask.

"Basin Creek's finest." She pushed the door back open and stepped outside. "At their ugliest." She did not even nod a goodbye, merely moved back, and shut the door.

After a slug of the last few ounces of cold, black coffee in the tin cup, Napoleon stood and walked to the coatrack. Buckled on the gun belt with the Remington, pulled on his black Prince Albert and hat, and stepped into the afternoon light. He could hear kids playing, some laughter coming from the Swede's Saloon, saw Seabrook about to enter the gambling den, and a farm wagon heading out of Basin Creek.

Turning, he walked to his cabin.

It was his own fault, Napoleon told himself. He had told Eugene that, being the oldest, he would have to take care of his kid brother and baby sister while his pa was working, but if he needed any help, he should run over to the seamstress's house. Miss Lois would be able to help him or tell him what he should do. Eugene wasn't yet ten years old. And Parker and Mary Ellen could be a handful.

Yet when he saw the town's finest ladies standing, all righteous and proper, across the street, Napoleon Drew understood it was not about Eugene. Or his other two children. The canopy-top surrey parked in front of the Drew cabin, with that matched set of blood bays, slurping up water from the water trough, told Napoleon all he needed to know.

The driver of the rig, the Negro with the French name Napoleon never could pronounce, sat on the stool he always carried with him. Sitting down, just reading a book. A big book, one of those with the hard covers, but not a book of law or records he had on the shelves of his office.

You didn't see that surrey out on weekdays—according to the calendar in Drew's office it was a Tuesday.

Sarah Doolittle would usually take her girls for a ride on Sunday afternoons, parasols in their hands despite the fancy top with the tassels and gold trim on the rig. Dressed resplendently in their best Sunday-go-to-meetings—though women in that profession never went to meetings. They usually went south to the swimming hole, or once in a while for an all-day journey up to Hoary Marmot Creek and back, where the girls would dare one another to cross that rickety old bridge.

Well, that's what Napoleon had heard anyway. He tipped his hat to the ladies, and turned up the path to the cabin.

The Negro looked up, smiled, and said, *"Bonjour, monsieur le policier."*

"Yeah." He hardly gave the man a glance and reached for the door.

"Vous trouverez tout le monde derrière votre château, monsieur."

Napoleon turned back to the . . . what was it that he called himself? A *chauffeur*?

"You will find them in the back." The man grinned those big white teeth and went back to his book.

Napoleon glanced inside anyway. Well, the table and the floors were clean. Then he heard the laughter and something else from behind the cabin.

He looked across the street, where two new women were joining the confab. Sighing heavily, he walked to the corner and turned. At least he got away from those probing, disapproving eyes of the town's *best* women.

He saw Mary Ellen in a tub, giggling and laughing, and Sarah Doolittle, not dressed in her finest silk and lace, but a worn canvas skirt and calico blouse, sleeves rolled up, a bonnet on her head. Suds clung to her arm as his three-year-old daughter splashed and laughed.

"Pa!"

Eugene bounded toward him, hair wet, barefooted, but wearing duck pants and a pullover shirt. He tossed the towel he had been rubbing over his hair to Parker. The six-year-old, also shining brightly from a good summer scrubbing, stuck one corner of the towel into his mouth and pretended the towel was some kind of musical horn.

"She made us take baths, Pa." Eugene slid to a stop. "She made us take baths. I wasn't even halfway dirty. Had a bath Saturday a week ago, I reckon. But she said we was taking a bath today. But it was fun, Pa. It was a fun bath. Ain't never had no fun bath before."

"Fun bath." Parker had removed the towel. He nodded eagerly. "I went first. 'Cause I was the cleanest."

"Was not!" Eugene turned and glared.

"Was too! Miss Sarah!"

"Boys." Sarah Doolittle just worked on scrubbing Mary Ellen's lathered hair. "We do not shout, remember."

"We got all our chores done, Pa," Eugene said. "Before the bath. Done it ourselves."

"Did not." Parker pointed at the tub. "She helped."

"I be including her when I said ourselves," Eugene protested.

"'*I was* including her,'" Sarah Doolittle corrected. "Not 'I be.'"

"Yes." Eugene stretched out the word in a long sigh.

"Yes what?" Sarah demanded.

"Yes, Miss Doolittle."

"Stand up," she ordered the young girl.

Mary Ellen grabbed the rim of the wooden tub, pulled herself up,and faked a shiver.

"Close your eyes and hold your nose." Then the woman who ran Basin Creek's brothel picked up a small bucket and dumped water over Napoleon's daughter, who shrieked and jumped up and down in the tub of sudsy water, yelling, "That's sooooooo c-c-c-c-cold."

Sarah Doolittle pitched the bucket onto the grass, reached down and scooped the naked girl out of the tub, set her on the grass, and ordered, "Then run around to dry off and put your clothes on." She looked at Parker and Eugene. "And you boys get back inside and open your Readers. I'll be inside in just a jiffy."

Napoleon stared in wonder as the kids did exactly as they were told. Not a peep. Not a scowl.

"We gotta study, Papa," Parker said as he hurried to the back door.

When the door closed, Napoleon looked back at Sarah, who was lowering the sleeves of her blouse.

"Would you like a bath, Napoleon King Drew?" she said with a delightfully wicked gleam in her green eyes.

"I had a bath," he told her. "Sunday morning."

"Too bad."

He nodded toward the street. "There appears to be some women who might want to take a bath."

Sarah Doolittle turned. Of course, she couldn't see through a log cabin, but she had to know. "I don't guess they're talking about Guillaume and my fancy rig."

"I didn't ask them."

She laughed. "Why not?"

He shrugged. "They can't vote."

"Yet," she added and winked.

He smiled.

"You asked Lois if she could watch over your kids till you could find a scullery maid," she said. "And usually that maid turned out to be Lois DeForrest. Today it turned out to be me. Because Lois asked me. If you are worried about an election in four years, I think you are safe, Sheriff Drew."

The election would be next year, but Drew didn't correct her. He liked hearing her voice.

"You might think about Lois DeForrest's good name instead of your own. If those fine, upstanding pillars of Basin Creek society learn that Lois knows me, even talks to me, the only work she'll get is sewing buttons on cowboy's shirts or darning their socks. I'll bid you good day, Sheriff. Tell your kids that school is out for the day. It's summer anyway. Summer isn't for school. It's for kids to be kids."

He watched her vanish on the other side of the cabin.

"Guillaume," he heard her shout, "we are going home."

A few moments later, he heard, "You'll find a bowl of stew on the stove. I imagine you can heat it up for supper yourself. Or maybe one of these fine, Christian ladies will be happy to do that for you, Sheriff Drew!"

He took off his hat, scratched his head, and tried to figure out what he had said to have riled Sarah Doolittle up so. Before he gave up, he slowly walked to the door and went inside. He didn't see any need in going back to the office and messing with all that adding and subtracting. He'd help the boys with their Readers, and point out the pictures to Mary Ellen.

That's what he was doing when Town Marshal Brent Garfield knocked on the front door.

The lawman spun his hat around by the brim with his hands, and wiped his boots on the old horse blanket that served as a mat. He backed up and nodded. "Napoleon, hate to bother you at home and all, but, well, Coulee King rode in a bit ago looking for you. He didn't think to come over here, so he found me in my office. But not before he stopped at the Swede's for a few bracers."

Getting drunk at the Swede's place sounded exactly like something that old cowboy would do. He had never come to see Napoleon Drew. Not when Napoleon was leading the vigilantes. Not when he had hired on as a stock detective. And certainly not in the month Napoleon Drew had been sheriff of Cutthroat County. Last week, on the other hand, it being the Fourth of July, Napoleon had gone looking for Coulee King, found him passed out on the porch swing at Sarah Doolittle's fancy house, and carted him back to the stone jail.

Napoleon waited, but all the marshal did was spin that hat around.

"And?"

The marshal just swallowed.

"Where's King now?"

"With the buckboard. At the Swede's. I figured I ought to fetch you."

"Why?"

"Well, Coulee brung in Billy John Hollister with him." He stopped messing with the hat and looked Napoleon straight in the eyes. "He's dead, Napoleon. Shot right through the middle."

Pushing away from the desk, Napoleon cut off the curse forming on his tongue and asked a question instead. "Did Coulee tell anyone other than you about Hollister?"

Garfield looked flabbergasted, and Napoleon knew it was a question he hadn't needed to ask.

"He told everybody at the Swede's." The marshal nodded in the direction of the saloon. "Reckon everyone's outside now, making sure nobody bothers Hollister's body till you get there."

A Tuesday afternoon. In early July. Most cowboys would be working, gathering a herd to trail to Fort Benton. But he needed to be sure. "Nobody from the Circle M was at the Swede's, was there?"

"Nah."

Napoleon stood, grabbed his hat, and found his gun belt. He was feeling somewhat easier until Garfield added more.

"But Homer Chesterfield ran to the livery to get Luke Jasper to saddle a horse for him so he could lope off to let Mr. Maddox know one of his cowboys has been murdered."

CHAPTER 17

She took the phaeton into Basin Creek that afternoon, planning to drop off three yards of moiré silk along with some taffeta and a bit of canvas at Lois DeForrest's cabin. Jeannie Ashton knew that Lois could make a right pretty and comfortable skirt.

Well, Jeannie could have done that herself. But it was a good excuse . . . and she could see how those children of Napoleon Drew were faring.

Yet well before she reached the cabins of Drew and Lois, she knew something was amiss in Basin Creek. But then, as she had often quipped, when was anything not amiss in Basin Creek?

She heard the shouts over the hooves and that squeaking left rear wheel she should have oiled before leaving her place. She saw Drew's three kids standing on the street corner, looking toward the main part of town, and Lois DeForrest behind them, her arms on the shoulders of Drew's pretty little girl.

The middle kid, Parker, turned toward the noise of that loud wheel, tilted his head, but did not wave. He didn't even smile. He had to recognize her. She had taken those kids, and sometimes Napoleon, on a buggy ride for a picnic at the swimming hole or just up and down the road to see some of the prettiest places on God's green earth.

Lois turned back. Her face looked sour, but she released her hold on Mary Ellen, stepped away from the children, and moved toward the phaeton, which Jeannie reined in. The squeaking stopped.

"What's going on?" Jeannie asked with urgency.

"What's going on?" Lois DeForrest was in one of those moods. Repeating the question. Then firing out the answer. "Mike McIlhaney. That's what's going on. He's spouting fire and brimstone against Napoleon. Trying to work folks into a frenzy. Of course, he's doing it when Napoleon isn't around. And look at that?" She pointed, almost spit in the street, and flattened her lips.

Jeannie made out the crowd in front of the sheriff's office but couldn't hear the voice of the man speaking due to a mix of cheers and jeers. She couldn't see the Swede's Saloon, but had to guess the owner of that establishment was happy. It was Tuesday. Nothing happened in Basin Creek on Tuesdays. Nothing happened in Basin Creek on most days, which was one reason Jeannie had never moved off somewhere else. *One* reason. Three reasons on top of the hill looking down on her home kept her there. Three reasons silenced till Judgment Day. And maybe a couple of other reasons, too.

One in town.

One at the Circle M ranch.

"Murdo?" Jeannie asked.

"No." The seamstress looked back at Jeannie. "He's not in town. Not yet, anyway. But he will be."

Eugene looked away from the crowd. His face was pale, but his ears were reddening in anger.

Someone was shouting into one of those horns. Like anyone needed to amplify their voice in a town the size of Basin Creek. She couldn't tell who was talking, but it could have been McIlhaney.

"My cattle. Your cattle. Your neighbor's cattle. The ranchers who put beef on your supper plates. Their cattle has been stolen. Rustled. You had a man for county sheriff, a good law-and-order man. A man whose name has meant honesty . . . integrity . . ."

"Drunkenness . . . depravity . . . obscenities," the seamstress whispered.

". . . and law and order. But the governor put a man-killer, a hangman, a cold-blooded rattlesnake into the sheriff's office. Napoleon Drew—the most despicable in a long line of deplorable Drews."

"They're talkin' 'bout Pa!" Eugene railed.

Jeannie drew in a breath. She was going to try to calm the nine-year-old down, but Lois DeForrest was faster in responding.

"Eugene, people have talked about your father lots and lots of time. You know that. And your father knows that. And what does your father always tell you?"

The kid pouted. Held his breath and shoved his balled fists behind his back.

The speaker went on. "But what kind of law? What kind of order. He guns down a man whose last name will always be in the history books as a founding father of what once was Montana Territory and is now the state of Montana!"

Mon-ta-na echoed as the crowd applauded and cheered.

As Eugene looked at the little boots on his feet, maybe Jeannie heard a few boos, then asked him, "What did your father tell you?"

"That people gots a right to talk all they want," Eugene said, barely loud enough for Jeannie and Lois to hear. "That sheriffs ain't never been popular with ever'one at the same time no time in history."

The megaphone must have been lowered. The noise turned muffled again.

"And?" Lois prodded.

The boy frowned. Parker jumped forth and yelled the

answer. "And words haven't hurt any Drew in two hundred years."

"Maybe more," Mary Ellen said, giggled, and jumped up and down.

Children sure can be precious, Jeannie thought.

"You Drews," Lois said, putting hands on her hips. "Here it is a perfect July afternoon, and you're standing around doing nothing but listening to a bunch of ignorant men and maybe a woman or two talk about things they don't even know nothing about. If I were you and your age, I wouldn't be pouting or listening to words you can hardly make out. And wouldn't—or shouldn't—be able to understand even if you heard them and had a Webster's handy. Go play. Go play. Play now because summer will be over soon and you'll be back in school listening to that boring schoolmaster. And before you know it, you'll be all growed up with nothing to do but get older and worn out. Go on. *Play*."

"Let's play hide and seek!" Mary Ellen tottered off toward Lois's cabin.

Parker ran off after her. Eugene frowned, kicked a stone, and followed, though his heart wasn't in it.

Jeannie climbed down from the wagon and walked to Lois.

"Now I know why I never married and had children," Lois said. She gasped, brought her right hand over her mouth. Her face blanched. "I'm so sorry, Jeannie."

"It's all right, Lois. It's all right." Jeannie put her arms around Lois and smiled. "Thing is . . . those are good kids." *So were mine. But you can't bring back the dead.*

Lois tried to giggle. So did Jeannie. But the laugh died after a raucous shout from Napoleon Drew's office.

"One of Murdo's cowhands was bushwhacked," Lois said.

Jeannie's heart skipped and she caught her breath.

"That jackass McIlhaney is forming a vigilance committee."

Mike McIlhaney had settled outside of Basin Creek three

or four years back. Started out as a small rancher, then started buying out homesteaders who'd learned that growing wheat in that area wasn't always possible. Fools had learned quickly it was downright impossible to make a living on a hundred and sixty acres. And small ranchers who gave up trying to compete against Murdo Maddox and the Circle M. Some folks looked at McIlhaney as a visionary who would take newly formed Cutthroat County to greatness. Most figured him to be another glory-hunting, power-hungry fool who would learn a lesson about that part of Montana Territory.

Push a Maddox, be prepared to be pushed harder. *Pushed down.* And most men who were pushed down by a Maddox, well, they found themselves six feet under and not getting up.

Jeannie tried to sound confident. "Napoleon has been hearing that kind of thing since he got talked into running for sheriff. Vigilantes have long been out of favor . . . since the gold-camp days ended and after those messy range wars."

The gold-camp troubles, in places like Alder Gulch near old Virginia City and Last Chance Gulch, where the territorial capital of Helena now sat, had been before Jeannie's time in Montana—and almost before she was born. She just heard the stories of those awful days of Montana—then part of Idaho Territory—while the Civil War was raging in the South and East. Men being hanged for suspicion of crimes. Even a sheriff named Plummer had been accused of heading a gang of cutthroats. He wound up swinging, too, all at the order of a so-called Vigilance Committee.

That was old history. So was the Committee of Safety's rule in Helena in the latter part of the 1860s.

But Jeannie certainly remembered cattleman Granville Stuart's activities with "Stuart's Stranglers" along the Musselshell not ten years ago. Cattlemen had formed stock associations and when they got no satisfaction from the law, they became the law. Became lawmen. Judges. Jurors. Executioners, too. Stock detectives had been hired, many of them already outside of the law themselves. They hanged men. They shot men. They burned homes and barns. Maybe twenty alone were killed in 1884.

Artie Ashton was one of the few who had escaped. He had come in to the ramshackle shack of a home and showed her the note he had found tacked to the lean-to: *3-7-77*

The origins of that message were uncertain. When Jeannie had mentioned it casually to Napoleon Drew, he had said it might have come from the Freemasons. He wasn't a Freemason, but had heard they had three officers in a lodge, seven members were needed for a quorum, but no one had ever explained what seventy-seven meant. The year somebody died maybe? Anyway, the only vigilantes he remembered were along Basin Creek, and those just handed men they disliked what was called a *white affidavit*. No numbers. No letters. Just a blank sheet of paper.

Those sent many a suspected thief or no-account riding south, north, east, or west at a high lope who weren't seen around those parts ever again.

"Come to think on it," Napoleon had said with a wicked smile, "those that stuck around weren't ever seen again, either."

Murdo Maddox, on the other hand, sounded as though he spoke with authority. He'd told her 3-7-77 were the measurements of a grave. "Three feet wide, seven feet deep, seventy-seven inches long."

Jeannie had never bothered measuring any grave, especially not Artie's up on the hill overlooking her home. She shook away thoughts of the past and realized the mob had quieted.

"Yes." Lois was talking again. "Yes, Napoleon has."

Jeannie had to think back to what she had said before she had drifted into memories.

"But now McIlhaney has hired Lat Carson."

Her knees almost gave out. You didn't forget that name,

not if you'd met Lat Carson. He had ridden up to the cabin north of the Musselshell back in '84. Jeannie, newly married, had stepped outside, expecting to find Artie unsaddling his horse, maybe showing off a deer he had killed. She could remember it all as if it had happened yesterday.

She stared into the almost colorless eyes and the gaunt face of a man suffering from consumption and shaded by a flat-brimmed black hat. She gasped. Couldn't stop herself. She even had to grab the frame of the door to keep from falling.

Which caused Lat Carson to laugh. Though she knew not his name at that time.

"Thanks for the kind welcome, Missus Ashton."

"I—" She lost the ability to speak English.

"Is your husband around, ma'am?"

"No." Wrong answer. *Artie had warned her more than once about that. "Yes. He's—" But lying had never been something she could master.*

The man, more corpse than alive, laughed, and stifled a cough.

"Which is it, ma'am? Have no fear in your answer. I seek neither pleasure nor displeasure from you. Just the truth."

"He's just over the hill," she said, and pointed to the farthest rise.

He nodded, and gathered the reins. "But a lie will work just as well, Missus Ashton." He tipped his hat again. "I'll take my leave. Just tell your good husband that Lat Carson of the Southeastern Montana Stockgrowers Association came by to pay him a visit." He eased the horse away from the shanty and turned it northeast—the opposite of where Jeannie had pointed. "But I'll see him some other time." His back was to her as he rode off.

"Maybe he'll see me." He gave another cold, emotionless laugh. "Or maybe he won't."

She heard his last words, and sunk to her knees.

When Artie returned, they packed what little they had—even left the milch cow—crossed the Musselshell, and hardly stopped until they reached Butte, where Artie went to work for a mine. He wouldn't try working for himself, on his own land again until he heard about the fine, good country up north at a settlement called Basin Creek.

"Where's Napoleon?" Jeannie's voice came out as a whisper.

"He rode out."

Jeannie breathed easier.

"The man who found the body brought it here. Napoleon gave him seven kinds of grief for that, but the man was Coulee King, and he didn't know any better. He had the body of a Circle M rider." Lois paused and tested the name. "Hollister?"

Jeannie shook her head. She didn't recognize the name. Murdo Maddox rarely mentioned one of his hired men by name.

"So now that the marshal is gone, McIlhaney is talking about the need for new law and order. He's forming a vigilance committee."

That actually made Jeannie feel more comfortable. "He's been talking about that for months."

"But no one was dead then."

That chilled Jeannie. Lois DeForrest had been in this settlement longer than Jeannie had.

"That new newspaperman, whose blood is probably blacker than his ink and his soul, is fueling things, too. That's what they're doing right now. You should have read what Batts put in this week's newspaper—if you'd call it a newspaper."

Jeannie waited.

"He wrote on the front page that McIlhaney needs to stop talking and start acting." Lois shook her head and sighed. "And before you drove up, I heard him say McIlhaney is acting now. Doing great things to bring law and order to Cutthroat County. They're calling the vigilance committee 3-7-77." She shook her head again.

A horse's snort turned Jeannie's head to the phaeton. She ought to get the horses some water, but then she saw a rider on a pale horse, easing down the road. Lois turned around, too. Both women stared.

Lois shielded her eyes. "I don't recognize him or the horse."

Jeannie didn't know the horse, but even at that distance, just the way the man rode, how he sat in the saddle, she knew him. She could never forget him. He had not changed much since that time on the Musselshell.

The horse walked slowly. The man looked like death. But those eyes, those dead eyes, were like that of a rattlesnake.

He rode easily, then reined up, and tipped his hat. A black hat with a flat brim. That pale face. The dead eyes. Lat Carson nodded, studying both women for barely a second but taking in everything about them.

"Ladies," he said with a cold, calculated smile.

The thunder of applause from the sheriff's office took his attention from Jeannie and Lois for just a moment. He smiled again, wet his cracked, thin lips with his tongue, and turned back to the two women in front of the phaeton. "I was going to ask you for directions, but that question is no longer necessary." He nodded toward the crowd. "I bid you—" His eyes had been on Lois. Now they turned back to Jeannie.

Resolve left her, and she stepped back.

"Have we met before, ma'am?" Lat Carson asked.

She could not answer.

"I have a gift for faces. But I cannot place yours." He shook his head. "That is a shame. I would treasure any memory of a face like yours." Quickly, those dead eyes shot over to Lois. "Which is not to say you're not a fine figure of a woman with a most lovely face yourself, ma'am."

His horse started ahead, then stopped.

"But let me leave you to your conversations and such. My business lies ahead. I hear my name already carried by the wind—and some big wind blowers." He laughed. "The name's Carson, ladies. Lat Carson. I'm the new stock detective for these here parts."

His horse walked slowly.

Lois DeForrest did not speak until she was certain he was out of earshot. And that did not happen until he neared Napoleon Drew's office.

Judge Van Gaskin, who Jeannie had not heard till that moment, yelled, "Folks. Here's our savior. Lat Carson." And the crowd showed approval with a bellowing roar.

Lois coughed. "That man . . . he looks like he's dead."

Jeannie swallowed. Her voice was barely audible over the cheers from the crowd. "He's not dead." Her next two words were practically inaudible. *"He's Death."*

The crowd noise even drew Eugene, Parker, and Mary Ellen back to the street. They had abandoned their game to see what the fuss was about.

Chapter 18

Murdo Maddox stopped the big black in front of the barn, dropped from the saddle, and handed the reins to the stable boy. A Mexican. You didn't find many Mexicans that far north, but Juanito was all right. Savvied English, though he rarely spoke much in any language. He had been with the Circle M for six months, and some folks said the kid was bucking for the record.

"Circle M stable boys," ranch foreman Deke Weems was fond of saying, "come and go these days like tumbleweeds."

Weems was old enough to remember back when no one had ever heard of tumbleweeds, before those stupid Russian immigrants planted all that Russian thistle across the country and ruined a lot of good grassland.

Murdo called out to the Mexican. "Put that saddle and bridle on a fresh mount, boy. I'll be riding back out as soon as I talk to—" He stopped and turned to the chimes of spurs.

Deke Weems and Ben Penny were walking toward him from the bunkhouse.

Weems. That was fine. The foreman was supposed to be there with Juanito and the cook. But Penny? Every man drawing a dollar a day—Weems and the cook got a hundred bucks a month—was expected to earn that pay. It was roundup time. They had a herd to get to Fort Benton. Beef, Maddox had heard, was drawing forty bucks a head, and he wanted to get this herd to the railhead before more cattlemen got to Benton and drove those prices down.

They stopped a few feet in front of him.

"What are you doing here?" Murdo asked Penny, not even attempting to hide the irritation in his voice. Irritation? No, it was full-fledged anger.

"Come huntin' for you, Mr. Maddox."

"Well, you found me." He was about to tell the lazy oaf to pack his gear and start walking to town. Maybe he could spend the rest of the summer swamping the Swede's Saloon or forking hay at Finnian O'Boyle's livery stable since Penny was about as worthless as Luke Jasper.

"It's Billy Joe Hollister, Mr. Maddox," the cowboy said. "He's been kilt."

Murdo let that sink in. He turned to Weems for confirmation, but the foreman just busied himself rolling a smoke.

"Homer Chesterfield rode all the way from Basin Creek to where we're holding the gather," Penny said. "He expected to find you there. His horse was played out and he ain't much of a rider nohow, so Kent Canary told me to get on my hoss and put the spurs to him and find you. I—"

"What was Hollister doing in town?" Murdo interrupted, knowing the cowhand would spend the rest of the afternoon telling him about his ride.

Penny blinked. He opened his mouth and tried to answer the question.

"Wasn't in town, Murdo." Weems struck a match against the buckle on his gun belt, and lighted his cigarette. He pitched the match to the ground, stepped on it for good measure, took one drag, withdrew the cigarette, and exhaled.

"Chesterfield said Coulee King brought the body into Basin Creek this afternoon," Penny explained. "Shot ten times. Maybe more. Deader than a mackerel."

Like Homer Chesterfield had ever seen a mackerel, alive or dead.

"Gunned down—"

Murdo raised his hand, and Penny knew better than to utter another word unless he was ordered to continue or asked a question.

"Shot ten times," Murdo said. "Is that what Coulee King said? Or what Homer Chesterfield said? Or what you said?"

The cowhand looked as though he had been struck dumb. He wet his lips. "Chesterfield said it. Something like it anyway. I think he got it straight from Coulee."

"I'm not sure I'd believe it from either of you." Murdo remembered his grandfather telling him never go off half-cocked. Murdo also remembered that he was not his dead cousin.

He looked at Deke Weems. "Billy Joe was . . . ?" He didn't need to finish the question.

"Dropping sulfur on Sacagawea Pasture."

A lot of cattlemen were doing that these days, usually in fall or winter, but Murdo Maddox kept boxes out in the pastures year-round. It had started off as a way to keep lice off the cattle's hides, but some ranchers had learned it also kept the animals healthy overall.

Murdo had seen his share of sick cattle over the years and knew healthy, fat-looking beef brought a better price at the railhead in Fort Benton. Murdo added six quarts of salt to each pound of sulfur, which wasn't unusual. He also added a peck of wood ash to the concoction.

"I don't think anyone in these parts would gun down a cowboy to steal a sulfur-salt mix," Murdo said.

"Ain't likely." Deke Weems blew white smoke into the air. "And that boy didn't have no enemies we know of."

Ben Penny just shrugged his shoulders.

Juanito was bringing a fresh horse, saddled and ready, out of the barn. Seeing him, Murdo said, "But the cattle we're rounding up for the drive to Benton . . . that's a long way from Sacagawea Pasture."

Even riding hard, the sun was starting to dip behind the Always Winter's tallest peaks by the time they reached Sacagawea Pasture. Murdo Maddox spotted the smoke rising from a small fire before Ben Penny or Deke Weems saw it.

Once they slowed their mounts to a trot, Penny started to pull his Winchester from the scabbard, but Murdo stopped him with a curse. "I don't think the men that killed Hollister would be sticking around to invite us to some jackrabbit for supper."

The cowhand shoved the carbine back into the leather.

They let their horses fall to a walk and covered the last fifty or sixty yards slowly, stopping when they could smell wood smoke. Whoever it was, he had picked a good spot for supper. A little coulee would protect him from the wind, and a handful of scrub trees were sprouting. Not much wood to burn, but there were plenty of cow chips. Chips dropped by Circle M beef.

Well, he wasn't cooking steaks on that fire. That was certain. Wasn't cooking anything.

"No rabbit, I reckon," Deke Weems said, and slowly pulled out the makings from a vest pocket.

Murdo did not grin. He cupped one hand on the side of his mouth and called out, "Hello the camp!"

They waited.

"Come on in, Maddox," was the soft reply.

"Who is it?" Ben Penny whispered.

Murdo knew, but he didn't answer. He just cursed again and kicked the horse into a walk.

Once he dipped into the coulee, he saw the man squatting by a fire. The horse had been unsaddled and hobbled. One horse. One man, who slowly stood from the fire and nodded.

"Any of you boys bring coffee with you?" Cutthroat County Sheriff Napoleon Drew asked.

Weems and Penny glanced at their boss.

"No." Murdo did not wait to be invited to light down and chat. He swung to the ground, tugged the reins, and let the horse follow him. His two hired men did the same.

"Then I guess it's just cold biscuits and creek water for supper." Drew shifted the cup to his left hand, and casually hooked his right thumb in his gun belt. Casual but cautious and professional. His right hand was just an inch or two from the holstered Remington revolver.

Those Drews. They were always suspicious of everyone.

Murdo knew it. When he was ten yards away, he stopped, nodded at Penny, and held out his reins. "Take all three mounts to the spring"—he pointed—"just behind those little trees. Let them drink their fill. Then picket them and let them eat."

"I didn't think to bring no grain, Mr. Maddox," the hired man said as he took the reins.

"In case you haven't figure it out, horses eat grass, too. That's all injun horses ever ate."

Embarrassed at the rebuke, Penny managed to nod and took the reins. He led his horse and Murdo's toward Deke Weems, who handed the reins to his horse to Penny and finished smoking his cigarette.

Murdo called out to the oaf of a cowboy. "Then bring them back and picket them near that swayback the law rides in Basin Creek."

Murdo walked toward the lawman, who'd ignored the comment about his horse. Murdo knew it was a right solid looking gelding, but a Circle M rider was dead. And Murdo's dander was up. "You expect to find the man who murdered Billy Joe Hollister warming yourself by the fire?" It was a pointless question to ask. And it left Murdo open for some sarcastic response.

But the man who had killed Murdo's cousin a month ago

shook his head . . . then pointed at the saddlebags lying next to his bedroll. "Some biscuits are in a cotton sack in the bag with the busted buckle. You boys help yourselves. I had my supper while waiting for you to get here."

Murdo ignored the saddlebags, but spurs told him Deke Weems was hungry. And Murdo knew that no-account Ben Penny would fill his belly, too, as soon as he had finished with the horses.

"Well"—Murdo sighed—"what have you learned about my man's murder?"

"Nothing." Drew squatted. "I don't even know where the boy got shot."

Drew glared. "I think a man shot ten times would leave enough blood to find out."

Maddox looked up and smiled. "Ten times?" He turned and looked at Ben Penny as he unsaddled the horses. Then he turned to stare up at Murdo. "I don't recognize that rider."

"His name's Penny." Deke Weems walked over holding a biscuit in his left hand. "Ben Penny. Hired on for the roundup."

Drew said, "I haven't seen any Circle M beef here. You're gathering beeves?"

"On the graze near Dead Indian Pony Creek." Weems uncorked his canteen to wash down the biscuit, but he left the crumbs on his mustache.

"So how'd Penny know Hollister got killed?"

Murdo answered. "Homer Chesterfield." He knew as gabby as Ben Penny and Deke Weems were, they would have told the lawman the life stories of Hollister, themselves, and all the cowhands working for Murdo.

Drew nodded. "Figures." He pulled a cigar from his vest pocket. "Well Coulee King found the body, not Homer. Brought the poor kid into Basin Creek this afternoon. And he wasn't shot ten times. Just once." He tapped the center of his chest. "All King could recall was that he found the body at Sacagawea Pasture. By the time I got to him, he was so roostered I couldn't get much out of him. And this is a big pasture. I figured I'd just wait."

"You can't solve a murder just waiting." Again, Murdo tensed. He was letting that slow-talking lawman get to him. Provoking him with just short answers. Playing with him. One day, Napoleon Drew would push Maddox too far. And they would be burying another sheriff in the county.

Calmly, Drew said, "I'm not going to go riding around in the dark. Even after the moon rises. I figured I'd sit here, wait till daylight. Seeing as you are here, maybe you can show me where the boy was working. Then we can find where he got killed. Figure this out the way Helena likes things to be done these days. Not running down the nearest strangers and shooting them dead or hanging them. Not like the way our pas done things. Right, Murdo?"

"By then, the boy's killer . . . or killers . . . could be almost in Canada."

"That's a fact. What was the boy doing?"

Murdo hesitated, then answered, "Putting out a sulfur-salt mix."

"Wagon?"

He nodded. "Buckboard."

"Working alone?"

Another nod.

"I haven't seen a buckboard."

"Like you said, it's a big pasture."

"Yeah. Always has been." Drew turned and looked off to the north." His head nodded once, and he pushed up the brim of his hat. "Guess that's why I didn't see any Circle M cattle . . . or anyone else's brand, either."

Murdo looked over what he could see in the remaining light.

Ben Penny was walking back from the horses and the spring. "I can circle around a bit," the cowboy suggested. "See if I can find—"

"No." Drew didn't even look over toward Penny. His eyes stayed right on Murdo. "Like I said, nobody's riding or walking anywhere till daylight."

Murdo kept staring east and north, but it was too dark to make out any Black Angus from a boulder or hillock or anything.

"Come morning, we'll see what we can find. About your cattle that ought to be here. And about that rider who got himself killed."

Ben Penny looked at Murdo, but the rancher did not take his eyes off the lawman.

"Hobble those horses, boy," Deke Weems told him. "Then come get one of these biscuits. The sheriff, he's a right good cook."

Drew laughed. "No, he ain't. But he knows a lady who's plumb crackerjack in a kitchen."

Murdo's hands balled into fists. He would beat the tar out of that smart-talking law dog. Just the way Maddoxes had been thrashing Drews since the beginning of the century.

But the lawman stilled Murdo's jealousy. "Miss Lois DeForrest sews buttons on my shirts and patches my britches, too." He drank from the canteen. "Come morning, we'll find some sign and figure out what exactly went down here."

Murdo walked toward the lawman and looked down. "You never were much of a hand at following a trail."

"You ain't, either." Drew capped his canteen and smiled. "That's why I asked Miles Seabrook to light a shuck north and bring back Keme."

Deke Weems put a biscuit in Murdo's left hand, and the rancher stared at it for a moment, then squatted in front of Drew and nodded. "Keme. Well, that's all right then."

1842

SPRING

CHAPTER 19

The trip had practically worn out Benjamin Franklin Drew and the breed boy. Well, it had aged Ben considerable, but now that he could see those big mountains to the northwest, he kicked the mostly black with some white pinto into a faster walk. Never knew what got into old Eb. Well, maybe he had. Ebenezer Maddox saw things clearer than Ben. Always had. That's why Eb had quit with trapping beaver all winter and fall, then getting drunk seven days or as long as the rendezvous lasted.

Good times then.

Now all gone.

Smoke drifted out of the cabin. Eb's cabin. And that hide man hadn't forgotten everything. Ben saw horses in the corral and a couple of teepees. He let out a laugh that would have frightened a silver-tip griz.

"I told you, Eb!" He looked back at the pup of a son he had. "I told him. Told Eb, I did. I said ain't nobody gonna come to live in this always winter land. No, sir. Nobody except Siksikaitsitapi and Shoshones. And crazy cusses like me and him." He waved the boy forward. "C'mon, Cody. Time you met your elders and your betters."

The boy seemed in no hurry. Pulling a string of mules and horses. Like that ought to slow a sixteen-year-old down. "By jiminy, boy, you keep a-tarryin' like this and it'll take us another year just to reach Eb's tradin' post."

The kid gave the lead rope a yank, but that was about all the effort he had in him.

Well, that was youth in the year of whatever it was. Boys like that—and Eb's son, from how Ben recollected—just didn't have the grit. But then, it wasn't like either Ezekiel or Cody had much of an upbringing. Maybe Zeke had it better, his ma being white, though she had been captured by the Siksikaitsitapi, as the Blackfoot-Speaking Real People called themselves. Most white folks called them Blackfoot, though Ben and Eb, back in the day, had figured themselves to be more Siksikaitsitapi than white after living so long with the Siksikaitsitapi and other Niitsitapi, the Real People—meaning all Indian tribes. Eb had to throw in a load of prime beaver pelts to get that gal, but he'd said she sure was worth it.

"Kick that pony, boy!" Ben shouted. He didn't wait to see what Cody did. He kicked his own horse, felt the wind in his hair and beard, felt like he was twenty years old again, and not the old fifty-whatever he was.

The horse galloped, and he prodded it to run even faster, slapping the barrel of his old Hawken's rifle against the horse's rump. He rode right up to the cabin and slid the pinto to a stop, yelling, "C'mon out, Eb, and see your better, you weak-livered, sorry skinflint of a store-tender. Come on out. See if I can't still out-wrassle you till you beg for your mammie. Come on out, boy, or I'll come in and drag you out like I done before Capt'ns Clark and Lewis all those years ago."

The door creaked open, and by then Ben was off the pinto, raising his Hawken over his head with both hands, laughing, and feeling prime again.

The smile faded when a slim boy in duck pants, muslin shirt, the sleeves held up with red garters, stepped out of the cabin. The face was tan, the hair sandy, the eyes blue. But he didn't sport any hair on his face.

Well, when a body minds a store, I guess he's gotta have a supply of razors. And it must be all right to try out the wares you're selling to make sure no customers accuse you of peddling sorry merchandise.

"Yeah," was all the kid said.

Ben had to think. How long had it been? "Yeah?" He lowered the Hawken. It felt a lot heavier these days than it had been when he and Eb had started trapping after leaving Lewis and Clark and setting out on their own with other independent cusses like John Colter.

"I'm Drew. Benjamin Franklin Drew. You ain't—"

"Ezekiel," the boy said. He saw Cody bringing the horses and mules.

Ben grinned. "Zeke. Boy, you've done shot up—"

"Ezekiel. Not Zeke."

The frown hurt Ben's lips. But he knew what would cure that. "Where's your pa, boy? I got stories to tell him and I got the rest of my life to hear his. I'm done with trappin'. Well, by glory, all us free trappers are done with that life."

There was hardly a beaver left to trap anyway. But more than that, folks had stopped paying prime dollar for beaver. Silk. Silk. Silk hats? Ben couldn't figure that out if he had fifty-five more years left in him. Which he sure didn't have. The rendezvous was a thing of the past. But Ben had a vision. He had always had visions. And he needed a solid thinker like ol' Eb to help him out.

"Where is he, boy? If he's drunk, I'll join him. If he's passed out, I can follow him right down that trail just like that time—"

"He's dead."

* * *

The chunk of granite marked the graves. A good ride from the teepees and cabin that served as the trading post Eb had said would bring folks to that far country.

But it hadn't happened. At least not yet.

Ben swung down from the pinto, and wrapped the hackamore around another rock. He heard his son dismount and walked closer to the granite, then knelt before it, looking at the letters. He wasn't sure how long he stared, but eventually he remembered he still wore the fur-skin cap, and he yanked it off. It smelled ripe.

No, the hat didn't stink. It was Ben who was ripe.

"Pardon me, Miss Linda."

Miss Linda. That's what Eb had named his wife. She had been living with the Niitsitapi for so long, she had forgotten her white name. Eb never said how he thought up *Linda*. Ben always thought she looked more like a Mary. But, well, she was Eb's wife. Not Ben's. Ben had married a Shoshone gal of a Siksikaitsitapi holy man.

He heard moccasins behind him, and pointed at the grave. "Reckon you don't remember Miss Linda, do you?"

"A little."

Ben sighed.

The boy stepped forward, then knelt closer to the granite. His right arm stretched, and his fingers rubbed the stone. "Those markings are her name?"

Ben felt ashamed. Some father he had turned out to be. Eb's boy was a wizard at figures and letters. His own kid was—He sighed. "Them ain't letters, Cody. They's numbers." The boy turned to look, and Ben tilted his head. "Well, that first thing to your left, that's a letter. It's a *D*. That means *Dead*. Or *Died*. Died 1839."

Cody grunted.

"Above that. That's her name. *L-I-N-D-A*." Ben let out a long sigh. "Died in 1839." His head shook. Three years ago. He had been gone three years. Zeke—*Ezekiel*—had told him his father, Ebenezer, hadn't lasted but six months after the spotted death took away Miss Linda.

Ben pointed at the stone. "Them other words and numbers. They spells out Eb's name. Ebenezer." He spelled it as though Cody had ever heard of the alphabet. Ben would have to fix that. Somehow. Though the thought of taking that half wild—by thunder, he was full wild—wilder than Shoshones and Lakotas, Cheyennes and those wild Siksikaitsitapi men and women, wilder than a she-griz whose cubs was being threatened. Just *wild*.

Wild like Ben. Wild like Eb used to be.

He walked on his knees closer to the stone, and put his hand over Ebenezer's name. "Died 1840."

Cody sighed. "Ever'thing I knowed died that year."

Ben sat down, pulled out his pipe, and nodded at that chunk. "I was comin' back to tell you all about the rendezvous, Eb. Ol' Bridger was there. You remember Jim, I know. No mountain man alive ever forgot that ol' kid. We all met in the Green River Valley. Same place as we done in '33. Now that one was prime, for sure. You was the smart one, Eb. Like always. A black robe named De Smet come with the caravan Jim led with Drips and that other feller with the funny last name. Never could pronounce it. F-something. Criminy, not more'n three years, and I can't remember a man's name. I'm getting as old as you was."

He looked at the numbers below his partner's name. "I am older than you was. By thunder, always thought you was older than me. You sure acted like an old fart." He laughed, sighed, and quickly brushed away a tear before the kid saw it.

"There was a woman and kids, too. Headin' to the Oregon country to . . . farm. I reckon I could have tol' 'em fools to forget about Oregon and come up north with me. Could've brung you some business. Though I don't know that this place is fit for farmin'. Who do you trade with anyhow? Other than red injuns."

He laughed again and shook his head. "Remember when we first saw this valley? This country? We and them Shoshones come up to get them hosses back the Siksikaitsitapi had stole from Capt'ns Clark and Lewis. You said this was the most beautiful land you'd ever seen. Said it was as perty as Miss Linda. And decided that's what you'd call it. Linda's Land. Linda's Land."

His chin dropped to his chest. "I guess it's her land now. She's part of the land. So are you, pardner. So are you. Linda's Land. That's right pretty. Poetic."

He looked at his son. "Don't you reckon it is, Cody?"

The boy's black eyes looked into Ben's own.

Ben chuckled. "No. You don't know about poems and such. Words. Gotta fix that, boy. You need yourself an education. Or you'll wind up like me."

He sighed once more. "Taken me three years to get from the Green River to Linda's Land."

Ebenezer Maddox was the one who'd kept bringing Benjamin Franklin Drew back to this country. Eb had pointed out the mountains, mountains that had snow on their peaks year round. "Those mountains are always winter," he had said, and the name eventually began to stick. Those mountains, the smaller range off to the east, the ones the Siksikaitsitapi called Ponoká, meaning Elk, helped turn this place into a bowl, a man named Irving had said.

"Must be a broken bowl," Ben had said then, pointing and laughing. "'Cause there ain't no sides that way nor that."

"Let's call this place Broken Bowl!" Jim Bridger had chimed in. But that name didn't take.

Somehow, *Basin Creek* did. That creek sometimes flooded but always had good water, clean water, fresh water, reviving water, and the place became known as Basin Creek—even though it really wasn't a basin.

Bridger and Ben had bet old Eb two jugs of trader's whiskey no one would ever call the place Basin Creek because white men weren't that stupid. And Indians were plenty smarter than white men. They had named the smaller range of mountains after elk, because elk lived in those mountains.

Ben smiled at his old pal's grave. *You usually was right, pardner. Never was much of a mapmaker, though. And folks will be cussin' you seven ways from Sunday if this name you give this right pretty country ever really sticks.*

Ben tried to stand, but couldn't. He had been on the back of that pinto for too long. "Well, Eb," he said, nodding at the granite and smiling again. "Couldn't get three dollars for a pelt. Remember when we got almost six back when we met at the Green that year? Whenever it was." He reached up, found the top of the stone, and used that to pull himself to his feet.

"I reckon the beavers won't be sad to see the likes of us go. Reckon they'll be happy as a pig in clover. See you in the morn, pard. See you in the morn."

Then he heard the horses. He glanced at his Hawken, saw the rider coming slowly, and told himself he was getting old and deaf. Cody reached for his knife.

"Easy," Ben whispered.

The rider was young. Siksikaitsitapi. Around Cody's age. He held out his right hand in a sign of peace, but Ben remembered when those red devils were anything but peaceable. Still, Ben raised his own hand and called out his name and Cody's name. He said he had lived with the Siksikaitsitapi for many seasons and it was always good to see one of the Blackfoot-Speaking Real People, especially when their numbers were not what they had been.

Smallpox, mostly, and other white man diseases, had done what flintlocks and Hawken rifles couldn't do.

"I know who you are," the rider said in guttural English.

Ben tilted his head and stared.

The Indian kicked the horse into a slow walk, reining up a few yards in front of Ben and his son. "I am called Keme."

"Keme." Ben mouthed the name, then smiled. "You have grown, son. Grown to be the spittin' image of your father." He cleared his throat and spoke to the young Indian in his own tongue.

The kid nodded.

"How is your father?" Ben asked, this time in English.

Keme's head shook. "Gone under. The rotting face. Four summers ago."

Rotting face. Smallpox. Ben shook his head. "He lived a good life."

"Yes," Keme said.

"How did you know I was here?"

The boy smiled.

Boy? No, he was a man. Lean, strong, and he had the scalps of his enemies hanging on his buckskin sleeves. The smile was Keme's only answer, and Ben needed no other explanation.

He remembered Ebenezer always telling him, "You can't keep secrets from them injuns. They know this land because it was—still is—their land. They know every rock and blade of glass. And they know when someone is in their country. Someone who belongs. And them that don't."

We belong, Ben told himself. Then he frowned. *We once belonged. But now . . . ?* "We should talk," he suggested. "Tell stories. You have much to tell me. I can't say I got a lot that would interest you." And he thought: *I never should have left Eb.*

"I would like that."

"You look like your daddy." Ben corrected himself, and used the Siksikaitsitapi name for father. "Come on. We'll talk at the post your pa helped me and Eb build."

"No." The word barked like a Hawken rifle. "Not there," Keme said quieter. "You come to the stream where you killed the Indian pony. We will talk there. I do not go to the white-eye post. Where they serve my people the evil water that turns them mean, foolish, useless." He spoke in the tongue of the Siksikaitsitapi, then added in English, "Pathetic."

"In two moons," he said. "At the stream where you killed the Indian pony. Bring the one who looks like you." He meant Cody. He turned the horse and rode away.

They watched Keme disappear.

"That's—?" Cody started.

"The son of the finest injun I ever knowed," Ben said, turning to his son. "If he's half the man his pa was, he'd rank up there with ol' Eb. But I got a feelin', he's gonna be a better man than his pa was." He put his hand on Cody's shoulder and squeezed. "Just like I know you'll stand taller and righter and better than I ever could."

Cody's eyes turned cold, but not at the compliment. "And Ezekiel?" he asked without trying to hide the bitterness.

Ben just sighed.

Cody helped him back to the horse, but Ben got into the saddle on his own. They rode back to the cabin and the teepees, and that's when Ben read the name carved into the wood above the door.

MADDOX TRADING POST
SACAGAWEA'S PASTURE

Two Indians walked out of the post, jugs in their hands, their eyes already glassy from the liquor they had consumed. The shorter one could hardly walk a straight line as they tried to get to their horses grazing by the corral.

Ezekiel stepped outside, smiling until he realized the two horses he'd heard carried not more Indians needing liquor but a worthless old mountain man and his half-breed kid.

"Pay your respects to my ma and pa?" the boy said.

"Yes, boy, I did." Ben did not look down from the words. "You done a fine job on that chunk of rock. Names and all. When they died."

"My blacksmith did that," Ezekiel said.

Ben nodded, though he really had not heard what the boy said.

He pointed at the sign. "What's that supposed to mean?"

The kid had to step out and turn around. He shook his head as though he was exasperated and spit between his teeth. "It says Maddox Trading Post."

"I can read, boy." Ben felt his neck warming, and it wasn't that hot of a day. It never got too hot in that part of the world.

"Well, you gave up your rights to having a stake in this business a long time ago, Pops. Remember? You laughed at my father when he said he was going to make something out of this country. Bring people to his country."

"That!" The word came out like the roar of the Hawken. Ben's finger shook at the sign, and he heard a horse stutter-step. Out of the corner of his eye, he caught Cody moving closer to him. The boy probably thought he was about to keel over from bad whiskey. He hadn't had but two snorts that morning.

"Not the post. I never wanted the post and told your pa so. I ain't fit to be indoors. I'm a free trapper." His right arm shot out and the finger trembled from rage. "Sacagawea Pasture? I ain't never heard of nothin' sillier than that."

"It's the name of this place."

He looked at the boy as though he were daft. "Your pa called this Linda's Land. After your ma."

"I know that. And what did it bring here?" He pointed at the two drunken Indians trying to mount their pintos. "Do you see anybody here? Other than me. And you. And them!"

Ezekiel's shout caused one of the Indian's horses to bolt off to the south. The drunk staggered after it, while the other, cackling and shouting guttural words at his pal, took the hackamore to his skewbald and followed.

He started singing a song, mocking the kid, but that ended when he heard what the son of Ebenezer Maddox, maybe the finest man—a man with vision, courage, and manners—Ben Drew had ever known, was saying.

"People talk about Sacagawea, old man," Ezekiel said. "They talk about Lewis and Clark. They write about them. I figured if I ever want to get out of this hellhole, Sacagawea will be my ticket. So this land is now being called Sacagawea's Pasture."

"Pasture?" Ben figured a laugh would work better on that louse than a curse or fist. "Pasture? What's that grass gonna feed, boy? Horses maybe. Pigs? Goats?"

"Maybe," the boy said, showing he could be just as sassy and prickly as that old mountain man pal of his dead father's.

"Buffalo." Ben laughed. "There be enough of them in this country."

"But pasture isn't what I'm selling, old man. I'm selling Sacagawea. And in time, that'll work. That'll get me back to St. Louis. And from there, wherever I want."

Ben looked back at his horse, then at his son, his blank-faced, dark-eyed son cursed with bad luck to have a fool trapper for a dad and a wild mama with red skin. "Boy, I don't know what got into you. But you ain't your dad's son."

"No," the kid said. "I'm not my dad's son. All I got is his name. Maddox. But I'll make that name mean something in this country. Mark my words."

DAY TWO

Thursday

CHAPTER 20

Billy Drew was beat. He had never been much of a coffee drinker, and hated soft drinks, so he had loaded up on Red Bulls. As fast as he had pushed the old Nissan Frontier, how he had made it that far without wrecking or getting a speeding ticket was nothing short of a miracle. He patted the steering wheel and whispered his thanks to his old junker. "You ain't too old, are you, Trickster?"

He laughed. Punch drunk, not enough sleep, and way too much adrenaline. "Got up to ninety-seven miles per hour."

Of course, his dad would throw a fit. It was an eleven-hour drive from Laramie to Basin Creek, and he had done it in . . . ? He glanced at his wristwatch. Yeah, his dad would kill him.

He had even lied to his old man about spending the night in Billings. When he had called his dad to let him know he was coming home, he'd already been on the road, calling him from a gas station. He had even lied about talking to his professor about missing the last two weeks of summer classes, but he had emailed that old fart, said he had a family emergency. The prof knew his dad was a sheriff in Montana, and likely would see the news and give Billy a break. Besides, he had an 89 average in the course.

But that part about not being needed for the wooden-bat summer college league? That was plain gospel. He had not mentioned his .125 batting average or his pickoff throw to first that went almost to the right-field wall and let two runs score for Fort Collins. That had led to fans yelling, "Go . . . home . . . Number Thirty-four! Go . . . home . . . Number Thirty-four . . . ! Go . . . home . . . Number Thirty-four!"

Well, he was heading home. Just to make sure his dad was all right. And that Mary Broadbent, sweet woman and good cop, would recover. *A bullet to her head.*

There hadn't been a shooting in Basin Creek in more than a year, and that had been a couple of drunken poachers arguing over who had shot an elk out of season. And the last time a law-enforcement officer had been wounded on duty? He couldn't even recall.

Billy shuddered. Found the can of Red Bull and made himself drink it.

Once he gassed up and emptied his bladder at Choteau, he slowed down to five miles over the speed limit. When he kept seeing patrol cars, he decided to keep his speed right at the speed limit. A Channel 16 News van raced by him.

He let off the gas a little more when he realized he was approaching US Highway 103. He would be in Cutthroat County once he passed it. But he always remembered it was where his mother had died. In that stupid car wreck. He closed his eyes just for a moment. At least, that was his plan. Then his eyes jerked open and he sawed the wheel, getting back into his lane. Luckily, no one was traveling toward him or following him.

Cursing himself, he waited for his heart to stop racing and his breathing to return to normal. That's the last thing his dad needed. Lose a wife . . . then lose a stupid son in a car wreck just miles from where the boy's mother had been killed.

Red Bull and real Cokes weren't all they were cut out to be for keeping folks awake. But then . . . driving a fifteen-year-old Japanese pickup wasn't the same as driving a Fiat or

Jaguar for as many hours he had been flying across two states. He tried to shake the cobwebs from his head.

The speedometer said 65. It felt slower than Christmas after racing up Interstate 25 and across I-90.

He thought about stopping to splash water over his face, but decided he didn't want to stop. Not that close to Basin Creek. He shut his eyes tight, just to clear them, opened them, and sighed. Just ahead, pulled off onto a dirt road that led to a ranch pasture was a Ford Mustang, hazards flashing, trunk open, and a young brunette standing in the right lane waving her hands over her head.

The last thing I need.

Billy flashed the lights and eased into the passing lane. No one was coming south.

The young woman waved her hands harder.

He hit the horn—hated the way it sounded in the old wreck—and waved his left hand, urging her to get out of the road. Fool kid. She'd get herself killed. She just waved harder.

His father's voice came to him. *"To serve and protect."*

"Crap." Billy let off the gas, and pressed the brake and clutch, downshifting and moving back into the right lane, slowing down and stopping just past the Mustang, seeing the flat left rear tire.

She was rounding the bed of the truck when he stepped out of the car. He heard her say, "Thank you, thank you, thank—" Then she stopped.

Billy shook the sleep out of his head and said, "Yeah, yeah, ye—" And he swore.

"Oh," she said.

He said something else. Something common among twenty-year-old college athletes and men in general.

"It's you," said Alyson Maddox.

"Yeah." Billy looked at the ripped tire. "It's me."

He hadn't seen her in years. She'd been two, no three,

years ahead of him in school. Stuck up was the way he remembered her. And, well, being a Maddox didn't help any. But he had forgotten just how attractive she was.

"My tire blew out." She nodded at the obvious.

"Yeah."

"I don't have a spare." Her head shook. She looked as if she had been driving for a while. "I mean. I have a spare. But it's flat."

"You should've checked before you hit the road."

"It's a rental," she told him. "You'd think . . ." She frowned.

"I thought you were living in Denver."

Her head tilted. "I am." That came out pleasant, but when she added, "That's why I'm driving a rental car," the sarcasm was apparent.

Aly must have realized she needed Billy's help as soon as she finished the rebuke. She wet her lips. "I flew to Great Falls from DIA." Then she tried a different tactic. "How's your father doing?"

Billy shrugged. "Holding up. And yours?"

"The same."

He nodded. "Guess your dad's a hero."

She acted as though she had not heard. "How's that deputy? Mary . . . ?"

"Broadbent." Billy gave another shrug. "Last I heard, she was still in critical condition." After a long pause, he asked, "Do you have AAA? I need to get to Basin Creek."

"Well so do I," she snapped. "And even if I had AAA, it would take forever for a tow truck to get here." She sighed and shook her head. "A family coming down from Glacier stopped. They said they'd let someone know in Choteau. That was thirty minutes ago. A van flew by—I think it was with a news outlet—and didn't even slow down."

He nodded. He remembered that van.

"And it's not like anyone has even one measly bar for Wi-Fi in this place."

Billy stared at the flat tire.

"Joyce Moore said you were playing baseball somewhere."

Joyce had been in Billy's class. He heard she had dropped out of college during COVID and gotten married to some jerk in one of the Denver suburbs. But he thought Aly Maddox was working at the airport. He couldn't recall her job.

"University of Wyoming," he finally answered. Looking north up the highway, then back down, he realized he was stuck. Just like Aly Maddox was. He had no other option and managed to nod.

"I guess . . . I guess I can give you a lift to the Wantlands Mercantile. Then I need to find Dad."

"Thank you."

Yeah, thank me. Stupid twit.

A noise down the dirt land commanded his attention. A highway patrol SUV rose out of a dip, headlights on but the emergency lights off. It was caked with dirt, and Billy guessed it had been driving around looking for the man who had shot Mary Broadbent. The car stopped at the fence, the engine died, and the door eventually opened.

Maybe, Billy thought, *I can get out of being a chauffeur for Miss Prissy and find Dad.*

"Good afternoon, Officer," Billy said in as friendly a tone as he could muster.

"Hi!" Aly sounded excited. She probably loathed the idea of having to be rescued by a Drew and then being seen in a wretched old foreign pickup truck driven by a Drew.

The patrolman looked a mess. The hat was crooked. The shirt seemed too big for him, and his pants were not state-issue. But then, he had likely had the day off, got pulled out of bed, and had been driving across ranch roads, or what passed for roads in that part of the state, all day.

The boots weren't state-issue, either.

He walked slowly to the fence, stared at it as though it were out of place, and then carefully found his way between strands of barbed wire. Obviously, no one had ever taught him how to open a wire trap, either, but then, that was a skill some working cowboys struggled to master.

"Officer, I flew in to Great Falls, rented this car, and the tire went flat. I don't know. I guess I might have run over a nail or something, maybe when I stopped in Vaughan for coffee. But the spare is flat, too."

A semi slowed down, heading south, and everyone looked as it passed. Hauling cattle. The trooper stared north for a long while, while Aly bit her bottom lip and waited, her right shoe tapping the dirt impatiently, until he turned around.

The wind blew with a surprising chill.

The cop's sunglasses were ill-fitting, like his shirt and hat. Billy was about to speak when the cop said, "I need to see your driver's licenses. Both of yours."

He looked at Billy first.

Aly opened her mouth, but quickly closed it. Billy told himself this was routine. A deputy sheriff had been shot and the shooter was still at large.

Aly must have figure that out, too, and she nodded. "It's in my purse in the car."

She started for it, and he let her go, focusing on Billy, who dug his billfold out of his jeans pocket.

My dad would ball you out seven ways from sundown. What if Aly has a gun in the driver's seat? That's a rookie mistake that can get a cop killed. And you're not even wearing a bulletproof vest. Billy tugged his license out and handed it to the trooper.

The trooper's head lowered, and he studied the license. "Drew?" His cold, strange eyes looked above the rims of the sunglasses.

"Yes, sir."

"Any relation to Sheriff Drew?"

"I'm his son."

The man nodded, raised his head, and saw Aly walking over with her purse in her hand.

Billy held his license and waited.

Aly held out her license, and the patrolman took it.

"Maddox. Alyson Maddox. What do you do in Denver?"

"I am an air-traffic controller."

The man's lips almost turned into a smile. "I don't think there are any airports in Cutthroat County."

"Oh, Garland Foster has a helicopter pad I have been told," she said like she was having a regular conversation. "And there might be a private landing. They say there was one, anyway, during Prohibition."

"What brings you to this part of Montana?"

"I am here to see my father."

The man looked at the license.

"Your father?"

"Ashton Maddox. You know. The Circle M?"

Braggart, Billy thought.

"I see." The man's voice sounded as dead as his eyes looked. He handed her the license, and put his hand on the handle of the automatic in the holster as another car passed.

This one slowed down. Rubberneckers. A station wagon heading south.

Billy's eyes stayed on the automatic pistol. That didn't fit, either. Something about this cop was all wrong.

"I need you to open the tailgate of your pickup, boy," the man said.

"It's unlocked."

"I said I need you to open it."

The cop's eyes made Billy shiver. He couldn't stop it.

"Come on, Billy," Aly pleaded. "I want to find my dad. And you probably want to see yours, too. *Pleassssse*," she begged.

He walked to the truck. For Christmas, his dad had gotten

him a really good cover for the Frontier's bed. A premium, hard-folding one with black matte panels and a tailgate seal. It kept his baseball equipment dry during the rain. And snowstorms.

He found the latch, opened the gate, and lowered it, then stepped aside. The trooper bent down and looked in only to find some plastic tarps, a catcher's bag, and a covered bucket of balls. Billy had also thrown in a gym bag with some clothes. And as a native of northwestern Montana, he had two jugs of water, a gallon of antifreeze, emergency lights, and several blankets.

But no shooter of deputies.

The cop nodded, and Billy started to close the gate, but was stopped by the policeman's bark. "Not yet."

He looked at Aly, who was beginning to lose what little patience Maddoxes had. Though he looked at her, his question was for Billy. "Your father's the county sheriff, right?"

"Yes, sir."

"I see." Eyes still on Aly, he said, "And you are the daughter of rancher Ashton Maddox."

Aly sighed, but nodded a confirmation. She had already told the cop that.

"Good." The cop's head turned south. Then north. Then fastened on Alyson.

Billy started to sweat.

The right hand jerked the automatic from the holster. The left snatched the back of Aly's neck and pulled her forward. She started to scream, but stopped when the muzzle of the pistol pressed hard beneath her chin. "If you move, boy," the man who was no state trooper said icily, "I blow her head off."

Billy stopped any and all motion. Except the fear that ran from head to toe.

"Listen to me." The fake cop did not look at Billy or Alyson, but kept his eyes on the northbound road. "Listen to everything I say and you"—he nodded at Billy—"and she"—he nodded at the white-faced Alyson—"will live through this day."

The wind blew as Billy made himself say, "I'm listening."

"The girl and I are getting into the bed. You will lock us inside. Then you will drive past all roadblocks. Everyone knows your dad is the sheriff, right?"

Billy nodded. But he also cautioned, "Everybody in Cutthroat County knows Dad. But there will be troopers and investigators from all over."

"You need to talk your way through it. Tell them the latch is broken. Tell them something. Or just charm your way through the roadblock. By what I heard on the radio, there will be one at the US highway up ahead. And one at where that whore of a cop got her head blown off. By me."

The man looked Billy dead into the eyes. "If someone opens that tailgate, the girl dies. Do you hear me?"

Aly whimpered.

Billy somehow managed to nod his head.

"Say it."

"I hear you."

"And I will shoot you, too, boy. This automatic will punch through your thin Jap tin and cripple if not kill you. Understand?"

"I understand," he heard himself say.

"The Circle M is before where I shot that cop," the killer told him. "You will go to the Circle M."

That made no sense to Billy, but he said, "The Circle M."

He looked at the girl. "How many men will be at the ranch?"

"I . . . I . . . I . . . I'm not . . . sure."

"Guess!"

"By the time we get there, no more than six."

"And your father?"

"You're not going to kill my father are—"

The barrel of the automatic cut off the rest of her protest.

"I will kill whoever I have to. Understand?"

"Yes," Aly whimpered.

"And I will not harm anyone who does what I say."

Billy didn't buy that for a second.

The head turned back to Billy. "Understand?"

Billy's voice cracked when he answered, too.

"We're getting into the bed," the man with the gun said. "You better keep your wits, boy. Or the blood will be on your hands. The girl will die. Many cops will die. I will die. You might survive with just a few bullet holes to remember me by. But the nightmares you will have for the rest of your life will make you wish you had died today, too."

CHAPTER 21

"I didn't kill him." Ashton Maddox kept both hands high above his head.

The man with the big guns just grinned. "I've seen fellas with less evidence than what I got here get that golden needle in Huntsville, pardner." He glanced at Harry Sweet's corpse. "And I bet that even in this hayseed part of the US of A that a mediocre forensics team can put your DNA on that murder weapon."

Sirens wailed up the dirt road.

The man with the guns sighed, and for a moment, Ashton thought the Texan had planned to shoot him dead. Claim self-defense. It sounded like something a rogue Texas Ranger would do.

"You're Grimes," Ashton said.

The man smiled and nodded. "Yep. But that's Ranger Grimes to you." He glanced down the road, then looked at Sweet's body. As his smile faded, he muttered a barnyard curse, shook his head, and turned back to Ashton.

Frowning, he said, "Well, curse my miserable luck." He sighed, cursed again, and sighed once more. He tilted his head toward Harry Sweet's body. "This sucker's been dead for hours."

The first state car came over the rise. A Cutthroat County

SUV followed. Grimes holstered his revolver and spread his hands from his body. "Don't do nothin' foolish. Maybe you ain't lyin'. Maybe you didn't kill this cowpoke. Or maybe you did it yesterday evenin', and come back today to get him hid."

The vehicles stopped.

Sirens still wailed, and dust rose.

The cavalry, Ashton thought, *coming to the rescue. No. That's not right. Coming to wipe out the Indian village. And I'm the Indian.*

Grimes spread his arms farther from his body, but keeping both eyes on Ashton and speaking to the state troopers—and Sheriff John T. Drew. "I'm a retired Texas Ranger," Grimes called, "working for the Citizens Action Network. I apprehended this man near the body of that man yonder. I have a permit to carry. I—"

"I know who you are," Sheriff John T. Drew said. "But why don't you just keep those hands right where they are." It did not come out as a question. "Then you can tell us exactly what happened."

Will Ambrose, a big shot with Montana's Department of Justice—and buddy-buddy with Sheriff Drew—ordered a state trooper to proceed down the road. The car drove past John Drew's Ford and another unit and gunned up the hill, sirens wailing.

Ashton looked at Drew, who stepped under and above strands of barbed wire, then held the top strand up to make it easier for the DCI cop and two troopers.

"Is it all right if I lower my hands?" Ashton asked.

"I think they are good exactly as they are for right now," Drew said. He looked at the Texas Ranger. "Yours, too, at least till we get some questions answered."

The Ranger chuckled. "Well, here's a confession, Wyatt Earp." He nodded to the old wreck of a line shack on the other side of the road. "You want to find that Mercedes that belonged to your cop-killer? Pardners, you'll find it right behind that thing some folks might call a mobile home."

Everyone stopped. Even Ashton looked at the trailer.

After ordering one trooper to investigate, Will Ambrose emphasized, "And don't touch anything!"

Drew seemed torn. After some inner debate, he stepped alongside Ambrose toward Grimes and the rancher. The sheriff took time, however, to stare hard at the Ranger. Mocking the Texan's drawl, he let him know the latest. "The deputy who was shot is still alive, *pardner.*"

Then both cops stared at the body of Harry Sweet.

Ambrose knelt over the corpse. "I'm guessing more than twelve hours. Maybe eighteen."

"I was talking to Harry just before Danny Adams radioed me about Mary." Drew spoke in such a whisper, Ashton could just barely make out the words.

"See anyone else?" Ambrose asked.

The sheriff's head shook. "No one." He cursed and slammed his right fist into the palm of his left hand. "I didn't think to look behind that shack."

"You didn't have any reason to." The DCI man turned back to a trooper standing outside his unit. "Radio Lieutenant Killius. Tell him to call George White in Havre. Tell White he needs to get down here right now. We have a cowboy dead with his head bashed in." White served as Cutthroat County's coroner. "And have him call Murdoch Robeson in Choteau. If the shooting of a sheriff's deputy won't get him up here, maybe a murder of a working cowboy will." Robeson was the county attorney.

John T. Drew stood in front of the Ranger and Ashton, patiently waiting for Will Ambrose to finish reminding his investigators it was a crime scene and protocol needed to be followed. At least, Ashton figured that's why the dumb brick just stood there, not saying a thing. But being a Drew, he probably just liked making Ashton stand in the noonday sun.

He was surprised the SOB hadn't already put handcuffs on him.

When Will Ambrose finally decided he had barked enough orders, he looked hard at Ashton, but Maddoxes were used to being stared at like that. "You want a lawyer?" the cop asked.

The Ranger stared at Will Ambrose like he was the dumbest oaf in the world. What kind of cop asks a suspect if he wants a lawyer? That's the last thing in the world a cop wants—a lawyer to tell the suspect to keep his trap shut.

Ashton answered with a smile. "I don't need a lawyer." Besides, the last thing he wanted was Taisie to see him on Garland Foster's land, being hounded by fifth-rate cops.

"What were you doing here . . . on horseback . . . on Garland Foster's land?" Drew asked.

Ashton had to think. Maybe he should call Taisie. If he could get a signal. Sighing, he reached into his jeans pocket and pulled out the chewing tobacco package. He told the truth, mostly the whole truth, with no embellishments or falsehoods that the law could cite him for later.

The look on Drew's face made Ashton feel better.

"You think Harry Sweet was rustling your cattle?"

"I thought I'd ask him about it."

Drew seemed prepped to fire off another stupid question, but a C.A.N. van appeared over the rise. The sheriff gave Ambrose a worried look, and Ambrose cupped his hands and yelled at a trooper on that end of the lane.

"Keep those men on that side of the fence!" he bellowed, then found the nearest uniform. "Get up there. Those nut jobs don't come near here. If anyone tries, arrest them. This is a crime scene and they're not going to screw this up."

The trooper took off in a sprint.

"Your evidence is slim," Drew pointed out.

"Like I said," Ashton whispered, "I came here to ask Harry about it. Not to kill him."

"And I said," Ranger Grimes drawled, "that maybe he came back to hide the corpse."

"No." To Ashton's shock, John T. Drew shook his head. "Ashton didn't kill Harry. He couldn't have."

The Ranger, the nearest troopers, and Will Ambrose stared at Drew—but none as incredulously as Ashton Maddox himself.

"He couldn't have." Drew repeated, nodding at the corpse. "I got the call from Danny over in Cut Bank near five o'clock yesterday. I was talking to Harry, and when I left, Harry was alive and well and herding some cattle west. We'll see what the coroner says, but when I left, Maddox here was performing CPR on my deputy. He was there being grilled long after Harry was bludgeoned to death." He faced Will Ambrose. "Wouldn't you agree?"

"We'll see what the forensics team says," Ambrose began, "but I'm betting you're right."

Ashton felt the cockiness Taisie loathed in him. "Then maybe you boys can let me get back to my ranch, and maybe you can harass somebody else or maybe you could even try to do your job and find the fellow who stove in this cowhand's head."

"And maybe," Drew said, "we can keep you up all night till we hear what time the coroner decides to say Harry Sweet left this world."

That was a Drew for you. Ashton started to say something to put the sheriff in his place, but just as Ashton's lips parted, a trooper jumped out of his SUV and screamed, "Officer down! Officer down!"

The troopers, even those trying to keep Dempsey's team from crashing the crime scene, turned. The cop, too panicked to use his radio, cupped his hands. "It's Hemby. Lon Hemby!" He pointed up the hill. "Carlson found his body."

Body. Another corpse. Those dumb cops might try to pin that death on me, too. Ashton frowned.

"Where?" Ambrose yelled.

"Four miles up this road."

Ambrose ordered some men to stay with Sweet's body. He told a corporal to radio for backup and crowd control. He told another uniform to get those vigilantes off this road and he didn't care how many heads he had to fracture to complete that assignment.

"Can I get back to my ranch, *Detective*?" Ashton demanded, emphasizing the last word.

"No," the cop said. "You ride with the sheriff." He recalled what he learned in state history about Maddoxes and Drews not really caring much for one another. "No, you ride with me." He nodded at Grimes. "*You* ride with the sheriff."

At least, Will Ambrose let Ashton ride in the front passenger seat. The cop said nothing to him, but talked on the radio about as fast as his unit sped up the road as they followed Sheriff Drew's Interceptor.

After checking his watch, Ashton sighed. At some point, he would probably have to call his ranch, or maybe his attorney, and find a way to arrange for his gelding to be picked up from Foster's pasture and hauled back to the Circle M. He had spent years with hardly any communication with law enforcement, and now it was becoming practically a daily occurrence.

Ambrose let off the gas, slowly pressed down on the brakes, and Ashton saw the flashing lights of the state unit on the north side of the road. The Cutthroat County unit eased around the state car and parked, blocking the road—intentionally—and the Ranger and Drew stepped out.

A uniform stepped out of the other unit, and that's when it struck Ashton. "Where's the dead trooper's car?"

Will Ambrose made no attempt at answering. He eased his SUV as far as he could get off the road and stopped just inches away from the patrol car.

The cop pointed. "Patrolman Hemby's in a coulee over there."

Ashton couldn't see a thing. Just wind turbines.

"How'd you find him?"

The cop's head dropped. "A coyote crossed the road, Detective"—he drew in a breath, held it, and sighed—"carrying Hemby's hat in his mouth." Tears welled, but quickly died as the cop shouted out in disgust: "Like it was some kid's toy!"

"Did you attempt CPR?"

"The top of his head was blown off, sir."

No one spoke for a few minutes. John Drew stepped through the barbed wire and made for the arroyo.

The wind turbines grunted their ugly song.

"Stay here," Ambrose told Ashton, then barked an order at the uniform. "Find out when Hemby last checked in. Get every bit of information on his unit. Then put out an ABP. If anyone gives you a hard time, you tell them if that doesn't go out ASAP they'll think the entire Always Winter range just dropped on their brainless heads. And I want roadblocks at every ranch road, hiking trail, off-road track this road hits."

Cops. Worthless, brainless minions.

Ashton waited at least two hours, sitting in the seat of various police cars, hearing the radio chatter, watching other cops, an ambulance, a white DCI van with a bunch of cops dressed in surgical gowns. And a helicopter hovering overhead. Ashton thought it was a police chopper, but one of the uniforms said it had to be from a news station.

Helena? Great Falls? CNN? The cops guessed.

Ashton tried his cell phone countless times, but he never even saw one bar on the screen. And within an hour, his battery was dead.

Eventually, they let him go. A cop took him back to the Harry Sweet crime scene. Some idiot with a bald head and crooked nose informed him that his horse would be kept overnight. They gave him a receipt. Told him he could pick it up in two or three days. Said not to worry, the gelding would be fed and watered, and that the saddle would be inspected but innocent men had nothing to fear.

This time, a sergeant read him his rights.

He knew the drill. Sign the waiver and maybe they'd let him go home.

The forensics team would be busy trying to find Harry Sweet's blood or DNA on the saddle, maybe fingerprints. Cops were thorough when it came to most murders. Montana, even Cutthroat County, was no exception. Especially when newspapers and TV stations could come up with some screaming headlines about wealthy ranchers and Old West bushwhackings.

Not all the cops were brain-dead buffoons. Some of them remembered him from cable news. Some of them knew he had performed CPR on a sheriff's deputy who had taken a bullet in the head. A few were hearing news a round from his revolver had punctured a gas tank.

That didn't make him many friends, though, when a pal who had graduated from the academy the same year as the late Lon Hemby reminded them that if the cop shooter had not run out of gas, he would not have had to kill Trooper Hemby and steal his unit.

Before five o'clock, a patrolman came up to him and said that Will Ambrose and Sheriff Drew said it was all right. He could go. "But don't make plans to leave Cutthroat County. Understand?"

"How do I get home?" Ashton asked. "Walk?" Like a Maddox would walk anywhere.

"The man running for sheriff." The cop pointed, and Ashton sighed at the very sight of the Citizens Action Network van. "He said he'll take you back to your ranch."

But Elison Dempsey said little, asked few questions.

Maybe he was as tired as Ashton felt. Finally getting a signal, he called the ranch.

Deke Weems was waiting in the F-450 at the road when the van got there. Ashton thanked Dempsey for the ride. Dempsey said they ought to have coffee and talk things over sometime, that Dempsey was on Maddox's side, and he sure would appreciate his vote . . . and maybe an endorsement.

Ashton purposely grunted something unintelligible and closed the van's door. Dempsey pulled away as Ashton walked to the truck.

Weems, who crushed out a cigarette, asked, "Where's your horse?"

"It's a long story, and I'm beat. Just get me home, Deke. I'll tell you everything over breakfast."

They rode together in silence. No news on the radio. Not even Ian Tyson or Willie Nelson music.

He didn't listen to the messages on his phone until after he had showered and after he had finished two healthy pours of Blanton's Single Barrel.

The first message was from Aly. She said she was on her way to the ranch. He frowned. That call was hours old. But Aly had not said where she was or when she might get there. He punched in her number, which rolled straight to voice mail. He left a message, "Call me," and hung up.

He looked at the phone. Looked at the bottle of bourbon. Then found his lawyer's name and hit the telephone icon.

She answered without a hello or her name. "You are one busy man, Ash."

"Can I see you?" he asked.

He heard ice clinking on her end of the line. Then she must have cracked a cube with her teeth—one habit of hers he did not like. But he liked when she did it. It meant she was doing it just to irritate him. She was like no woman he had ever known.

"Want me to drive over?" she asked.

"No, Taisie. I can be over in forty-five minutes." He started to hang up, but remembered his manners. "If that's all right with you."

"I'd love to see you. You know that. But there are all kinds of cops and reporters in town. You wouldn't believe the crowd at the casino—or the bar. All it would take would be for one person to notice your SUV and the camera lights would be about as bright as the blast of a hydrogen bomb."

Ashton Maddox's day just kept getting worse.

"But," she said, "no reporter's going to follow me."

Though most of them would likely make a pass, he thought.

"So I could come over to your place. There's no one watching the gate, is there?"

"There wasn't when I came home." He wasn't sure he liked that idea, though. He didn't have a full crew of hired hands, but—

"Unless you—" She sighed. "I am tired of feeling like a kept woman. Kept secret, I mean."

Cowboys were generally respectful of women, though, Ashton reminded himself. One thing that hadn't changed over a century and a half. Cowboys didn't talk out of turn when it came to women. Proper women, anyway. Every hired hand on the Circle M ranch knew they had better keep their traps shut about certain things if they wanted to stay on the Maddox payroll.

He gave her the gate code.

"Why, Ashton Maddox," she said in that alluring voice that drove him crazy. "I think you might just like me."

"I'll probably be in bed," he said, "by the time you get here."

"Good," he heard her say right before she disconnected.

CHAPTER 22

"Let him go." John T. Drew waited for Will Ambrose to turn around.

His friend stared at him hard, face showing surprise. Drew just waited. He was bone-tired.

"I can't believe you said that, John," Ambrose said.

"You got nothing to hold him on. He was trying to keep Mary Broadbent alive when Sweet got killed."

"Oh."

Drew frowned. He could interpret the *Oh*. *So when a man tries to save your deputy's life—a deputy that, if you believe the gossip making its rounds across Cutthroat County and all the way to the Montana DOJ, a deputy who might be more than a deputy—you cut your archenemy a break.* Still, he just waited.

"Talley," Ambrose called out to some patrolman. "Cut Maddox loose. Just Maddox. But give him that cliché about not making any plans to go anywhere without checking with me . . . or Sheriff Drew . . . first."

"Yes, sir."

Ambrose did not look away from Drew. "You got the lead on Deputy Broadbent's shooting, but I'm taking charge over Lon Hemby. He was a good cop. Twenty-plus years of service."

"We're likely looking for the same man," Drew said.

His cell phone buzzed. He pulled it from his pocket and felt his heart skip when he recognized the number. "I have to take this, Will," he said, and walked toward the bar ditch, away from investigators. He pushed the button, and took hold of the top of a fence post with his free hand. "Missus Broadbent."

She was crying. "John—" The word caught in her throat.

Drew closed his eyes, trying to think of something to say. He couldn't, so he just waited.

"They're taking Mary into surgery, John."

The sigh he released sounded like an engine releasing steam. His left hand let go of the oaken post, and he sucked in another huge breath, then exhaled, quieter this time. Mary was still alive. At least for now.

"How are you holding up?" he asked.

"I . . . don't . . . really know." Mrs. Broadbent choked back another sob. "That little man who's in charge . . . Doctor . . . Doctor . . . Doctor?"

"Haddad."

"Yes. He said that he and that other doctor . . ."

Takahash. No. No, that was the name of another specialist from another hospital back east. The one in Missoula was . . .

He'd lost that name, and said, "Yes," hoping it would stop Mary's mother from trying to think of some surgeon's last name.

She went on. "Well . . . he said her vitals had stabilized enough they thought this would be the best time to remove the bullet. They said . . . they said"—she sniffled some more—"they . . . well, the bullet had shifted a bit. They thought they should get it out now. Because if . . . if . . . if it moved . . . again . . . it . . ."

He heard her crying, then words echoing from an announcement, and muttered voices most likely in the waiting room.

"Here." That was a man's voice, nearby.

Mrs. Broadbent said something.

Static. A man's voice clearing. Then, "John."

"Mr. Broadbent," Drew said.

"Yes. The doctors took Mary into the operating room. They said it would likely be some hours. They said it had to be done. They said . . . they said . . . they said it was their best chance, but . . . but . . . but . . ." He let out a heavy sigh.

Drew heard what Mary's father couldn't say. *But don't get your hopes up.* "Why don't you two get out of the hospital? Get some fresh air."

He just heard Mary's father's heavy breathing.

Drew knew he was giving advice he wouldn't take if it had been him waiting in that medical center. But he also knew a change of scenery, seeing something other than surgical gowns and sick—sometimes dying—strangers, and hearing sirens, code blues, coughs and doctors, nurses, and receptionists speaking jargon only they could understand, would do them a world of good. "Get some fresh air. Maybe go for a walk."

"I can't . . . we can't leave, John."

Drew nodded. "I know."

"What's happening with the investigation?"

Well, there are two dead men, a loner cowboy and a state trooper who should have retired. The shooter of Mary is still at large. And I'm not making sense out of any of this. "We've got the state's top men on this. We're making progress."

"Any idea who shot my baby girl?"

"We know what he looks like. And—"

Will Ambrose and a sergeant were walking toward him.

"Mr. Broadbent." Drew stepped away from the fence. "I have to talk to some investigators. I'll let you know of any developments." He did not wait for the worried-sick dad to answer. "Just keep me updated. I'll try to get down there when I can." He hated to do it, but he disconnected, and dropped the cell phone into his pocket.

"They found Hemby's unit," Ambrose said.

Drew waited.

The sergeant said, "Just south of the county line."

"Let's take your Ford," Ambrose told Drew.

Drew was quiet during the ride. Remembering . . .

"Do you ever worry?" Mary asked.

Drew looked up from the container of Chinese food—takeout from the Chinese joint in Medicine Pass. Jimmie's Chinese. That pretty much said all you needed to know about the state of Chinese food in Cutthroat County. "About what?"

She shrugged. "Getting shot?" She managed a smile, but he could tell she wasn't joking.

"I don't worry. And you shouldn't worry. You just have to be careful." He watched her, amazed at how she could work those chopsticks. He was using a plastic fork. Roundabout, the fat cat, sat patiently, eyes on the food, waiting like a dog for some morsel to fall.

"If you're scared—"

"I'm not scared. Not even worried. I think I'm a good cop."

"You are." He dropped the fork in the noodles.

Her eyes locked onto his. "Did she . . . ?" Those eyes fell onto the plate of egg rolls they'd heated up with her microwave.

"We never really talked about it," he told her. With regret he thought, and I never worried she might get killed in a car wreck.

Somehow he put that behind him, reached for an egg roll, but moved away from it—a good thing, since the egg rolls, even heated, tasted worse than what Jimmie's called Lo Mein.

Drew put his right hand atop hers. "Don't worry about me, either." He squeezed her hand. "I'm a pretty good cop, too."

* * *

Drew eased through the roadblock at the intersection of US Highway 103 and Montana 60 where Denton Creel was assisting, and cruised down no more than a couple of miles to the myriad flashing lights of state patrol units and, of course, two TV vans and the sickening sight of the C.A.N. van. At least the troopers were keeping the Citizens Action Network goons on the other side of the two-lane.

Drew eased the Interceptor slightly off the road and parked behind a state unit. After killing the engine, he stepped outside, moved around the Ford, and joined Ambrose and Sergeant Wally Fields as they walked to a moose-necked patrolman, who made his report to Ambrose.

"No sign of anyone, Lieutenant. Corporal Andreassen . . ."

Drew tuned them out and focused on the unit, which was parked behind a Ford Mustang on a northbound pullout. The trunk was open on the Mustang, and a rear tire was flat. He could make out a sticker on the windshield that told him it was a rental car. "Who rented the Mustang?"

The trooper stopped, turned, and swallowed. It was Ambrose who answered, apparently having just learned that kernel of news a moment ago.

"Alyson Victoria Maddox."

"Of Denver," the thick-necked trooper added.

Drew slowly sighed a barnyard epithet.

A brunette investigator rose from a squat behind the Mustang. "Lieutenant, you might want to look at this. We might have a lead on Hemby's killer. We found a driver's license."

Will Ambrose started toward her, and Drew followed, but the woman stopped, staring at Drew. "I don't think he should see this."

"What kind of crap is this, Rachel?" Ambrose barked. "Maybe this is just outside of Cutthroat County but—"

Her face blushed.

"Go on." Drew didn't care about what a driver's license said, and this was not Cutthroat County, though knowing the sheriff of Teton County, Drew figured any help would have been appreciated. He left the state guys and the woman, and walked to the Mustang.

The tire had blown. That much was obvious. He looked for footprints and saw markings most likely left by a tennis shoe, boot heels that had to have belonged to Ambrose Maddox's daughter, and heavy imprints from the murderer of Officer Hemby. Drew felt like kicking himself. He should have brought Hassun with him. That old man could track anything. But he had asked the Blackfoot elder, with permission from Ambrose, to check out the pasture where Harry Sweet had been murdered.

The sheriff frowned, then looked back to where the investigators were staring at something on the ground, something between the Mustang with the blown tire and the state unit, lights off, engine most likely cold. He moved into the space, but not close to the circle of kneeling cops. He saw tire treads that were too big for the Mustang, and he didn't think those were made by the state vehicle. Not a car. An SUV maybe. Or a van. He looked across the street at the C.A.N. rig. A pickup.

"John."

Drew looked at Ambrose, who waved him over. The woman held the driver's license in her gloved hand. A numbered yellow flag marked where the license had been found. Rachel turned her hand so he could read the Montana driver's license.

The curse spat from his mouth, and his fingers balled into fists. "That stupid—" He had to catch his breath.

And ran that morning's telephone conversation with Billy through his mind. *Dad, I'm coming home. . . . The Rustlers don't need me. . . . I can talk to my professor. . . . Don't argue. I'll stop for the night in Billings.*

Drew swore again. It struck him that he was probably only a mile south of the turnout when he had answered Billy's call. "I'll stop for the night in Billings," Billy had said. It was better than a six-hour drive from Laramie to Billings. And more than five more to get from Billings to there. Considering that ancient truck the boy drove, the math just didn't calculate.

Which meant his son had lied. He had to have been heading up I-25 when he had called.

"MVD," the big trooper said, "says William Drew drives a—"

"Blue Nissan Frontier. 2008." Drew finished the sentence, but didn't recall the plate number. "Black cover over the bed."

The cop cited the license plate. "They must have gone south," he said. "Because of the roadblock up ahead."

Drew swore again, and stormed off toward the Interceptor. He did not wait for Ambrose or anyone else, fired up the engine, and pulled out, sending dust and gravel flying. Burning rubber on the pavement, he hit the lights and siren as he sped to the roadblock at US 103.

He stopped in the road, leaped out of the car, and yelled, "Denton."

Creel was slugging down bottled water. He tossed the empty through the window of his SUV, and hurried over, the other officers staring with curiosity. Drew heard the rumbling of another unit, and figured it was Will Ambrose and whomever. Another vehicle was close behind, and that, he regretted, had to be the Citizens Action Network van. Drew didn't look around.

"Did Billy come through here?" Drew bellowed.

Denton Creel paled, and Drew regretted the outburst.

"Yeah, John," the deputy said, and glanced at his wristwatch. "Thirty, forty minutes ago. I saw him. Just waved him through."

"Anybody with him?"

"No, John. He was alone. Said he had driven all night to get here."

"You didn't ID him, Deputy?" That voice came from behind Drew, and he whirled.

"Who invited you into this conversation?" Drew bellowed.

Elison Dempsey took two steps back. One of the men with the vigilante put his hand on a holstered automatic, and Drew cut loose with more profanity than one would hear on a late-night comedy routine on Showtime.

"Officer." Drew found the closest state cop that hadn't ridden up with Will Ambrose. "Get these men away from this checkpoint. And make sure that one with his hand on that pistol has a permit to carry. *Now!*"

Turning back toward Denton Creel, Drew sighed.

"Did you check the back of the pickup?" Will Ambrose asked in almost a whisper.

Creel's head shook, then spoke softly. "It was Billy, John. He was alone. Said . . ."

A long, heavy silence followed. "It's all right, Denton." Drew wasn't sure how he had managed to get that sentence out.

Because it was a long way from being all right.

A long, long way.

CHAPTER 23

Billy Drew pulled up the emergency brake, kept the Frontier's engine running, and stepped out of the pickup. There was that big Circle M sign and the dirt lane that led down to what all the kids in school used to call Disneyland. He looked up and down Highway 60, but saw just Big Sky country, drew in a deep breath, tried to settle his stomach, and called, "Alyson?"

"What do you want?" That wasn't her voice. It was the homicidal maniac.

"I need the key code to open the gate," he said. He could barely make out the murderer's, "*Tell him*."

She did. He walked to the pad, hit the numbers, and the gate began moving. Billy climbed back into the cab, waiting till the gate had stopped before he drove through. He kept driving, watching in his rearview mirror to make sure the gate closed. As if something a Maddox paid for wouldn't work to perfection.

When the Frontier dipped down a rise, he braked again, shut off the engine, and stepped outside.

"Now what?" the killer demanded.

Billy swallowed. "I'm going to need Alyson up here with me."

A profanity came from the beast's mouth. Followed by a cry from Alyson. Billy tensed.

"You think I'm a fool?"

Billy swallowed. "Mister, if I drive up alone, the cowboys here will send me back to the highway. And not necessarily in one piece."

The killer cursed him.

Alyson whimpered. Maybe she told that psycho that Billy was right. Gave him a quick history of the relationships between the Drews and the Maddoxes.

When a silence stretched for more than ten seconds, Billy explained, "All I have to do is tell whoever checks on me that Alyson's Mustang blew a tire, the spare was flat, and that I happened by. I can do that much. It's the truth. I picked her up. Took her home."

"He's right." Alyson's muffled voice could just be heard through the hard bed cover. "I'll invite him in for coffee."

Billy and Alyson were on the same wave link. "They'll go back to their bunkhouse. You stay here—"

"And you call the cops. I'm not an idiot!" the killer bellowed, adding a few impolite words.

"Mister"—Billy swallowed down bile and fear—"I'm not going to do anything that'll risk Alyson's life." He tried to chuckle, but failed. "Or mine. Or do or say anything that might get a few working cowhands murdered."

He was greeted with the Montana wind, but the killer remained quiet.

"I'll park the truck with the tailgate facing the garage. It'll be easy for me—and Alyson—to come out. Like we're getting her luggage. The boys in the bunkhouse won't pay much attention. They're cowboys. Cowboys aren't curious. They're just hard workers. And this time of day, they just want to drink some beers, watch TV, play cards, and go to bed. They get up before daybreak, mister."

Alyson begged him. The maniac stayed quiet.

"We get you inside." Billy stopped. *And then what? The psycho blows his brains out. No. He wouldn't risk the shot. But he could cut Billy's throat. And Alyson's. And then what?* Billy bit his lip, balled his hands into fists, and shook with rage.

"This was your idea," he heard Alyson tell the murderer. "We wait."

"And your father?" the man asked.

"He won't be home," Alyson said. "It's Thursday. He'll be with . . . that . . . woman."

Billy didn't know what she was talking about. "Mister"—he tried again—"this is your only way out of here. It's a freakin' miracle I got through those roadblocks without—" He cut himself off.

He had dropped his driver's license when he climbed into the Nissan so his dad, or anyone, would know he had been here. Providing some pack rat didn't take the license to its nest. Of course, now he realized how stupid he had been anyway. When he reached the checkpoint and saw Deputy Denton Creel, he could have given the deputy a signal. Written a note as he drove, slipped that to Creel or one of the state troopers. Anything.

Of course, Creel hadn't given Billy time to drop some kind of clue.

"Hey, Billy. I thought you was in Laramie."

"I was, sir."

"I'm glad you're here. It'll do your daddy a heap of good."

Billy had been thinking of some way he could alert Creel of the danger. But the deputy had stepped back and waved him through.

"He's all right, boys. That's the sheriff's son."

Memory gone, Billy exhaled.

"All right, boy," the killer called out. "But if I see anything that annoys me, the girl dies first. And before I die, so will you."

Helping Alyson out of the pickup bed, Billy stared at the muzzle of the automatic pistol in the man's hand. Those eyes were dead.

The killer climbed out of the bed, too, looking around, then smiling. "I have a better idea."

Billy's stomach seesawed.

The automatic's barrel pointed at a two-track that led off the main road to, if Billy's memory was right, an old swimming hole where Basin Creek boys, and sometimes a girl or two, would sneak in for a skinny dip.

Skinny dipping was not on the killer's mind. "Where does that lead?" the madman asked.

"Swimming hole," Aly answered.

He nodded. "Then here's what we shall do. We'll take the truck there till dark. Then we will all drive up to your house."

Billy shook his head. "Mister, the cops are gonna know that Aly's missing. The ranch will be the first place they look."

The man nodded. "And when they find no one there, they will look elsewhere. But if they decide to look at that swimming hole, you die. The girl dies. You will drive the truck there. I will keep the girl with me. I will wipe out the tire tracks. Then we will join you. And wait till dark."

Wait until dark.

Well, Billy thought, *maybe he could get away with Aly, and hide in the dark.* But it had been a long time since he had been at the swimming hole. And—

The motor of a car was sudden. Bringing the automatic up, the killer swore, then shouted at Billy and Aly, "Move and I'll blow you apart. Just stay right where you are." He ducked, hiding in front of the truck.

Again, Billy thought about running. But he couldn't. Not yet. And for a moment, he thought he might throw up. What if that was his father coming over the ridge.

It wasn't.

He didn't recognize the little SUV.

But Aly must have. Because she swore softly.

Taisie Neal saw the pickup pulled off on the side of the path, and slowly braked her Honda to a stop. She didn't recognize the young boy in jeans and tennis shoes, but she knew the girl.

That's why the curse slowly slipped out of her mouth. "Well," she said softly, "it was bound to happen sometime." She shifted into PARK, killed the motor, and stepped out of the CR-V. "Alyson," she said. A lie came to her. "I was bringing some papers for your father to sign."

She killed that thought. And turned to the boy. Her head tilted. She found the resemblance quickly. "You're . . . John Drew's son?"

Her eyes darted back to Alyson, and she shook her head, trying to figure out just what in blazes these two kids were doing here. She glanced at the path that led to the water hole. But they weren't wearing bathing suits.

Skinny dipping? . . . Don't be silly. Or scandalous.

A smile crept across her face. And died there when a horrible-looking man stepped from the front of the truck, and aimed a pistol at her chest.

"Welcome," he said in a voice that chilled her to the marrow of her bones.

They took both vehicles to the edge of the water hole, Miss Neal riding with Billy in the Frontier, and Aly stuck with that cold-blooded SOB in the lawyer's white Honda.

"What's going on?" Taisie asked.

"I think he killed a state trooper." Billy spoke rapidly. "Aly's car blew a tire. I stopped. He showed up. I don't know what's going on. I'm sorry—" His voice cracked.

She thought he might break into tears. "It's all right, Billy. We'll get out of this." She just didn't have a clue as to how that might happen.

Parking as close to the hole as possible, Billy did as he was told. He waited till the killer and Aly had stepped out of his truck.

When Aly and the murderer joined Billy at the edge of the water hole, Billy sighed. The police hadn't showed up yet. Maybe they wouldn't. No, they had to. Unless they realized that lives were in danger.

The killer held out his free hand, and Billy let the keys to the Frontier fall. The man simply tossed those over his head, and Billy heard the splash as the keys met the water hole.

"Lady," the killer told the lawyer, "a nine-millimeter hollow point will punch a big hole in you. If you try anything." He looked at Billy. "If anyone tries anything, all three of you die. Her blood will be on your hands. You understand?"

Billy nodded.

"Say it!"

"I understand."

"Say it again. So I know that you know I mean what I say."

"I understand. Completely."

"*A lot* of people will die. Or no one. It's up to how you play this hand when the time comes."

Billy tried to swallow, but his throat had gone dry.

"I've lived a long life. I know I will die at some point. But I plan to take as many men and women with me before I go."

Billy couldn't move.

"You have lived this far." He turned to face Miss Neal. "I could have killed you. But hostages may be needed."

Billy found his nerve and voice. "Listen. We're not going to try anything. But if you want to get to that house to hide, we ought to get there quickly."

The killer grinned.

"We are not going to the house, boy. We were never going to the house. The cops, fools that they are, will be all over that place."

Billy tried to grasp that, but he couldn't make any sense out of it. The Circle M ranch covered a lot of sections—maybe not as much as it had a century ago—but still a lot of ground.

"I will not kill you unless I have to." That was a lie.

The killer turned to Aly. "Where is section fifty-four at Dead Indian Pony Creek?"

She blinked. Billy tried to think, but he was no expert on the Circle M.

"I . . . don't know." Aly's voice was starting to break.

"Don't play me for a fool." The killer's voice was sharp, and he raised the automatic and aimed it just inches from Aly's face. "Your face won't be so beautiful if I put just a bit of pressure on this trigger."

"But . . . I . . . don't—" She stopped, closed her eyes, mouthed a short prayer, and opened her eyes. Nodding, she turned. "The creek is that way. But I don't know the section numbers. There's a map"—she stopped, then sobbed—"in Daddy's office. But . . . please."

The muzzle of the pistol touched Aly's forehead.

Taisie cleared her throat, and saw the killer's cold eyes turn toward her. She pointed in the same direction Aly had. "It's a bumpy ride. Through several gates. The turnoff is a few miles down the road."

"How do you know?" He called Taisie a nasty name she had heard many times back when she was a public defender.

Fifteen years ago. When fresh out of college, she'd had dreams of doing something good with her law degree . . . before she decided money was more important than her dreams. "I am Ashton Maddox's attorney." That was true. "I handle all his legal matters." That was also true. "He has shown me around."

"On picnics?" The monster smiled.

"Two or three times."

"I bet." He lowered the revolver. "Get in the truck." He nodded at Taisie.

"That's not an extended cab," Billy said. "We all can't fit."

"That's why I will lock you and this skinny little twit in the bed. And you can see how uncomfortable a ride that is, boy." He waved the automatic again. "Now move. We're going to that pasture."

Billy thought about all the action movies, thrillers, cop shows he had seen growing up. The hero always came up with some idea. Saved the girl, himself, and the day. But he remembered his dad saying, "Real life isn't like the movies."

He whispered how his dad often punctuated that bit of wisdom with . . . *"Lots of times, real life just plain sucks."*

George Grimes was bored out of his mind. He was stuck at this crime scene in the middle of the biggest patch of country he had ever seen. He had never been awed by anything, he figured, except himself, and maybe that woman he had met in Lajitas that time. Yeah, she had been awe-inspiring.

He started to regret he hadn't taken off with that idiot Elison Dempsey in his C.A.N. van. Grimes had liked being a Texas Ranger. The DPS gave a Ranger a good bit of autonomy. The captain told you what to do. You went out and did it. At least, that was before everybody in Texas government got all wishy-washy when it came to cops and the rights of friggin' criminals.

Already late in the day, about time for his first shot of Jack, and he was with a bunch of pansies who thought they were forensics experts. One of the geeks had come up to him and talked to him for fifteen minutes about hair follicles.

Somehow, Grimes had managed to stay awake, but he feared he might have to ask one of those freaks for directions to where he was supposed to be staying in that Podunk little burg down the road. On the other hand, a couple of the lady cops weren't half-bad looking, and after a bottle of Jack, they might look even like that gal from Lajitas. Maybe one of them, or both, would like to spend an evening with a Texas Ranger.

"You know, ladies," he had said earlier, "Montana ain't as big as Texas."

They hadn't laughed.

Then he saw the big Indian. The one who had figured out a bullet had punctured the gas tank on that Mercedes. The one who had just come back from scouting around the site where the cowboy had gotten his head bashed in. Grimes leaned forward and stared. The Indian was looking southwest. But when Grimes looked in that direction, he saw a whole bunch of empty.

He found the sun. It would disappear behind the mountains soon. Dark came early in that country, even during Daylight Savings Time. The Indian didn't have a truck. Grimes laughed. Didn't have no injun pony, neither.

The Indian stared. At nothing.

Grimes walked over to a cooler, opened it, found no beer, just bottled water. He drank one, then found a female cop and asked her if it was all right if he went beyond the fence and used the bathroom. Urinate, he meant, though that's not the word he used.

She gave him the look of a grandma who had been raised by a Bible-thumper, and he laughed, crushed the bottle, and tossed it into a friggin' recycling bin the cops had set up. Moving to the fence, he unzipped his jeans, emptied his bladder, shook himself dry, and wiped his hands on the back of his Wranglers, then zipped up and turned around.

The injun just stared.

Well, that was something to do, he thought, and walked over to the big brave. "What's that catchin' your eye, Chief?"

The big man stared as though he were deaf.

"I say, what's got your curiosity, Chief?"

The Indian kept looking. But this time he spoke. "My name is Hassun."

"Sounds like a Jap name."

The Indian turned, and Grimes realized he might be picking on the wrong guy.

"It is not."

Grimes patted his pockets for a pack of cigarettes, found nothing, and changed tactics. "I was going to ask if you wanted a smoke."

The Indian kept looking. "You don't have any."

"Well, you'd be right." Grimes remembered crumpling the pack and tossing it into the recycling bin.

Without looking away from whatever the Sam Hill was grabbing his attention, Hassun pulled a pack of Native American Spirit Black, and held it out toward Grimes.

His first notion was to say, "*What you doin' smokin' Black when you could be smokin' Red?*" but stopped himself. He pulled one out, let the Indian take the pack, and found his lighter. The taste wasn't half bad. He let it kill some lung tissue, exhaled, and looked toward where the Indian was staring. "I don't know what you see out there, Tonto."

"Hassun, Ranger Walker."

Grimes spit out some of that Indian-made cigarette taste. "I ain't no karate kid. And I ain't like that wuss that played me in the movie, neither. What you lookin' at?"

"Dust."

Grimes squinted. "I don't see nothin'," he complained after a long minute or more.

"I know." The Indian, Hassun, raised his right arm and pointed.

Grimes looked in that direction, tried hard, and shook his

head. He took another pull on the cigarette. "I still don't see nothin'."

"You won't. It is gone."

"Some rancher, I suspect."

A guttural engine and the sound of wheels on pavement turned Grimes's attention. He turned and saw a black Range Rover—looked like a custom job, probably running something over two hundred grand, but it looked more like a woman's car. Not like those Range Rovers of old. The rig stopped, the engine died, and a man stepped out.

George Grimes lost interest in the big Indian and his dust fantasy. He smiled as old Garland Foster himself looked around, but hardly even gave Hassun and Grimes a passing glance. A big man like him, and he didn't have the nerve to step into a crime scene without permission.

"Where's Sheriff Drew?" he demanded.

One of the female cops said, "He and Lieutenant Ambrose were called away."

"For what?"

No one answered. Grimes grinned, enjoying the Indian smoke and the reddening of the back of the rich man's neck.

"One of my hired men has been murdered, and I want to know what the devil is being done about it."

The news crews hurried to get all this on film. Arguments like this increased ratings.

"Lieutenant—"

"Isn't the sheriff running this investigation?"

The camera lights glared. Grimes crushed out his smoke.

No one answered. A uniformed corporal suggested Foster wait in his Land Rover until the sheriff or lieutenant returned.

"And when will that be? A man who worked for me for years has been murdered."

"So has a state trooper." The female cop had some backbone after all. "With twenty years' service. And a deputy is fighting for her life."

Uppity old Garland Foster was losing this fight all of a sudden. That made George Grimes mighty happy.

Foster recovered. "Hired cowboys aren't policemen. They aren't supposed to be shot dead and left for wolves."

Grimes crushed out his smoke with the toe of his boot. "Watch this, Chief," he told the big Indian.

"You call me Chief one more time," he heard the big Blackfoot growl. "And it will be your last time."

Ignoring the big chief, Grimes walked over toward the millionaire. "Howdy, Foster Brooks, you old drunk, you. You ain't gettin' no cooperation from these fine north country peace officers? Maybe I can help you."

Foster's face reddened to match his neck when he turned around. Why, George Grimes figured he hadn't seen that much hatred on a face since he busted that dope-pushing Greek's mother.

"You came up here after all," Foster said.

"I was needed," he told the TV cameras.

"My, how the mighty have fallen. Texas Ranger one day, rent-a-cop the next."

The TV boys would have a field day with that.

It was just fine with George Grimes. He would get some publicity. "I'm in charge of this operation," he lied, "pending the return of Sheriff Drew and Captain Ambers."

"Lieutenant . . . Am-brose," the cop in petticoats said.

Foster turned back to the female cop. "What can you tell me about poor Harry Sweet?"

"Poor?" Grimes slapped his thigh. "You mean somebody workin' for a rich gent like you is poor? Say it ain't so, Joe?"

He heard a chuckle from a newsman, and saw a couple of cops crack grins.

"What is—"

"This is an ongoing investigation, Mr. Foster." The female cop cut off the man richer than God. "That's all that I can tell you."

Foster tensed. He raised his hand and wagged his finger, still facing the brunette. "One of my men is dead. Murdered. I'll have justice one way or the other."

"Same justice," Grimes said, loving every minute of this, "that you got when your Mex wife got knocked off?"

Foster whirled around. "You'll go too far one day, Grimes, and wind up six feet under."

"I know it," Grimes said. "But I'll go under clean."

"Tell the sheriff, or whoever's running this half-baked investigation, that if I don't hear from him sometime tonight, I'll call the governor. And maybe the attorney general in Washington, D.C." Foster stormed back to his SUV, waving off questions from the TV men, and even that reporter or editor or publisher of whatever he was for that Basin Creek rag.

The Land Rover pulled out and the tires squealed as it roared back north.

Grimes winked at the cameras that weren't following Garland Foster, and then winked at the female cop.

She gave him the finger.

He bet they wouldn't show that on the nightly news.

1891

July

CHAPTER 24

Her dreams had been pleasant—despite a stressful night—but Jeannie remembered none of them when she awakened in a blackened cabin. A strange cabin. Not hers. She could tell that much from the smells and the sounds. It was not the quietness of her place. This was . . . Basin Creek. Lois DeForrest's cabin, where she had spent the night. She lay on a pallet on the floor, rolled over, and saw the stove.

Quickly, Jeannie went to work. She never liked to rush into a morning, but on that summer day, she had no choice. First, she stoked the coals, fed them with kindling and pine straw, and then added a log.

"Jeannie?" Lois called sleepily from the loft. "What time is it?"

She laughed. "Too early. Go back to sleep. I need to get home. But thank you for all your hospitality."

"Let me . . . get—" The seamstress yawned heavily. Then she began snoring.

Jeannie worked with a purpose. She got the stove heated, too, for coffee. She had to have coffee. Then she dressed, found her watch in a purse, and frowned at the time. She made herself drink one cup of coffee, found a bonnet. If she left something behind, Lois would take care of it. She had to hurry.

The sky was turning gray in the east, but the sun had not broken through quite yet. She could smell chimney smoke, and saw a few lights in windows and at businesses that opened early. Doris Caffey's café. The hotel. O'Boyle's livery. She walked to the livery. Theodore Tawny, Napoleon Drew's deputy, had taken her phaeton there yesterday afternoon.

She hated to do it, but she had to kick the soles of Luke Jasper's right boot to wake him. He was snoring in the hay, but he sat up, rubbed his eyes, then raised his sleepy head before jumping to his feet and brushing off his muslin shirt and tan pants.

"I'm sorry to wake you, Mr. Jasper," she said.

"No, no, no . . . I needed to get up anyway. Mr. O'Boyle don't like it for nobody to be sleepin'."

"Well, I am sorry anyway. But could you harness my team?"

"Yes'm."

"And I'd like a horse to rent. Please saddle one for me and tie him up behind the phaeton."

He scratched his head. "You want to rent a hoss? And have me tie him up . . . behind your buggy?"

"Exactly." He forgot to cover his mouth when he yawned. "I'll bring the horse back this evening at the latest." The phaeton might have trouble crossing Sacagawea's Pasture.

"Yes'm."

She did not expect to find torches at the edge of town. And armed men standing in the road.

Stopping the phaeton, she watched a cowhand in chaps and a tall hat, walk over, his right hand resting on the butt of a holstered revolver, and his left hand bringing a straw to his mouth, where he chewed on it for a few seconds, then the hand brought the straw down, back up for another chew or two, then back down. Back up . . . and down once more.

"Good morning," she said, interrupting his habit.

Nodding, he dropped the straw, wet his lips, and said, "Yes'm. You can't be leavin' town today, ma'am."

She laughed. "Upon whose orders?"

"The judge's."

"Judge?"

"Yes'm. The judge." He didn't even know Van Gaskin's name.

"Has there been a cholera outbreak, young man?"

His eyes widened, but just for a few moments before he reassured himself he was not facing an ugly death. "No." He even managed a smile. Some of the other armed men stepped closer. "No. That ain't it. It's just . . ."

A meaner brute hitched up his gun belt and said, "There's gonna be some stuff happenin' up north a bit today, lady. Mr. McIlhaney and the judge don't want no innocent folks gettin' hurt." He tipped his hat and grinned underneath a filthy mustache. "You see how it is."

"I see. But I do not live north of here." She pointed, fairly accurately, in the direction of her home. "My home is south."

"It don't matter."

She leaned toward the brute. "I think it does. And I know Horace Van Gaskin quite well." Which was a lie. "And I know Mike McIlhaney." *Well enough to despise him.* "And I have even had the honor to be acquainted with your good friend Lat Carson." She prayed that cold-blooded soulless monster was sleeping somewhere else. "One word from me, you two-bit gunmen, and you'll be flogged if I am not allowed to return to my home. Which," she barked, and raised her quirt, "is *south*. Not north. Now step out of my way."

The younger one, probably just a thirty-dollar-a-month-and-found waddie, walked to the left. "Let her through, Jim," he said to someone behind the torches.

The brute glared.

"She ain't gonna do nothin'," the cowboy told him. "She's just a woman. Goin' home."

The man frowned, but he stepped aside. Jeannie snapped the quirt, and her horses pulled the phaeton past the torches, the gray from the livery following. None of the fools guarding the road had the brains to question why she was leading a saddled horse behind her rig.

When she reached the road, she turned south. But only for a hundred and fifty yards. Then she stopped. Waited. Turned the rig around, and rode north as quietly as she could.

Dawn broke before she reached Sacagawea Pasture.

Jeannie pulled hard and let the horses slow the phaeton to a final stop. She could see the smoke rising off to the east, and knew that had to be Napoleon Drew's morning campfire. She secured the leather lines, adjusted the bonnet covering her head, and stepped down from the rig. The gray tethered behind the phaeton snorted, ready to be released, but Jeannie wanted to give the team that had gotten her there a reward.

She let both have two cubes of sugar, patted each, and walked back to the seat where she had placed two mixing bowls. These she took to the harnessed horses, and set on the ground. One more trip back to her carriage, and she returned with a canteen, which she uncorked and filled both bowls.

"Drink and rest," she told them as she corked the canteen and threw it over her shoulder. "Stoney and I will be back in a jiffy." She untied the gray and pulled herself into the sidesaddle. Frowning, she flicked the reins and led the gray off the road and into Sacagawea's Pasture.

Riding sidesaddle absolutely disgusted her, but there was a slight chance—if she knew Napoleon Drew and Murdo Maddox—both men would be at that campfire. She kept riding.

Voices proved her instincts had been right.

A cowboy greeted her with a cocked revolver, but he quickly lowered the hammer, and let the big weapon find its way back into the leather holster. He removed his hat, opened his mouth, and blinked, but did not speak.

Jeannie reined in the gray. "Good morning, Mister . . . ?"

The man blinked again. Finding his tongue, he managed to choke out his name. "Penny. Ben Penny."

"Will you help me down, Mr. Penny?" she asked, though she had no problem dismounting from a sidesaddle or a man's saddle. But it was the age of Queen Victoria, and even in Cutthroat County, little things were expected.

The cowboy pulled the gray behind him as they walked toward the campfire. She saw no coffeepot, not even a skillet, near the fire.

All conversation stopped when Napoleon saw Jeannie. All hats were removed from heads.

"Jeannie!" Murdo shouted. "What the devil are you doing here?"

"I saw your campfire," she said. Which was true. Her eyes turned to the sheriff. "But I thought you would be farther than here."

Which she had . . . until one of Mike McIlhaney's cowhands—or *gunhands*, as some folks called the rancher's hired workers—had ridden into Basin Creek with news that the sheriff hadn't gotten any farther than the southern edge of Sacagawea Pasture. That bit of news had made it to Theodore Tawny, probably at the Swede's Saloon, and Tawny had told Doris Caffey. The café owner had left her cabin to tell Lois DeForrest, who had invited Jeannie to stay overnight. Jeannie was glad to. It was a shorter ride to Sacagawea Pasture from town that it was from her place south.

"You going somewhere?" the sheriff asked.

She nodded her head north. "I thought it would be a fine day for a ride to Dead Indian Pony Creek. It's pretty this time of year." She smiled at Napoleon Drew, whose face turned to granite, and then she looked back at Murdo, who looked as though he were remembering the picnics they'd had there.

"This isn't," Napoleon said, "on the way to that creek."

Murdo's foreman Weems frowned. "You ain't ridin' that hoss all the way up there and back, is you, Missus Ashton?"

Jeannie laughed. "Goodness, no. I have my phaeton on the road."

"You alone?" Murdo asked.

"I was." She bowed. "I have the most charming company now."

The sheriff, still frowning, repeated his statement: "This isn't on the way to Dead Indian Pony Creek."

"We'd offer you coffee, ma'am?" Murdo's cowpuncher said, "but . . . well . . . we ain't got none."

Murdo and Napoleon gave him deadly looks, but Jeannie saved him by shaking her head.

"Had I known that, I would have brought you all some. I would love to stay, but I have a long ride, and, these days, it probably is not wise to leave my phaeton on any road." She looked around, saw Napoleon Drew's hard eyes, and tried to charm him with a smile. When that didn't work, she sighed.

"Deke," Murdo told his foreman, "escort the Widow Ashton back to her rig."

The cowboy bent to pitch his cigarette into the fire, and started toward her.

"Napoleon," she said.

The foreman stopped. Napoleon stared at her.

Facing Napoleon, she said, "A man rode into town yesterday. He calls himself Lat Carson."

The sheriff's lips tightened.

"Lat Carson." Deke Weems turned around. "I ain't heard his name since that scrape down in Johnson County a coupla years back."

Napoleon said nothing.

"Horace Van Gaskin swore him in as a county stock detective," Jeannie revealed.

The sheriff stayed quiet, and his face remained stone.

"They were forming a posse last night. The judge and Mike McIlhaney were buying plenty of liquor for anyone who wanted to ride down rustlers and owlhoots."

"They ride out of Basin Creek yet?" Napoleon finally spoke.

"I think they had the same idea you have," she said. "They hadn't left, as far as I know, when I rented a rig and this gray just before daybreak. It might take them longer considering all the whiskey the judge and McIlhaney let them have last night. But I thought you should know."

"Lat Carlson." Murdo Maddox tested the name. He turned to the sheriff. "I had no part in his coming up here."

"I know that," Napoleon answered quickly.

"McIlhaney." Murdo spat out the name. "He wants to be top dog. And the judge"—he started to curse, but stopped himself—"aims for being governor."

"Thank you, ma'am." Napoleon hadn't taken his eyes off Jeannie. "But you best get back home."

She smiled. "Not until I see the overlook at Dead Indian Pony Creek."

"I wish you wouldn't go up there alone," Murdo said.

She bowed at him and widened her smile. "Why don't you come with me, Mr. Maddox? We could have a picnic."

He frowned. "I can't do that, Jea . . . Missus Ashton." Turning back to Napoleon Drew, he said, "I have to help the sheriff here find the scum who killed one of my men."

A horse whinnied. The gray answered, causing Jeannie to get a firmer grip on the reins. The young cowboy, Ben Penny, reached for his revolver as he turned to the sound of a slow-walking horse.

Murdo Maddox told him, "Keep it leathered."

Penny did not draw his weapon.

"It's all right," Napoleon reassured everyone.

The horse was a pinto, the head and mane solid black, with black on its belly and legs. The rider was lean, leathery, wearing buckskin britches, old moccasins, and a store-bought shirt. His hat was black, flat-crowned, with feathers on both sides, and he wore a bone breastplate over his shirt. Long silver hair hung in braids. The horse carried him slowly toward Jeannie.

The rider was old, his face creased with wrinkles, but he carried himself with power. He pulled hard on the hackamore, stopping the pinto. "I have come."

That's all he said.

"Keme." Napoleon Drew walked toward him. "It is good to see you."

Keme. It was a name she knew well. But in all her years in Cutthroat County, she had never seen him.

The Indian nodded once. His eyes swept past the others in the camp.

He was not what she expected. From the stories she had heard, she knew he had to be old. Quite old. But still, from the tales she had heard, she expected him still to be robust—Hercules, Apollo, or some godlike legend.

He sat his horse well, and the pinto was well-trained. The man carried no weapon. Not even a knife or bow.

"The man who I sent to you?" Napoleon asked.

Keme said, "He found me."

"You will help us?" Murdo asked.

"I am here." Keme did not look away from Napoleon Drew. "My grandson."

But the sheriff looked away from the Blackfoot. His eyes stopped on Jeannie. "We'll be leaving now. You best go back to your place."

"All right." She looked at the sidesaddle with distaste, but she just needed to tolerate that for a ride back to the phaeton. "Good luck," she told the men when she had managed to fit herself properly and so dignified on the torture devise. After turning the gray around, she rode out of the camp and across the grassy land till she saw her rig and her own horses waiting.

There, she drank water herself, tied up the gray behind the rig, and looked south.

She had heard no riders, so the vigilance committee had not yet left Basin Creek. For surely they would follow Napoleon's posse. Maybe they were all sleeping off that drunk. Maybe reason and common sense would win out. Maybe the good people of Basin Creek would stand up to the tyrants. Maybe, as her father used to say when he didn't think she could hear, Hell would freeze over.

Men—Western men, especially—never thought about reason.

But . . . she didn't want to ride back toward Basin Creek and run into McIlhaney's bunch, especially those guards whom she had told she was going home.

She picked up the empty mixing bowls, tossed them into the phaeton, found more sugar cubes to reward the team for patience and the gray for a pleasant enough gait. Then she drank water from the canteen herself, and climbed into the phaeton.

The horses pulled the rig back onto the road. She let them trot. And rode north. She could be at the bridge over Dead Indian Pony Creek in four or five hours. It was a beautiful place, after all. And she could be back in Basin Creek, return the gray to the livery. With luck, she would be back in town in time for supper. Doris Caffey served better food than she could cook anyway.

Chapter 25

Once Jeannie Ashton had left, Napoleon told Maddox's hired hand to kick out the fire and cover the pit with dirt. They were riding out.

Keme, however, said, "Grandson, I have not had any coffee."

That caused Murdo Maddox to laugh—and Drew's ears to redden . . . but he held his temper. And at least he didn't blush in embarrassment. He muttered an apology, and told the Blackfoot elder there was no coffee. And not much in the way of breakfast.

Keme shrugged and got to business. "The white man you sent says a white man has been killed."

"That is what we were told. I did not find the body before sundown and thought it best to wait for you."

"What if I did not come?"

Napoleon's eyes sparkled. "I did not even consider that a possibility."

Keme made no comment, and Napoleon explained the situation as best he could. "The dead man worked for him." His head tilted toward Murdo Maddox. "That is why he and his two hired men ride with me . . . with us, I mean."

"Yes." Keme turned toward the rancher. "It is good to see you, Grandson."

Murdo Maddox stiffened for a long while, but at last his head bobbed and he said, "Grandfather, it has been a long time."

"Four winters," the old man said, and he turned to Napoleon. "Five winters have passed since I last saw you, Grandson."

The lawman went rigid. "Has it been that long?"

"You call them *years*. My people, we Siksika—and many of the other tribes who are not blessed by the Great Father to be Blackfoot—count by *winters*, the hardest of the seasons. And an old man like me remembers when he last saw his two adopted pale-eye grandsons. The grandsons of my own blood . . . they are all dead."

"Chogan?" Murdo called out.

Which would be just like that louse, Drew thought, eavesdropping on a conversation.

"Yes."

Old Blackbird. About twice as old as Drew, they had wrestled many times back when they were younger. Drew never had figured out how to best that wiry old Indian. But Murdo Maddox had.

Drew took in a deep breath, his memories taking him back to those years. "And . . . Apani?"

The old Blackfoot stared at Drew for a long while. "Your grandmother, too, has joined her ancestors."

Their adopted grandmother. *Butterfly*. Toothless, though beautiful. Strong, though small. She could outsing the younger women in the village, could outsing her daughters, and smoked venison with the best of Montanans, white or red.

"I am sorry," Drew said, and added, "Grandfather."

"There is no need to be sorry. Her spirit lives with me. Soon, I will join her. But not today. Today I come to assist my grandsons." He turned toward Murdo. "Come. Mount your ponies. We have work to do this day." Keme walked toward his pinto, grabbed the hackamore, and leaped onto the horse's back as though he were a young warrior.

Deke Weems took care of putting out the campfire, and Drew moved to his horse, checked the cinch, and swung into the saddle. Keme was already riding northeast. Drew and Murdo caught up with the old-timer. Pulling up just behind the Blackfoot, Drew rode on Keme's left, and Murdo on the right.

Deke Weems and Ben Penny rode behind them.

Ahead, Keme grunted, and let his head bob once. "It is good to see my grandsons ride together again."

Drew unclenched his jaw, and let hot air escape his body. He wondered if he had made a mistake asking for help from the old Blackfoot.

"Lord have mercy," Deke Weems whispered.

They found the wagon three miles from where they had camped.

Murdo unsheathed the Winchester, jacked a round into the chamber, and squeezed off a shot that sent four buzzards back into the air. "The boy," he said, jacking a fresh round into the carbine, "could've been buried. He . . ." His voice trailed off as a saddled horse whinnied and pulled hard on a tether in a copse of trees.

Napoleon Drew touched his Remington. Murdo levered the Winchester.

Then a man slowly stepped out into the clearing, patting the dun horse with his left hand before slowly stepping into the open. He kept his hands wide apart from his body, the gun belt, and revolver. "Been waitin' for you, Sheriff," he called out, and grinned. He was about as white as the horse.

"You didn't see him, injun?" Deke Weems whispered.

"I did not."

Keme stared at the figure. "He is quiet. Confident," he

whispered. "He did not come this way to reach this place." The Indian's head shook. "I have never seen this man or this horse."

"I haven't either," Napoleon said. "But I'm betting the man is Lat Carson."

After clearing his throat, the lawman called out, "All right if we join you"—he decided to take a chance—"Lat Carson?"

The stranger's laugh held no humor. "Like I said, Sheriff, been waitin' for you. I'm glad my reputation and handsome face has gotten this far north."

Napoleon, Murdo, and the cowhand rode easily to the buckboard, the corpse, and the wagon and pale horse.

As soon as they could see the corpse, Murdo resumed his disapproval. "Hollister didn't have to feed those—" The rancher was spitting mad again.

"He didn't feel a thing," Napoleon said coldly. "The worms will get him, too, when you plant him here." But he was thinking the white-skinned man had already traipsed over any sign that might have helped Keme.

"You weren't always so coldhearted," Murdo told him. He lowered the hammer on the Winchester but kept the long gun close.

"Sheriff Napoleon Drew," the pale man said. "Heard about you. You must be the big fart in this country." He grinned up at Murdo. "Though you ain't quite as big as I figured."

The man eyed Keme. "And an injun tracker." He spit in the grass.

Napoleon turned to Keme. "You want us to wait here?"

His head nodded curtly, then Keme slipped off the pinto and handed the hackamore to Murdo.

The leathery Blackfoot walked slowly, head turning left and right. He gave Lat Carson no consideration, acting as though the killer was invisible. About thirty yards from the riders, he stopped and knelt, fingering something beneath the grass.

"Light down, friends," Carson said.

The white men dismounted, while Keme worked.

Napoleon studied the country around where Billy Joe Hollister had been killed. The buckboard, the horses or mules cut out of the harness and long gone. The body had fallen near the wagon.

"They must have shot poor Billy Joe off the seat," Ben Penny said. "Bushwhacked him without a call."

"That's how I figured it," Lat Carson said. The hired gunman leaned against the side of the buckboard, rolling a cigarette, the brim of his hat pushed up.

Out of the corner of his eye, Napoleon saw Murdo's head bob.

But the rancher added, "Or they dragged his body to the wagon."

The cowhand nodded. Deke Weems was busy picketing the horses. Lat Carson lighted his smoke.

"That's why we brought Keme," Murdo added.

We? Napoleon shook his head. *We?* I *sent for Keme. You would have ridden over here and spoiled anything that old Blackfoot could have told us.* He kept quiet though.

"That cowboy's killers are just getting farther away," Lat Carson said.

"I don't think they'll be moving too fast," Napoleon said.

"Why?" Deke Weems, finished with the horses, lowered the cigarette he was about to lick and light.

Murdo answered first. "Because we still haven't seen one head of my cattle."

While Keme methodically studied the area surrounding the wagon, Napoleon walked to the corpse, glancing at the bed of the wagon. "You two cowhands"—he waited for Deke Weems and the younger waddie to look up, then pointed at the wagon bed—"there's a shovel here. You might as well dig a grave."

"That's right kind of you," Murdo said, "Sheriff."

Napoleon did not satisfy the rancher with any reaction. Instead, he stepped around the wagon and knelt by the corpse. Carrion had worked over the poor kid, so he spat out bile and pulled the bandanna over his mouth and nose. He moved on his knees and leaned over the cowboy's chest, sticking a finger in a hole that had not been made by wolves, coyotes, or buzzards.

A shadow crossed the dead cowhand, and Murdo Maddox said, "God." Then he cursed the killers, or maybe he was just cursing the whole world.

"Shot from behind." Napoleon sucked in wretched air and turned the body over onto its side.

The entry wound was higher than the massive hole in the kid's lower chest. He raised his head, thinking the men—or man—who did this would not have moved the wagon too much except while unhitching the team. The wagon was pointed southwest, so Napoleon looked northeast, and saw a knoll that reached above the line of small trees where Lat Carson had picketed his white horse. Two hundred yards. Maybe two-fifty. "Maddox."

"Yeah?"

"Is the brake set?"

The rancher sighed, but he moved back to the side and looked across the driver's box..

"Yeah."

Drew nodded.

"What you getting at?" Murdo asked.

"Just a hunch." Napoleon stood, wiped his hands on his chaps, and turned toward the Circle M bunch. "Billy Joe climbed into the wagon. Probably as soon as he sat down, the killer put a large-caliber bullet through his back. Didn't get a chance to release the brake. Or the horses or mules—whatever he had for a team—would have bolted."

"Or the killers brought the team back here." Lat Carson had walked over to join the party.

Napoleon stared up at the ugly killer. "That's not likely." Like anyone in his right mind would try to take a wagon back to a dead man to unhitch a team. He saw enough gorging of the grass and sod there to know the animals had not wanted to be there to begin with. If the killer or killers had been smart, they would have led the wagon away from the dead man. But most killers, he figured, weren't smart.

Although this one was a calculating professional. Calculating and cold.

"You shoot a Sharps. Don't you?" Napoleon stared at Carson.

"Fifty-ninety," he answered. "It puts a fella down so he don't get back up." Smiling as he removed his cigarette, Carson pointed the smoke at the dead boy. "I'd say that it was a fifty-caliber that blowed the supper out of that boy's belly. Maybe even a fifty-ninety like mine." He bent forward just a few inches. "Or a fifty-hundred. Possibly a fifty-seventy if he hollowed out the lead. But I ain't the detective that you be, Sheriff."

"Sharps," Deke Weems said. "Most of them went out with the buffalo. But you still see a few around." He reached for the shovel, dragged it to the edge, and pulled it over the buckboard's side, then turned to his boss. "You want us to bury Billy Joe here?"

The sheriff and the rancher turned and looked down the pasture toward where they had camped. Where many old-timers had been buried. Where Ebenezer Maddox had been laid to rest, and his wife, and even Ezekiel, Murdo's grandfather. But not Ben Franklin Drew, who had been old Eb's partner and lifelong friend. Not Ben Franklin Drew.

"Bury him here," Murdo said after a long thought. "Ground's

softer. And it's easy enough to find in case his folks want to bury him in the family plot."

"He never mentioned no family," Ben Penny said.

Deke Weems grunted. "Well, we'll check his bunk when we get back to the ranch. See if there's anyone who needs to be wrote to." He looked at his boss. "You'd be the one to write that letter, wouldn't you?"

"Yeah. If there's someone to write."

Weems nodded at Ben Penny. "We got one shovel, boy. You want to dig? Or bring the body to the hole?"

The young cowhand's face turned almost as pale as Lat Carson's. "I . . . I'll . . . I'll . . . dig." He took the shovel.

"Is this how you boys chase down a cold-blooded killer in Montana?" Lat Carson asked as the Montanans squatted in the shade of the wagon while Ben Penny dug the grave. He swore when his comment got no reaction, and pointed to the north. "Trail's easier to read than capital letters."

"Says you." Deke Weems rolled another cigarette.

That got a grin from Napoleon, and when he looked up, he found Murdo Maddox smiling, too.

"Whoever shot that boy, he and his compadres took some of the cattle in this pasture and drove them that-a-way," Carson said. "We can catch those killers sure enough. If you would get off your arses."

"I don't remember inviting you to join this posse." Napoleon pushed himself to his feet. "The way I heard it, you got a bounty for every so-called rustler you brought in. In Wyoming."

"Colorado, too," Murdo said.

"And Texas," Deke Weems added.

"Feel free to ride out and collect your first Montana bounty." Finding his gloves and pulling them on, Napoleon walked to the grave and waited for Ben Penny to dump sod onto the mound and look up. "You've dug enough. I'll finish. Get some water and rest up." He held out his hands for the shovel, took it, and moved it to his left hand, and kept his right out, waiting for the cowboy to grab it.

When Penny finally understood, he accepted the hand and let the lawman help pull him out of the hole. "Thanks."

Napoleon nodded, and jumped into the grave. He went to work.

They had wrapped Billy Joe Hollister with a tarp they found in the back of the wagon, and Deke Weems was shoveling sod over the body when Keme rode up. He stared at the covered body and shook his head.

"I will never understand the custom of you white men," the old Blackfoot said, staring at his two adopted grandsons. "You trap the spirit when you cover him with Mother Earth. Then, when he has begun his journey to the Sand Hills, he may be put beneath our Mother Earth." He nodded at the copse. "Trees. Put his body in the branches of a tree. Or leave him in the open. It is easier. It is the way of my people."

"And a good way," Drew said. "But not the way of my people."

"Well." Keme dismounted. "At least your clothes are old and your hair short. That is proper mourning."

Napoleon nodded while Murdo tried not to grin, probably thinking the only time a cowhand wore clean clothes was after a trail drive when his duds were too torn up and stinking, or at the end of the month when he had money in his pocket and wanted to look good for the chippies in town.

"What do you think about the men who did this?" Napoleon asked.

Keme turned slightly and pointed northwest. "Three men. Two mules." He nodded at the wagon. "Ten beeves. They go that way."

"That's what I told you suckers hours ago," the hired killer said.

"All right." Napoleon turned to Murdo. "We'll ride out soon as you say the words over your dead cowhand."

"We'll say the words later," Murdo said.

"Best to put some stones over the mound," Napoleon said. "Keep wolves from digging him up."

"That can wait."

And I thought I was the coldhearted—

"I will stay." Keme interrupted Napoleon's thought.

The sheriff turned and stared at the old Blackfoot and could not hide his surprise.

"The trail is easy to follow," Keme said.

"I told you fools that, too," Lat Carson said.

"It will be all right," Keme said. "I want to look around some more. And I will find you." His nod was a period to the statement.

Napoleon knew better than to protest.

"Go," Keme ordered. "I will finish burying this young warrior. In your foolish way. And I will make sure no animal digs him up before his spirit has started the journey to the Sand Hills." He nodded again. "Go."

CHAPTER 26

The Frankie Maddox—killing sheriff rode point. Murdo Maddox wasn't going to put up any argument over that. Lat Carson rode a few yards behind the sheriff and Murdo took the rear, letting his two cowboys ride off to the side and slightly behind the stock detective.

They remembered what Murdo had told them before they left Billy Joe Hollister's grave. "Whatever you do, don't let Carson get behind you for more than a second."

Keme was right. A half-blind kid from Helena could have followed that trail. But Murdo could reason it out. They were rustlers. Cattle thieves weren't generally so cold-blooded. Lat Carson, he figured, had never even thought about stealing cattle. Those waddies had come upon poor Billy Joe, had to kill him, and were most likely making a beeline for Canada or hoping to lose them in the country to the west.

These waddies had come upon poor Billy Joe . . . Murdo cursed himself. "You ain't that stupid."

Billy Joe had been shot from behind with a large-caliber rifle. *Bushwhacked.* Shot dead in cold blood. No, they had not just come across that good young pup who knew what it meant to ride for the brand—especially the Circle M brand. Murdo stopped trying to reason things out. They were on the trail. They would find his cattle and the rustlers. Those fools should have stuck to stealing beef from Mike McIlhaney and the small ranches in Cutthroat County.

Finding the sun, Murdo sighed. He thought about Jeannie. Knowing her, she would be coming close to the trail that led to Dead Indian Pony Creek. He pushed back his hat and looked straight ahead, making out the foothills that led to the Always Winter range. If the rustlers kept this trail, the posse—if one could call it a real posse—would cross the road to the reservation and—The thought made him tense.

The rustlers wouldn't head straight west. Not toward Dead Indian Pony Creek. They would turn north. But they wouldn't be stupid enough to stay on the road. If they tried to push Circle M beef through the reservation, the Blackfoot Indians would hold them until they heard from Murdo himself. No running irons had been found at the camp where they had killed Billy Joe.

Ahead, Napoleon Drew reined in his horse.

"What you stoppin' for?" the hired killer called.

Deke Weems and Ben Penny stopped a few yards behind Lat Carson.

Good. They'd remembered not to get behind the stock detective's guns. Murdo kicked his horse into a trot, but slowed it to a walk when he rode between his two hired men. He looked toward Weems and said, "If Carson touches his revolver or that Sharps, kill him." The horse never slowed, and Murdo did not slow his horse until he reached Lat Carson.

"What's he stopping for?" the killer demanded, his face knotted but not reddening in anger. The skin remained the color of the dead.

"It's Big Coulee," Murdo said, and rode past the gunman, stopping at where Sacagawea Pasture disappeared and what some folks called the End of the Earth began.

The hoofprints of horses and cattle left the grass, and moved down the slope into the coulee, which stretched on for a hundred yards, deeper and deeper, and then bent and moved toward the northwest.

"As slow as you jaspers have been ridin'—like it's a funeral possession or headin' to church—we could've caught up with them rustlers before they disappeared into that big ditch."

Murdo ignored Carson, and reined up on Napoleon Drew's left. "You figured this?"

The sheriff shook his head. "Not really. Come to me a few miles back." He spoke in a whisper.

"Good place to disappear," Murdo said, "but not if you're in a hurry."

"If I'd killed a Circle M rider," Napoleon said, "I'd be in a hurry."

Murdo almost smiled. That, he had to admit, was a mighty fine compliment. Especially coming from a low-down Drew.

"What you think?" Finding his canteen, the lawman took a drink, and held the container out toward Murdo, who shook his head. Maybe he would have accepted a bottle of bourbon . . . but not water from the man who had killed his cousin.

"Same thing you think?" Napoleon secured the stopper and draped the canteen's canvas strap over the saddle horn.

Still muttering curses, Lat Carson kicked his horse forward. "What's the palaver? What's the holdup?"

Napoleon pointed his chin at the big drop. "Big Coulee."

"So?" Carson pointed. "Tracks lead into it."

"I can see," Napoleon said.

"You scared?"

The sheriff shrugged. "Cautious."

Murdo decided to chime in. "It widens two miles that-away. But before it widens, there's a narrow defile where one gun or two could have a regular turkey shoot. We'd have to pass through it."

"You think rustlers would plan an ambush?" Carson

laughed. “They’ll be raisin’ dust on account they know I’m comin’ after ’em.”

“You weren’t coming very fast,” Murdo said. “You were waiting where one of my hands got killed from behind.”

The killer tensed. His right hand started for his revolver, but he stopped. “I’m gonna let that pass, pardner. This time.”

“Those rustlers haven’t been in much of a hurry”—Napoleon Drew pointed at the tracks—“since they left Billy Joe’s grave.”

Carson opened his mouth, then shook his head. “I don’t know why I waited for you. I could have got your cows back and collected me some reward on dead rustlers.”

“Why didn’t you?” Drew asked.

The man frowned. He swallowed down whatever he thought about saying, and changed his tone. “We could ride up top, get past that narrow spot where you think someone will be layin’ for you. Catch ’em unawares. How’s that sound?”

“Not bad,” Drew said.

“Boss!”

Murdo turned toward Deke Weems, who was pointing down the trail. Standing in the stirrups, Murdo looked hard and saw the rider coming at a fast trot. The horse was a pinto. The rider was Keme.

“Let’s hear what my grandfather has to say,” Drew said, and he eased his mount away from Big Coulee’s edge.

Keme slowed the pinto to a walk and eased toward the gathering of white men about fifty yards from Big Coulee.

“Finished buryin’ that back-shot cowpuncher?” Lat Carson said, still in the saddle, rolling a cigarette.

The elder’s head moved up once, then down, then back up, and he looked at Napoleon Drew. “I found trail.”

Carson laughed. “Well, the trail we left, and the trail the rustlers left, was pret’ easy to find, injun.”

Keme did not look at Carson. The old Indian's eyes locked with the sheriff's, but he spoke to the stock detective. "That not the trail I find."

Carson coughed out a laugh. "What trail did you find, redskin?"

Now the Blackfoot turned to the hired gun. "Yours."

Murdo thought the man-killer's face got even paler.

"You found the dead boy who rode for my grandson," Keme said.

"That's right." But the killer's hand dropped toward the stock of the Sharps in the scabbard, then wisdom came to him, and he moved the hand away from the single-shot rifle and rested on the butt of the holstered revolver.

"You good tracker," Keme told Carson. "You ride from white-man road straight to dead white boy."

The killer's mouth tightened briefly, then became a thin smile across his dead skin. "You don't know what the Sam Hill you're talkin' 'bout."

"Maybe so. But the tracks not lie. They left with the cattle"—Keme pointed—"toward what you call Big Coulee, but what we call the Hole Where No Wind Blows. And, as you know, the dead white boy was killed with Loud Gun That Makes Big Hole."

"You're wrong, injun. Dead wrong."

Napoleon nodded and calmly drew the Remington, thumbed back the hammer, and pointed the .44's barrel at the pale man's chest. "You better hope so. Because you and I are ridin' into Big Coulee. If I hear one shot, I'll blow your head off."

"No." It was Murdo who spoke.

The sheriff kept the barrel pointed at the now-sweating hired gunman. "What are you talking about?"

"I'll ride into Big Coulee with him," Murdo said. "Billy Joe worked for me."

* * *

"I'll need your hat," Murdo told the sheriff.

"You think those swine know the color of our hats?" But Napoleon removed his hat, wiped the sweatband with his finger, and held it out. Murdo took the hat, removing his at the same time, and the swap was made. He had to push it back a bit. All Drews had heads too big for any human's body.

"Badge, too." Murdo shook his head at how ugly his hat looked on the lawman.

Napoleon unpinned the tin star, considered it, then with a shrug, he dropped it in Murdo's hand. The rancher pinned it on the lapel of his vest.

"We don't look alike," Napoleon pointed out.

"I thank the good Lord for that every day," Murdo said, though he wasn't trying to be funny. He was nervous. And Murdo Maddox did not like being nervous. He turned serious. "They won't be looking closely. I don't think they'll risk a spyglass or anything. Might give away their position."

"And our chaps, vests, and shirts are close enough in color," Napoleon said.

"Good. I'd hate for this story to spread all over Cutthroat County." Murdo's joke, however, fell flat.

"We'll ride hard ahead." The sheriff repeated the plan he had laid out earlier. "Get past the narrows. That's where they'd set up an ambush. Don't you think?"

"Maybe." Murdo shrugged. "Well, from the tracks, there are only four of them."

"I gotta figure some others joined them from the reservation road."

Murdo let out a mirthless laugh.

"I need to deputize you," the sheriff said. "To make it all legal."

Murdo's laugh was genuine as he looked at the sheriff. "Think they might get suspicious? Me . . . as *you* . . . riding alone with him."

Drew shrugged. "Like I said, I'm willin' to ride down there. It was my idea, after all."

"Yeah. That's why they'll think it's you." Murdo shook his head. "You're a better hand with a gun than I am."

The lawman coughed out a laugh. "Well, I appreciate the compliment. But you got more guts than me."

Murdo tried to grin, but that wasn't in him at the moment.

"You're makin' a mighty big mistake, you ignorant fools," Carson said, then entered Big Coulee first, an empty Sharps in the scabbard. He carried his revolver in the holster, but they had unloaded that, too. Even pushed the cartridges through the loops in his shell belt so he would have no weapon.

"Wouldn't be my first," Drew said, and nodded at Murdo. "Luck."

"You, too." Murdo kicked the horse and followed the killer.

When they reached the bottom, Murdo nodded at Carson. "You take the point. At a walk. You ride faster, you die. You take off your hat, you die. You do anything I take as a signal—"

"I die." Carson spat. "But you'll die, Maddox, before this day is done. And I'm gonna spit in your eye before I put you under."

"Open your mouth once more," Murdo told him, "you die."

At least they were out of the wind. The walls grew higher, and the coulee began its twist as the dry bed began to narrow. If not for that part of the dry wash, Big Coulee would have made sense for rustlers to hide out in. Dust wouldn't rise. The walls would keep most of the noise cattle made below the rim. They could move a stolen herd practically to the road.

But the narrows. That was different. Cattle would have to go through one at a time. Ten head . . . that wasn't too bad. And they weren't longhorns from Texas. They were good Circle M beef. Scottish bred. Big animals, not as leathery. They could squeeze through. And a rider on horseback would be a sitting duck for any man perched above the rocks at a bend.

One shot.

One dead man.

The sand kept down the noise of the shod horses.

Murdo found the sun and guessed the time. Then blocked time and everything else from his mind as he focused on the man riding in front of him. He drew the Winchester, rested it against his thighs. He had even put an extra shell in the cylinder of his revolver.

Six beans in the wheel.

No cowboy in his right mind kept the hammer under a cartridge.

Ahead of him, Lat Carson straightened.

"Spur that horse," Murdo told him in an even voice, "you die."

They entered the narrows.

To Murdo Maddox it felt like a coffin.

CHAPTER 27

"Listen, cowboy," Lat Carson said, his voice bouncing off the walls, the hooves of their horses sounding abnormally loud.

"Shut up." Murdo's voice echoed. "One more word," he said in an urgent whisper, "and I blow your fool head off."

Fifty yards later, before the first true turn of the coulee where the land sloped off deeper, and where the passage could only be made single file, Murdo spoke again. "Rein up."

Carson turned in the saddle, his face a mask of confusion. "Huh?"

"I won't say it again." Murdo stopped his horse, and brought the Winchester's stock to his shoulder.

The stock detective pulled on the reins.

"Now dismount." Murdo spoke in a whisper.

Uncertain about anything except the .44-40 aimed at his chest, Lat Carson dismounted. Murdo waved the Winchester barrel up, and the killer raised his hands, holding the reins to his pale horse in the left hand.

Murdo swung down easily, then eased the hammer down and laid the carbine against a boulder. "Take off your hat, shirt, vest, and that filthy bandanna." He drew his revolver to make sure his instructions were followed to the letter, and as Carson began to undress, Murdo Maddox did the same, keeping far enough away from the assassin and keeping his eyes on the killer. The sheriff hadn't seen much reason to swap every stitch of clothing with Murdo, but Murdo figured to give himself every advantage he could think of to live through this day.

"You figure you're smart, don't ya?"

Murdo shook his head.

"You don't even like that hard rock of a law dog. He shot down your brother in cold blood."

"Cousin," Murdo corrected. "And my cousin was an arrogant fool. And a drunk. His own daddy, my uncle, said he wouldn't live to see thirty years, and probably would shame the Maddox name."

The Texas killer spit out more history that sounded like he was begging. "Y'all been feudin' for generations. That's how I hear it. Now why don't you listen to me? We can cut you in and—"

"You should have thought of that before you killed one of my cowpunchers. I'll never shame the Maddox name."

The killer's face kept getting paler. Or maybe it was just the light that far down in Big Coulee.

"It ain't how you figured, Maddox. It ain't—"

"Turn around." Murdo aimed the revolver to make sure Lat Carson did as he was ordered. He stuffed a handkerchief into Carson's mouth, causing him to gag, then used an extra bandanna to gag the blowhard. After that he prodded the pale man's back with the barrel of the revolver and steered him to the sheriff's horse.

Lat Carson figured out the plan, but he couldn't voice any objection—or shout some warning. If Napoleon Drew's clothes looked ridiculous on Murdo, they were twice as bad on the sickly assassin.

But that was part of the gamble, Murdo figured.

The men waiting to shoot down a posse wouldn't be paying that much attention. High enough up, they wouldn't want to use a spyglass for fear of the reflection giving away their location. And they weren't professional killers like Lat Carson—or Napoleon Drew. They'd want to end the fight as quickly as possible.

Wishful thinking? Murdo wasn't sure, but he had dealt himself into the game. And he would play out his hand. "Mount up," he ordered.

The gunman did as he was told, but he was sweating. Sweating and turning whiter and whiter.

"You'll keep riding point," Murdo said, as he started to put on the cold-blooded killer's shirt, vest, bandanna, and hat. Again, the fit wasn't right, but it would have to do. "Try to spur my horse and get out of my sight, I shoot you dead. Try anything, I shoot you dead. If I see one thing that makes me nervous, I shoot you dead."

Murdo shoved the empty carbine into the scabbard of Drew's horse—the horse Lat Carson was currently sitting on—checked the cylinder in the holster on Carson's hip and made sure it was empty. "Anything you do that I don't like—even if it's just a loud, rippling fart, I shoot you dead." He nodded—"You're riding point"— and he swung into the saddle on Carson's pale horse.

Seeing the dust rising east near the edge of Sacagawea Pasture, Jeannie Ashton pulled hard to stop the phaeton, and stared long and hard. She remembered the stories told by the Blackfoot and Shoshones, and even Lakotas when they had traveled to that country. Remembered stories about their ancestors told by Murdo Maddox and Napoleon Drew.

Indians who had stampeded herds of buffalo over the edge of Big Coulee. The Hole Where No Wind Blows always sounded much more romantic, and accurate, than the drab *Big Coulee.*

Suddenly, she thought of something else. *Cattle had been rustled all across Cutthroat County, but no cattle had been found.* And Big Coulee was a fine place to hide.

The dust could be anything. But most certainly not buffalo. Those big shaggies were practically gone from Montana, almost extinct across the whole United States. Could be a spooked herd of elk. Cattle. Circle M cattle. Or maybe—she looked up the road. The livery horse tugged on its tether and snorted.

Or maybe . . .

It was still a long way to what passed for a bridge over Dead Indian Pony Creek. And maybe a mile or two only to the rim of Big Coulee.

She looked back at the horse. "You want to ride a bit, boy?" she asked, and climbed out of her rig.

"Grandfather," Napoleon Drew said as he tethered his horse to a shrub.

Keme waited with the big Sharps.

"I have been a stupid fool."

The old Blackfoot's face revealed nothing.

"All those small ranchers losing cattle here and there. No cattle showing up. No brand inspectors reporting anything suspicious up at Fort Benton. Mounties not reporting anything in Canada. And the last place anyone would look to find rustled beef would be the Circle M."

"My other grandson," Keme spoke solemnly, "is not one to steal your smelly cattle."

"No, Grandfather. I agree with you. But a smart man could hide a lot of cattle in"—he spoke the Blackfoot words—"the Hole Where No Wind Blows."

Deke Weems stopped pushing cartridges into his carbine. "Rustled beef couldn't stay there forever."

Napoleon nodded his agreement. "Ambush the sheriff and the biggest rancher in the county, though, leave them dead in Big Coulee, and a man would be able to push those cattle somewhere. The agents at Fort Peck are a lot more accommodating. They don't ask questions. Don't pay close attention to brands."

Ben Penny cleared his throat. "Maybe we ought to . . . well . . . maybe one of us ought to go get some more guns."

"You go right ahead, cowboy." Napoleon checked the rounds in his revolver cylinder. "Ride out. Fetch us some help. But I'm not leaving Murdo down there to get slaughtered." He eased the Remington into his holster. "Besides, he's on my horse."

Weems fed a final cartridge into the carbine. "Go on, Ben. The injun and sheriff and me can handle this."

Ben Penny shook his head. "Reckon not. The Circle M pays me."

The saddle was uncomfortable and the hired killer's pale horse was no Circle M gelding. Wasn't even as good as the sheriff's ride. Murdo Maddox started regretting he had volunteered, but he let the horse have enough rein to pick its own path when they entered the narrows.

In the open, deep country of Big Coulee, the sun had felt like an oven, but the shadows turned everything cooler. In fact, Murdo shivered for a moment, and not because of nerves. The hooves amplified sound in the thin pass. His throat went dry. He wondered if Drew and the others had found a position yet. Or if the sheriff had just set him up to get killed.

The plot had some holes, he figured. Lat Carson was supposed to lead the posse into an ambush. Would a gunman risk his own hide? Maybe. If he was being paid enough. But shots could have been heard. He shook his head. No. That was another saying Murdo had heard from the Blackfoot Indians. *No sound ever rises above the Hole Where No Wind Blows.*

Murdo shook his head. *It isn't that deep, he told himself.* But they were getting deeper.

* * *

Keme nodded.

Napoleon Drew peered into the abyss. He felt someone beside him, and turned to find Deke Weems.

"How far down, you reckon?" the Circle M foreman asked.

"Far enough to kill you if you slip."

The cowhand shook his head. "Always figured I'd die from falling off a horse."

"Horses aren't good at climbing." Drew watched the young cowboy named Penny tie one end of a lariat to a stump. Three lariats had been tied together. Sixty feet each, more or less. One hundred and eighty feet, taking away the fifteen feet from the stump to the abyss.

A drop of a hundred and sixty-five feet. Or thereabouts.

That wouldn't get them to the bottom. But it shouldn't be that far of a drop to that ledge. And from there . . .

Keme dropped his hackamore and another rope. They watched it fall, landing on the ledge without a sound.

Ben Penny tugged on the rope once more, cleared his throat, wiped his palms on his chaps, and walked to the edge. "Who goes first?"

"I will." Keme had fashioned a sling from a vermilion sash and some rawhide, securing ends around the barrel and stock of the big Sharps. It looked ridiculous, but it might hold.

"Grandfather?" Napoleon said softly. "Are you sure?"

"If I fall, I will not scream. Then it will be up for you to decide if this plan is worthwhile." With that, he grabbed the rope and started down.

It had been a long time since Napoleon Drew had prayed, but he started whispering one. He was sweating.

"What about the horses?" Ben Penny said.

"We leave them," Deke Weems told him.

"But we'll need horses if . . . when . . . we get down there."

"We'll have them," Weems said. "From the men we're going to kill."

Jeannie liked this horse. He was a good horse, and since she had rented it from Finnian O'Boyle's livery in Basin Creek, that surprised her. She would have to thank Mr. O'Boyle and Luke Jasper for picking him for her to ride. Not only did this gelding have an easy lope across Sacagawea Pasture, he handled a steep trail into Big Coulee like he was part mountain goat.

She had never known it could be that easy to get to the bottom of the coulee. The trail was steep, but it wasn't narrow in the least. Cattle had been driven down there. She saw the feces and the markings in the sand. Hoofprints from shod horses, too. She could read those clearly.

When she reached the bottom, she heard only the snorting of the horse and her own heavy breathing.

What amazed her was the beauty. She had heard stories about Big Coulee—about buffalo being stampeded to their deaths—but always imagined it as some dry arroyo one would find in the Southwest. Yet she saw cottonwoods off to the far side, and the grass looked thick, and smelled sweet. Probably because of the wet winter they had had.

It was a good place for cattle. And then it struck her. It was a good place to *hide* cattle.

The horse lifted its head, sniffed, and whinnied.

Jeannie pulled hard on the reins, reached down, and patted the gelding's neck. "Easy. Quiet, boy. Be—"

She heard an answering whicker, and saw two men round the corner. One reached down and pulled a rifle from the scabbard.

Jeannie turned and looked up at the trail. Then she sighed. There was no point in trying to climb that. Instead, she pulled the hat down tighter on her head, planted the biggest and fakest smile she could drum up, and kicked the horse into a walk.

She headed right for the two . . . rustlers.

They were polite enough. One thing about Montanans—the men, good, bad, or indifferent, treated women with respect. Especially attractive widows.

These two tipped their hats, asked her what brought her down into Big Coulee, and invited her to ride over to their camping spot where she could enjoy some coffee and maybe corn dodgers if the boys hadn't eaten them all up.

It wasn't quite an invitation, of course.

By the time she had reined up in front of the two cowhands, both men held their rifles. Not aimed at her. But the message was clear.

The one on the bay turned and led the way. Jeannie followed him.

The man riding the palomino followed her.

No one said a word, and suddenly the beautiful base of Big Coulee no longer looked so luscious, so much like a Garden of Eden.

It was hot in the sun. But she felt chilled.

If I were planning an ambush in this patch of hell, Murdo Maddox thought, *this is where I'd do it.*

He reached up, pulled the hat down lower, and managed to drop his head, but his eyes were not on the trail. The pale horse had better eyes for finding the right footing than Murdo. He needed to find out where someone might be drawing a bead on his middle button.

And yet no gunfire came.

As the pale horse emerged from the narrow passageway, he thought the know-everything sheriff—and even old

Keme—had thought wrong. That nobody was at the bottom of Big Coulee.

Lat Carson screamed, "Drew is at the point, boys! Shoot that law dog down!"

That's what Murdo had expected. That was the plan. He spurred the horse and dived to the right, hitting the ground as the gunshots sang out. He rolled, came up, saw a bullet whine off a stone. The ambushers were to his left. The sheriff's horse galloped past, taking Lat Carson away. By then Murdo saw where he needed to be. He rolled first, and just in the nick of time. Sand exploded as a big bullet rocked the ground where he had been.

Drew's hat was gone. The pale horse was following Lat Carson. Murdo found a hole—no, not even a hole, but a shallow depression from roaring water a month ago, a year ago, a century ago. That was all the shelter he could find, but it would have to do.

He came up. Bolted. Dived as another bullet scorched the back of his neck. When he hit the ground, bullets struck all around him. But none hit him.

God—or the Devil—or one of Keme's people's spirits—sure were looking after him.

Somehow, he was alive. He jacked a round into the Winchester and waited for Napoleon Drew to do what he was supposed to be doing, along with two Circle M riders and that old trustworthy Blackfoot.

Sucking in all the air he could hold, his ears ringing from the blasts of rifles, whines of ricochets, and the echoes of everything, Murdo waited for some yell from Weems or Penny . . . or anyone.

All he heard was the sound of gunshots. And bullets striking all around him.

DAY TWO

THURSDAY

CHAPTER 28

"Chief."

The big old Indian turned and gave George Grimes a cold look, but the retired Ranger just grinned.

"Hassun," the old red devil said. "You call me *Chief* again, you will regret it."

Grimes chuckled. "Bet it would be quite the tussle, Haz-Sunnnn. The Trillah in Manillah. The Rumble in the Jungle. All over again."

When Hassun did not appear to appreciate Grimes's humor, the Texan sighed and shook his head. "How much daylight we got left?"

The Indian looked at the sky. "An hour. Maybe. Why?"

"Well, there ain't much happenin' here. And I don't think your sheriff friend would appreciate my company with all that's gone down recently. That poor boy's got his hands full. But you ain't doin' him no good just standin' here, watching trucks go by and listenin' to she-male cops talk about boy-friends and computer crap." He waited for the big Indian to say something. But gave up on any further conversation.

Finally tired of waiting for that big chief to blink, Grimes said, "Why don't we go back to that pasture where that cowboy got his head bashed in?"

"That won't help find Billy."

Grimes nodded. "Well, I don't reckon that kid's near that pasture. Nor that rancher's daughter." His eyes brightened. "Do you know the girl? Is she hot? I mean, she's young, I know. But . . ."

There was that stare again, and Grimes decided to cut the act. "Haz-Sun. Here's what I think. And this time I ain't funnin' you, ol' boy. I'm serious as a heart attack. How's this sound to you? A cold-blooded killer finds hisself in a pickle. He runs out of gas, and hides his gas-empty car in a pasture. Kills a cowboy. Kills a cop. The cop I can figure. He ain't got much choice. Shoots the poor sucker dead, strips off the cowboy's shirt and gun and stupid Montana hat and all that. Keeps the charade goin' as long as he can. Then kidnaps a coupla kids. You foller me, hoss?"

The Indian said nothing.

"Havin' a confab with you—" Grimes shook his head. "Why kill that cowboy?"

"He saw him." But the big chief didn't sound so certain.

"The cowboy didn't have to see him. This guy's a pro. Like me. Like you even, Haz-Sun. I don't see this killer as no cowpuncher. He ain't goin' over to that pasture in hopes of stealin' a hoss and ridin' all the way to Canada."

The Indian still didn't blink.

"This man's a pro. Don't you reckon? A pro like me. And your buddy, the sheriff." Grimes was on a roll. "He kills the cowboy because he has to. But why?"

"You the Ranger," the big Blackfoot told him. "You figure out."

"That's what I plan to do, pardner. But why don't we drive back to that pasture? Those forensics folks already know you got a free pass to look over all 'em cow turds and grass and hoofprints. Maybe you can read a bit more sign."

The Indian did not appear to be interested.

Grimes swore, shook his head, and tried another tactic. "Well, I thought it would sure beat just standin' out here in the wind and waitin' for the next car to come by in an hour or two."

A half-dozen emergency vehicles parked on the highway and in front of the gate that led to the Circle M headquarters. John T. Drew opened the hatch of his Interceptor and began suiting up in tactical gear. Then he opened the case and pulled out the .223-caliber AR-15 rifle.

Heading south, a beat-up Ford truck from the late 1960s or early '70s slowed down, and the passenger window rolled down. Two troopers walked over to the truck, which Drew figured was coming down from the Blackfoot rez. A trooper looked inside, while the one on the other side of the blacktop looked into the rusted-out bed.

"What's happening?" The voice sounded Native.

Both troopers stepped away from the pickup. The one on the other side shook his head at Drew and Ambrose, and the closest one just waved an arm and said, "None of your concern. Proceed, sir. And have a safe evening."

A safe evening. Maybe somebody *would have one.*

Before he had died, Drew's dad had mocked the new gun, saying there was nothing wrong with the M-14 rifle he carried, though he would always prefer the Winchester .30-.30 and the .45-caliber long-barreled Colt revolver.

Drew had gone through training at the Montana Sheriffs and Peace Officers Primary SWAT Academy two years earlier. Long days, ten hours minimum, often up to thirteen, but it had been a good course, though he had shot at nothing but targets with the semiautomatic rifle. And had hoped he would never have to use the vicious rifle except for target practice and training exercises.

Other troopers were doing the same thing. Will Ambrose was talking to a couple of suits who huddled over a computer screen in a highway patrol van watching the video from a drone they had launched. For a moment, Drew wondered what his dad would have thought about a drone.

The cell phone buzzed, and he looked at the number, hoping it would be Billy's. Drew had called a dozen times, and each time was immediately rolled over to voice mail. He hadn't left a message. The number he saw sickened him, but he tapped the green icon and said, "Mr. Broadbent." He held his breath, waiting.

"She's still in surgery, John. A nurse came over a minute ago to say there's no change, but said that Mary's strong. She'll need strength."

Drew bit his lip to keep from exploding. He glanced up, saw Ambrose and a female detective walking toward him.

"Everything else all right, sir?"

"Yeah. Her mom's worried sick. So am I. It's just—" He sighed heavily.

"I have to go, sir," Drew said curtly. "Keep me updated, though. If I don't answer, just leave a message." He ended the call, slid the phone into a pocket, and fired off a dozen curses at Mary's dad for a meaningless call, then cursed himself for blowing up at the poor man. He would apologize later. To both of Mary's parents. Right now, he had work to do.

"It's all right," he told Ambrose and the tech.

"John," Ambrose said after stopping about six feet in front of the sheriff. "There's no sign of your son's pickup at the ranch house."

Drew's stomach turned into knots. He bit his bottom lip. "The barn?" That was a stretch. He knew it. But it was an option.

"I don't think so, Sheriff," the tech told him. "There's no clear view from overhead, but the door to the barn is open. We zoomed in as tightly as we could. Couldn't risk lowering altitude in case someone spotted the drone. Nothing resembling tire tracks. One cowboy led a horse to the barn, went inside, came out, and walked to the bunkhouse—" She probably would have kept right on talking, explaining why the chances of the Frontier being hidden in the barn, and offering a dozen other possibilities.

But he stopped her by raising his hand.

Then he looked at Ambrose, who shook his head and asked, "Any idea where else they might be?"

Drew could think of 760,000 acres. But the truck hadn't gone past the checkpoint where Mary had been shot. There were patrolmen and women cruising all over Cutthroat County. The shooter wouldn't be stupid enough to hide in Basin Creek. Drew clutched the AR-15 hard in his hands.

If the cop-killer who had also slain Harry Sweet had Alyson Maddox and Billy hostage, it made perfect sense he would have taken them both to Ashton Maddox's place. *Unless he killed them both and dumped their bodies somewhere.*

Drew closed his eyes and shook his head at that thought.

And thought of something else.

He had picked up Mary at the apartment and taken her to the Busted Stirrup.

"Is this a date?" she asked with that twinkle in her eye.

He frowned. The cat hissed at him. He hissed back, hoping for a laugh, or a smile. From Mary. Not the dumb, fat cat.

"It's—" He made the mistake of looking into her eyes. "It's . . . a date," he told her. "If that's all right with you."

She shrugged. Then giggled like she was in eighth grade. "It's most certainly all right with me." She threw on her jacket, found her compact, stuck that in her purse, and stepped outside, closed the door, locked it, checked to make sure it was locked, turned, and smiled.

"I'll behave."

He laughed. His stomach acted as though he was in eighth grade. No, tenth, when he'd picked up Mary Beth Lewallen and drove her all the way to that old burger joint in East Glacier.

Somehow he reached for Mary's hand, and she fit hers right into his. He was much taller, but their stride was almost the same. He realized he'd parked too close to her apartment. They didn't have far to walk.

He gave her hand a gentle squeeze. She squeezed back.

He swore. Stopped. Stared at her and pulled his hand away, shaking it. Part of it was an act. But he was completely honest when he told her, "You don't know your own strength, do you?"

"Of course I do," she said brightly. "Semper Fi, Sheriff. I'm a Marine."

A patrolman at the gate ended the memory. "Vehicle approaching! Vehicle approaching!"

Drew stared as a dozen cops dropped to their knees and aimed myriad weapons at the dirt road. The woman tech stepped behind a van. Will Ambrose unholstered his revolver and began speaking into the microphone. Drew walked forward, stood in front of his Interceptor parked directly in front of the gate, and butted the AR-15's stock against his shoulder.

The sun had vanished behind the Always Winter's tallest peaks, but it was still light enough to find a target.

"What the—!"

Ashton Maddox braked the Ford Expedition as soon as he topped the incline and saw what looked to be the entire Montana Highway Patrol and Cutthroat County Sheriff's Department in front of the main gate. In his life, he had stared down a pistol barrel twice, and a rifle barrel three times. But he had never seen that many weapons aimed at him and hoped he never would again.

Someone—it had to be Will Ambrose—spoke into a megaphone. The words were muffled. What he had paid for that SUV, he demanded a quiet ride. He killed the image. He didn't need to hear what that cop was telling him. The assault rifles made it absolutely clear.

After killing the motor, he opened the door. He hadn't fastened his seatbelt yet. He usually waited to do that till he was past the gate. Slowly, he stepped out of the Expedition, keeping his hands up and away from his body.

Will Ambrose lowered the megaphone. "Is anyone in that SUV?"

"No. What the devil are you doing on my property? What—"

"We are on the county easement, sir."

That peckerwood of a sheriff walked up to Ambrose's side, holding an assault rifle. At least it was aimed at the ground. An army of cops, though, kept their weapons pointed at Maddox and his rig.

"Open the gate, Ash."

"Why don't you tell me what the devil's going on?"

"Open the gate."

He felt sweat on the back of his neck, and it was a cool day. He inched closer to the Expedition. Keeping his left hand raised, he stuck his right arm inside the SUV and punched the button on the opener fastened to his visor.

The gate slowly opened.

When Ambrose and some of those storm troopers started in, Ashton slammed the Ford's door and yelled back at them. "Show me your search warrant before you set foot on my property."

The state cop stopped, and so did his storm troopers.

But John T. Drew came ahead, still holding the nasty-looking rifle, but keeping the muzzle aimed at the dirt. "Where's Alyson?"

"She better be in Den—" Ashton stopped, feeling the anger leave him in an instant, replaced by unequivocal dread.

If he hadn't been worried sick over his own son, Drew might have felt sorry for the rich rancher. The color had drained from Ashton Maddox's face when he'd learned about his daughter. His head shook hard to remove the confusion, the cobwebs, the sickening feeling that numbed his entire body. Just as it had Drew's for a while, before he had to man up, as the saying went, and remember he had a job to do. Though right about then, he wished no Drew had ever pinned on a county sheriff's badge.

"I was looking for"—Maddox shook his head—"I thought maybe Taisie forgot the gate code." The tone was almost dreamlike.

Drew had never seen Maddox not in complete control. "Taisie? Taisie Neal?"

Ashton nodded. "She was coming over."

Darkness started coming quickly. Headlights were turned on on the emergency vehicles, and troopers began putting up orange pylons on the highway, and portable lights.

One officer asked if this was wise, giving away their location. Drew had a bigger concern. The lights might attract all those news crews, but maybe not. They were all likely watching themselves on the televisions at the Busted Stirrup or the Wild Bunch.

Maddox blinked slowly, still trying to come to grips with what he had just been told. He found his cell phone, probably the FAVORITES page, and tapped the screen, then brought the phone to his ear.

He swore, and Drew could guess why. It was rolling straight to voice mail—the same result he had gotten in countless calls to his son that day.

"Taisie. Call me. Now." Ashton took the phone away from

his ear, hit another button, and listened again. He swore. “Sweetie. Call me.” When he disconnected and put the cell phone away, he was back in control. “What are you doing here?” He stepped toward Will Ambrose. “There’s nobody here except me and my hands. You cops need to be finding my kid. And Tai . . . and my attorney.”

Drew was already punching his phone. He waited till he heard Denton Creel. “Denton, where are you?” He nodded at the response, then frowned. “No. Nothing. Listen, I want you to run by Taisie Neal’s house. You know where she lives, right? Good.” He looked at Maddox. “She still drive that little Honda?”

Maddox nodded. “Yeah. White.”

“Know the plate number?”

The rancher shook his head.

Ambrose said, “We’ll get that to Creel before he reaches her house.” He turned and barked a command to a female trooper, and she was on her radio just seconds later.

It had turned so dark, they needed flashlights.

Another car was coming. Rubbernecking, it slowed down like all drivers did, but the big pickup stopped.

Spotlights bathed the truck.

The driver stepped out, and Drew sighed. The last person he wanted to see was George Grimes. Then the passenger door opened, and Hassun stepped onto the gravel.

CHAPTER 29

"Ouch!"

Alyson Maddox brought her left hand up to her head that had slammed against the pickup bed when the Nissan stopped. She figured she already was bruised all over from bounding around in this stinking truck. She saw nothing, but felt the warmth of Billy the Loser Drew.

And heard him whisper, "Are you all right?"

No, she wanted to cry, but instead she shushed him. Her eyes saw only black, but she stared at the tailgate, then sighed as the front door to the truck opened.

"Where are we?" he asked.

"The second gate."

He inched toward her. "So you do know where we're going."

"Shhhhhh."

To her surprise, this Drew boy actually listened. She waited, hoping Taisie would have trouble with the wire trap. Then maybe . . . maybe . . . Maybe what? What chance did Alyson have of breaking out through the bed cover. All that would do would get her killed, most likely, though she was pretty sure she wouldn't live much longer anyway. But that freak would also kill Taisie and the Drew jock. Not that she cared for either one, but—

One door shut, then another. Alyson sighed, then muttered an oath. That's right, she remembered, Taisie grew up in North Dakota . . . on a ranch . . . but she had forgotten how to drive pickup trucks in pastures.

Alyson bounced around again, and Billy put a strong arm around her. She started to shove him off, then suddenly she wanted to be held by someone. Even a dirty Drew.

"There are two more gates," she told him. "Then it's a really long way to the timberline and the hills. The creek is just a few yards into the woods."

"Do you think he's meeting someone?"

"No." But all sorts of thoughts raced through her mind. A helicopter landing to get him out to safety. *Don't be ridiculous,* she told herself. *This isn't a James Bond movie.*

There were no trails, other than those made by the cattle as they moved up to the summer pasture or back down to the winter graze. Off to the west, any man trying to escape the law would find himself up against a bigger law—the law of nature. The law of the Always Winter range.

The truck would be found easily once her dad sent someone to check on the stock. The cops probably had already located that lawyer's Honda by the swimming hole. She didn't think the killer would be taking them all the way to the section to kill them, just to make some kind of statement. The man was crazy. No, he was just a cold, calculating killer.

"The bridge?" Billy asked.

She bounced around more, and he held her tighter, even pulled her against his body.

"The bridge." She tested his question. Alyson hadn't been to that bridge in years.

"Eighth grade history. The mayor—he was teaching school then"—she heard herself saying—"that some men rustled Circle M cattle by taking them up Dead Indian Pony Creek. Then hid them in Big Coulee."

"No," Billy Drew said. "You're mixing up two stories."

Her head hit the bed again. She cursed. He held her tighter.

"Dead Indian Pony Creek. The Blackfoot got away using Dead Indian Pony Creek. Big Coulee was when—"

"Who cares?" She practically shouted that, but breathed deeply, telling herself to keep control, keep control.

He held her tighter. And she let him.

"But," she whispered, "the highway patrol—they have roadblocks all over." Her head shook before he could think up some lie to make her feel safer. Like anyone could feel safe there. Since there were too many ranch roads in Cutthroat County, you'd need the National Guard to watch them all. Especially at night.

Alyson knew they wouldn't cross the bridge and head into the high country, but they could travel back to the county highway. But then what?

They remained quiet, getting bruised and battered, but he pulled her even closer and it was nice, she decided, to be held. On what probably was going to be her last night on this earth alive. She dammed the tears that wanted to come out and bit her bottom lip to stop all of that self-pity. But she still let Billy Drew hold her.

The pickup stopped. The engine kept running. The two doors opened.

This gate. Then one more.

Then they'd be at . . . *the end of the road?*

"You ain't bagged that cop-killer yet?" The dirty Texas Ranger laughed.

And Ashton Maddox wished John Drew would have torn the SOB's head off.

Instead, the sheriff looked at Hassun and asked, "You found something?"

The old Blackfoot shrugged. “Maybe something. Maybe nothing.”

“Awww.” George Grimes patted his pockets for a cigarette, but found nothing. These days he would have a hard time bumming one off a cop. Giving up, the wretched man coughed a couple of hacking coughs before recovering and pointing up the highway. “The chief and me went back to the pasture where that puncher got whacked.” He nodded up at the tall Hassun as though he admired the Blackfoot, which struck Ashton as odd. Texans admired nobody—except, maybe, other Texans.

“You got a right good tracker here, boss man. He had me shining a flashlight and he still found some things none of them hifalutin fooo-wren-sicks experts could figure out in a month of Sundays.”

“Get to the point, Grimes,” Drew ordered.

But it was Hassun who spoke. “The white man who died stepped off his pony. He led the pony—this is how I read the signs, anyway—toward the unknown man. The unknown man shot him. The pony ran away. Come back later.”

Drew considered that, but one of Will Ambrose’s minions shook it off with a laugh. “That doesn’t tell us who killed the cowboy.”

“It tells us that Harry Sweet knew the guy,” Drew said, testing the sentence on himself as well as all those cops with him. He hated seeing that publicity-hungry arrogant Texas SOB grinning in the headlights.

“Come on,” the cop countered. “Everybody I’ve talked to said Sweet was a good ol’ boy. He saw a stranded man and—” Those words died in the cop’s throat.

Will Ambrose probably spoke what that young detective was already thinking. “You think anyone in Cutthroat County would walk up to a stranger . . . on foot?”

Officer Win said nothing else.

Hassun turned and looked at the detective. "I go back now."

"To the rez?" Ambrose asked.

"To the pasture where cowboy died." Hassun stared hard at Grimes. "Take me."

The Ranger didn't like that idea at all. "What on earth for?"

"Cowboy drive cattle, right?" He looked at Drew, who nodded.

"Where those cows go?"

Will Ambrose's and John T. Drew's phones buzzed again. Drew saw the Broadbent number and swallowed down the fear, but he answered. Ambrose was walking away, listening to whoever had called him.

"John."

Drew cleared his throat, but before he could even grunt, Mary's father said, "She's out of surgery, John. That Haddad fellow just came out. He said it was clean and quick and . . . the bullet's out." The man started crying. "Both doctors said the damage looks minimal. She's not out of the woods yet but . . . Oh, God, oh thank the Lord. We're praying."

Drew saw Ambrose lower the phone. The lieutenant mouthed, *Hang up now.*

"Thank you, sir. Thank you." Drew ended the call. And thought, *Semper Fi, Sheriff. I'm a Marine.*

"We're idiots," Ambrose said, and pointed. "Corporal Hazen just found Miss Neal's Honda in front of a water hole off a road just two hundred yards from us."

"This is it?"

Taisie Neal sighed. "It's the last gate. We still have a few miles to go before we're at the creek."

The killer stared out the windshield, seeing what the pickup's headlights showed and nothing else. "Get out," he told her.

She left the Nissan's engine running, opened the door,

wondering if as soon as she opened the gate he would kill her. Behind her came the noise of the psycho opening his door and stepping outside. She figured he was resting his arm against the angled frame that held the windshield, taking careful aim, waiting for her to make some stupid move.

The only stupid move she had made all night was driving over to Ashton's home. And it had been her idea. She was shocked he had even agreed to the idea, but, well, it must have been a long day for him. A long week. And now it was getting even longer.

Another freaking wire trap. If she hadn't grown up on a North Dakota ranch, the assassin aiming an automatic pistol at her back would have likely shot her in the back long ago. She worked on the post, and stared at the night sky . . . praying to see a helicopter or plane, maybe a drone.

That made her wonder if any law-enforcement agency in the big state had drones.

Then . . . How would evidence gathered by a drone hold up in a court of law? Would a search warrant be required first? Drones had been criticized as an invasion of privacy, but warrants, of course, cared nothing about privacy, as long as you could find a reasonable judge to think issuing a warrant was legal and legit and couldn't be overturned by a higher court.

Shut off that legal brain, she told herself. *You're going to be murdered before daybreak. It's a miracle you're still alive now.*

All she saw were brilliant stars. *Well, at least I'll see something beautiful before I'm killed.*

The post dipped below the hard wire, and Taisie dragged the barbed-wire gate to the far side of the road. The night was cool. She should have thought to have thrown a jacket in the Honda, but then she had not expected to wind up on section fifty-four. And she wasn't in her Honda. She was driving an old pickup that smelled of jockstraps and horny teenage boys.

She sucked in a deep breath, turned, and studied the ground instead of the headlights. She couldn't make out the man until she got closer, and then he was slipping back into the passenger seat and closing the door.

The gun remained aimed at her when she got into her seat.

She paid him no attention. Just closed the door, found the gearshift with her right hand, and the steering wheel with her left. Pressing the accelerator, Taisie drove past the gate, and did not stop to shut it.

That might be her salvation—or maybe it would save the lives of those two kids bouncing around in the bed of the ancient pickup.

At the first gate she had opened, then driven through, the madman had asked, "What about the gate?"

She'd laughed. "Cowboys are lazy. They leave the gate open till they drive back through."

This should do it. She could practically feel the bullet entering her brain. She breathed in. Out.

The man chewed on that for a minute.

"But no cowboy came through here. Tomorrow—"

"Tomorrow they'll be on the other side of the ranch, practically all the way down to Flathead County." She was pushing her luck. "And if Norris, the dumb oaf, sees the gate open, he'll just close it and cuss out all of Ash's men on the payroll. None will say they did it. None will say they didn't do it." She cursed them as ignorant oafs.

She had left every gate open. Breaking the law of every cattleman, farmer, cowhand, sheepherder, goat tender in the United States. It was understood you left a gate exactly the way you found it.

This man was dumber than Taisie's fellow students at the Chicago-Kent College of Law. But this man had also shot a Cutthroat County sheriff's deputy.

"It's going to get bumpy, mister," she told him. "Would

you mind putting that piece away. We don't have that much farther to go."

She regretted the last sentence. It could be the end of the line for her. And the killer did not listen to her.

Instead he raised his arm and put the muzzle just a few inches from her temple. "Then," he said softly, "you best not hit any big cow turds."

1891

July

Chapter 30

The Good Lord looks after fools and Cutthroat County's first sheriff, Napoleon Drew thought. *So far, at least.* He watched old Keme inching along the flat outcropping, toward the narrows.

Ben Penny landed next, quietly as possible. "How'd you know about this place?" the cowboy whispered.

Napoleon looked above, watching old Weems inch down the rope. The lawman held his breath. If someone saw Weems climbing down, the surprise would be over. Deke Weems would be dead. And so would, in all likelihood, Keme . . . Napoleon . . . the young cowboy . . . and Murdo Maddox.

But Weems moved down. Dropping the final ten feet, he landed on the ground with a soft curse, and pushed himself up. Napoleon watched the swinging rope. Someone might still spot that, but once it stopped swinging, it would blend in with the rocky wall and be hard to see from below.

Keme was still moving like a sloth. Then he checked his rifle, and looked at the curious cowboy. "Long ago," he whispered to Penny, "a band of Shoshones came here. To take some Blackfoot scouts. The story has been told for ages that the Blackfoot village had camped here."

"To hide?"

Napoleon's head shook. "They had driven some buffalo over the edges. It's how they hunted way back then. But a Gros Ventre brave had seen the Shoshone. The Gros Ventre and Blackfoot were allies. He warned them, and they climbed up here. Waited."

The old foreman was moving toward them now, carrying his rifle, keeping low.

"But you said we'll be above those ambushers, right?" Penny asked.

"We will. If we guessed right. The Blackfoot didn't climb this high. But that was a hundred years ago. At least. Likely even longer." Napoleon pulled off Maddox's hat and laid it on the dirt, then nodded at the cowboy's hands. "Take your gloves off. You'll shoot better without them."

The kid obeyed.

Something his father said came back to Napoleon as he blew the dust off his rifle. *"'There's no such thing as new. Anything that happened in history will happen again.'"* "We'll be shooting downhill," he told both men. "Aim below your target." Then he began crawling after Keme. "And don't shoot Maddox." *What were the odds of a Drew ever saying that?*

"What are we going to do for horses?" Ben Penny whispered.

"Try not to hit the horses," Napoleon told him. "Especially mine."

He stopped a few feet behind Keme, who slowly rolled over, his face suddenly grim. "They are here," he said softly, and held up his left hand, spreading out all the fingers.

Five men.

All right. Napoleon would have to kill two. At least. Keme could take one with the Sharps. Paid to ride and rope and brand, not kill their fellow men, Napoleon hoped the cowboys could take down two. Three. They would have to kill Lat Carson, too.

But then Keme said, "This is not how I remembered the narrow place."

Feeling a tightness in his throat, Napoleon held his Winchester out to Deke Weems, who took it with reluctance, and then the sheriff inched forward till he could see below.

Part of the wall must have collapsed, tightening the narrows even more. He rubbed his mouth with his right hand. Two men stood atop the fallen rocks. A third was practically out of view inside the narrow pass. The fourth assassin took longer to find. Keme pointed, and, squinting, Napoleon found him perched like an eagle in a juniper trying to grow about twenty feet up the wall.

All four of those shots would be difficult for the best of marksmen. And because of how the wall had collapsed, they wouldn't know when Maddox and Carson were near, except for the gunmen starting to aim.

The fifth man was easy, though. He stood far back, out of the narrows and where their horses had been picketed.

Napoleon scanned the rest of the area, looking for someone Keme, old as he was, might have missed. But there was no need for that. There were just five men.

"Kid," Napoleon whispered as he slowly sat up and backed up against the canyon wall.

Ben Penny stared, eyes red and wide.

"Draw a bead on the horse tender. We're not going to wait for Maddox. When I say 'now,' kill that one. Then we'll open up. Keme, take the one atop the rocks to the left. Weems, the one on the right. I'll kill the one in the tree. Then we all have to fire at that one hidden in the shadows. Only chance is to aim at the far wall. Just pour lead into those stones, and hope we get lucky with a ricochet."

The color drained from Ben Penny's face. "I just shoot?" He looked like he might vomit. "Don't give him no chance."

"They aren't planning on giving your boss a chance."

"But that one's just guarding the horses."

"Which we'll need."

He knew something like this would happen. But he couldn't blame the young cowboy. "Weems, you kill that one. I—" A shout and the reverberations of echoes stopped his order.

"Drew is at the point, boys! Shoot that law dog down!"

And the gates of Hell opened.

A grinning Mike McIlhaney rose from the cookfire when the rancher's cowhands—*rustlers*, Jeannie Ashton corrected—escorted her to the campsite in the widest part of Big Coulee where she saw a few cowhands already working their running irons on the cattle that had been driven into the perfect hiding place.

With a smirk on his face, he removed his hat, and gave a mocking bow as the riders reined up. "As I live and breathe, if it isn't the Widow Ashton coming to pay a call on her good neighbors." He nodded at the coffeepot. "Light down, lady. Help yourself."

She painted a smile and bowed slightly. "I'm afraid I won't be staying that long, kind sir."

A black-bearded man beside McIlhaney grunted.

McIlhaney sighed. "I'm afraid you will, Jeannie, darling. I'm afraid you'll never leave Big Coulee." He settled the hat back on his head. "As the saying goes, 'Curiosity killed the cat.'"

Another cowboy who was heating the branding iron in another fire stood up. He worked up the courage before asking the question, "You ain't plannin' on shootin' no woman . . . are ya?"

McIlhaney did not even give the boy a glance. "Maybe you'd rather spend a few years in Deer Lodge for rustling. And that's only if we aren't hanged, which is much more common in these parts than getting tried by a jury of our peers."

The black-bearded man turned back and stared at Jeannie. "I know a better way of killin' a fine, good-lookin' woman like that."

His grin revolted her. But she managed to look down at the rancher, and she gave him a wicked, condemning grin. "Now I know how you managed to get a cattle herd so quickly."

"I bet you do, ma'am. After all, wasn't your husband a rustler?"

She spit into the dust.

"Too bad, lady. We could've made a good team."

"I'll see you dead," she told him.

McIlhaney had no chance to respond. For gunshots echoed from somewhere up the coulee.

She had to hold the reins tight. And another cowboy walked forward and grabbed the bridle to her rented horse.

"What's . . . that?" She barely managed to get the question out—for she already knew what the answer had to be.

"That is the sound," McIlhaney said, "of a sheriff and a pompous rancher dying."

Work the lever. Squeeze the trigger. Work the lever. Squeeze the trigger. That's all Napoleon Drew could do. He had made the first shot count. The man in the juniper had whirled around, caught a bullet, and dropped the rifle, then somersaulted on the long drop down. If the .44-40 bullet hadn't killed him, the fall most certainly did.

The rest of his bullets were placed against the coulee wall. But if any one of those struck the squat assassin hidden in the shadows, Napoleon couldn't tell. White smoke from the hot

Winchester practically blinded him. The roar of weapons deafened him.

When the hammer struck but the stock did not kick his shoulder, he knew he was empty. And cursed the luck.

Lat Carson rode Napoleon's horse through the bend. He kept screaming, "It's an ambush, boys."

But the kid, Penny, fired a shot. Missed. He levered another cartridge into the chamber, fired again.

Drew wished he carried a .44-40 revolver, so he could reload from his shell belt. But the Remington .44 was worthless there. He came up. Penny fired a shot after him. Keme, with the Sharps, rose, but dropped the big cartridge before he could place it in the breach. He sighed, bent, found the heavy bullet, and stood again.

Deke Weems sent a shot after the rider, and started to waste another bullet, but Napoleon said, "Let him go. You'll just waste a bullet."

Then he turned around and looked as gun smoke and dust slowly dissipated. Staring into the bend of the narrows, Napoleon cupped his mouth with one hand and yelled, "Maddox? Maddox? You alive?"

The echoes of his question he could not hear. He could barely hear his own shouts for his ears rang from volley after volley.

No one moved below. He saw the dead horse tender, spread-eagled on the ground, the horses pulling hard at the tethers, but they had also been hobbled. He would have to thank the ambushers for being so obliging.

An arm dangled over a rock on the top of the cave-in, but Napoleon couldn't find the other man. And the one in the narrows? Napoleon cursed. He had no way of knowing. A glance to the west showed him the fading dust of the stock detective. "All right. We have to get down in a hurry. There might be more men we have to kill." He nodded toward the fleeing Carson.

Then he saw a man emerge from the turn in the narrows. The Winchester came up, until he remembered he had not reloaded. It didn't matter. The man was Murdo Maddox.

Which had to mean that the well-hidden ambusher was dead.

"Get your arses down here pronto!" the rancher bellowed.

DAY THREE

FRIDAY

Chapter 31

That high up in the foothills, the first glimpse of dawn arrived slowly, and the birds began flapping their wings while their songs and tweets finally gave the lawmen something to listen to other than the flowing of Dead Indian Pony Creek. Eventually, John T. Drew took off his night-vision glasses and rubbed his eyes. He tried to recall the last time he had slept—really slept, not just catching a brief nap—and rubbed his eyes.

It was cold. July could get cold that far north, so early in the day. His stomach reminded him of the last time he had eaten. Somewhere in the woods, he heard a cough.

"Quiet," a trooper whispered.

Will Ambrose had ordered radio silence. He had two snipers on each side of the creek, high up in the woods, wearing camo fatigues. He had ordered two other DCI men, one a Crow named Alton from Pryor; the other a former Green Beret. Both men were armed with AR-15s, but they weren't there to kill. They were the eyes.

Already having forgotten the name of the Green Beret, Drew started to yawn, but the cry of a mountain lion stopped that, making John T. Drew wide-awake. That Crow cop had sounded just like a cougar.

Closer to the bridge, Will Ambrose looked toward the path where Drew sat.

After blinking away the last of the sleep, Drew quietly moved his head and stared down the incline at the river. A few birds took flight. All noise stopped. That's how good that Indian's impression of a cougar had been. It might have filled those people walking in the creek with trepidation . . . if more than one person walked in the creek. He had to accept the real possibility Billy was dead. That Maddox's daughter was dead. That the lawyer from Basin Creek was dead. That the only person coming through the water was a cold-blooded killer.

His heart pounded, no matter how hard he tried to still his emotions.

And for one moment, he wondered what Ashton Maddox had to be feeling. Ambrose and Drew had been adamant the rancher had to stay with a bevy of law-enforcement officers far down what passed for a road near Neely Road, also known as State Highway 60. Only when he had threatened to arrest Maddox and have him jailed in Basin Creek did the man finally relent.

Drew breathed in and out as quietly as he could. His eyes focused on the dark water below. A trout jumped in a shallow pool somewhere. All he heard was the rippling current . . . and his pounding heart.

"Stop."

Alyson obeyed. She felt the pressure of the gun against her spine.

She could make out Billy Drew a bit behind her and to the left. That lawyer she couldn't see.

"It was a mountain lion," Billy said.

Her heart felt as though it might crack her ribs. She tried

to swallow, but couldn't. All that cold water numbing her toes, her calves, and she was parched.

"The birds have stopped," the killer said.

"Because," Billy tried, "of the lion."

"They should be spreading the alarm."

Somehow, the baseball jock managed to snort. "I think that lion just did that, mister."

The pressure left her back, and Alyson breathed in as much as she dared.

The cold voice behind her spoke to Billy Drew. "I don't need you, boy. One hostage is enough."

"You need Billy," Alyson heard herself saying. "He knows where the trail is that leads out of this . . . nightmare."

The man's curse told her what he thought of her opinion.

"It was a lion," the lawyer lady said. "Come on. We've been inching along all night. I can't feel my legs past my knees. I want to get out of this creek as much as you do. It can't be much farther, can it?"

As the automatic jabbed her spine, Alyson gasped.

"Walk," the killer ordered.

George Grimes was still ticked off at Am-broke, who was nothing more than some uppity highway patrolman, and John T. Drew, a lowly county cop. Keeping Grimes, the greatest Texas Ranger since McNelly, or even Hamer, at the state highway with the big Indian Hassun and a bunch of state cops, not one of them with a rank above corporal was such an insult. Plus, he was out of cigarettes. Had to bum a sissified Marlboro from a woman trooper who was ugly as sin.

And he was freezing his butt off.

But the sun had started to peak over the eastern mountains. He was as far down the dirt road as the state boys would let him be. He considered finding old Hassun and sneaking with the big Indian into the woods, creeping up to the bridge where the cops expected that murdering jerk to be wading up Dead Something Another Creek.

But he wised up and realized that was a good way to take a friendly bullet in the head. Or get arrested for obstruction of justice or something like that.

That Maddox rancher, well, he was down there, too. He almost had as much reason to gripe as Grimes, being the daddy of a kidnap victim and all.

"Lieutenant." The call came to another she-male cop on her radio.

"Amelia," the cop spoke into her mic.

"An SUV just turned onto the road."

George Grimes crushed out the smoke, smiled, and made a beeline toward the state blacktop.

Billy could see the trail. Off to the right and clear as day, even though daylight was just meandering through the trees and hills. Of course, if rustlers had driven sixteen head up that slope days or even a week or two ago, the trail would have been easy for anyone to spot. But the psycho with gun didn't appear to notice it.

Maybe because he was on his cell phone again, having ordered everyone to stop and keep their hands on their heads.

"You won't have a signal here," Taisie Neal told him.

"I'm texting," the man growled.

"It won't go—"

He silenced her with a motion toward the gun he had shoved into his waistband.

If only I could get closer, Billy thought. *Tackle him. That would give Miss Neal and Aly a chance.*

The man cursed, raised his hand in a rare flash of anger and started to throw the phone into the creek. He had made all three of his hostages toss their phones into the swimming hole. Not that they would have had a signal that deep in the wilderness.

But the kidnapper stopped himself from throwing the phone and swore. "Battery's dead," he said to no one in particular.

"From searching for a signal," Miss Neal reminded him. "I told you—"

He aimed the gun at her chest. Billy held his breath.

"And I told you, one hostage is enough to get me to Canada."

No, Billy thought, *not yet, anyway*. Not until Billy or Aly showed the killer the way out of the creek. That sealed the deal. They would have to keep walking. Billy prayed Alyson would keep her trap shut when he stayed in the creek, underneath the bridge. He had to figure out what he could tell the madman if he asked about that bridge—the old bridge. The newer one was a mile upstream.

Upstream was, actually, the treacherous part of the creek. Farther up he and Harry Gibbs, when they were sophomores in high school, had seen a sign on a trail that led to the creek.

Expert kayakers only beyond this point
Turn back—or die

"Well, well, well." A grinning George Grimes ran his finger across the dusty hood of a black Cadillac Escalade. The driver was the only one in the big, hundred-grand-plus diesel. The state trooper glanced at Grimes, who wiped his finger on his pants, and walked over to the driver's side.

"Garland Foster, as I live and breathe. What gets you out of bed? Wanted to see one of these Montana sunrises? Or get the first look of your windmills turnin'?" Grimes nodded across the road. "Some of them things ain't spinnin'. You forget to pay your electric bill?"

Garland Foster spoke softly, and Grimes laughed.

"My, my, my . . . such language." He nodded at the cop. "And in front of a lady."

The millionaire looked at the trooper. "Listen, I saw people on this road. And nobody is on this road at this time of day. I am on my way to Basin Creek."

"You mean you ain't here to help us catch some kidnappers?" Grimes asked.

Even in the gloaming, Foster's glare was unmistakable. "What kidnapping?"

"You must've been watching the stock-market channel instead of CNN." *This,* Grimes thought, *was fun.* "It's been all over the news. Montana ain't had this much publicity since Custer met up with ol' Geronimo."

Foster ignored him and asked the trooper, "May I back up and get to my breakfast meeting?"

The cop returned Foster's driver's license and stepped away from the Caddy. The millionaire, after giving Grimes the middle finger, rolled up the window, backed the Escalade onto the highway, and sped off.

"There hasn't been anything on the news about the possible kidnapping," the officer in charge told Grimes.

He laughed. "That's called detective work, missy. Tryin' to see if someone slips up. But ol' Garland Foster, he's too smart for that. He's too smart for his own good."

1891

July

CHAPTER 32

She saw the dust before the horse and rider. Everyone spotted the dust first. Jeannie Ashton sucked in hot air, and held it.

Horse and rider came around the bend at a full gallop.

Bringing up one hand to shield her eyes from the sun, she stared. The rider had to be a third of a mile away. He shouted something, but the words were a jumble of nothing.

"That's—" McIlvaney used his hat to block the sun.

The black-bearded man eared back the hammer of his rifle.

Jeannie whispered, "Oh."

Another cowhand struggled with the saddlebags near his bedroll, pulled out an old pair of binoculars, and brought them up.

"He ain't slowin' down," someone drawled.

"That's the sheriff's horse!" cried the boy with the binoculars.

The rifle came up to the lecherous cowboy's shoulder.

The rider's voice finally reached them. "We gotta get outta here."

"Hold up!" McIlhaney bellowed, but the rifle blast came before he finished the order.

The horse went down hard, throwing the rider over its

head. Gasping, Jeannie turned around quickly, refusing to watch.

"Lord have mercy," a cowhand whispered.

Her stomach turned, but she breathed in, out, steeling herself. Once the bile began to settle, she drew in a deep breath, and made herself look back down Big Coulee.

The dust hung for a long time in the Hole Where No Wind Blows. The horse was dead. The form of the rider did not move.

The cowboy jacked a fresh round into the Winchester, and, grinning underneath the thick beard, he looked back at his boss. "That takes care of your sheriff, boss."

"You fool," McIlhaney whispered. "You stupid fool."

The killer's lips tightened.

"Look!" The cowboy with the binoculars pointed. Then shouted with glee, "That's Marty. They did it. They did it!"

The horse and rider did not move, but just past the bend, five riders approached slowly. Too far away to recognize. The horses spread out. They rode slowly.

A few minutes later, Jeannie's heart quickened. "Well," she said, and almost smiled.

They circled wide around the dead gelding. He was a good horse. *But at least he took Lat Carson with him,* Napoleon Drew thought. He had seen lots of men with broken necks—lynched mostly, but a few from accidents or horse wrecks. But he had never seen one twisted that badly.

Napoleon would need a new hat. See if he could find something at the mercantile that would fit. He would pick up his sheriff's badge later. He wiped his right hand on his chaps.

The men who rode for McIlhaney would bury his horse.

Bury him good and deep. And they would bury whoever else decided to be a fool.

"That's far enough, Sheriff!" McIlhaney brought up a rifle.

Drew pulled on the reins. The rustler's horse he rode responded well. Maybe he would keep it as a replacement. Those owlhoots would not be riding for some time. Some of them, well, the next horse they sat might be under a gallows tree.

"You don't want to come any farther," McIlhaney shouted. "Or my man here blows this woman's head clean off."

The riders stopped.

Murdo Maddox stood in his stirrups. "That's Jeannie," he whispered, and felt his stomach twist into knots.

"You're under arrest for cattle rustling," Drew shouted. "You boys don't want to make it murder, too." He heard the laugh.

"You got it wrong, Drew. We got you outnumbered."

"Do you?" It was Keme who spoke. Then he sang out some loud war chant or something, and sank back into the saddle of the horse he rode. "Look!" he shouted.

Murdo didn't know what the old Indian was talking about. Nor, apparently, did the Cutthroat County sheriff. But they all looked to the rim around the northern side of Big Coulee.

Some rode horses. Some were afoot. Where there was wind, feathers waved. And that was just on the north side. Murdo turned to the south and saw more Indians. It wasn't the entire Blackfoot nation, but for a people who had been decimated by smallpox and other diseases, it might have been close. They began singing or chanting, whatever one called it.

A war song?

The Indian agent farther north must have been losing his mind right about then. Jeannie wondered how many Blackfoot men remained on the reservation.

Napoleon Drew kicked his horse into a walk. Murdo Maddox did the same. The others stayed behind, their rifles ready.

Three of the rustlers ran for their horses.

Hearing a hammer being pulled back behind him, Drew said, "Let them go. We have who we want." He and Maddox covered the distance at an easy pace, then reined up and let the reins fall over the gelding's neck.

"You're letting us go, Drew," McIlhaney said. "Or Mert here blows this lady's head off."

"You're not going anywhere." Drew put his hand on the butt of the Remington. "But hell."

"The lady dies if you don't back away!" McIlhaney yelled.

When the black-bearded man shifted, Jeannie took the chance. Her right foot came up, then slammed down on the killer's boot. Figuring it was the dumbest move she had ever made, she bent her head and upper body as far forward as she could.

The gun roared.

Her neck burned like hot lava, but she was on the ground, rolling over, seeing the gunman cock the revolver and aim at her. She was as good as dead.

But at least she would die on her own terms.

But the man's eyes lifted and so did the gun.

Smoke and flame belched out of the barrel, and then she heard only explosions. Her eyes closed. And opened. She was alive. Jeannie came up, turned, and saw McIlhaney on his knees.

Clutching his belly, blood spilled from his lips.

She brought her left hand to the back of her neck, screamed at the touch, but felt little blood. "Murdo!" she yelled.

Her eyes found the dead man. She gasped, then realized it was one of McIlhaney's men.

Murdo Maddox was on his knees, his horse galloping

away. His right hand gripped his left shoulder. His face was paling.

She looked up as Napoleon Drew dropped to the ground and let his horse—or the horse he had borrowed—gallop away from the fight.

"Murdo." Jeannie caught her breath and rushed to Maddox.

Napoleon Drew watched her run and wrap her arms around that son of— He wouldn't think of that and took a few steps toward McIlhaney, who'd sunk to his knees and raised his head. His lips parted, but no words came out, just blood trickled out. Then the eyes lost their light, and the man fell to his side.

"You fool," Napoleon heard Murdo say.

"You're the fool," Jeannie told him. "Both of you."

Drew turned back, and saw her holding Murdo's head against her shoulder, tears running down her face.

He drew in a breath, and found Keme.

"She has chosen," the old Blackfoot said.

"Yeah." Drew holstered the revolver.

DAY THREE

FRIDAY

Chapter 33

The lawyer, Taisie Neal, he saw first. On Sheriff John T. Drew's right, she was moving slowly in the flowing water. A few tense moments later, he made out Alyson Maddox and the cold-blooded SOB right behind her. Biting his bottom lip, he waited, then exhaled as softly as he could when Billy appeared. All of them . . . alive.

For the time being.

Light began to shine, but barely, through the leafy branches, the towering pines. Drew's mouth and throat felt like he had been in a desert for months. He tried to wet his lips, and slowly turned toward Lieutenant Will Ambrose, who was staring directly at Drew.

The DCI lieutenant's mouth moved and Drew read the lips. *It Is Your Call.*

Drew did not hesitate. His head moved up and down once, then he watched Ambrose's chin drop right above the mic. His friend whispered, "If you have a clear shot, take it."

"Stop."

Taisie Neal did as the killer ordered, and slowly looked at the cold-blooded man, who aimed the automatic at Billy Drew, who had slowly turned in the cold stream.

The gunman nodded, and Taisie knew why. Billy had not turned toward the trail that took fly-fishers down the lane to the creek. She might not be a native of Cutthroat County, but she had been up there with Ashton for some serious necking, and Billy's daddy had told her all kinds of stories.

But she had to hand it to the boy. The kid had guts. He was trying to take them all upstream.

But the man who had the gun was no dummy. "That is the trail."

Billy shook his head. Nodding underneath the rickety old bridge, he said, "That's the old one. There's—"

"Nothing up that stream except rapids and fish."

"Mister"—Billy was standing his ground, running a deadly bluff—"I've lived here all my life, and I'm telling you . . ."

The cold man smiled. "I studied maps before I came here, boy."

Billy's face appeared to whiten.

"You lived here all your life. And here you will die."

When he brought the gun up, Alyson kicked his left shin with her leg. The man was pulling away, taking aim at Billy, who dived as the automatic spat out a noise that sent birds flying.

Run! Taisie thought. Instead, she dropped to her knees and picked up the first stone she could find.

The killer must have slipped. So did Alyson . . . just as thunder boomed and echoed in the confines of the woods. No. That wasn't thunder. It was . . . a gunshot.

Alyson fell on her side.

The madman cursed. He had been aiming at Billy, but that deafening report caught his attention, too. "I will kill the girl! If you fire another shot." His dead eyes were bright with fury and the gun he held was coming down at her head.

Billy came up to his knees with a smooth stone in his

hand, and he side-armed it as he fell back into the cold water. He broke his fall with his free arm, screaming, "Hit the dirt, Aly!"

But she was already in the water, looking up at the killer, just as the stone hit him in the chin. The man twisted, then another stone splashed near him.

"Run, Aly!" Billy yelled.

She tried to get to her knees, but the killer was bringing his automatic down. Then he was flying backward, his pistol unfired. That booming noise from somewhere in the forest drowned out the gurgling water and Billy Drew's own pounding heart.

The first shot was muffled. For a second, Ashton Maddox did not know exactly what it was. Then came a louder report—and even that far from the bridge, he knew it had come from a high-powered rifle.

He started running up the road, but stopped. Another roar came from the forest. He would never get there. He wouldn't even be able to get through the barricade twenty yards up the lane. Changing directions, he ran to one of the DCI vans, shoved one small trooper out of the way, and bulled his way to where a woman with sergeant's chevrons on her sleeve was yelling.

"What's going on?" Ashton bellowed. "What's—"

"Shut up, sir," the sergeant roared. "Lobo One, this is Command. Lobo One, come in. This is Command."

"Command, this is Lobo One."

Ashton's mouth went dry.

"Suspect is down, Command. Repeat suspect is down."

He waited.

"All other parties are all right, Command. Tell Ashton his daughter is all right. So is the lawyer."

"How's the Drew kid?" Ashton couldn't believe what he had just asked.

The sergeant didn't have to ask. "Everybody's fine, Command. Suspect is dead. All hostages are safe."

He had not cried in years, but he bawled like a newborn, and wasn't ashamed in the least.

The coffee was how many days old?

It didn't matter. John Drew poured himself a cup, and stared at Mary Broadbent's desk. He tried to remember the last time he had been there, gave up, and glanced at the clock. At least the newshounds weren't so interested in him—not even the Montana press, or what passed for a newspaper in Basin Creek. He had heard one clip from Billy, saying that if his coach in Laramie had seen him make that throw, well, he would be signing a minor-league contract with the World Series champs.

But Will Ambrose had been getting the most attention. Like it was all over.

Drew's cell phone buzzed, and he saw the number, and put the call on speaker. "Mr. Broadbent."

"John."

He expected a bevy of questions about the dead man. Was this the same man who had shot his daughter? Why had he done it? What was . . .

"Mary was conscious, John. Just for a minute or two."

Drew straightened. Of course. He was such an idiot. The Broadbents wouldn't be watching TV. All of their attention would be on their daughter.

"She . . . re—" Mr. Broadbent's voice broke. "She recognized us."

"That's good," Drew heard himself say.

"She wanted us to tell you something." Then he started speaking to his wife, telling her he was getting to that.

Drew sighed.

"John."

He braced himself.

"It didn't make any sense, John. Maybe it's the drugs. But she recognized us. And asked about you."

"What did Mary say?"

"Well . . . it's . . ."

Drew tried that exercise Mary had told him about. *Breathe in. Breathe out. Breathe in. Breathe out.* Which he didn't think she had learned in the Marine Corps.

"She said, 'Trailer. SUV. Man. Man who shot. Dashcam.'"

Drew looked for a pencil, found one, and scribbled that down, waiting for Mr. Broadbent to finish. "And?" he prodded as gently as he could.

"That's all, John. Does it mean anything? I guess not. You got the guy, right. You're sure that's the one."

"It's an ongoing investigation, sir." Drew couldn't leave it at that. Not to Mary's parents, and added, "But . . . he's the one." Drew looked at what he had written. *Trailer. SUV. Man. Man who shot. Dashcam.*

"That's it, John. That's all she said. Does it mean anything?"

The door opened, and Dan O'Riley stuck his head in, clearing his throat. Drew covered the mouthpiece with a hand and looked up.

"CNN. You need to come see this, John. Now."

Drew nodded and once again, though politely, cut off the call with Mr. Broadbent. He left the wretched coffee cup on the desk, and stepped out. Following the county manager into his office, he heard the irritating voice of Garland Foster.

DAY FOUR

SATURDAY

Chapter 34

It hadn't all been Garland Foster. News reports had Alyson Maddox talking about her ordeal. Will Ambrose took most of the questions from the newshounds. Even Billy Drew got to brag about how he had made one of the greatest baseball throws in his career—with a stone, and in a creek. For a lighter look, there was a ten-second clip of Billy saying it was like an Old West incident when cattle were driven up Dead Indian Pony Creek by rustlers. Alyson countered that he had the story wrong, that the cattle were hidden in Big Coulee. Phyllis Lynne, Basin Creek's librarian, had said Alyson was correct.

Even though he had managed to keep himself out of the spotlight, John Drew had been congratulated.

Twenty minutes before last call, the Busted Stirrup was almost back to normal when John Drew entered the dive that evening. Most of the national press had rushed off to Missoula or Billings or Great Falls to catch a flight back to wherever they called home. Others were either still working on their stories or drinking at the Wild Bunch Casino.

He leaned against the bar and ordered a Moose Drool. The

bartender nodded, reached into the ice box, pulled a bottle out, opened it, and set it on the bar.

When Drew reached for his wallet, a smoke-ravaged voice said, "It's on me, boss man."

George Grimes sat beside him, telling the bartender, "Jack on the rocks. More Jack than rocks."

Drew thought about leaving the beer and the bar, but he was just too tired.

"Ol' Garland Foster stole some of your thunder, didn't he?"

Drew thought about what he had seen in O'Riley's office. Garland Foster had been speaking in front of the town hall, regretfully saying he had found incriminating evidence about his longtime foreman, Harry Sweet. Then the cameras showed Foster in Big Coulee, the wind turbines and a backhoe in the background. Only a millionaire like Garland Foster could find a way to get a backhoe into that big ditch.

What was it the Blackfoot Indians called it? The Big Hole Where No Wind Blows.

Well, down in that coulee, Garland Foster was blowing pretty hard. Harry Sweet had been the mastermind of a rustling ring that wasn't. Cattle had been stolen from various ranches, and hauled to Garland Foster's ranchland—unbeknownst to the millionaire—where the cattle were killed. "A wretched, horrible, inexcusable crime," Foster said. Then they were buried.

Even some of Foster's own cattle had been shot, left to be buried in the coulee.

"It was, I believe, an attempt," Foster told the cameras, "to tarnish the reputation of Sheriff John T. Drew, and I would not be surprised if the Citizens Action Network was responsible."

"He sure sucked up to you, boss man." Grimes fired up a cigarette.

Drew picked up the bottle, lifted it, set it back down.

Elison Dempsey had been on all the networks immediately

after that statement—cable news wasn't always biased or completely irresponsible—refuting Foster's accusations. Drew had managed to avoid any press, and he had ordered Denton Creel to refer all calls to the county attorney.

"How's your deputy?"

Drew sighed. "She was conscious for a minute or two today. But the doctors say they like her chances to make a full recovery."

Grimes snuffed out the cigarette and killed the double of sour mash. "Good for her." He motioned for another round. "I told Dempsey to kiss my fat arse. Don't want nothin' to do with them idiots."

"'Trailer. SUV. Man. Man who shot. Dashcam.'"

Frowning, the Ranger turned as the bartender filled his tumbler.

Drew turned and said, "What would that mean to you?" then repeated the seven words.

"Not a blasted thing." Grimes nodded his thanks at the bartender, and brought the glass toward his lips, but lowered it. "You off your rocker? You ought to go to bed. Drink that beer, pardner. It'll help."

"That's what the father of my deputy said. Told her dad to make sure he told me that."

The Texan shrugged. "Well, she took a nine-mil slug in her noggin, boss man. She's doped up on drugs. You saw the dashcam video. There was no trailer around. And the shooter wasn't drivin' some monster SUV but a sleek Mercedes sedan."

"With a fake license plate from a Wyoming man who's in England."

The old Ranger sipped the whiskey. "What'd she say again?"

Drew said, "'Trailer. SUV. Man. Man who shot. Dashcam.'"

Grimes took a healthy swallow, bit his lower lip, and shook his head. "Still gibberish."

"Yeah." Drew stood. "Help yourself to my beer."

"I never touch the stuff," Grimes said, but killed his Jack Daniels and grabbed the bottle. "Where you goin'?"

"To Mary's unit."

Drew went through the door, hearing the bartender yelling, "Hey, you can't take that beer outside. It's against the law."

And heard George Grimes's comeback. "That law don't apply to Texans, sonny."

The Montana Highway Patrol was using Rudy Pierce's Car, Truck & Tractor Repair as the lab, but now that the case was all but closed, only a couple of troopers were on duty. Sheriff John T. Drew had a free pass and signed in. George Grimes scribbled something next to the illegible name he had written down, which looked like *Mickey Mouse*. It didn't matter. The trooper would identify George Grimes, just like everybody in Cutthroat County could.

Mary's SUV was covered with a highway patrol tent. How the police had managed to put that up in the wreck of a garage baffled Drew, but he put on the plastic gloves, the surgical cap, and everything else, even those plastic wraps over his cowboy boots.

"Do it," he told Grimes. "We're by the book. No one's walking on some technicality."

Grimes laughed, cursed, but grabbed the nearest gown.

Drew sat in the driver's seat. Grimes leaned in and watched as the sheriff maneuvered the camera to fly through the jumpy film of Mary getting a bullet in her head, Ashton Maddox performing his heroics, then fuzzy pictures of nothing. He let the film run and then . . . darkness. A trailer on some road, a big SUV on the roadside. The flashing lights atop Mary's Interceptor. Beside the trailer was a cowboy.

"Harry Sweet," Drew whispered. Then he saw a sedan, but less than half of it was in the frame. It could be a Mercedes. A man walked around the side of the trailer.

George Grimes swore. "That's your killer."

Mary glanced at the guy, then focused on Sweet, who lit a cigarette. They chatted. The man leaned against the trailer as she turned to speak to someone off camera. Then she walked out of the camera. The man stared after her, and the video went black.

Drew rewound it. Went through it again, slowing it down, then watched once more. He swore, and switched it off. "Can't see the SUV. Can't ID the man Mary talked to."

"Your deputy can ID him. Even money says it's Garland Foster."

Drew turned, pulled himself out of the Ford, and shut the door. He stared hard in the dim light at the Ranger. "Why?"

The Ranger chuckled. "Let's say that trailer was filled with cattle were gonna be killed . . . or taken to market . . . till Foster got nervous."

"A millionaire doesn't need to rustle cattle."

The laugh became harder, then turned into a nasty cough. Grimes snorted up and swallowed phlegm and grinned that nasty smile of his. "This never was about cattle, boss man. Don't wanna brag, but this—"

"Not here," Drew said, raising his hand. He walked away from Mary's unit, pulling off and trashing the surgical gear.

The cat rubbed against George Grimes's pants leg, so the Ranger barked like a dog. Mary's cat didn't care.

Drew found a can and opened it, and that took the cat away from Grimes, who started to fish out a cigarette before Drew said, "No smoking."

The Ranger cursed. When the cat started eating a really late supper, Drew sat on the edge of the sofa.

Grimes propped his butt up on Mary's desk. "You ain't got a lick of evidence, pardner. Not one that'll hold up after one of Garland Foster's ten-grand-an-hour attorneys tears your D.A. a new a-hole. You savvy?"

Drew just petted the cat, though it didn't seem like he was really a cat person. "The man who shot Mary is in that video."

"I reckon we can positively ID him, too. But that man is dead. Killed by one of Montana's finest. But even a dimwit attorney would say that's why he tried to gun down your pretty cop. Harry Sweet . . . remember . . . he's the rustler. Or cattle killer. Tryin' to drive up the price of beef. Tryin' to get folks to eat more mutton. Who the devil knows? But . . . it all falls back to Sweet and rustlers and, according to Garland By-Gawd Foster, the C.A.N. boys."

Finding his pack of cigarettes, Grimes frowned, and dropped the pack back into his shirt pocket. "He shore throwed them boys under the bus, didn't he?"

Drew just stared at a photo of Mary on the dresser. Grimes glanced at it. "Friggin' Marine, huh?" He laughed. "Don't fret none, boss man. That gal . . . she's gonna pull through just fine."

Finally, the sheriff stood. "Foster," he said.

"You got nothin', pardner." Grimes coughed, snorted, and started to spit on the carpet. But swallowed instead. "What was he doing?"

"Only two men in this county," Drew said, "could afford that kind of hit man. Ashton Maddox is a prima donna, but he wouldn't try to whack his daughter and lawyer, especially since I see he has more than a professional interest in Taisie Neal."

"Can't blame him for that. She's a fine-lookin' gal." Grimes cursed at Roundabout and the cat scurried to find shelter. "But . . . what can you prove? Nary a shred of evidence and not even a clue. You got an election locked up. Don't that mean somethin' to ya, boss man?"

Drew cursed and walked to the door. "I'm going home."

Laughing, Grimes walked behind him, blew the hiding cat a kiss, and stepped into the early morning chill. "Sheriff," he said after Drew closed and locked Mary's door, "I've been at this a lot longer than you, hoss, and there's one thing you gotta learn and learn to live with." Free of cats and non-smokers' prejudices, the old Ranger lighted his cigarette, took a long pull, and blew smoke toward myriad stars. "The bad guys . . . sometimes, they get away. Foster'll slip up another time . . . now that me and you know he ain't just some wind-energy crackpot."

CHAPTER 35

George Grimes opened the door softly, heard snoring, and stepped inside. He started to close the door, decided against it, and clicked on the flashlight. Shades were open, and red lights were blinking on those newfangled windmills. Turbines, he meant.

Well, a king liked to look over his kingdom.

He reached the trunk in front of the window, leaned against it, and faced the bed. The light clicked off. The sleeper snored.

And Grimes yelled, "Rise and shine! Rise and shine!"

"What the—" Garland Foster sat up in his big bed. "Who's . . . Harry?"

"Over here, pardner." The flashlight clicked again, lighting up the Ranger's dark face. "Remember me."

The millionaire gasped. "Grimes."

"You win a cee-gar, pardner." The flashlight turned off.

"Get out." Foster's whisper sounded hoarse.

"You put on a good show today—yesterday, I mean. Did I hear you right, though? Just now. Did you say, 'Harry?' As in sweet ol' and stinkin' dead Harry Sweet?"

The rich man said nothing. Grimes chuckled.

"Get out."

"I will. Don't worry. And I wore my gloves. So I won't leave any fingerprints."

The man drew in a deep breath, which made Grimes happy as he could be.

"Here's my theory, Garland. Tell me if I'm even close. Those idiots come in with this idea of forming a vigilante group—like this is back in the Wild West days. And then some cows turn up missin' because Harry Sweet has learnt your windmill operation don't pay him much money. He starts stealin' some beeves, and you don't mind. They can hide in that big ol' arroyo—what y'all call a coulee here—and if the brand inspector or your county sheriff catch him, you plead plumb ignorance."

The millionaire said nothing.

Grimes snorted, spit on an expensive rug, and went on. "And then all of a sudden, those idiots with the Citizens Action Network start thinkin' 'bout bringin' in your ol' buddy from way back when, George Grimes, movie hero and Texas Ranger legend. Which shore might just ruin your reputation if George Grimes was to start talkin'. Lord knows everybody knows George Grimes has a gift for gab."

"Ol' George Grimes might spread the rumors 'bout how you had your Mex wife murdered before she could start talkin' to the Mex cops 'bout some illegal activities you had. Collected that insurance policy, too." He chuckled. "Makin' a ton of money off condos in Florida? That didn't bring in half of what you got helpin' a cartel or two. Ain't that right? How many hits did you have pulled on folks in Mexico and even here in the good o' US of A? And takin' some of your dope to peddle in Paris, and in England? No wonder you can afford to invest in Don Quixote's archenemies.

"No, you brung in your best man—and he sure was a good one—in cities. Dallas. Miami. Mexico City. Juárez. Celaya. Uruapan. He sure wouldn't have no problem bumpin' off a hick Texan like good ol' George Grimes."

"You're . . . wrong."

Well, it was good to know that ol' Garland Foster hadn't gone deaf and dumb. Or back to sleep.

"Am I wrong 'bout this? You contacted your ol' pal Santiago Scholz—that's what the feds say his fingerprints revealed. Mex-Kraut hired killer. Interpol was interested in him, too. Invite him up so he can kill me before I start monkeyin' up your works.

"You met him at night when you were also bringin' in some steers you swiped from Ashton Maddox. You and Harry Sweet, who, turns out, weren't so sweet. But what happened?" Grimes reached over and turned on a tall lamp, bathing the sprawling bedroom in dim light. Then he drew a throwaway .22 revolver and grinned.

"A pretty cop showed up. Sheriff's deputy. She was just bein' friendly, seein' if y'all needed some help. But she sees Señor Santiago Herr Scholz. Might not even remember him, it bein' so dark. But you can't have that. She might put some pieces together. So she's gotta die. Even before ol' Ranger George Grimes gets murdered."

"You'll never prove it." The millionaire made a bold move, throwing the covers and sitting up.

Grimes laughed. "Thing is, Garland, I don't plan to. Yep, it's all circumstantial. But I can't let you go 'round shootin' peace officers—and if I let you live, you'd have to kill me. It's survival of the fittest. And, even with my sour-mash belly and smoked-up lungs, I'm fitter than you." He aimed the .22.

And the rich man screamed, leaped out of bed, and moved to run out of the bedroom. "Don't do it!" he yelled. "I'll pay you anything you want." He tripped, fell onto the thick carpet, and rose. Pleading. "A million dollars! Deposited anywhere!"

Grimes stood and walked slowly, keeping the .22 pointed at the floor, his face void of emotion, except for the keen eyes.

Foster rose to his knees, tears streaming down his face. "You can't—" He looked for help, but saw an empty mansion. "Two million. Three."

Grimes turned to cough, and that let Foster leap to his feet and run out of the room. But it was a big house and a long way to the stairs.

Yet the millionaire reached the top of the staircase as Grimes walked out of the bedroom. He kept the .22 aimed at the floor, and his finger out of the trigger guard.

"Don't." Foster turned, hit the first step, the second, then started to scream. But that was cut off, when he tripped and tumbled. Grimes lowered the hammer on the .22 and walked to the balustrade.

The light came on downstairs, and Grimes swore. He brought up the throwaway gun, and aimed. Garland Foster lay sprawled on the floor. His twisted head was on the last stair, and he appeared to be looking out the window. At the blinking red lights on his wind turbines.

At the front door, Grimes saw another late-night visitor. He was out of uniform. And he held a .22 revolver, just like George Grimes.

Cops, Grimes thought, *can be so predictable.*

After he stepped onto the porch, John T. Drew closed the door.

"Fell down the stairs," Grimes said, and patted his pockets for a cigarette. "Broke his neck."

Cutthroat County's sheriff felt sick. The crisp Montana air didn't help.

"What were you gonna do, Sheriff? Beat a confession out of 'im?"

Drew stared ahead.

"You can arrest me if you want. I'll plead temporary insanity. Get a new movie made 'bout me."

Drew said nothing.

"The problem with you, John Drew, is your conscience. That man who shot your little lady was wanted by Interpol. He worked for cartels. So did that son of a—" He drew in a deep breath and slowly exhaled. "This is how they'd a-done it on the rez. This is how they'd a-done it in most parts of Texas. Justice is done, boss man. I done you a favor."

Finally, the sheriff faced him.

"I can live with what I done, Sheriff. But you couldn't. So . . . can you live with this?"

Drew didn't answer. He walked into the darkness, then stopped. "I guess you'll be leaving now."

Grimes laughed. "I don't know, Sheriff. I kinda like it up here. This Montana. It might grow on me."

"Let it grow on you someplace other than Cutthroat County."

"Hey, you still gotta beat Elison Dempsey in an election. You might need my vote."

"You haven't lived here long enough to vote. And I don't want your vote."

Grimes heard the lawman's footsteps as he walked away. "That law don't apply to Texans, pardner." But heard no laugh.

Once Grimes went down the steps, he wondered where the sheriff had parked his car. But that didn't matter. Grimes knew where he'd left his. And there was a bottle of Jack waiting for him.

"Sheriff." He waited. No reply came, so Grimes went ahead and asked. "I been hearin' 'bout this feud. Between Drews and Maddoxes. So after what happened today, do that mean the war between those two clans is over?"

John T. Drew did not answer. He kept walking and finally realized he still carried a .22 with the serial number filed off. He stopped and stared at the gun, then flung it into the pasture and continued walking toward his Interceptor.

I don't even recall what started that feud. I don't think anybody today really knows.

1843

Fall

Chapter 36

The Indian was drunk on whiskey from the Maddox trading post. Waving his arms and slurring the words, he sang as he staggered toward Cody Drew. Cody reined in the pinto and waited. The man grinned, spread his arms wide, pointed at the smoke rising from the log cabin's chimney, and begged for something he could trade for more whiskey.

He was Blood, as the white men called them, *Kainah* in the tongue of Siksikaitsitapi. He was not Siksika, as Cody considered himself—a Northern Blackfoot. But part of the Siksikaitsitapi confederacy.

Angrily, Cody pointed northwest to the land of the Blackfoot Speaking Real People. "Go," he said in English. Then spoke in his mother's tongue. "Go home. Go."

The Indian frowned, then cursed a white-eye curse, spat at the pinto's forefeet, and staggered off. For a long while, Cody sat in the Blackfoot saddle, staring at the post at Sacagawea Pasture. After a heavy sigh, he kicked the pony into a slow walk and watched the white-man cabin with the white-man sign his father hated because of the white-man words.

The place had not changed. No new settlers had arrived. At least, no new white settlers. A few lodges stood off in the distance, not too far away, and Cody wondered if those were for Siksikaitsitapi who desired to be closer to the blinding whiskey the son of his father's partner and longtime friend sold.

It was not his business. It did not matter. He'd come to trade with Ezekiel Maddox. At the empty rail, Cody slid from the pinto and wrapped the hackamore around the pole. At least the son of Cody's father's friend had chiseled a trough out of a cottonwood trunk and filled it with water. The horses could drink water—and not the whiskey that befuddled Cody's true people. *Befuddled. Sometimes blinded. And occasionally killed.*

The door opened, and Ezekiel Maddox stepped out, but the smile he had painted on his face to greet an Indian died. "Oh." The trader straightened and looked past Cody, probably for Cody's father, but saw just the drunken Blood making his way to his lodge far away or to wherever he would pass out.

"Today," Cody said, "is the day of my father's birth."

"So?"

"I trade . . . for . . . something." He thought. "Something good to give him."

Ezekiel's head tilted. "A birthday present, you mean."

It was not phrased as a question, but Cody nodded.

"Well." The trader's eyes brightened. "Come on in." He stepped back, holding the door open, and Cody followed, but could not help but catch the scent of the whiskey on young Ezekiel's breath. The trader's eyes were dimmed, too, as had been the Blood's.

The door was left open allowing more light into the dark room stuffed with plunder, most of it worthless, except for what Ezekiel Maddox took in as trade. The trader staggered to a big table, pointing at cloth and pans and trinkets. "Look around," he said, and found a jug, which he brought to his lips. "What do you like?" He laughed. Then set the jug on a barrel. "But first, what you got to trade me?"

Cody pulled the knife from its sheath, took the blade, and held it to Ezekiel, who studied it, and finally accepted the handle. After studying it for a minute, testing the sharpness with his thumb, he laid it beside the jug.

He picked up and held it out for Cody. “Have a bracer.”

Cody shook his head.

“Come on. It’s your pa’s birthday. You ought to celebrate. Lord knows that drunken ox will be in his cups if he’s not already.”

“No.”

Ezekiel set the jug down, and nodded at Cody’s waist. “Well, knives aren’t worth much. Everybody’s got a knife. You’ll have to throw in the sheath, too. It’s old, but the beads make it almost pretty. That might get you”—he looked around and, finally, pointed at a shelf in the far corner—“a tin cup. They’ll all hold whiskey.”

“I want something special.”

Ezekiel snorted. “Special. A knife and sheath won’t get anything special. Maybe that hoss you rode in on. Throw that nag in and, now, that might get you a bolt of calico. Maybe a Blackfoot squaw could make your daddy a pretty shirt.” He laughed, picked up the jug, and held it toward Cody again.

“Drink up, Cody. I’ll—”

It had been a stupid idea. It probably would have been foolish even if Ezekiel had been sober. Cody walked forward, and the white thief’s eyes brightened as he thought Cody was coming to take the jug, but he cursed when Cody picked up the knife and slid it into his sheath.

“I will find something else for him,” Cody said, and headed toward the door.

“Suits me.” Ezekiel laughed. “After all, how do you know ol’ Ben Franklin Drew is your actual daddy. I mean, those Blackfoot squaws back then—and to this day—would spread their legs for—”

Cody whirled, swung a fist without realizing it, and Ezekiel slammed against the barrel, almost knocking it over. Cody charged. Never saw the jug come up as Ezekiel smashed it against Cody's head. Cody fell against the table, then saw the jug coming back at him, but ducked. The stoneware container slipped out of Ezekiel's grasp and shattered against a case of rusted muskets. Cody reached for the sheathed knife. But Ezekiel was already charging, lowering his shoulder, catching Cody at the waist and driving him through the open door.

They crashed over the hitch rail, flipped over, and landed on the cottonwood trough.

Squealing, the pinto pulled the hackamore loose, and galloped away. Cody rolled over, his back and side hurting like blazes. Dropping to the dirt, he tried to catch his breath.

A boot caught him just below the ribs, and he grunted, rolling over on the grass. Out of the corner of his eye, he saw the wild-eyed trader diving toward him. His hands caught Ezekiel's shoulders, and he rolled atop the drunken louse. But the trader somehow managed to flip Cody over and away.

Cody rose to his knees as Ezekiel caught his breath.

Then both men grasped each other, dropped to their sides, and rolled over and over. Cody came up on top. He reached for his knife, found the handle, and pulled it out.

Then something grasped his wrist. The knife fell into the grass, and Cody felt himself hurled over. He hit the ground, rolled, and crashed against one of the posts that secured the hitch rail.

Through blurred vision he saw Ezekiel charging him. And as he pushed himself up, a bear of some sort wrapped its giant arms around the trader, lifted his feet off the ground, and hurled him headfirst into the cabin.

"Stop it!" the bear yelled. "Stop it you dern fools! Stop—" The bear stopped, gasped, and fell on its back.

Cody's eyes cleared. He shook the aches from his head, and saw . . . it was not a bear. "Pa!" He ran, slid to his knees, and lifted his father's head.

Lying on the ground, face up, Ben Drew clutched his chest with one hand. He kept trying to catch his breath.

"*Ninnaa*!" Cody screamed. "*Ninnaa*!" His mother's people's word for *Father*.

A shadow crossed the old mountain man's face, and Cody looked up, seeing a bloody, dirty Ezekiel Maddox staring down.

"Help," Cody heard himself pleading.

The trader started to bend over, then straightened.

Ben Drew stopped gasping for breath as a smile formed deep in his thick beard. "The sky," he whispered. "Look at that sky. And there's my sweet bride. There's . . ."

The smile remained, but the light vanished from eyes that did not close until Cody laid Ben's head on the ground and let his fingers slide the eyelids down. He stared for what felt like days. When he managed to look up, he found himself staring at Ezekiel Maddox.

"You don't bury him here," the trader said, spitting out blood and phlegm. "That graveyard's for decent white people."

Cody wiped blood from his busted lip. "I wouldn't bury him near a Maddox."

And he didn't.

He laid Ben Franklin Drew in a fine tree on a high rise, in the way of the Siksikaitsitapi. But Cody remembered how much his father had thought of Ebenezer Maddox and Linda. From the hilltop, old Ben Drew could look down on the rocky ledge overlooking Linda's Land where old Eb and his wife rested.

At least until Benjamin Franklin Drew's spirit found its way to the Sand Hills.

1891

July

Chapter 37

Abe Killone led about a dozen of his cowhands and what had to be a dozen or more men from Basin Creek—even the Swede and Luke Jasper—into the widest spot of Big Coulee before Napoleon Drew got out of the Big Hole Where No Wind Blows.

Keme and his people rode off a short while later. No reports came from the agency that any Blackfoot had ever left the reservation.

The way the editor Ira Batts wrote it up in the *Cutthroat County Messenger* made Killone the hero, claiming that Killone had saved Sheriff Napoleon Drew's posse from "becoming another 7th Calvary at Little Big Horn."

Lois DeForrest, reading over Napoleon's shoulder, pointed out that the newspaperman had misspelled *cavalry*. Judge Van Gaskin, the story continued, resigned his appointment, citing a need to return to a sick family member in Baltimore.

The governor, on the other hand, had wired congratulations to the sheriff and the people of Cutthroat County. Murdo Maddox was back at his ranch. Jeannie Ashton was most likely at her place.

And for a moment, Napoleon Drew felt sorry for himself. But that ended when the sheriff's children entered the cabin and said the teacher and all the kids at school were calling their daddy a hero.

"I don't know about that," he told them.

"I do," Lois said, then she ordered the children to go outside and wash up.

Napoleon watched them scurry to the water bucket, then he turned and stared at Lois. She smiled and put a hand on his left shoulder.

And Napoleon Drew, the first sheriff of Cutthroat County, didn't feel so sorry. Not a bit.

DAY NINE

Thursday

CHAPTER 38

When her eyes opened, Mary Broadbent breathed in deeply and slowly exhaled. *My Lord,* she thought, *I'm alive.* She closed one eye. She could see out of the left one. Closed that eye. *I'm not blind.*

She tried to move her right arm to touch her forehead, but that proved harder. When she slowly turned her head, which she couldn't move too far, she understood why. So many tubes and contraptions were attached to her arm, she felt like she was being transformed into . . .

She had to remember. She *had to* remember. Her brain had to . . . Mary smiled. "An android." She heard her voice. She wasn't mute either.

Another noise caught her attention. She wasn't deaf, either.

Boots clopped toward her and a man came into view.

"Hey," she whispered. Her voice sounded like she was ninety-nine years old.

Sheriff John T. Drew closed a book. His Adam's apple bobbed, and he inched closer. "How do you feel?"

Her answer was blunt.

"Well," he said, "I'm glad your mom didn't ask you that."

"Mom's here?"

He nodded. "So's your dad." He pointed somewhere.

She wasn't sure exactly where she was.

"I sent them to get . . . just to get out of the hospital. Get a meal. That little breakfast place we went to . . . three, four months ago."

"What day is it?"

Drew told her the date. He moved his right hand and she felt his fingers on her arm, above all the tubes and blinking things. "You came to a few times. Remember anything about that?"

"John." Her head started to hurt worse than ever. "John. There was . . . the man who shot me . . . I saw—"

"I know." He leaned over and she felt his lips below the massive bandage over her head.

"You woke up. Told your mom and dad. They told me. Well, your father did. We got the guy. It's all over."

"I told Mom?"

"And your dad."

"You got the guy?"

She was getting sleepy.

"We got him. It's all over. Everything's fine. You just need to get well."

Her mouth needed moisture, but she had to make sure. "H-Harry . . ."

"We know about Harry Sweet. We know about Garland Foster. He hired the man who shot you. It's a long story. But it's all over, Mary." His voice cracked a bit. "You're going to be fine." He was standing again.

And it looked like he might even be crying. But that wouldn't be like the John Drew she knew.

"Did they shave my head?"

He laughed, wiped his nose and eyes, and shrugged. "I can't tell."

"Johnny?" She was fading again. Just so tired. But there was so much she wanted to know—what happened? What day did he say it was? How was her cat? She didn't have amnesia. She remembered she had a cat, Roundabout.

"Johnny?"

He leaned forward, and she felt his lips on hers. Her eyes closed, and Mary thought she was smiling. "Do . . . Johnny? John? I mean, Sheriff. Do I still have a job?"

His voice sounded like he was in a tunnel. But what he said, before she returned to that deep sleep, made her feel stronger.

"Of course you do. Cutthroat County needs all the good cops it can get. And a sheriff like me sure needs a smart, strong deputy like you."

She thought she was smiling. Her head didn't hurt so much. She hoped she would remember this, and wake up still feeling his lips on hers.

"*Semper fi,*" she whispered. "I'm a Marine."

And she drifted back to sleep.

TURN THE PAGE
FOR AN EXCITING PREVIEW!

JOHNSTONE COUNTRY. NEXT STOP, HELL.

Civil War veterans Mac and Boone put the brakes on a crooked railroad boss's evil plans—using only their wits, their guns, and a few well-placed sticks of dynamite. . . .

All of America is buzzing about the new railroad line being built across the western frontier. Funded by a wealthy shipping magnate back east, this hugely ambitious project will expand his growing empire to the California coast—and crush his competitors in the process. This might seem like a golden opportunity for a lot of folks. But not Yankee spy "Mac" MacCoole and Rebel dynamiter Hokum Boone. Heading home from their latest job, they stumble onto the dark truth about this new railroad: the workers are prisoners, their families are enslaved, and their cruel rail boss is laying down tracks with their blood, sweat, and tears—on a one-way trip to Hell.

Thurston Kane is a cruel railroad boss using immigrants as "free" labor. The men are treated like mangy dogs, the women are shackled and sold to the highest bidders—even the children and elderly are mercilessly worked to the bone. Mac and Boone are enraged by what they're seeing. They're also armed to the teeth—with a Henry repeater, Colt's Dragoon hand cannon, sawed-off shotgun, and a few sticks of "widow-makers," aka dynamite. Their first order of business is to free a wagon full of chained women. Then they start laying tracks of their own—to derail this once and for all . . .

They say you can't stop progress. But no one ever said you can't blow it all to kingdom come.

Chapter 1

"Seems to me you ought to pay closer attention when I share a sweet memory of my cherished youth." Hokum Boone picked the lint from a knob of chaw he found in his possibles bag and stuffed it in his cheek.

His business pard and best friend, Keller "Mac" MacCoole, suppressed a smile and glanced to his right, well aware that the longer he refrained from responding, the more worked up ol' Hoke was liable to get. It worked every time. Mac took his time tugging out a black, finger-length cigarillo that looked less like a cigar and more like something a sick dog might have left behind in an alleyway. He licked the end, then popped it between his lips and scratched a match head with his thumbnail.

It flared, and as soon as he set fire to the end of the cigarillo, Hoke did what Mac expected. He set to moaning and clucking and growling as if Mac were working him over with a cudgel.

"You all right over there, Hoke?"

"No, I ain't all right, and you damn well know it! Every time you set fire to one of those godawful stinkers, I'm liable to expire from a case of the agonizing tremors I feel deep down in my innards!"

"You're certain it's not that hunk of old, used chaw you found in your pocket that's making you feel awkward?"

"No, I tell you! I hardly ever save my chaws for later."

"I know," said Mac, snapping his big fingers. "It just may have something to do with the fact that you are wrapped in a suit of greasy buckskins that haven't seen a good scrubbing, and neither has the varmint trapped in them, for many, many moons. Hmm?"

"No again! And I'll tell you a thing or three, Mister Think He Knows Everything! It just so happens that buckskins have natural smell-deadening qualities. You ever wonder why you are likely surrounded by deer and elk and such most all the time but you hardly ever smell them?"

"Except when they're in rut." Mac plumed a cloud of blue smoke over toward Hoke, who gigged his paint, Chummy, ahead a step to avoid the noxious cloud.

"Rut, my foot! You are in rare form today, MacCoole, and toying with danger! And besides, I happen to know you only smoke those stinkers to annoy me." Hoke almost grinned. Almost. The rangy woodsman knew he had to keep his ornery demeanor from slipping, lest he appear weak.

Mac wrinkled his own nose at the rank smoke he was generating and puffed again. They were not like any of his finer cigars, that was for certain. "You know, Hoke, I do believe that was the first true thing you've said all day."

"You mean to tell me you don't believe what I told you about Cousin Merdin and the half-woman, half-tree creature? Why, everybody in Hoddy's Gulch knows it for a fact, but then again, I'd expect doubts from someone such as yourself who hasn't had the good fortune or good sense to spend time in Hoddy's." Boone smiled at the memory of the place. "I ever tell you that the Gulch was named for my great grand-pappy?"

Mac nodded. "I do believe that earthshaking revelation has passed from your lips a time or three, yes."

"And you're a better man for hearing it, Mac MacCoole. Let me tell you."

"I can't disagree, Hoke, that at the end of my days I will look back on this life and I will say to myself, 'Mac, you have had a vast assortment of fascinating experiences, seen a host and a half of astounding sights, and heard sounds the likes of which you will recall far into the afterlife."

"Uh-huh, that's the truth," said Hoke, nodding.

"But none of those vivid, sweet recollections," continued Mac, trying not to grin. He knew Hoke would glance at him soon, and continued when he did. ". . . will ever compare with Hokum Boone's assortment of windy tales."

"Windy tales? That's what you think these are? Why, they are pure fact! Gold, I tell you! Why, people hear them and shake their heads! I don't doubt but they are thanking the Almighty for allowing them to hear such astounding truths!"

For a spell, neither man spoke as they plodded along, riding from the northwest back to their home base in Denver City. They were fresh off a mild town-taming job for a wealthy widow woman who owned an entire mining town in a valley in Oregon Territory.

Other than her trusted manservant, who Mac and Hoke suspected was also her longtime lover, Madame Steiner had claimed she could trust no one. And if what had been happening to her at a steady and alarming clip was an indication, she was correct. It seemed that the old girl's inherited fortune had been set up such that she had, up to then, little reason to root into her finances.

But it turned out she had been the long-term victim of unscrupulous, unsavory characters, namely a mine foreman, Eddie Tinkerson, and his rapacious wife, "Sweet."

And then, Madame Steiner's townsfolk, who all had been living a meager existence, beholden to Steiner and her business, noticed they were being short-changed on their weekly rations of flour and fatback bacon and sacks of beans. And trouble had begun. They were being short-changed on other supplies as well, discovered as Madame Steiner investigated further. She finally had cause to look deeply into the earnings of her many local mines, and what she found appalled her.

Steiner was at her wit's end when an acquaintance wrote telling of a couple of men who roved the West taking on jobs considered too unlawful for the law, and too dangerous for most other mercenaries to take on. But Mac and Boone were hardly ordinary men.

They received a missive from Madame Steiner explaining the situation and requesting their assistance. It seemed that money would not yet be a concern, though if the situation kept up it might well become a worry.

As the men had had little going on at that time, and had grown restless and, for Boone, at least, increasingly financially strapped, they wrote back to Steiner forthwith and accepted the work.

They rode to Steiner's Mountain, naturally, and had made good time. Within a week, they found themselves gracing the front steps of Madame Steiner's mansion.

It had taken them the better part of a month to infiltrate the inner group of Eddie and Sweet Tinkerson. The mine foreman had initially regarded them with suspicion, but as the days wore on, they proved indifferent and then useful to Tinkerson's larcenous ways.

One night, they plied Eddie with the last of Mac's decent bottles of whiskey he'd brought along. The thief had become a bit loose with his tongue, enough so they learned more in one evening than they would have in a month of further snooping about his nefarious deeds.

It turned out Tinkerson had been raking Steiner over the coals for years. At first he'd only dared to filch a little at a time, and always covered his tracks with the utmost in care. Then he began sending wagons loaded with ore down the backside of the mountain they mined.

As time had progressed, he realized no one was going to harangue him about his loosely kept books of accounting, so the greedy rat grew greedier. With Mac and Boone on the job, Eddie and Sweet's operation ground to a skidding halt.

Back on the trail and making for home, each man was mired in his own thoughts. Sometimes those thoughts overlapped, as with an old married couple. After a few long days on the trail, usually Boone would circle back and to say something about how they met all those years ago in the war, in a battle to the death, in the midst of a dank, dark swamp.

They had been surrounded with slithering, snapping creatures. And in the wet, fetid heart of that swamp, the two men had savaged each other, delivering a thousand nicks and cuts and gashes. None alone had been fatal, but if they had continued each would have surely laid the other low given a few more hours.

But in one of their mutual halts to catch breath and wet lips, the blood adversaries—Hokum Boone as a Grayback and Mac MacCoole as a Bluebelly, heard shouts—dare they guess? Perhaps some sort of distant yells of hoorah from beyond, up the long hill and back into the light of afternoon on the battlefield above.

They were beckoned, heralded by officers of each side standing side by side and shouting to them to cease their battling because the war had come to a halt. Lee had called it a day. It was over.

Those two men, one in blue, the other in gray, and each oozing red, had officially met. From then on they had become fast friends, then business partners, then best of friends, confidants, and foils for each other's foibles and jokes and follies.

Their trail banter, as had been exchanged on that day, was of the ribald and humorous, rubbing, ribbing quality.

They were, after all, flush with cash, following yet another successful mission during which their shared thirst for derring-do and adventure and excitement had been slaked. Plus, there was the bonus of them being able to help deserving parties to overcome forces seeking to do them harm.

Madame Steiner had smiled and waved and wept as they rode off, so grateful had she become to them. Her manservant, Willard, had even cracked a smile on his normally stoic face.

They'd stocked up on trail goods—bacon and flour and cornmeal and apples and dried fruits and tobacco and whiskey . . . and various other items—at the nearest noncompany town down the valley aways, which they would enjoy on their slow journey back to Denver City.

The weather was fine. No storms on the horizon that they could discern. Their horses, Mac's big Appaloosa, Lincoln, and Hoke's smaller but steady paint, Chummy, were in fine form, and they were on no man's clock save their own. And theirs, for the time being, had ceased to tick. Late starts and early camps were the order of the week. And that suited each man right down to the ground.

And then they met the women. After a fashion . . .

CHAPTER 2

Five months ago

The portly gentleman in Highland tweeds and plus fours puffed on a large meerschaum pipe. A commissioned piece, its ornate surface had been carved to resemble the man himself, complete with waxed mustaches, muttonchops, and trim beard.

Pipes and fine tobaccos were an indulgence Winterson Blaswell could well afford. He was, after all, a shipping magnate with primary offices in Boston and Providence and one of the wealthiest men in America. His mansion in Providence dominated a sizable wedge of premium real estate overlooking the busy port.

As he gazed out on the bustle and ebb and flow of commerce in the harbor, much of the trade of which his business accounted for, Blaswell smiled and grunted in satisfaction. He ruminated as he sent forth clouds of blue smoke into the high-ceilinged office with its richly carved paneling and thick imported rugs.

He had done rather well for himself since coming to America as a young immigrant from Latvia. He'd recognized various needs in life, needs others also recognized, but for which most people merely yearned.

He, on the other hand, had an innate skill—he'd heard

others call it a gift, though he never said this of himself, no, no—for finding solutions to problems, finding ways of turning needs into wants, and then supplying them.

Take ice, for instance, a worn tale he had often told his daughter, Philomena, at dinner of an evening. Oh, he knew the poor girl had heard the story of his rise to fortune a thousand and one times, but once he'd tucked into a third glass of red wine during their meal, he could not help himself, he simply had to boast, even a little.

And Philly, named for the birthplace of her dear, departed mother, always listened with a half smile, so like her mother's. It made Blaswell feel as if she really were hearing it for the first time and not merely indulging his bragging whimsies.

If there was one thing he could wish for, the one thing money with all its wonders simply could not buy, it was to spend another day, another hour, a single minute, with Philly's mother, Edna. Dear Edna, gone from their lives these last four years now, taken by a case of creeping chronic pleurisy.

"Trade it all," he whispered to his reflection in the window. "Trade it all . . ."

From behind him, a voice cleared.

Blaswell spun to see his right-hand man, the young Thurston Kane, standing with the inevitable sheaf of papers held before him, no doubt requiring his signature.

Kane was a decent young fellow, dapper, tending in his wardrobe selection toward the outdated but serviceable. This was also reflected in the man's speech and mannerisms. Despite this, or perhaps because of it, Blaswell liked the young man. He reminded the portly businessman somehow of himself some years ago. From poor stock, Kane had worked his way up and out of the bonds of poverty. He was shrewd and keen to learn. *Eager,* thought Blaswell, *and hungry.*

Best of all, it appeared as if Thurston Kane was fond of his Philly, too.

As she was no longer a child, but creeping into the first

years where the word *spinster* might well be muttered in the salons and drawing rooms of Blaswell's wealthy, if snide, acquaintances, Winterson thought perhaps it was time the girl were married.

The one impediment he noticed had been and continued to be her looks. The poor thing was not what anyone might consider attractive to the opposite gender. Not that Philly was homely, but neither had Winterson nor dear Edna been possessed of facial appeal.

This trait, unfortunately, had passed to their one and only offspring. But he most decidedly could say that what she lacked in looks, Philly made up for in mental acumen. Had she been born a male, he might be inclined to allow her what she always pestered him for—to help run his burgeoning empire.

Thankfully, Thurston Kane had come along. That might well solve both problems—the marrying off of Philly and the future of his empire. For Winterson Blaswell knew he would not be around forever. His attacks of gout had flared with more frequency of late, and the thumping of his heart, like a locomotive on an uphill grade, woke him now and again in the night.

Of this latter, he told no one. The former, he knew from his doctor's advice, could be solved by reducing his intake of sweet meats and whiskey and wine, even tobacco. "Perish the thought," he would say. "I did not work so hard for so long to abandon the rewards of such a life now!" Then he would smile and light up his pipe. Or a fine cigar. And hoist another after-dinner snifter.

"Sir?"

"Kane, yes, a good morning to you, son."

They both seemed to like this ritual, though it was well into late morning. Blaswell had grown accustomed to having Kane around, and in the short ten months or so since the young man had arrived and shown such promise, Blaswell had gradually loaded down the lad with more and more duties, telling himself the more he was able to do that, the more time he would be able to devote to important matters, such as establishing the new rail line, which would allow Blaswell to breach, develop, explore, and unfold untold new markets. Already his efforts, moving from planning to implementation with the recent establishment of an office in San Francisco, were making national headlines.

With all this exciting new momentum bristling in the air of the opulent office that morning, Blaswell and Kane surveyed the big map spread out yet again upon the central table.

"This will be the first and most important section of the new rail line, Kane. The bedrock, the very foundation spur that will eventually run from Chicolo, north of Sacramento, over the Sierra Nevada range, north to Oregon and Idaho. Why, not only will it reach into the newest and most promising agricultural lands and gold fields in all of North America, it will crack them wide open! Why, then it's all a matter of speculation, my dear boy. In short order, I dare say nobody in these burgeoning United States and beyond will be unfamiliar with the name Winterson Blaswell!"

The portly gent smiled broadly, rocking on his heels as if he were about to tumble right over backward. He set down his prize pipe lest he swing a waving arm and smack the gentle creation into a bookcase.

"Yes sir," said Thurston Kane, doing his best to maintain his serious demeanor. "Though I am hardly a judge of such matters, I will posit a notion that you must have already entertained yourself."

"And that is, my boy?"

"Well, that perhaps you should run for office."

"Do you mean mayor of Providence or some such?" Blaswell chuckled.

"Well, no sir. I meant on the statewide level. Or perhaps,

dare I say it, at the national level. Why, a man of your vision could easily hold the highest office in the land."

"Kane, Kane, you are a clever young man, that much is certain. But, though the office of President is not open to one such as I—I was born in Latvia, lest you forget—"

"Sir," said Kane, "pardon me for interrupting, but such laws are changeable. What is America if not a place of change?"

"Well, yes, that is true. But look, enough of that now, my boy. You have certainly given me food for thought. Yes, yes, of course I had entertained notions of perhaps one day sharing my, dare I say, expertise in building and shaping an enterprise into more civic-minded duties. But the time is not yet ripe. What it is time for is to plan next steps in the rail line.

"What I need now is someone on the ground out there. We'll set up an office, a base of operations in San Francisco, of course, but this person will have to arrive well ahead of time and meet those contracted firms we have lined up. There will be much to do, much to do. Once they are in situ, as it were, this person will need to meet the ships bringing the first loads of immigrant labor forces we have sent for from China."

Blaswell rubbed his pink hands together and smiled. "I tell you, Kane, being able to give all those families this opportunity! It's something I never had, arriving here as a penniless youth. Oh, think of the leg up we'll give them."

"Indeed," said Kane, thumbing through the papers on the table before him.

"Yes, yes! We shall establish encampments for them in which they will be able to work, live, cook . . . oh, the lot of it. Living, daily living. Only they will no longer be scrabbling for a meager livelihood in their natal lands! No, they will be in the United States of America, my boy. Working for a living, earning lucre to give their offspring the very best this bounteous land can offer!"

He thumbed his lapels and looked out the window. "And we will be there at the outset to guide them. Why, jobs building a railroad is just the start. I envision entire towns all along the routes. And one day those modest villages will become booming centers of progress and commerce, and populated with the very people we helped to bring here. Think of it, Kane, all of them contributing to this American Dream!"

"Yes sir," said Kane. "And all of them beholden to Winterson Blaswell and Company." As Kane said this, his eyes shone and he nodded in agreement with himself.

But his boss was not smiling. "Well, that may well be a byproduct of our efforts, surely, but it is not the primary motivation. You see that, don't you, Kane?"

"Oh, oh, of course, sir. I only meant that—"

But Blaswell was off, roaming the room again, setting fire to what Kane thought as his damnable pipe, and about to embark on another windy discourse about the wonders of his life.

Kane made to head him off before it was too late. "Sir, if I may . . . we need to discuss the applicants. I believe I left you the stack of their applications listing their qualifications."

"Applicants, Kane?"

"For the manager's job, sir. In California."

"Oh, yes, well," Blaswell waved a hand at the papers on his desk. "They are all fine men, I'm certain. But I have another idea in mind that I would like to discuss with you, Kane."

"Oh?"

"Yes. You see, it involves you, personally. It's no good having our enterprise being commandeered by a stranger. I need someone I can trust out there, man! This is the largest undertaking in our years-long methodical plan to broaden beyond the East. Whoever this is will represent the name Blaswell clear across the country. It is of the utmost importance that this person be eminently trusted and trustworthy. Do you understand?"

"Of course, sir, that's why—" He held up the papers.

Blaswell shook his head. "No, no, Kane, I'm not speaking

plainly enough for you. I see that now. What I need, what the company needs, is you, Kane. We need you out there. Don't you see? You're the only one I can trust such an undertaking to."

"Me sir?" Kane suppressed a wide, wide smile. Doing so was the single-most difficult thing he'd had to do since beginning work for Winterson Blaswell.

"Yes, Thurston. You." Blaswell stood behind his desk and leaned forward, his pudgy fists resting atop the blotter. "I suppose I don't have to mention how close you and Philomena have become in recent months. I may be her father, son, but I have eyes. The one thing I have hoped, for some time now, was that she should find a suitor who might be worthy of her, and of what she will . . . not to put too fine a point on it . . . but what she will one day come into." Blaswell bowed his head and waved his hands wide to take in the room. It was a gestured attempt at humility.

One Kane had seen before. One he knew was intended to encompass the entirety of Blaswell's massive holdings. And Thurston Kane did not take it lightly. He was suitably impressed.

Kane was not born into wealth. Far from it. In that regard he and Winterson Blaswell were much alike. But where Blaswell grew up believing in the innate goodness of his fellow humans, Thurston Kane grew up believing in the innate worthiness of himself and in the innate worthlessness of most others he met.

He felt that he, and he alone, deserved everything life could offer, nothing less than all of it. And if he was not to become heir to a fortune, then he could by god marry one.

That he had found such a person was no surprise to him. Finding Philomena Blaswell and then courting her was all part of his personal business plan. That she had a face like a mud fence, well, that could be tolerated and dealt with for as long as was necessary. Then provisions could be made to clear that fence from the landscape. *Time,* he told himself. *All in good time.*

By the time he had worked for Blaswell for a month, Thurston Kane felt he knew how the old man thought, how he went about things. Oh, sure, his employer could still surprise him, but for the most part he was confident he could land a solid guess as to Blaswell's next move in most any situation.

In fact, Kane often played a little game with himself, just for fun. He would predict what Blaswell's response was going to be before he consulted him on a topic, be it a new business venture, plans for the rail line project, or one of the many various shipping issues that invariably cropped up in a day's time.

Kane reckoned he was at a 90 percent success rate. And then Blaswell would lob in a skewed response that would throw off Kane's average. But that made it all the more fun.

And so, Thurston Kane was extremely gratified in the days following Blaswell's revelation that he wished Kane to head up the Blaswell Railway expansion enterprise on the West Coast. It was a decision Kane was not in the least surprised by, though in the days leading up to the announcement, he had been increasingly worried lest he do something to perturb his portly employer before the offer could be made.

He was also certain it would be a test to see if Kane was indeed worthy of marrying his beloved daughter, the horse-faced Philomena. *Ha,* thought Kane. Blaswell had on several whiskey-fueled occasions all but hoisted the slight woman into the air and handed her to Kane with his best wishes and kind regards.

Nonetheless, Kane decided he would work as hard on this project as he ever did on any project . . . perhaps harder. More to the point, he would make darn certain the immense task was completed ahead of schedule and, most important of all, so far under the projected budget there would be no doubt Kane was the very match for Philomena.

And that, in turn, would secure his future as all but heir to the Blaswell empire. He supposed he must also speed up the wooing of Philomena if she, also, were to take him seriously as a suitor.

She was less predictable than her father and had surprised him at times with her frankness and opinions over matters she should not have concerned herself with. This annoyed Kane, as he felt, as did Blaswell, that a woman's place was at home, fretting and wringing her hands lest her man, the breadwinner, the patriarch, come home late from the office.

"Ah, time enough for such concerns, Thurston," said Kane to himself as he beckoned a hansom cab on the eve of his departure. One last meal at the Blaswell residence, one last opportunity to kiss the hand of Philomena. It certainly beat kissing her face.